Praise for

BRENDA NOVAK

"All the characters [in *Dead Right*] are well-defined....
This novel is incredibly taut and tense, with some
nice sexual tension between the principals—
and the denouement is harrowing."
—*RT Book Reviews*

"Believable characters and gripping action—
nonstop suspense at its very best."
—*New York Times* bestselling author Carla Neggers

"Any book by Brenda Novak is a must buy for me."
—*Reader to Reader Reviews*

"Brenda Novak's *Cold Feet* is storytelling at its best—
engaging and entertaining but believable.
It just doesn't get much better than this."
—*All About Romance*

"Brenda Novak's seamless plotting,
emotional intensity and true-to-life characters
who jump off the page make her books completely
satisfying. Novak is simply a great storyteller."
—*New York Times* bestselling author Allison Brennan

"Novak knows how to relate a suspenseful tale.
[The heroine's] almost palpable fear fuels this gripping tale."
—*Publishers Weekly* on *Every Waking Moment*

"Novak expertly mixes her usual superior
characterization with a chilling sense of evil."
—*Booklist* on *Dead Silence*

BRENDA NOVAK

WATCH Me

MIRA®

ISBN-13: 978-0-7783-2904-6

WATCH ME

For questions and comments about the quality of this book please contact us at Customer_eCare@Harlequin.ca.

www.MIRABooks.com

Printed in U.S.A.

To my brother. If only you knew...

Dear Reader,

Sheridan Kohl, the heroine of this novel, has spent the past several years building The Last Stand, one of the best victims' charities in the country. Driven by her own experience with the ravaging effects of random violence, she really believes in the cause. Although she thinks what happened to her is in the past, she's trying to make a difference for others. But a new development in her own case sends her home to Tennessee, where she must face the man she left behind—and at the same time she learns how very present the old danger is.

Cain Granger is the man she left behind. He's a character based very loosely on my own brother. A man I barely know. A man who loves animals and the outdoors with unrivaled passion. A man who feels more comfortable alone than in a crowd. A man who has always struggled with his lack of a father. A man who, in his anger, takes no prisoners. It requires the love of a woman like Sheridan to make Cain whole. Maybe writing this story was my attempt to give my brother the happily-ever-after I so wish for him.

In the first two books of this series (*Trust Me* and *Stop Me*), you came to know Sheridan's partners in The Last Stand—Skye Kellerman and Jasmine Stratford. They're part of this novel, too, but they also have their own stories to tell.

There are lots of fun things to do, read and see at www.brendanovak.com. Please visit if you'd like to take a virtual tour of the offices of The Last Stand, read a prologue that doesn't appear anywhere else, download a free screen saver for signing up on my mailing list, read interesting interviews with police and other crime fighters in my Crimebeat blog, browse merchandise with the "The Last Stand: Where Victims Fight Back" logo, enter my monthly drawings for fun mystery boxes and other prizes or check out the items in my annual Online Auction for Diabetes Research. The diabetes auction is my own passion, my own effort to give back. Together with my fans, author friends and publishing contacts, I've raised over $350,000 to help those, like my son, who struggle with this disease.

I try to respond to everyone who contacts me, so feel free to e-mail me via my Web site. For those who don't have e-mail access, please write to P.O. Box 3781, Citrus Heights, CA 95611.

All the best,

Brenda Novak

1

The belief in a supernatural source of evil is not necessary: men alone are quite capable of every wickedness.
—Joseph Conrad

Was he gone?

Sheridan Kohl lay in a heap on the ground, her clothes, her cheek, the entire left side of her body, wet from the moist earth. The taste of her own blood sat bitter on her tongue, but the fecund smell of the thick vegetation growing all around reminded her of her childhood. She'd grown up in eastern Tennessee, in the small town of Whiterock.

Not that this was the kind of homecoming she'd expected.

The scrape of a shovel let her know the man who'd attacked her was still close. So close she dared not move or even whimper.

After a few turns of his spade, his breathing grew labored, and she heard him grunt every so often.

Scrape...plop. Scrape...plop. The digging obviously wasn't easy, but it was rhythmic enough to tell her it was progressing. Although he wasn't particularly tall, he was strong; she knew that already. Even after she'd managed to get free of the rope that had bound her wrists, she hadn't been able to fend him off. Her determination to fight had only made him angrier, more violent. She was sure he would've killed her if she hadn't gone limp.

She gingerly explored her top lip. It was split, but that was probably the least of her injuries. Unless she angled her head just right, blood rolled down her throat, choking her. She could barely open one of her eyes. And his fierce blows to her head had left her dazed, unable to think coherently. On some level, she knew she needed to get up and run now that he'd turned his attention elsewhere. But she couldn't stand, let alone make a dash for freedom. It was painful just to *breathe.*

The promise of complete darkness and total silence hovered at the edge of her consciousness. She longed to embrace it, to drift away and leave her broken body behind. But her best friend seemed to be standing at her shoulder, shouting: *Get up, damn you! Don't allow this, Sher. Gain the upper hand no matter what you have to do. Fight for your life!* For a moment, Sheridan even wondered if she was sitting in one of Skye's self-defense classes back at the victims' charity they'd started five years ago.

But then she felt the rain, lightly sprinkling her parted lips, forehead, eyelashes. She was in the forest in the middle of the night, alone with a man wearing a ski mask.

And he was digging her grave.

* * *

The dogs, barking and jumping against the chain-link fence, woke Cain Granger from a deep sleep. He told himself it was probably just another raccoon or possum, and rolled over to go back to sleep. But when the racket didn't stop, he realized it could also be a bear. He'd spotted a couple of black bears in the area the week before; they seemed to be foraging closer and closer to the house.

"I'm coming," he grumbled. Forcing himself to get out of bed, he yanked on a pair of jeans and some work boots. It was the height of summer—too hot and sultry to bother with any more clothes, even in the mountains. A bear would have no opinion on how he was dressed. But by the time he'd grabbed his tranquilizer gun and reached the dogs' pen, he didn't see a bear or anything else, at least not in the immediate vicinity.

"Quiet down!"

The dogs stopped barking, but they didn't come toward him. All three coonhounds stood rigid as statues, sniffing the air and pointing with their noses, as if they were tracking.

Cain frowned at this odd behavior, but he was too tired to do much about it. If the bear wasn't close enough to cause any harm, he didn't care to mess with it. Drugging and transporting such a large animal was a major feat; he knew because he worked for the Tennessee Wildlife Resources Agency, and it was the kind of thing he did for a living. "I'm going back to bed," he told the dogs and started toward the house, but Koda, his oldest and smartest hound, gave a warning growl that brought Cain up short.

Koda didn't spook easily....

Instead of returning to the house, Cain opened the gate and all three dogs raced toward him, shimmying and shaking, but not barking because he'd already chastened them for making too much noise. "What's up?" he asked, patting each of them. They generally loved his attention, reveled in it as long as possible, but tonight they tried to slip between him and the fence so they could head out into the forest.

"Hold on." He was planning to put them all on leashes, but Koda didn't want to wait. The black-and-tan bounded to the edge of the clearing, then glanced back for permission and whined.

"If it's a bear, you'll get your ass kicked," Cain told him, but Koda wouldn't attack a bear. Not on his own. The dogs would corner and hover until he arrived—and hopefully they'd be quick enough to get out of the way if a bear charged them.

He relented with a wave. "Fine," he said, "do it."

And that was all it took to send the hounds racing out ahead of him.

Taking a flashlight from the shed, Cain jogged behind them, using the noise they made as a guide.

It wasn't long before the tenor of their barking changed. They'd found something.

Picking up his pace, he shone the flashlight to avoid obstacles. The moon hung full and bright overhead, but it was beginning to rain, and the extra light helped when he had to weave through the shadowy trees. A lot of stumps, pinecones and broken limbs littered the ground. But there weren't many people in these mountains. That was why Cain loved them so much.

The dogs grew louder, more excited, as he neared the far corner of his property. Whatever they had was on *his* land.

He put the tranquilizer rifle to his shoulder, in case he needed it, and came up behind Koda. But they hadn't cornered a bear. They hadn't cornered anything threatening at all. From the looks of it, they'd surrounded a life-size *doll*.

Was this a joke? The boys in town, with whom he occasionally had a few beers, liked to pull pranks....

"Take it easy." He spoke low in his throat, his tone warning the dogs to calm down and back off. Reluctantly, they inched away—and that was when Cain saw that it wasn't an inflatable doll or a mannequin or any other inanimate object. It was a woman.

"What the hell?" Whoever she was, she'd been badly beaten. She wasn't moving, wasn't responding to the noise and activity around her.

Was she *dead?*

Cain used his flashlight to search the surrounding trees. He appeared to be alone with the woman, but the existence of a discarded shovel and a partially dug hole a few feet to his right told an unsettling story. Apparently, someone had murdered this woman and brought her out here to bury her.

No wonder his dogs had been going crazy.

"Son of a bitch." He should've come sooner. Maybe he could've saved her.

Setting his gun on a nearby log where he could get it in a hurry, he commanded his dogs to get out of the way and knelt beside her. Her limp wrist felt small and fragile in his hand. Thick black hair had fallen over her face; he could see, even in the darkness, that it was matted with fresh blood.

What must she have gone through? Who was she? And why had this happened?

Cain was so sure she was already dead the faint fluttering of her pulse surprised him. But it was there— thank God, it was there.

Breathing a sigh of relief, he silently begged her to hang on while he tied his gun to Koda's collar so the black-and-tan could drag it home.

He had to get this woman some help. Fast. But there was no time to put her in his truck and drive seventy miles to the closest hospital. She'd never make it.

Lifting her gently, he carried her to the clearing near his house and animal clinic. He'd have more room for her in the clinic, an easier place to wash her up. But as clean as he kept it, he couldn't imagine putting a human being where he'd been nursing sick and injured dogs, cats, horses and the odd coyote, deer or bear. Opting for the house, he shoved the front door open with his shoulder, then brought her to the spare room, where he laid her on the bed.

Her head lolled to the side, smearing blood on the bedding, but the mess didn't matter. He'd never seen anyone so close to death. Except Jason, one of his stepbrothers.

Ordering the dogs who'd followed him in to stay out of the house, he hurried to the living room and called for emergency services. A helicopter would never be able to land in the wooded area where he lived, but he could meet the airlift at the Jensen farm just outside of town, like he had for that camper who'd had a heart attack two years ago.

It only took a moment to arrange it, then he tried to contact Ned Smith, Whiterock's chief of police, but the dispatcher didn't know where to find him.

"Want me to wake Amy?" she asked, offering him an alternate.

"No." Cain didn't even hesitate. Amy was also a cop, but she was Ned's twin sister—and Cain's ex-wife. He definitely didn't want Amy in the middle of this. She had no experience with violent crime. Neither did the other two officers on Whiterock's small force, which was why he didn't suggest the dispatcher continue down her list of available officers. Cain wasn't sure Ned would be any better, but he *was* chief of police. "Just get hold of Ned and tell him to meet me at the hospital in Knoxville. As soon as possible."

"The hospital?"

Cain didn't have time to explain. "That's right."

Afraid the woman he'd found in the forest might die before he could reach the helicopter, he hung up and went back to the spare bedroom to get her. "You're going to be fine," he told her. Carefully he smoothed the tangled hair out of her face, wiped away the mud and blood—and realized, to his shock, that he knew this woman. It'd been twelve years since he'd seen her. But he'd slept with her once. Right before she'd gone to Rocky Point with Jason.

2

When the hospital paged him to the nurses' station, Cain thought the county dispatcher had finally located Ned Smith. But it was Owen Wyatt, the older of the two stepbrothers he had left, trying to get hold of him. Cain had called Owen from the hospital as soon as he'd arrived, at least forty-five minutes after the emergency helicopter had transported Sheridan. Someone back home needed to know what had happened. And, as the only doctor in town and the family member Cain liked best, Owen was the most likely candidate for helping him deal with the situation in Ned's absence.

"I got your message," Owen said.

"Let me call you from a pay phone."

"Wait—what's going on?"

Cain glanced at the nurses trying to work around him. "I'll call you back." He didn't have a cell. At times like this he regretted it, but he didn't get good reception where he lived and worked, so it wasn't worth the expense.

Five minutes later, he stood in the lobby, leaning against the wall closest to the pay phone, and had Owen on the line again. "Where were you?" he demanded, almost before his stepbrother, who was four years his junior, could say hello.

"What do you mean?"

"It was three-thirty the last time I tried you. I expected to drag you from your bed. What, were you on a house call?" It should've surprised Cain to hear his answer. But it didn't.

"I was on a house call, all right. Robert came home drunk and drove into Dad's gardening shed. I had to help get him out of his old Camaro and stitch the gash over his temple."

Cain's other stepbrother had a drinking problem and was always in some kind of trouble. He was the youngest in the family, but at twenty-five he was old enough to take care of himself. Instead, he lived in a trailer on his father's property, spent every waking hour playing online games rather than trying to hold down a job, and when he wasn't gaming, he partied. Cain had no sympathy for him. Maybe Cain had been a hell-raiser in high school, but he'd been on his own since he turned eighteen. He'd put himself through college and had never expected anyone else to clean up his messes. "Why didn't you answer when I tried your cell?"

"I left it in the car. You should've seen Robert." He made a noise of disgust. "What an idiot."

"Nothing new there."

"No. So…what's going on?"

The adrenaline that had fueled his mad race to the hospital was dwindling, allowing fatigue to set in. "Someone attacked Sheridan Kohl a few hours ago and left her for dead."

A short pause followed. "Did you say Sheridan Kohl?"

"That's right."

"I'd heard she was coming back to town, but I hadn't realized she'd arrived. And...who would do such a thing?"

"I have no idea."

There was another pause. "How do you know about it? Her being hurt, I mean."

"I found her. Whoever attacked her dumped her near the old cabin at the far edge of the property."

Owen surprised Cain by cursing. Generally the strait-laced type, he used big words, not cuss words.

"What was that for?" he asked.

"This makes me uncomfortable."

That was an understatement, and understatements were far more typical of Owen. "You're telling me."

"Have you called Ned?"

"Of course. First thing."

"Well, considering the way you two feel about each other, I had to ask."

Cain had gone to school with Ned, but they'd never been friends. After Jason's murder, Cain had been so busy self-destructing he hadn't had time for friends—real friends, anyway. He'd partied harder than ever, risked life and limb with crazy stunts, fought anyone and everyone who'd venture to take him on and messed around with a different girl almost every weekend. Then there was his brief marriage to Ned's sister. That alone made it a damn shame the Smith twins had become fifty-percent of Whiterock's police force. "I called, but I haven't been able to reach him," Cain said.

"Why not?"

"How the hell should I know?" An old woman entered the lobby and slumped into one of the plastic chairs. Cain moved the handset closer to his mouth and lowered his voice. "If you want the official answer, he's temporarily 'unavailable.'"

"He's probably with his new secretary."

"Mona?" As far as Cain was concerned, a guy would have to be drunk and blind to get naked with Ned's secretary. She didn't even keep herself clean.

"That's my guess. She doesn't look like much, but from what I hear she's willing to do anything. I saw him feel her up as she was getting into her car at the Roadhouse last week." Owen clicked his tongue. "Poor Brian. He needs to leave her."

"I think he should thank Ned and hand her over." The woman in the lobby looked up, and Cain faced the wall.

Owen cleared his throat. "You know what people will think when they hear about this, don't you?"

Scowling, Cain shoved his hands in his pockets. "I don't care what they think."

"No, you never have. So let me spell it out for you. It was only three weeks ago that the two Wallup boys found that rifle in the cellar of *your* old cabin."

The rifle that subsequent ballistics tests proved to be the one that had killed Jason. How could Cain forget? "I'm aware of that. But it's ridiculous. I didn't touch her. I didn't even know she was back until I found her lying in a heap, covered with blood and dirt and leaves."

Owen released an audible sigh. "No one'll believe that. Word that she was planning to return has been circulating for the past week."

Cain wished he'd taken the time to change. His hair, which was getting a bit long around the ears and neck, had dried, but his jeans were still damp enough to be uncomfortable. "I'm telling you, I didn't hear about it. Besides, she hasn't been back in twelve years. Why would she come now?"

"Why do you think? Someone told her about the rifle."

Cain assumed it was Ned. He and Ned had been rivals ever since Cain had broken Amy's heart. "Why would that bring her back?"

"Because she wants to solve the case."

"You mean she wants to see it solved."

"No. When Ned told me she was coming, I looked her up on the Internet. She's part of a victims' help charity in California."

"So she's a social worker?"

"More like a caseworker. About five years ago, she started The Last Stand with two other women, also victims of violent crime. They each have different specialties. Sheridan's bio said she handles the bookkeeping but also works with private investigators, police, psychologists, self-defense experts, what have you, to find missing persons, protect the innocent, put violent offenders behind bars, do anything that's needed, really. I got the impression she knows a lot about the criminal-justice world, that she's sort of a jack-of-all-trades. I mentioned her victims' work to Dad. I can't believe he didn't tell you."

The fact that his stepfather hadn't mentioned Sheridan's background or her impending visit made Cain a little apprehensive. It was something they might've discussed—before the discovery of that rifle. "Realistically, what's she going to be able to do?" he asked. "Nothing's changed. That rifle went missing before Jason was shot. Bailey Watts reported it stolen five days prior. And it's been wiped clean of prints. We don't know any more than we did the day we buried him."

"Ned thinks he's found a previously overlooked suspect, and he's gathering evidence." He paused. "And that suspect—quite conveniently—is you."

Cain fidgeted with the change in his pocket. "Anyone could've put that rifle in the cellar. The cabin's been empty since I finished the new house six years ago. I've only used it to store a few things or spend an occasional night."

"I'm not going to lie to you, Cain. There's been a lot of discussion lately, ever since that rifle was found, about your state of mind after your mom died. About how you behaved."

Cain had behaved badly. He knew it, and so did everyone else. But since his real father had skipped out before Cain was ever born and hadn't left a forwarding address, Cain had had nowhere to turn after his mother was gone. He'd been reduced to asking his stepfather if he could go on living in the house until he finished his senior year. John had agreed, but Cain had been tolerated about as well as a noxious odor. "I was angry."

"You cut classes, you started drag racing, you slugged a male teacher who tried to send you to the office. Those aren't things people tend to forget."

Cain glowered at the woman who'd been watching him since she entered the lobby and she finally glanced away.

"Do *you* think I shot Jason?" he asked Owen.

"Of course not. I know you better than that. Point is other people are beginning to wonder."

Ned had put him forward as a suspect years ago, but no one had taken the accusation seriously. Was that changing?

"These days when I say, 'Cain would never go so far,' I don't get agreement, I get doubt," Owen was saying. "'People do terrible things when they're confused.'"

Cain's grip on the phone tightened. "*Who's* saying that?"

"Why bother naming names? I'm just warning you to be careful."

"And how am I supposed to be careful, Owen?" Cain felt his eyebrows knit. "I didn't know that rifle was in my cabin. And with Sheridan, what else could I have done? Let her die in the woods?"

"Of course not. But…they'll look for any excuse to pin it on you. That's all I mean."

And now her blood was not only on his clothes, it was in his house.

"Tell me you don't have any swollen knuckles," Owen said.

"It wouldn't matter. Whoever did this used something besides his fists. A board. A bat."

"How do you know?"

The woman in the lobby was twisting around to look at him again. He lowered his voice even further. "I can tell by the injuries."

"Someone had to use a club to get the better of a woman *her* size? What kind of man would do that?"

"A weak asshole. But a dangerous one. Someone

who wanted to be sure he had the upper hand and didn't lose it. Which is why I'm surprised she's still alive."

"Maybe he thought she was dead."

"He wasn't finished. Hearing me coming with the dogs scared him off."

"Then it's a good thing you found her when you did."

"It's a good thing he was gone when I got there," Cain muttered. "Or she wouldn't be the only one needing a doctor."

"That's exactly the kind of comment that can get you into trouble, big brother."

"It takes more than an offhanded comment and a little circumstantial evidence to convict someone of attempted *murder*. What motive would I have for hurting her?"

The woman in the lobby got up and left. Apparently, she'd heard enough.

"Ned thinks she's hiding something," Owen replied. "Thanks to her supposed 'untold knowledge' and the discovery of that rifle, folks will believe you wanted to shut her up."

Alarm traveled up Cain's spine. Sheridan *was* hiding something. In all her conversations with police, she'd never revealed their brief involvement. Cain wasn't sure why—if she'd done it to protect him or if she'd merely been looking out for herself. She had only been sixteen, he seventeen and a half, when they met up in the Johnson's camper during that party. Her strict, religious parents would've disowned her if they'd known what she did with him.

"Tell me this," Owen said.

"What?"

"Is she still beautiful?"

"With all the scrapes and bruises, it was tough to tell."

"I bet she is. She was *always* beautiful. That's what got Jason into trouble. There wasn't a boy in town who didn't want her."

She'd been Jason's type—well-adjusted, happy, popular. So why had she given *him* her virginity? Cain had no idea. But he didn't want to think about the mistakes he'd made. He'd been young and stupid, too ready to capitalize on her schoolgirl crush. After that night, he'd never called her, but only because he'd known instinctively that he'd crossed the line when he touched her.

"What happened to Jason wasn't her fault," he said.

"Whose fault was it?" Owen asked.

Cain's. But not in the way everyone thought. "It was crazy. Random."

"You're saying whoever it was stashed that rifle in your cabin?"

"I told you, I have no idea how it got there. Anyway, why would I want to kill my—" for the first time in a long while Cain felt the need to differentiate "—*your* brother?" Jason had been everything a parent could want, and Cain had been the opposite. Cain had envied Jason. But he never would've hurt him.

"You wouldn't, but no one else understands you the way I do. They only know you've had some…issues. It doesn't help that half the people in this town are afraid to deal with you on any issue that doesn't involve animals. That makes them willing to believe almost anything."

Cain hadn't lost his temper in years. But Owen was

right. Most men stepped to the side to avoid getting in his way. Even certain women kept their distance. Others, he couldn't seem to get rid of. There were days when he turned out of his drive onto the county road to find Amy, his ex-wife, sitting in her car, waiting just to catch a glimpse of him. "That's not enough to prove I tried to kill her. If I wanted her dead, Owen—if I was capable of going to such lengths—she'd *be* dead. I would've gone ahead and buried her. I certainly wouldn't have called for emergency help."

"Considering that rifle, Ned will be suspicious. That's all. Keep it in mind." Owen coughed. "So, when are you coming home?"

Cain didn't know. Sheridan's fragility made it difficult to just leave her there and go. He doubted she'd be very excited to see him, but he was all she had. "I don't know."

"If she dies, it might be better if you're not hovering around."

"She's not going to die."

Silence. Then Owen said, "I hope you're right. I'm exhausted." He punctuated those two words with a yawn. "I'd better go."

"Wait." Cain caught him before he could hang up. "Does Dad think I shot Jason?" Hating the vulnerability revealed by that question, Cain braced himself for the worst. John Wyatt had never approved of Cain, even after Cain had cleaned up his act and gone to college.

"I don't know what he thinks," Owen said, but his voice held no conviction and that revealed the truth.

3

It was midday when Cain returned home. Ned had shown up just after Cain had admitted Sheridan, and he'd made a fuss—probably to deflect any speculation about the time he'd spent messing around last night. He'd asked all kinds of questions Cain had no way of answering and made a point of letting the doctors know he'd be staying in close contact, waiting for the first moment Sheridan was capable of holding a conversation.

Cain figured Ned would be waiting for a few *days*. The doctors were keeping her unconscious to relieve the swelling in her brain. Fortunately, that swelling wasn't bad enough that they'd had to drill holes in her skull, but it could get worse, so they wanted to keep her perfectly still. Whoever had beaten her had done a damn fine job. Besides the head injuries and the cuts and scrapes from being dragged through the woods, she had a bruised liver and a damaged kidney.

Cain hadn't wanted to leave. It felt like he was abandoning her. But he couldn't tolerate being around Whiterock's chief of police for more than five minutes, and Ned wouldn't go anywhere as long as Cain was in the room.

It was better that he'd come home. He'd agreed to

show Amy where he'd found Sheridan, and he'd volunteered to take the hounds out to see if they could pick up the scent of her attacker.

Koda, Maximillian and Quixote were waiting for him at the gate of their pen when he got out of his truck. They whined as he strode toward them: they didn't like being left behind, but they were fine. If he'd ended up staying away much longer, he would've called Levi or Vivian Matherly, his closest neighbors, and asked one of them to stop by. But it hadn't been necessary today.

Predictably, the hounds' unhappiness evaporated the second he lifted the latch. Then their tails began to wag and all was forgiven.

"Let's get you fed." He set about filling their dishes. Quixote and Maximillian immediately went to their bowls and got down to the business of eating. Koda took advantage of their preoccupation to nuzzle up to Cain.

"What're you doing over here, huh?" Cain asked his favorite dog, crouching to rub the dog's ears. "I know you're as hungry as they are."

Koda barked in response and Cain chuckled. Sometimes he was sure this particular dog could read his mind. "You're the best of the bunch," he said as Koda's warm tongue caressed his hand.

The sound of a motor and the crunch of tires on gravel announced Amy's arrival. She was early. Cain hadn't had time to shower or shave, and his eyes burned with fatigue, but he stood up and faced her as she parked.

"You're back," she called as she opened her door. "Looks like my timing is good."

Cain made himself acknowledge her with a nod, but

he suspected she'd actually been hoping to arrive before he did so she'd have a chance to snoop around. Since the miscarriage and their subsequent divorce, she was always watching him for fear he'd hook up with someone else.

Maybe if he had a love interest, Amy would give up and move on. But it was three years since the woman he'd been dating on and off had moved to Nashville to pursue a country music career, and he hadn't been with anyone since. The longer he remained single, the more Amy managed to "bump" into him.

Realizing he'd been upstaged, Koda barked once and trotted over to his dish, where he began to wolf down his food—apparently trying to catch up with the others.

"Take it easy, it's not going anywhere," Cain admonished.

All the hounds brought their muzzles up and pricked their ears, watching him for the direction they received from his body language as much as his verbal commands. Cain nodded for them to finish, and this time Koda ate a little more slowly.

"It's amazing how well they obey you." Amy was wearing her police uniform. Her badge identified her as Officer Granger, but that name didn't seem any more natural than her recently enhanced curves. Eleven years ago, an unexpected pregnancy had forced Cain into proposing to Amy. Their marriage had lasted only three months, but because he'd never loved her, those three months had been hell. Why hadn't she reverted to her maiden name?

"That's what they're trained to do," he said.

"No amount of training would make them obey me like that. You have a way with animals." She smiled bitterly. "And women."

"Amy—"

She scowled at the warning in his voice. "No need to say anything. This is business. I know."

He hoped she'd keep that in mind. But years of experience told him that their encounter would slide into the personal at some point. It always did.

"Let me put on a clean shirt and brush my teeth, and I'll be right out," he said.

Her eyes followed him as he walked to the house. He didn't need to look back to know that; he could feel her attention. If she was around, he could *always* feel her attention. "Why'd she have to join the police force?" he grumbled once he was inside.

The blood in the bathroom sink and on his shirt served as an unnecessary reminder of last night's horrific events. It was a miracle his dogs had been able to rouse him—and that whoever had beaten Sheridan hadn't finished her off.

She could still die....

That thought caused a ripple of anxiety as he washed his face and hands and brushed his teeth. He was just stripping off his T-shirt while walking to his bedroom when he heard Amy address him from the end of the hall.

"Is there anything I can do to help you get the dogs ready?"

Cain turned in surprise and couldn't miss the way her gaze moved hungrily over his bare chest. *Shit...* "No," he said. Then he went into his bedroom and pointedly closed the door. With his luck, she'd come in and offer to help him change his boxers, too....

She was on her knees, examining some blood on the carpet when he came out.

"You brought her in the house?" she asked, glancing up.

His stepbrother's words seemed oddly prophetic given this question from Amy, but he shrugged off the sudden foreboding. He'd done what he had to do, what anyone would've done in the same situation. "For a few minutes."

"Wasn't it obvious that she needed to be driven to a hospital?"

"It was *obvious* she might not make it that far and that I had to call for an airlift." He stared her down, refusing to show any doubt about his actions. Amy hated him every bit as much as she loved him, and she could switch from one emotion to the other in a second. If she was going to fault him for his actions, he wanted her to know she'd have a fight on her hands. It was better to discourage her from the beginning, before her twin brother could get involved.

Fortunately, taking the offensive seemed to work. She frowned at the blood and stood up. "All set?"

He was hungry. Once he'd decided to return and do some tracking, he hadn't bothered to stop and eat. The coffee he'd bought at the hospital was chewing a hole in his stomach, but he didn't want to spend an extra second in Amy's company. Even the sound of her voice changed to a higher pitch when she was with him. Every word raised the hair on the back of his neck.

"Let's go," he said. He could eat later.

* * *

"It's gone." Cain searched through the undergrowth near the half-dug grave.

Amy was busy taking pictures of where Sheridan had been lying. He could see broken limbs, matted leaves and blood. "What's gone?" she asked.

"The shovel."

Letting the camera drop around her neck, she walked over. "Where was it?"

"Here." He pointed to the left of the hole.

"You're sure?"

"That's not something that would be easy to mistake."

"How'd you see it in the dark?"

"I had a flashlight. But I could've seen it anyway. There was a full moon."

"It was raining in town last night."

Her apparent doubt made him grind his teeth. "We got a light drizzle, too, but the moon was out."

"You think he came back for his *shovel?*"

"*Someone* took it." Cain wished he'd been there when the man returned. It had to be someone he and Sheridan knew. It was too much to believe a stranger had tried to kill her on his land a few weeks after that rifle had shown up in his cabin.

"Let's talk about motive," she said.

Cain whistled to round up his dogs, who were sniffing the trees, marking their territory. "What about motive?"

"Who'd want to do this to Sheridan Kohl?"

"I have no idea. As far as I know, no one's seen or heard from her since she left."

"Could be an old grudge."

"She was popular in high school, well-liked."

"So was Jason," she mused.

"It's probably the same person."

"You don't think there could be two men in White-rock capable of this kind of violence?"

"It's possible, but unlikely," he said. "Don't you find it odd that Sheridan was involved in *both* incidents?"

"I guess. But we have to look at all the possibilities. Coincidence is one of those possibilities." She tried to tame the wisps of curly auburn hair that'd escaped the thick braid hanging down her back. With little effect. The wayward strands continued to frame her broad, heavily freckled face.

There'd been a time when Cain had found Amy *slightly* attractive, but that was years and years ago. Before the wedding. When she was younger and thinner and didn't have those harsh frown lines around her eyes and mouth or that look of desperation in her eyes.

"It was no coincidence," he insisted. "She either knows something someone doesn't want her to tell, or she has an enemy who's been out to get her since the night she and Jason were shot." With his foot he poked through the damp needles and leaves near a cluster of pine trees. "And I'm leaning toward the 'keeping her quiet' motive. There wasn't a single person who didn't like her."

Amy hesitated long enough to tell him that she'd recognized the respect in his voice. "*I* didn't like her."

"Why? The two of you didn't even socialize. You came from completely different worlds." Amy had belonged to his band of rebels; Sheridan had headed their school's chapter of the National Honor Society.

"We had one thing in common," she said.

"What's that?"

"You."

Uncomfortable with where this conversation was going, Cain cleared his throat. "I don't know what you're talking about."

"Her hair was all mussed one night at a party when she was last seen with you. Are you telling me you *weren't* the reason?"

Now he understood who was fueling the suspicion that he might've had a jealousy motive for shooting Jason. He should've guessed it was Amy. If she couldn't have him, she wanted to make his life as miserable as possible. "Sheridan wasn't the type for that," he said.

"Maybe not with other boys."

"Why would she be any different with me?" That was the big question, wasn't it? One he'd never really been able to answer. He knew she'd had a crush on him, but that was the part he couldn't understand. He shouldn't have been appealing to a straight arrow like her.

"Maybe she wanted you. Maybe she was willing to lift her skirts, hoping you'd fall in love with her, become her boyfriend."

"Stop it." That was a little too autobiographical, coming from Amy. And his experience with Sheridan had been nothing like Amy was insinuating. Sheridan hadn't been trying to manipulate him, certainly not that night. Something honest and pure had passed between them. Which was probably why he'd never called her afterward. She'd been the only girl to pose a threat to the part of himself he'd been trying so hard to protect after his mother's death. "I barely knew Sheridan."

"So you didn't sleep with her."

"That's none of your business."

She arched an eyebrow. "An evasive answer makes you seem guilty, you know."

Amy had pushed him into a corner. If he lied and Sheridan came out with the truth, it would look as if he was being dishonest about everything—the shooting, last night's beating. But he couldn't help defending Sheridan's reputation. He refused to throw what'd happened between them into the dirt for the whole town to gossip about. Especially now that Sheridan was back and would have to deal with that gossip and the judgment and disapproval guaranteed to go along with it. "I didn't sleep with her, okay?"

Thick mascara far too dark for her fair coloring coated Amy's eyelashes, in sharp contrast to the light blue of her eyes. "I have a hard time believing that."

"Why?" he challenged, throwing up the shield of insolence that came to his rescue at such times.

"Because some women would do *anything* for you."

The passion behind those words gave Cain the impression that she was making him an offer. If he'd take her back, she'd become his most ardent defender and the suspicion surrounding him would disappear. But that wasn't a trade he was willing to make. His feelings for Amy hadn't changed. They never would.

"Sheridan would've known better than that," he said.

Amy's eyes held his, so full of abject longing he finally had to yank his gaze away. And that was when he saw it—a piece of wood lying in the trees behind her. It had a dark, almost blackish substance on one end, a substance that looked like dried blood.

"I just found his weapon," Cain said, astonished by the ease with which the object had suddenly stood out when active searching had yielded nothing.

Disappointment crept over Amy's features, and immediately turned into a highly focused, razor-sharp hate. But Cain was used to the way her emotions vacillated and cared more about what he'd found.

He started toward it but Amy was closer. She got there first and nudged it with her toe. "He hit her with *this?*"

Much to Cain's relief, Amy seemed to have regained control of her reactions. "He used more than his fists."

"The fact that he used a convenient weapon suggests he didn't go after her with the intention of killing her."

"He had a shovel. I don't carry a shovel in my trunk. Do you?"

Amy bent to pick up the club, but he stopped her. "Leave it."

"Why?"

"He probably threw it down to free his hands for digging. Then he heard the dogs."

"So what does it matter if I touch it? I can't get prints off a log." Crouching, she plucked a long, black strand of hair from the bark and held it up.

The sight of Sheridan's hair and blood on the end of that club called to mind the sight of her lying on the ground—and the feel of her against his bare chest, so limp in his arms. "It would carry his scent."

"As well as hers," Amy argued. "How can the dogs distinguish between the two?"

"The same way they distinguish between all other scents." Kneeling beside her, Cain called his hounds over and gave them each a good sniff. Then he told them to "find" and sent them into the woods.

Koda started tracking right away. He led the others uphill, which surprised Cain. He'd expected them to go east, toward the road.

He hurried after the dogs, with Amy jogging behind him. She caught up only when he stopped to examine several footprints on the muddy bank of Old Cache Creek. "He crossed here," he said, and ordered the dogs to do the same.

Maximillian didn't like the water. He hung back until the last moment but plunged in when he saw that even Cain was going to wade through it.

"What was he doing way up here?" Amy called after them.

Cain didn't respond. He was scanning the area as he cleared the creek, trying to think like the man who'd used that club.

"Maybe he's some vagabond who's been camping out in these mountains," she suggested, answering her own question.

No, it was someone from Whiterock. Cain's gut told him that. The shooting, the rifle, the beating—there was some connection. "He isn't a camper. He ran this way because he thought I might come after him."

"*Did* you?"

"No, I went for help. When he figured out I wasn't

coming, he probably wound back to the road and drove off."

"Maybe he fell and got hurt and is still out here," she said.

Cain cringed to think that Amy was the best the Whiterock police had to offer. "He wouldn't have come back for his shovel if that was the case."

The color in her cheeks camouflaged some of her freckles as she wiped the sweat from her temple and moved farther up the bank of the creek they'd just crossed. "Then this is a waste of time. I say we head over to the road and check for tire imprints before too many other vehicles go through and destroy our chances."

When she started off in that direction, he called to the dogs, but only Maximillian and Quixote joined him. Cain whistled, giving Koda a second command, but the black-and-tan didn't return for another minute or two. Head and tail lowered apologetically, he finally came to a stop about five feet from Cain—but Cain realized there'd been a reason for the delay.

"Whatcha got, boy?"

Creeping forward, head still down, Koda dropped a shiny object at Cain's feet.

Cain glanced over his shoulder at Amy's retreating figure. For once, she wasn't watching him. She was leading Maximillian and Quixote toward the dirt road that led past his place to Levi Matherley's.

Keeping his back to her, Cain bent to retrieve the shiny object. He hoped it was a piece of jewelry belonging to the man who'd attacked Sheridan, and that it could eventually be traced to its owner.

But the reality made his jaw sag. It was *his* watch. The one he'd left on his nightstand before bed last night.

"You coming?" Amy called.

Cain shoved the watch into his pocket. The man who'd nearly killed Sheridan had been in his house while he was driving to the hospital.

4

Sheridan couldn't open her eyes. The light was too blinding, too white. But she was fairly certain she wasn't having a near-death experience. There was no tunnel, no loving Christlike figure waiting to embrace her. The air was cold, she could hear distant movement and voices, and she could smell antiseptic and just a hint of... *cologne?*

Raising her eyelids slightly, she looked through her lashes to see walls covered with blue-and-yellow wallpaper. Judging by the IV tube going into her arm, the TV suspended from the ceiling, the rails on the bed and the rolling metal tray down by her feet, she was in a hospital. Which hospital, she had no idea. But that seemed less important at the moment than the fact that she wasn't alone. A man stood at the window, gazing out. She was pretty sure he was the source of the cologne.

There was something unsettling about that scent, about this man's presence....

Did she know him? He seemed vaguely familiar. But she couldn't recall a time or a place or a name. He had unruly dark hair and a lean, muscular build with broad shoulders and golden tanned skin. Well-toned arms showed beneath the short sleeves of a white T-shirt, and—she tilted her head for a clearer view—he looked better in a pair of jeans than any man she'd ever seen.

She doubted that detail would've occurred to her if she were lying at death's door.

He shifted, seemed to catch sight of her from the corner of his eye and turned.

She knew him, all right. She would never forget *that* face. It was Cain Granger.

"Thank God," he breathed and came immediately to her bedside.

The relief and concern in his manner made her wonder if she'd missed the chapter where they'd become friends.

"What…happened?" The words had to be forced from a tight, scratchy throat, but she didn't hurt anymore. The pain had been replaced with a sort of weightless euphoria that suggested she was under the influence of some very strong medication.

He took her hand and toyed with the tips of her fingers as if they knew each other much better than they did. "You don't remember?"

Sheridan couldn't put the whole story together, but fragments of various scenes flitted through her mind— a pair of muddy boots, a shovel, the rain. Those were the bad memories. Then there were some that, except for the pain, wouldn't have been bad at all: a rock-solid chest and sinewy arms cradling her, a soft bed and the same scent she'd identified when she woke up a moment ago. "You… I was…in your bed."

"That's right. Briefly."

"But…it wasn't you who…who did this to me." She struggled against the confusion that nearly over-whelmed her.

A dark scowl brought out the stormy green of his eyes. "No. I found you after you were hurt, after who-ever did this ran away."

"Oh." That made sense. She'd definitely seen his face at some point. And heard a helicopter.

"Do you remember now?" he prompted.

He seemed anxious for reassurance, but before she could piece together the separate images floating around in her brain, a shorter, stouter man appeared in the doorway wearing a police uniform.

"Look at this. She's up!" he bellowed, removing a cowboy hat as he entered the room.

A cowboy-hat-wearing cop wasn't something she'd expect to see in California, but it wasn't so unusual here. She might've smiled, except the muscle that flexed in Cain's jaw told Sheridan he wasn't pleased about the interruption. Dropping her hand, he stepped away.

In the few seconds it took her new visitor to reach her bedside, Sheridan realized she knew this man, too. She'd gone to high school with him, the same as Cain. Unlike Cain, however, he'd lost a lot of hair and gained a lot of weight.

"Ned?" she said uncertainly.

"Hey." Holding his hat in one beefy hand, he rested the other on her bedrail and smiled, revealing the gap he'd always had between his teeth. His twin sister had one just like it—for being fraternal twins, they looked surprisingly similar—unless she'd had it fixed since Sheridan had seen her last. "How ya feelin' little lady?"

She glanced at Cain, but he wasn't watching them. He'd taken up his post along the wall and was once again staring pensively out the window. She could see his profile, the long sweep of his dark lashes, his bold, prominent chin, straight nose and well-shaped lips—

"Sheridan?"

She dragged her attention away from Cain. "Yes?"

"How are you feeling?"

"Better. I think. What's wrong with me?"

"Not much now. Doc says you're healing nicely. The swelling in your brain has gone down. You had some internal injuries, but that's all going to be fine, too."

"How long have I been in the hospital?"

"A week."

That sounded like an eternity. "Where're my parents?"

"I don't know. We've tried to reach them, but the phone at their place in Wyoming—it is Wyoming, isn't it?"

She managed a careful nod.

"No one answers."

Why not? she wondered. They were always there, as reliable as rain.

And then it occurred to her. They were on a two-week cruise to Alaska. They wanted to get some traveling in before her younger sister had her baby, which was due… She'd lost track of time; she didn't know when. "They're on vacation," she said.

"That explains it."

A man's hand, holding a piece of wood, flashed

through Sheridan's mind. But that had to be part of a dream…. "What happened to me?"

"Someone attacked you. That's why I'm here. I'm Whiterock's chief of police."

Attacked her?

The figure with the club reappeared in her mind. Evidently he wasn't a figment of her imagination. She'd been attacked before, years ago, but the situation had been different back then. How was it that this kind of violence had visited her again?

Maybe this time she'd see justice done. "Do you know who did it?" she asked.

Ned's lips formed a hard, flat line. "Not exactly. But we have our suspicions."

That was no solace. They didn't know, which meant more of what she'd experienced twelve years ago—more wondering, more waiting, more fruitless hoping. "Who do you suspect?" she asked, but Cain interrupted.

"The wrong man. He's wasting his time, that's all he's doing."

"We'll soon find out, won't we?" Ned said. "Surely she saw more this time."

They were relying on *her?* A strange panic set in because Sheridan couldn't identify the man who'd attacked her. She couldn't recall anything about the incident. At least nothing clear or sequential. Nothing that made sense or hinted at reasons and names. Just those bizarre, upsetting images. "I don't think so," she said helplessly.

"Tell me everything you remember since you first drove into town, darlin'."

Her mind searched for a starting place, a string to follow to the point where everything went wrong. She was currently living in Sacramento, working with The Last Stand—a victims' charity she'd founded five years ago with Skye Willis and Jasmine Stratford. No, not Stratford. Not anymore. Jasmine was married and living in New Orleans with her husband these days.

Her thoughts were so tangled….

"Why'd I come back to Whiterock?" she asked. With a bit more information, she might be able to put it all together….

"You wanted to come after I called you about the rifle," Ned said, but that elicited nothing.

"I did?"

"You said you've learned a thing or two about investigatin' crime since you moved and wanted to help me solve Jason Wyatt's murder. That was three weeks ago."

She couldn't remember three weeks ago, but she could remember Jason. That part of the past came rushing back like a horror video on fast-forward: Cain's stepbrother putting his arm around her in that steamy truck, trying to kiss her. Her unwillingness to let him. The way she'd wiped a spot on the window with her hand, hoping for a glimpse of Cain. Then the door being wrenched open—

She squeezed her eyes shut as the barrel of the rifle materialized in her mind. *Stop. Stop. Stop!* She wasn't ready to relive that nightmare.

"Sheridan?" Ned pressed.

Sweat dampened the valley between her breasts. "I— I'm not myself yet," she murmured. "Maybe… maybe you should come back later."

Cain turned. She could feel him observing her closely, assessing the situation in that silent, watchful way of his. He'd changed some, filled out, grown harder around the edges, more rugged. But his mysterious, aloof air was vintage Cain.

Ned let go of the bed rail and began rolling the sides of his hat toward the crown. "When?" he said. "I'm not sure if you're aware of it, but this hospital's seventy miles from Whiterock, darlin'.'"

"Stop calling her 'darlin','" Cain growled. "And so what if waiting means you have to make another trip? She doesn't need any pressure from you. She's had it hard enough."

She was relieved to have someone stand up for her. Right now, she needed that buffer. But she could also understand Ned's impatience. He had an investigation to run, and he expected her to react like the professional she'd promised him she was and not the victim she'd become.

Somehow, frightening and painful though it was, she had to delve into the half memories that shrouded this most recent incident. But she couldn't create clarity that wasn't there. "Can you tell me more, some detail that might remind me?" she asked.

"Cain found you next to a half-dug grave in the forest near his old cabin. You were so beat-up he thought you were dead."

His words reminded her, all right. She could barely breathe. "I—I…"

Cain cut in. "Damn it, Ned, give her a break."

The rest of Ned's good ol' boy veneer disappeared.

"So you can get to her first?" he snapped, the twang of his accent growing more marked. "Plant thoughts and memories that aren't her own? Hell, no!"

Had Sheridan been more herself, she would've argued that no one could play with her memory that way. The truth was there; it was just temporarily locked inside her mind. But she felt too uncertain to argue about anything. "I'm going to need some time," she said.

Ned wasn't happy with her response, but most of the tension in the room existed independent of her. There was some kind of feud going on between him and Cain. Why? They'd known each other in high school. But they hadn't hung out together. They'd barely—

"You married her," Sheridan said, finally piecing one small mystery together.

Cain knew exactly who and what she was talking about. She could see it in his face. But Ned was still caught up in trying to get his own answers and didn't clue in quite so fast. "Excuse me?" he said, wearing a scowl.

"Amy," she explained. "Tina Judd wrote me a year after I left town." Before her mother demanded she sever even that relationship. "She said Cain had married your sister. You two are in-laws—"

"*Were* in-laws," Cain interrupted. "Amy and I are divorced."

That didn't surprise Sheridan. Amy had never been right for Cain. She was far too grasping. Sheridan wasn't sure *anyone* was right for him. He held too much power in every relationship, or at least those she'd seen.

"You weren't made for marriage." As soon as she said it, she realized that was probably something she shouldn't have spoken out loud, but with the medication, her brain hadn't stopped her mouth in time. And once it was out, it was out.

Cain quirked an eyebrow at her as Ned laughed. "I guess she knows you better than I thought," he gibed.

Whether the remark was appropriate or not, she was relieved to be able to reach into the past, even if it wasn't the part she most needed to remember. "Dogs. That's what you really loved, wasn't it? Animals?" He gave his heart to his pets, but his body had been a whole other story. He'd gotten an early start with the girls....

And yet...Sheridan could still remember how gentle he'd been with her that night in the camper, how sweet. He'd been seventeen years old, only eighteen months older than she was at the time, but he hadn't bumbled his way through an experience she found awkward at best and painful at worst.

Odd that she could recall so clearly how hard he'd tried to hold himself back when she could barely come up with her own name.

"Considering we barely knew each other, that's more than I expected you to remember about me." Cain's voice was so clipped and his body language so indifferent, she figured he'd forgotten about those few minutes in the camper. Or the memory didn't mean anything to him.

Most likely the latter. He'd been with a lot of girls. What was thirty minutes with a naive little virgin?

"I guess there are some things a girl never forgets," she said, the words, as well as the memory, bittersweet.

She saw something in his eyes, something that

seemed to indicate he remembered every detail as well as she did. But she refused to let herself care one way or the other. He obviously hadn't changed. Why was he even in her hospital room? Ned had said she'd been unconscious for a week. What could Cain Granger possibly want that would keep him around for so long?

"I hope the details concerning your attack are some of those things," Ned said, single-mindedly bringing the conversation back to the original topic. "We have to find the guy who did this to you."

Sheridan curled her fingers into fists. "Why did this happen to *me?*" she asked Ned. "Why me *again?*"

"That's what I want to know," he replied. "The only answer I've got is that this has some connection to Jason's shooting." He continued talking, but what he said had no meaning to her. She couldn't deal with what'd happened to Jason, not in conjunction with this. She cringed every time she heard his name. That memory had always been painful, but today it created an emotional overload like she'd never experienced before.

Instinctively, she turned her face into her pillow, trying to avoid his words, to avoid any thought of Jason, but he kept talking, saying things she didn't want to hear. *Go away.* She'd awakened to so many questions. Questions that left her feeling lost and disoriented.

She needed an anchor—and looked up to find Cain.

"Whatever's going on is based in the past," he said when their eyes met. He was speaking over the blustery Ned, but Sheridan didn't care. She had to tune Ned out, couldn't tolerate his overbearing manner.

"I wish I could tell you more," Cain added. "But

that's all we know. Someone believes you can expose him—or he's been out to get you from the beginning."

"But I don't know anyone who'd want to hurt me. What could I have done to cause it?"

"With some people, you don't have to do anything."

Now silent, Ned shot Sheridan a sullen glance for allowing Cain to upstage him. But at the moment, Sheridan didn't have it in her to worry about, or apologize for, the lack of courtesy. "There was no warning," she said numbly. "Nothing to alert me to any danger. The last thing I remember is packing my suitcase to come to Whiterock."

"I'm guessing you weren't in town very long when this happened," Cain said. "Where were you staying?"

"My uncle's house," she replied at the same time Ned said, "The old Bancroft place."

Yes, the old Bancroft place. She could picture it. She seemed to be getting her bearings, remembering more and more. "Uncle Perry died a few years ago and left it to my mother," she told Cain. "My folks have been renting it out, but the man who lived there since Uncle Perry died moved two months ago and my mother doesn't want the responsibility anymore. When she heard I was coming, she asked me to clean it up and put it on the market."

"Did you notice anyone watching you? Following you?" Ned asked.

She focused as hard as she could on what she'd done after packing her bags, but the details she'd recalled were already slipping into the shadows. "I—I can't say." She didn't even know where her car was. Had she left it in Sacramento and rented a vehicle once she flew into Nashville? *Had* she flown into Nashville? That was the most logical place, but most of the practical considerations of the past few days—or was it weeks?—were lost to her.

She'd never realized how much those details mattered, how much they grounded a person, until she couldn't remember them.

Cain studied her closely. "It'll come back," he said as if he understood that losing those memories was nearly as terrifying as the violence that had put her here.

It'll come back. She clung to those words as she closed her eyes. She needed to block out the fear and uncertainty growing stronger inside her.

The phone in her room rang, and Ned picked it up. "It's for you," he said, holding the receiver out to Cain. "It's Owen."

As Cain spoke to Owen—telling him she'd just awakened and was going to be fine—Sheridan let herself drift off. She was almost beyond the fear and discomfort, almost at the dark, quiet place where she'd spent the past week. But then she felt a heavy hand on her arm. "Sheridan?"

She opened her eyes to see Ned's ruddy, freckled face only inches from her own. "I'm pretty sure Cain's the one who did this to you," he whispered while Cain continued to talk on the phone. "Can you tell me why he might want you dead?"

She thought of one very obvious reason. She'd been trying to make him jealous when she encouraged Jason to take her to Rocky Point. She'd only wanted Cain to see her with his stepbrother, to make Cain regret not calling her. "M-maybe he blames me for…for Jason."

"Why would he?"

The sedatives were getting the better of her again. It was difficult to make her mouth form the words. "Because…I…was…there." She sounded like a CD player with the batteries running on low.

"Because you and Cain had some sort of secret relationship, right?"

She heard Cain's voice in the background. *I'd appreciate it if you'd call Janice Powers and Juan Rodriguez and let them know I won't be around today. They both have appointments with me for their dogs….*

Sheridan wanted to listen instead of struggling to find an answer. "What?"

"He shot Jason out of jealousy, didn't he?" Ned insisted. "Then he did *this,* because he's afraid you might reveal his motives."

"No."

"You're sure?"

She didn't like the change in Ned's voice or manner. But, with effort, she managed two more words. "I'm…sure."

Was that a frown creasing his forehead? Sheridan squinted to clear the blurriness in her vision. But he was too close—and only leaned closer, his breath smelling of stale coffee as it fanned her cheek. "Do you have any idea who did?"

The dark form with the ski mask emerged in her memory as if suddenly stepping out of a fog.

"What do you want?" she cried. "What have I done?"

He wouldn't respond. He was afraid she'd recognize his voice. That had to be it. She could tell he wanted to speak. The way he jerked her around, used any excuse to inflict pain, showed his contempt, his derision.

"Why are you doing this? Who are you?" she asked.

Filled with a hatred that was palpable, his eyes gleamed at her through the holes in the mask. But, again, he didn't answer. His hands closed around her throat for the second time, cutting off her air. She was going to die. She...couldn't...get...free. He was...too...strong. Again. No...air... NO...AIR!—and then he let go.

Gasping, she stumbled, and he kicked her, knocking her to the ground. That was when she came up fighting. It was her only choice. She used her feet, mostly, and her teeth, when she could. She even used her head as a battering ram—knocking him off balance once.

That was her only victory. Besides getting loose, of course. She'd been pulling and twisting on the rope that bound her hands behind her back ever since she'd regained consciousness. He thought he could do this to her and get away with it? No! She fought for the rights of victims every day; she was determined to fight for her own, to resist each blow.

And then, by some miracle, the ropes came loose and fell away. She dragged in one gulp of air—that was all she had time for—hit him in the face as hard as she could and lunged toward the trees.

But she didn't escape. He caught her by the hair and dragged her back. And then he spoke, but it was such a low growl she still couldn't identify the voice. "Stupid bitch! Now you're going to pay."

She did pay, but not the way she thought she would. He didn't try to rape her. He just kept striking and striking—

"Do you?" Ned pulled her back into the present. "Are you going to answer me?"

Sheridan had begun to shake. She didn't want to face any more. But she had to. If she wanted to catch the man who'd hurt her, she had to give Ned more.

God, she longed to remember some detail about her attacker's body or movements. But the whole episode became one terrifying blur. He was simply a man of medium height dressed in black. "N-no."

"Then how do you know it *wasn't* Cain?" he asked.

The heart monitor revealed how fast her heart was beating. *Beep...beep...beep, beep, beep...*

Cain was still on the phone. *I'll come by tonight and say hello, see what you need on that alternator. Might be late...*

"I'll figure it out," she promised. She wished the noise would stop. That she could catch her breath. That Ned would leave. Her throat ached as if her attacker's hands had just been there....

"When?" Ned pressed. "*When* will you figure it out?"

"Soon."

He tightened his grip on her arm. "Listen to me," he said, but at that point someone else entered the room. A nurse.

"Is everything okay?"

He released her. "Fine. I was just trying to learn a few things about the incident that put her here."

"I think it's too soon for that. She really shouldn't be bothered right now."

"She was the one who wanted to talk," he said as Cain hung up.

Sheridan didn't bother trying to contradict him. Physically and emotionally spent, she couldn't even open her eyes.

"I'm afraid I'm going to have to ask you both to step out of the room," the nurse said.

"I'll check in with you this afternoon," Cain muttered.

A moment later Sheridan sensed that both men had withdrawn. The nurse's shoes squished as she walked around the bed, tucking in the blankets.

Relieved by the woman's matter-of-fact presence, Sheridan let go of reality and the blinding sunlight pouring through the window, let go of the fear and the confusion. But Ned must've poked his head back into the room, because she heard him speak again.

"By the way. What are the chances that she'll recover?"

Sheridan wasn't ready for this answer. But she had to listen, had to know the truth.

"I'd say they're good," the nurse replied. "I talked to the doctor barely an hour ago. He's very pleased with her progress."

Ned cleared his throat and this time his voice fell to a whisper. "And her memory? Do you think she'll ever be able to recall what really happened to her?"

"That's hard to say. Many patients with head injuries experience ongoing problems. Dizziness. Depression. Disorientation. Memory loss. Those problems can last for a few weeks or several months, even longer."

That gave Sheridan a lot to look forward to....

"But there's a possibility it could come back to her, right?"

"It'll depend on how well she's able to cope with the trauma. She could develop acute stress disorder, post-traumatic stress syndrome or a whole host of other things. But the doctor's optimistic that won't be the case."

God, please, no more problems. It'd taken her a decade to get over the shooting.

5

A raging headache woke Sheridan in the middle of the night. She lay perfectly still for several seconds, trying to cope with the pain. Where was she? Something bad had happened....

And then she remembered. She'd nearly died. Someone had beaten her until she couldn't fight back anymore, then left her for dead in the mountains of Tennessee.

Now she was in the hospital in Knoxville. The same hospital where they'd taken her at sixteen, when she'd been shot.

At least she knew that much. It was more than she could recall the last time she'd awakened.

Encouraged by the improvement in her mental acuity, she decided not to ring for the nurse to request more pain medication. Hurting like this was better than the disorientation caused by the sedatives, mostly because she didn't know how much of her confusion to blame on the analgesic and how much on her injuries. She needed some time to assess her situation, to get her bearings.

Taking a deep breath, she glanced at the medical equipment surrounding her, feeling more alone and adrift than when she'd been admitted to this hospital twelve years before. Back then, she'd had her worried parents constantly by her side, could hear the soft rumble of her father's snoring if she happened to wake at odd hours. Tonight, there was no snoring. She was an adult and her parents didn't even know she'd been hurt. They were on a cruise ship. Her sister was in Wyoming expecting her first baby. And Sheridan's friends were several states away. Skye and Jonathan lived in Sacramento and Jasmine in New Orleans.

Sheridan knew her friends and family would come if she called them. But she doubted she could make a long distance call from the phone in her room, and she had no idea what'd happened to her cell. Whenever she tried to remember, panic set in.

Despite the jab of pain, she turned her head toward the window and gazed out at the moonlight filtering through the tall trees. Somehow, she could still smell Cain's cologne. And it made the hospital seem less sterile, less frightening. All she had to do was get through the next few minutes, she told herself. Those minutes would turn into hours, which would soon bring the dawn. After enough hours and enough days, she'd recover—and she'd do for herself what she did for other victims: make sure the person who'd hurt her was put away.

The fact that Jason's killer had never been caught threatened to erode her fledgling confidence, but she was older than she'd been back then. She had control of her own life and some experience in criminal justice. This time, she'd fight back—no matter what. She wouldn't just go on her way, hoping the police would take care of it. That had been her parents' approach and it hadn't worked, had it?

Nausea roiled in her stomach. Closing her eyes, she focused on Cain's cologne because it seemed like the only raft in this undulating sea of uncertainty, fear and pain. "Hang on. Just hang on," she breathed.

"Sheridan?"

The voice that came out of the dark made her heart jump into her throat—until she realized it was Cain's. Evidently, she hadn't imagined the smell of his cologne. He was there, cloaked in shadow, sitting in the chair in the corner. And she got the impression he'd been with her for some time. Judging from his lack of movement and the scratchiness of his voice, she'd awakened him. "Cain?"

She heard a rasp as he dragged a hand over the beardgrowth on his chin. "Yeah, it's me."

"It's late, isn't it?" she asked in confusion.

"Two or three in the morning."

His presence bolstered her spirits even more than she would've expected. He wasn't part of her family or her circle of friends, but he was company. "I didn't know I had a visitor."

"I tried to wake you earlier, but you didn't stir."

"It's the drugs. I'm still groggy." Careful not to move her throbbing head, she eased herself onto her side. She couldn't see his face, but now that she knew where to look, she recognized his feet beneath a hospital-issue blanket. "What are you doing here?"

He seemed to weigh each word. "I don't want to frighten you, but whoever did this to you is still out there."

"You think he might come after me again?"

"He might not be happy to hear you survived."

Although it hurt to do so, she couldn't help lifting her

head to get a better look at him. She hadn't considered the possibility he suggested; she'd been too busy worrying that she might not fully recover. Until now, she hadn't been coherent enough to consider much of anything. But what he said was certainly possible, since she had no idea why she'd been singled out in the first place.

"So…are you a cop or a security guard or something?" she asked. She couldn't imagine him working with Ned, but there had to be some reason Cain was the one still here, protecting her.

"No."

"Then how'd you get the job of keeping an eye on me?" She wasn't *his* problem. Until she opened her eyes to find him staring down at her after the attack, she hadn't been in touch with him since Jason's death. She'd sent him that note, telling him how sorry she was. He'd never responded, and she'd moved with her family. That was it.

"I guess I've appointed myself."

"Where's Ned?"

"He said he was too tired to drive. I think he got a motel."

"And?" She could tell he was holding something back.

"And probably a prostitute. Ned's not one to waste a hall pass from his wife."

"It's nice to know he's so concerned about my welfare."

"He doesn't worry about anything until it happens. And then he looks for someone to blame."

Ned had told her he thought Cain was the man who'd attacked her. But if he truly believed that, why had he left her alone with him? "He doesn't like you, either."

"No."

"Why?"

"I broke his nose a few years back."

"Were you drunk?"

"I wasn't, but I'm pretty sure he was."

"What happened?"

"I don't know. I wasn't paying attention until he took a swing at me."

Considering Cain's reputation, Ned would've had to be blind drunk to start a fight with him. "I hope you weren't his brother-in-law at the time."

"I was only his brother-in-law for three months. As far as I'm concerned, that isn't long enough to count."

Sheridan couldn't imagine Cain married to Amy. She wanted to ask him what'd changed after she'd left, what'd brought them together, but she knew it was too personal a question. "Has Amy remarried?"

"Not yet. She's seeing Tiger Chandler, though."

Sheridan remembered Tiger. They'd gone steady when they were sophomores and part of the following summer, until she started taking her little sister to swimming lessons at the public pool, where Cain worked as a lifeguard. Pretty soon, Cain was all she could think about, so she broke up with Tiger, after which he refused to talk to her. They hadn't had a single conversation since. He wouldn't even say goodbye when she'd moved. "Tiger's still single, huh?"

"He's been engaged a few times but never married."

"What about Ned?"

"He hooked up with Jackie Mendosa right out of high school. Adopted the kid she already had. They have two others."

There was so much more she wanted to know. After her family relocated, her parents had taken her to a trauma counselor who'd recommended she sever all connections with Whiterock and anyone who'd remind her of the attack. Her parents had agreed and insisted she put the whole thing behind her.

That gave Sheridan time to heal. But she'd never been able to forget the people she'd left behind.

"What's Owen doing now?"

Cain's feet moved as he shifted in the chair. "He's a doctor."

Picturing the knobby-kneed, geeky boy who was so smart he'd been put two grades ahead made Sheridan smile. "I'm not surprised. He sat in the front row in three of my classes and could answer *any* question— at fourteen."

"I could admire that if he had any common sense. He's a good doctor, but—" Cain chuckled "—he can't scramble eggs. If it wasn't for Lucy—"

"Lucy?"

"His wife. He met her in college. Now they live in town with their three boys."

"You like her?"

"She's perfect for him."

That sounded happy. Sheridan had always liked Owen. But the pain in her head was growing worse, and with it the fear that she'd never be the same. *Do you think she'll ever be able to recall what really happened to her?… It'll depend on how well she's able to cope with the trauma….*

Could she cope? It'd been difficult enough to regain

her sense of well-being the first time around. But these doubts terrified her, so she struggled to shut them out, to keep talking. "Ned's disappointed that I can't tell him more," she said.

"Like I said, Ned's lazy. He doesn't want to have to figure it out for himself."

"My memory will come back. I know it will…." Realizing that she'd begun to slur her words, she worked harder to enunciate. "I'm going to see…whoever did this…is put…behind bars."

"Are you okay?" He sounded a little alarmed.

The whole room seemed to be spinning, but she refused to throw up in front of Cain Granger. "I'm… fine. Just…tired."

She let her eyelids close but when he got up, they flew open almost of their own accord. "Cain?"

He hesitated. "What?"

"Are you leaving?"

"I'm getting a nurse."

"No, I—I don't…need…more medicine. I think that's what's making me sick."

He slid his chair up to her bed and sat on the edge of it, this time in the moonlight where she could see him. "What do you want me to do?"

"Nothing. Just stay…with me…for a while, okay?" She had no right to ask him for anything. Jason would never have been at Rocky Point if she hadn't invited him up there to make Cain jealous. She'd cost Cain his stepbrother. But she couldn't handle the guilt. Not right now. All that mattered was this moment. She had to keep it simple just to survive.

"I'm not going anywhere."

His response should've calmed her. But she heard the deafening blast of that rifle at Rocky Point, the rattle of Jason's struggles for breath, the burning sensation of the bullet penetrating her stomach. The details somehow mingled with the details of last week's beating until she could no longer separate one incident from the other.

Stupid bitch, now you're going to pay!

The man with the club had whispered that to her. But he was also the man who'd shot her, wasn't he? Ned thought so. Sheridan did, too. Only he'd changed over the years. His thirst for blood had grown stronger, or he would've been satisfied with using a rifle, like he had before.

Her friend Jasmine, who was a forensic profiler, would've said exactly that. Sheridan had heard her analyze enough violent offenders to know what conclusions she'd draw from such an up close and personal attack. Whoever it was hated her. But why?

With a nervous glance at the door, she reached through the bars of her bed and encountered the soft hair on Cain's forearm before she found his hand. He was so solid, so warm. "Can you…hang on to me for a…for a few minutes?" she asked. He'd said he wasn't going anywhere, but he couldn't stay indefinitely. She wanted to be sure he wouldn't leave before she could stand to be alone.

He didn't actually answer the question, but his fingers curled protectively around hers. "Everything will be okay."

"I know that," she lied. "I just… Don't let go. Don't let go until I fall asleep."

His fingers tightened, as if to convince her. "I'm right here."

Then the blackness swelled up, washed over her and dragged her down.

Cain sat in the dark, watching Sheridan sleep. Every time he covered her up, she managed to push the blankets away. They were bunched at her waist now, but she seemed comfortable so he left them there. The purple bruises on her face, neck and arms were turning green and yellow in places. With the addition of the scabs over a multitude of cuts and scratches, the unwashed mess her black hair had become and the gash on her forehead, which had required ten stitches, she could almost pass for the bride of Frankenstein. And yet Owen was right—it wasn't difficult to tell that without those injuries she'd be as stunning as ever, maybe more so.

Now that the lights were off, the cuts and bruises nearly disappeared in the pale light of the moon, hinting at what she'd look like when she healed. She had the same oval face and widow's peak she'd had before, but her eyes seemed bigger, maybe because her cheeks had lost their rounded curve. The cute dimples of her younger days were mostly gone, but Cain didn't mind. He preferred the subtle sculpting of a leaner face. With full lips and a nicely shaped nose, she didn't need any other assets, but she'd obviously had some orthodontic treatment since she'd left Whiterock. The slightly crooked tooth he remembered from her wide cheer-leader smile—the same tooth he'd once touched with his tongue—was now as straight as the others.

He couldn't stop his gaze from wandering lower as he assessed the changes in her body. Having lost ten or fifteen pounds since high school, she was thinner. As a result, her breasts seemed larger. Beneath her thin hospital gown, they fell naturally to each side.

Looking at her like this brought back memories of another moonlit night, when she'd been lying naked on the bed of a camper in the woods.... That vision gave him such a jolt of testosterone, he stood to cover her yet again so he wouldn't feel like a lecherous creep.

As he placed her hands beneath the blanket, he noticed the torn and broken fingernails that proved how hard she'd fought to save her own life, the chafing around her wrists from the rope, and experienced a flood of fresh anger—

"Cain?" Her eyelids fluttered open.

"What?"

"I'm still…awake," she murmured, the words barely coherent. "Don't go… Don't leave me…"

"I won't," he said, and on impulse kissed her forehead as if she were a little girl. Then she was asleep.

He sat in the chair near her bed. He had a lot of work to do at home. But he didn't want to leave in case she woke up again.

The memory of her thin, delicate fingers seeking his hand convinced him that she needed him. And as long as he sat there with her, he believed the strength of his will might make a difference to her recovery. When she was back on her feet, he'd turn his attention to finding the man who'd done this. Lord knew Sheridan couldn't count on Ned. Ned had joined the police force to be able to swagger around town with a badge and a gun.

The door opened and a nurse came in. "It's time for her meds," she whispered and checked Sheridan's blood pressure and other vital signs before inserting a needle in the tube of her IV. Once the nurse was done, Cain knew Sheridan would be out for quite a while and was finally able to relax enough to sleep. But a scuffle and yelling out in the hall woke him in what felt like mere minutes.

"Who are you? What're you doing here?" someone cried. Then there was a crash and several female screams.

Throwing off his blanket, Cain jumped to his feet and dashed out the door. In the hall, he saw an overturned cart of medical supplies and several hospital employees rushing around in a panic.

"Call security!" someone hollered.

"He went down the stairs!" someone else cried.

A doctor dressed in scrubs stood against the wall not far away, looking stunned as he watched the pandemonium.

"What's going on?" Cain asked.

"I saw a guy who was acting a little strange walk past me," the doctor said. "When I tried to stop him, he bumped into the nurse pushing this cart, knocked her and it over, and took off running for the stairs. Two orderlies went after him."

Cain's stomach knotted with tension. "What was he doing?"

"Nothing, really. I mean he was dressed in blue scrubs, which isn't unusual. But he had a surgical mask over his face and it looked like he was wearing some kind of wig. That's what made me notice him."

Pivoting, Cain ran back into the room and snapped

on the light. He was so used to nurses and doctors coming in and out. Had he missed something?

He yanked back the covers, half expecting to see a knife in Sheridan's chest. But there was no knife, no blood.

Pressing two fingers to her neck, he prayed for a pulse....

And found one.

"Is everything okay in here'?"

Cain turned to see that a nurse had pushed the door partway open. "Fine," he said, and she hurried on.

It *was* fine, he told himself. Sheridan was safe. But he hadn't been vigilant enough.

Thank God he had another chance.

6

"What's all the fuss about?" Marshall demanded.

Cain rested his elbow on top of the pay phone in the hospital lobby, once again wishing he had a cell phone. He'd needed to make sure that Levi Matherley was taking care of his dogs, and he'd decided to check on his grandfather while Sheridan's doctor was with her. Maybe Cain's relationship with John, his stepfather, had been strained from day one, but the opposite had been true of Marshall. They'd hit it off the minute Cain's mother had taken Cain, as a twelve-year-old boy, into Wyatt Hardware to make the introductions. "So you've heard about all the excitement," he said now, attempting to rub the exhaustion from his eyes.

"You think I don't get any news in here?"

Marshall lived in a rest home. Because of the onset of Alzheimer's, it was the best place for him. But it wasn't easy for Cain to see his normally self-reliant grandfather in a situation neither of them liked. Marshall was lucid most of the time; it was just the odd moment when he found himself lost and confused.

"I think you manage to get whatever you want in

there," Cain said with a laugh. "Including a string of girl-friends, judging by the cards I saw on your desk last visit."

"Girlfriends!" His voice boomed through the line. "You know I'd never cheat on Mildred. I've been faithful to that woman for more than fifty years."

Cain tried to ignore Marshall's response. Mildred had died before Cain was even in high school. Marshall forgot that fact more than any other. Probably because that was the fact he wanted, more than any other, to change.

"How's she doing, anyway?" his grandfather asked. "Why doesn't she ever come to see me?"

Cursing the disease that was slowly robbing Marshall of his memory, Cain grimaced. *God, why do I have to watch this happening to the person I love the most?* He never knew what to say when Marshall lost touch, but generally preferred to go along with the conversation rather than risk embarrassing such a proud man. "She's doing fine. I'm sure she'll be by soon."

"I miss her," he said. "Life just isn't the same without her."

There was an awkward silence, because Cain could no longer pretend. He missed his grandmother, too. She'd been every bit as loving and supportive as Marshall. If only she'd lived…. It would've made a big difference—to him *and* Marshall.

"But she's dead, right?" Marshall said at length. "I know that, I know that," he murmured as if he needed to repeat it in order to convince himself.

He was back. Already. Sometimes he slipped in and out of reality so quickly Cain could almost convince himself that Marshall wasn't getting any worse. "Yes, she's gone."

His grandfather cleared his throat, and Cain suspected he was hiding tears. "But Sheridan Kohl isn't gone, is she? I remember her parents, you know. They came into the hardware store all the time. A nephew of theirs ran my Nashville store before I sold out. They were good people. A bit uptight for my taste, maybe. Still, good people. They must be relieved their little girl's okay. And it's all because of you."

This brought a smile to Cain's lips. Others might doubt him—but never Marshall. "They don't know yet. They're on some cruise. And it might be a bit premature to celebrate her safety."

"Why's that?"

"There was an incident here at the hospital last night. A man was spotted right outside her room, wearing a wig and doctor's scrubs. He took off when a real doctor tried to speak to him."

"You think he wanted to harm her?"

"I think he came back to finish the job."

"So what are you going to do about it?"

Cain had been wondering that ever since the incident occurred. He couldn't protect her in such a public place—and couldn't stay at the hospital indefinitely. "I'm going to take her home with me."

"That should be interesting," Marshall said.

Cain had never nursed a woman back to health. But over the years, he'd worked with so many ill and injured animals, he figured it wouldn't be that different. Having her in his own sphere of influence would give him greater control. He could take care of her until she was well enough to care for herself. "I'm sure it will be. If I can talk her into it."

"My favorite show's coming on," Marshall suddenly announced.

Cain chuckled. Marshall scheduled his life according to TV programming. "Okay, I'll let you go."

"Call me later."

"I will," he said. Then he hung up and hurried back to Sheridan's room so he could catch the doctor.

When Sheridan woke up, it was daylight and she found Cain sitting next to her bed. His hands dangled between his knees, his hair stood up on one side as if he hadn't had the chance to comb it and the shadow of beard covering his jaw had darkened considerably.

"How long have you been here without a break?" she asked.

"Nearly two days."

"I'm sorry. I should've told you to go home last night." She was still drowsy but feeling better. The sunlight coming through the window chased away her remaining doubts. She could smell food drifting toward her from the covered plate on the rolling table now positioned at her elbow. For the first time since the attack, she felt hunger pangs. "Want to share my lunch?"

"No."

He seemed preoccupied. "Is something wrong?" she asked hesitantly.

"I want to get you out of here."

She forgot about lunch. *"What?"*

"Whoever did this to you…it's not over."

The brief sense of well-being brought about by all that sunshine disappeared. "What do you mean?"

"Someone who wasn't a doctor or a nurse tried to come in here last night, after we both fell asleep."

"Tried?"

"He looked suspicious so someone confronted him and he took off."

A deep uneasiness caused goose bumps to jump out on her arms. "You're saying whoever did this to me isn't giving up."

"I don't know. Maybe it wasn't connected, but I don't want to take the chance that it was."

She could tell he was reluctant to scare her; she could also tell he fully believed it *was* connected. "This killer is determined."

"It takes a lot of audacity to try something in a public place."

"Or a strong desire. That's why—"

Voices at the door interrupted her. Ned entered, followed immediately by a woman who looked less like a linebacker than he did but was still a far cry from petite. Sheridan knew without any introduction that this was Amy. She recognized her from her resemblance to Ned, but she would've remembered Amy regardless of her brother—despite the extra weight, the practical braid that kept her long red hair in order and the dark blue uniform.

Hoping to read his reaction to his ex-wife, Sheridan studied Cain, but in the blink of an eye, his expression became too neutral to reveal what he was thinking.

"What's going on?" Ned demanded.

"As you know, we had a little disturbance at the hospital last night," Cain said.

"What the hell's that supposed to mean? On the phone, you made it sound as if someone came after Sheridan again."

"I think that's exactly what happened. Fortunately, there was a doctor in the hall right outside who thought it was strange to find a man walking through the hospital wearing a wig."

Amy moved closer to the bed and folded her arms across breasts that hadn't existed in high school, at least in their current size. Her eyes darted toward Cain for the fifth time since she'd walked in. Amy was obviously as infatuated with him as she'd always been, but she seemed professional enough when she spoke. "They didn't catch him?"

"No. A few orderlies chased him but he got away."

Ned cursed and shook his head. "I can't believe this."

"So what do we do now?" Amy asked.

Cain shoved a hand through his tousled hair. "I'd like to take her home with me."

Sheridan's jaw dropped. This must've been where Cain was leading the conversation before Ned and Amy walked in, but she hadn't seen it coming.

Ned responded before she could. "No way!"

Cain got up and rounded the bed. "Why not?"

"Because I'm hoping she can help me solve Jason's murder. The last thing I want is to have her cozy up with you."

"I plan on doing everything I can to solve Jason's

murder," Sheridan said. "But that has nothing to do with Cain. Where I stay makes no difference."

"So you're saying you *want* to go home with him?" Amy asked.

"No, of course not. I don't want to inconvenience him or anyone else. Surely there are other alternatives."

"What makes you think she'll be safe at your place?" Ned asked.

"It beats a hospital," Cain said. "Too many people coming and going. There's so much noise and activity, I can't tell when something doesn't belong."

"I'm sure whoever it was won't return," Amy chimed in.

"We can't assume that," Cain said. "The fact that he came here once tells me he's bold enough to try anything."

Amy's eyes darted between them. "So we'll post a guard."

"And who'll pay for that?" Ned muttered.

Sheridan felt obligated to offer, but she couldn't pay for it out of her personal account. She and Skye and their new partner, Ava Bixby, drew salaries that barely covered their living expenses. "My charity can probably pick up the tab. That's what we do, fill in the gaps for stuff like this and, considering the situation, I guess that would apply to me, too. A victim is a victim."

"There's no need for anyone to pay," Cain said. "If I take you home it'll be free."

"But her doctor will never go for it," Ned said.

"I've already spoken to him." Cain leaned against the side of her bed. "He agreed with me. He believes she might actually recover more quickly in a homelike setting. And he's willing to have Owen check on her and report back to him."

Amy was visibly struggling to hide her anxiety at that suggestion. Obviously, Cain's ex-wife didn't want Sheridan anywhere near him. "If she can be moved, why not send her home to California?"

"She can't travel that far," Cain said. "Not yet."

"And I'm not leaving Whiterock," Sheridan told her. "Not until the man who hurt me is behind bars."

"So you're going to Cain's?" Ned asked.

Sheridan pulled the blankets higher, seeking their reassuring warmth. "It's my best option."

Ned sent Cain a sly look. "Why are *you* taking such a personal interest?"

"I want closure, as badly as she does," he said. "I want to know who tried to frame me by putting that rifle in my cabin."

"There's a chance her memory won't come back," Amy pointed out. "She won't be any good to the investigation unless she can remember what happened."

"Excuse me?" Sheridan was about to explain that she'd dealt with over a hundred criminal investigations in the past five years, that she'd have *something* to offer regardless of what she remembered. She probably had more experience dealing with violent crime than the whole Whiterock police force combined. But Cain had already answered, and Sheridan knew Amy didn't care what *she* had to say. She cared only about Cain.

"At least she won't be vulnerable," he said. "She'll have a safe place to heal."

"Who's going to keep her safe from you?" Amy snapped.

Cain rolled his eyes. "I'm no threat to her, and you know it."

She glared at him. "You're a threat to *every* woman, Cain."

He ignored the comment. "I've got a quiet place that's away from roads and buildings. And I've got the dogs. They'll tell me if anyone's coming."

Ned exchanged a glance with his sister. "I don't like it," he said. But his tone had changed, and Sheridan sensed that he was only trying to support Amy. His professional objections had been neatly overturned.

"Someone could shoot your dogs. And then where would you be?" Amy asked Cain.

"Anyone who shoots my dogs had better pray I don't catch them."

Ned touched Sheridan's arm. "You'd be safer with a guard."

"Your doctor's willing to release you. You don't need Ned's permission," Cain said.

"My brother knows what he's talking about." The distress on Amy's face almost made Sheridan feel sorry for her. She wanted Cain so much she couldn't even take a pity project in stride.

But if Sheridan couldn't go back to Sacramento, Cain was all she had. She certainly didn't know anyone as capable of keeping her safe. He was the one who'd pulled her out of the forest, who'd saved her life. Besides, she'd been through too many battles since she left Whiterock to run from this one.

"I'm not afraid of Cain," she said. But she wondered, even as she made the decision, if she wasn't asking for the same kind of heartache Amy had endured since high school. There were times, even while she was making love with the man she'd nearly married, that she thought of Cain.

Maybe she'd never gotten over her own infatuation.

Cain stood at the entrance of Sheridan's late uncle's house, which was obviously furnished just the way it'd been on the day he died, despite the interim renter. The door had been locked, but the key was stashed under the mat, so anybody could get in. He saw no sign of forced entry. Whoever had grabbed Sheridan had either opened the door after she'd unlocked it or simply used the key, as Cain had. Or maybe she'd let him in.

Ned and Amy, or one of the other two policemen on the Whiterock force, had visited the house while Sheridan was in the hospital and made a mess dusting for prints. Powder in contrasting colors covered almost every surface. But they hadn't found anything useful. He knew because he'd called Ned to see if they'd located Sheridan's purse, and learned that they had—the contents were spilled all over the kitchen floor.

Now that the police were done, Cain planned to gather up her belongings and take them to his place, where Owen was looking after her in his absence.

A radio played in a back bedroom. Cain assumed it'd been on since Sheridan arrived. Maybe she'd been hoping to make the house feel less empty. Set on a rhythm-and-blues station out of Nashville, it broke the silence, but given the stagnant air and closed-up feeling of the place, the music seemed more forlorn than comforting.

Several flies escaped as he walked in. Bees hovered amid the kudzu that had taken over the front planter areas. The yard smelled like warm earth, but a far less pleasant scent emanated from the kitchen, where Cain discovered a brown-paper sack of groceries sitting on the counter. Blood soaked the bottom of the bag.

After what he'd seen the night he rescued Sheridan, the sight made him uneasy. Surely whoever had dragged her out of here hadn't left some sort of disgusting present....

No, the police would've found it first. He'd obviously seen too many horror movies.

A quick inventory of the contents revealed nothing worse than a pound of spoiled hamburger. Apparently, whoever attacked Sheridan had made his move just after she'd returned from the grocery store. Maybe he'd followed her home.

He frowned as he noticed blood spatter on the kitchen window and could instantly tell that it had nothing to do with the rotting meat. There'd been a struggle here. A chair had been knocked over. Everything in Sheridan's purse was spilled out on the floor. Even the fridge doors were hanging open. The rattling, over-worked motor managed to provide a faint puff of cool air in the otherwise stifling room, if he stood right in front of it, but the ice cream in the freezer had melted. And water pooled underneath. The police hadn't both-ered to turn off the radio and close the fridge?

"Callous assholes," he muttered. Amy had probably left it this way on purpose. She wasn't happy about

Sheridan's staying at Cain's place. But seeing the house exactly as it'd been the night Sheridan had been attacked gave him a clearer sense of what'd happened. At least he knew where the trouble had started.

Unfolding one of the paper sacks Sheridan had emptied before being interrupted, Cain began picking up the cosmetics, papers, pens and other things that'd been in her purse. Her compact was cracked, a tube of lipstick had melted and the battery in her phone was out of power. He wondered if her friends and family were trying to reach her, what they must be thinking after so long without word.

As he stood to go in search of her luggage and cell phone charger, he spotted a wallet he'd missed. After dragging it out from under the table, he realized it contained photos—photos he had no business seeing, but he was curious enough to look at them anyway.

There was a picture of her younger sister in a wedding dress, her parents standing by a Christmas tree, and her with two other women posing in front of a glass door that read *The Last Stand*. When he saw a picture of Sheridan sitting at a formal event with a man who had his arm around her, he took an extra second to study their body language. Was this man significant to her? Was he worried because she hadn't been in touch? *Had he made love to her the way Cain had twelve years ago?*

Shoving that question—and the persistent memory that went with it—to the back of his mind, he flipped to the next photo. And froze. It was Jason's sophomore picture.

Why was she walking around with a constant reminder of what she'd been through?

The sadness of his stepbrother's death hit Cain as

hard as it had the day it'd happened, as if no time had passed at all. Jason had been the best kid Cain had ever known. He'd been more positive and functional than Robert, more socially adept than Owen. He'd been the all-American athlete, the guy who should've been voted Most Likely to Succeed—had he lived to graduate.

Cain could still remember Jason's excitement over having a date with Sheridan. He could also remember the gnawing jealousy—

"Hey, anyone home?" a male voice called.

Cain put the photo book in the bag. "Come in."

The creak of footsteps sounded in the hall before Tiger Chandler ducked his head into the kitchen. "I thought that was your truck. There goes the neighborhood, eh?"

Cain returned his smile. "It went to hell a long time before I got here."

"No kidding." Although Tiger wasn't the kind of guy who went to the gym, he had a stocky build and was naturally strong. Cain had seen him in a bar fight and knew he could be formidable. "You the cleanup crew?"

"More or less."

He wrinkled a nose that was too small for his face. "Smells like you've got your work cut out for you."

"Smelled fine till you came along." Cain grinned as he used a paper towel to wipe the melted lipstick off his hands.

Tiger rubbed the blond tips of his bleached hair, which he'd gelled into spikes. "I didn't think you were the type to play with makeup."

Cain righted the fallen chairs. "Don't worry. I left the panties and high heels for you."

Tiger laughed, but sobered as his eyes wandered around. "So this is where it happened, huh?"

"Looks that way to me."

"She'd only been in town for a night and a day. How's that for a welcome party?"

Taking a rag from the drawer next to the sink, Cain began wiping off the table. "How do you know how long she was in town? Did you talk to her?"

"No, Amy got the date from the contract on Sheridan's rental car."

"Whoever did this moved fast."

Tiger's expression turned grim. "He definitely came with a purpose in mind."

"The question is *why?* Why Sheridan? Why now?"

"I can't tell you. I mean, we didn't part friends." He seemed to realize that put him in Sheridan's "enemy camp." "But I'd never attack her," he added.

Cain set the sack with her belongings on the table he'd just cleaned and dusted off the chairs. "Have you had *any* contact with her over the years?"

"Nope. I don't think anyone has. She was pretty freaked out when she left. The whole family was. They packed up and took off and never looked back."

He tossed the rag into the sink. "She'd been shot for no reason. And she watched my stepbrother die. That would be traumatic for anyone." Steeling himself against the stench, Cain got another sack, placed the spoiled meat inside and carried it out to the garbage.

"So what's she like?" Tiger asked when he came back. "Has she changed much?"

She'd grown more beautiful. And she probably

wasn't as sexually inexperienced. But Cain wasn't about to speak those thoughts aloud. Finding a broom in the utility closet near the entrance to the garage, he started sweeping. "I don't know. She's been pretty incoherent since it happened."

"It's interesting that she's at your place."

"Why?" Cain paused to glance up at him.

"I always thought maybe she had a thing for you."

No. She'd been trying to get back at her controlling parents by doing exactly what they were afraid she'd do. At least, that was what Cain liked to tell himself. It was the only explanation that made him feel better about ignoring her after such an encounter. Acknowledging that she was infatuated with him made him feel too guilty. "Why did you think that?"

"When she broke up with me, she told me she liked someone else, but then she never got with anybody. Any other guy would've snapped her up in a minute."

Cain went back to sweeping. "That was just an excuse to get rid of you."

Tiger didn't go for the joke. "Maybe, but her little sister made an interesting comment once."

Cain wasn't sure he wanted to hear what it was. The trust Sheridan had handed him that long-ago night had terrified him. He'd rather not have any proof that there was real feeling behind it. That would only make it harder to convince himself she was merely rebelling. "Little sisters say a lot of things."

Tiger hesitated, then appeared to shrug it off. "Right. You two were so different in high school, I could never imagine you together."

Neither could Cain. And yet…

"It's nice of you to do this for her," Tiger said.

Why *was* he doing it? Why was he letting himself get more and more involved? He could hear the question in Tiger's voice, but he didn't completely understand, either. Maybe it was because, for the first time in her life, the girl who'd had it all needed someone—needed *him*. "It wouldn't be pleasant to come home to this after everything she's gone through."

"She's coming back here, then?"

"I'm assuming she will, when she's strong enough."

"Would you mind if I stopped by your place to visit her sometime?"

Cain didn't want anyone bothering her. Not for a few days. But he knew Tiger would misinterpret simple concern for her well-being as something more if he said no. "Of course not."

"Okay, I'll see you around."

After Tiger left, Cain finished dusting, vacuuming and scrubbing. Then he packed her luggage, hauled it out of the bedroom and locked up. He hadn't been able to find Sheridan's phone charger and was just wondering if she might've forgotten it in California, when he opened the door of his truck and found a gigantic box of condoms on the seat.

There was a note on top. And he was pretty sure it was Amy who'd written it. *At least wait until she can walk…*

7

John Wyatt hadn't been sleeping well, so he'd taken a week's vacation from his janitorial job over at the high school. He'd been at the school for so many years, he had plenty of vacation time and needed to use some of it anyway. But he should've settled for a day or two. Anything more left him with too much free time. He had no idea how long he'd been staring at the picture of the son he'd loved more than anything in the world. He only knew Jason was gone. For good.

Sometimes, even after twelve *years,* it was hard for John to believe that. He'd wake up in the morning, thinking he had a son who was everything a man could ever want, a son of whom he could be proud. And then he'd realize that the only children he had now were Robert, who wasn't much to admire at all, and Owen, who was so intellectual and reserved he was almost... *odd.* He didn't count Cain, of course. John had never counted his stepson.

He shifted his eyes to the small box he held in one hand, hesitated, then flipped open the lid. A half-carat diamond ring sparkled against a blue velvet background. He'd bought it for his girlfriend, Karen, nearly a month ago. He'd planned on asking her to marry him, planned on walking into her classroom in the middle of her high-school English class and proposing in front of all her students. He knew the kids would get a kick out of that, knew she'd enjoy the attention. She deserved something big like that for her first proposal.

But that was before the rifle that'd killed Jason had been found in Cain's cabin.

With a bitter chuckle, John snapped the lid shut and got up to toss the ring back into his underwear drawer. He'd propose eventually. He and Karen were meant to be together. She was the reward he deserved for all the years of unhappiness since his first wife died giving birth to Robert.

It wasn't the right time for an engagement. The news wouldn't make the big splash he'd anticipated. It couldn't compete with that rifle reappearing, and the return of poor little Sheridan Kohl.

A fresh wave of hatred made him clench his teeth. It was *her* fault Jason had been at Rocky Point in the first place. Her fault—and Cain's—that Jason was dead. That was enough to hold against his stepson, but Cain was responsible for even more than that. He'd ruined John's second marriage. How often had Julia taken her son's side in an argument? Practically always. Julia wasn't nearly as docile as his first wife. John had been happy with Linda. If he'd had his choice, they'd be married to this day. Then none of these terrible things would've happened. He wouldn't have met Julia at that cheesy strip bar in Nashville where she worked as a waitress, and fallen for her beauty. He wouldn't have had to take care of her while she died of breast cancer. He wouldn't have been saddled with a stepson he'd never even liked. He wouldn't have had to suffer his own father's many reprimands for "not treating Cain fair."

But it was losing Jason that ate at him, that made it almost impossible to look at Cain.

The phone rang.

Dropping onto his bed, John glanced at Caller ID, then picked up. It was Karen.

"Aren't you coming to get me for lunch?" she asked.

John blinked, suddenly aware that quite a lot of time must've passed without his noticing. His eyes cut to the digital alarm clock. Sure enough, it was after noon. Sometimes he got so caught up in his thoughts he lost track of the present. That he'd done so *again* frightened him. Was it the beginning of Alzheimer's?

God, he didn't want to be like Marshall, didn't want to end up being pitied by his own children. "Yeah, ah, of course," he said, trying to regain his mental footing.

"Then, where are you? Don't tell me you got involved with your welding again."

He'd started a side business via the Internet, selling lawn decorations he fashioned out of scrap metal and made to look like animals. Usually he just spent Saturday mornings in his welding shed, but he was doing more work there now that he had some time off. "Actually, I did." He didn't want to tell her he'd forgotten their date; it was only a half hour ago that he'd sent a text to let her know he was coming. And she was fifteen years younger than he was. He didn't want to scare her, make her fear he had mental problems. Then she'd never marry him.

"Where's your cell? I called, but you didn't answer."

It was in the living room, where he couldn't hear it. "I must have the ringer turned off."

"Well, turn it on. And hurry. I'm not going to have time if you don't get here right away."

Massaging his temples, he told himself other people occasionally forgot lunch appointments, too. "I'll be there in five minutes," he promised.

Judging by the brightness outside her window, it was at least late morning, maybe early afternoon, during her first day at Cain's. But Sheridan heard no one in the house. She lay there for several minutes, listening to complete silence. Was she alone?

Rolling onto her side, she checked the nightstand for a phone.

There wasn't one. She was in a guest bedroom that probably saw little use; she could understand why it might not have an extension. But she wanted to call The Last Stand, to talk to Jonathan or Skye or Ava, and follow up with a call to Jasmine.

What would she tell them? They'd all advised her not to come back to Whiterock. Jon, especially, insisted there was only pain and misery for her here. He didn't believe a rifle devoid of prints would yield any new evidence. But Sheridan had wanted answers badly enough to make the trip despite that. And now she was lying injured in Cain's spare bed. Once her friends heard, they'd either rush to her side, which is imprac- tical now that most of them had families of their own, or plead with her to return.

Sheridan didn't welcome either response. She refused to interrupt their lives, since this had been her own decision in the first place. And she wasn't about to return before she was ready. The attack on her had created more questions—and more determination to answer those questions.

Almost glad she didn't have access to a phone, after all, because it put off having to tell her friends, she smoothed down her hair with both hands and called out, "Hello? Anyone home?"

She hated being so dependent and helpless, hated feeling that she was causing Cain more work and trouble than she had any right to expect from an old acquaintance, but she needed a drink, and both he and the doctor had warned her not to get up by herself.

Fortunately, Cain didn't seem to mind the extra trouble. From the gentleness with which he'd fed her and helped her sponge-bathe last night, she got the impression he enjoyed caring for her, the same way he enjoyed caring for all the other living creatures on his property. At the very least, he took it in his stride.

No one answered her call, but a black snout poked through her half-open door and she realized she was about to meet one of Cain's dogs.

"Hello," she said, but the hound didn't come in right away. He hesitated as if waiting to see if Cain would respond with an order *not* to enter. When that didn't happen, he widened the opening by wiggling his body and came in. Then he stood there, cocking his head to one side, apparently trying to figure out who she was and why she was in his master's house.

"You must be one of the dogs that saved my life."

A tall, thin man with a boy's bushy hair and a pair of nerdy glasses—a man who could only be Owen—stepped into the room behind the dog, carrying a tray with a cup and a bowl on it. "This is Koda."

She shifted in the bed. "From what I hear, I owe him a lot."

"He's a good dog, but it wouldn't matter even if he wasn't. Cain can turn any hound into a good dog, make him obey with a whistle or a nod. The hounds I used to own would never shut up, and they raced after anything with a scent." He paused thoughtfully. "As a matter of fact, Koda used to be mine. He wouldn't do a thing I told him. But if Cain asked him not to eat, he'd voluntarily starve to death."

She tried not to laugh—it hurt her head—but she chuckled. "How've you been, Owen?"

"Better than you, for the past week or so, anyway."

"That wouldn't be hard."

"No."

"Cain tells me you have a stellar wife and a couple of kids."

His cheeks reddened. "I have a few more mouths to feed."

Sheridan smiled, mildly surprised to see how much more successfully Owen could relate on a social level now that he'd matured. In high school he'd been so much younger than the other students. He'd always avoided one-on-one interaction, preferring to keep to himself or hover at the fringes of a group. If Sheridan ever approached him, he'd stare at his shoes and mumble monosyllabic responses in a mostly one-sided conversation.

"He said your wife keeps you on track."

"Only because I don't dare cross her." He grinned as he put the tray on a nightstand that was extra-large and as masculine as the rest of Cain's furniture. From what Sheridan had seen, in Cain's home comfort won out over style. Yet there was a woodsy, cabinlike atmosphere throughout, and every room was clean.

"You've brought lunch, I see," she said.

"Cain had to go to town. He asked me to look after you—and gave me strict instructions that I was to wake you and have you eat if you weren't up by noon. I was giving you five more minutes, so your timing's good."

"Is he a paramedic or a vet or something?" Other than ascertaining that he wasn't a cop, she hadn't questioned Cain about what he did for a living. She'd either been loopy with drugs or too preoccupied with doubts and fears about her recovery. But the care he'd shown her from the beginning suggested he had more confidence in dealing with injuries than most people did.

"No, he works for the Tennessee Wildlife Resources Agency. He looks after the large tract of public land adjacent to this property."

"The forest?"

"The main body of it. In addition to that, he patches up other people's animals—any animals, really—just because he's good at it. Fortunately, he hasn't yet put me out of business by turning his talents to healing people," he added with a rueful smile.

"So I'm an exception?" She was now officially "Cain's patient," it seemed.

"You're just another bird with an injured wing," he

said. "And the good news is that Cain always opens the cage when you're ready to fly."

Sheridan didn't know how to respond to such a strange comment. Did Owen intend more warning than reassurance? Sheridan thought so. "What happened between him and Amy?" she asked.

Koda gave a low growl, as if he didn't like the conversation, but a quick glance in his direction confirmed that he was just interested in her food.

"Go gnaw on the furniture," Owen told him, but Koda merely sat down and wagged his tail.

"I don't think you'll be able to convince him to do anything Cain wouldn't like," she said between spoonfuls.

"I couldn't get him to obey me at all. That's why I gave him to Cain."

She swallowed before sending him a hopeful smile. "Are you going to tell me about Amy?"

He seemed annoyed by the question. "Why do you want to know about Amy?"

The sudden change in his manner made Sheridan frown. "Basic curiosity. I've been gone for twelve years. Last I knew, she was following him around like a love-sick fool, but he wasn't interested."

"He was interested enough to get her pregnant."

A latent twinge of jealousy clamped down hard but she managed to smile through it. "Is that why he married her?"

"It wasn't for love."

"You don't think she tried to trap him, do you?"

"With Amy, who knows? She'd do anything to have him, even now."

Based on what she'd seen, Sheridan agreed. "So…is the child living with her?"

"She miscarried a few weeks after they eloped."

"Does anyone know for sure if the baby was real? She could've made that up."

"Cain's not stupid," he said. "He went with her to get an ultrasound before he married her. There was a baby."

"Was he excited at all? About the baby, I mean?"

"I don't think excited would be the right word."

She pushed her hair away from her eyes. "So what did he do after she miscarried?"

"He divorced her."

"The miscarriage didn't make him sad?"

"Cain didn't talk to me about it. He's very private, so I doubt he talked to anyone. But I'd guess he was so young that one ultrasound wasn't enough to make it real. He acted like the pregnancy was an obligation. An obligation from which he was granted a reprieve."

"So he was relieved."

"I had the impression he was very relieved. He did mention to me once that his relationship with Amy wouldn't provide a very strong foundation for a family. But of course we already knew that."

"His desertion must've hurt Amy." Sheridan felt sorry for her. But if Amy had gotten pregnant intentionally, she should've expected problems. Trying to corner a man like Cain was beyond risky; it was downright foolhardy.

"Judging by her bitterness, I'm sure it did."

"So…"

He lifted a hand to silence her. "If you stick around long enough you'll hear plenty about Cain and Amy.

She won't let go of the past, won't let go of *him*." Taking a break from the soup, he helped her drink some warm beverage she didn't recognize.

"What's this?"

"Cain's own blend of herbs brewed into a tea."

"Not bad, considering it's medicinal."

Owen set it aside. "What about you?"

"Me?"

"Are you married?"

She wanted to feed herself, but her movements weren't steady enough for soup and she was afraid she'd dribble it all over the bedding. The beating had impaired her motor skills, which gave her one more thing to worry about. "Nope. Not even dating."

"Why not?"

"I've let my work take over." It was a sad commentary on the state of her life at twenty-eight, but The Last Stand had become her only passion. She and Skye and their new partner Ava, who'd started a few months ago, worked night and day, and it still wasn't enough to meet the tremendous need for the services they provided.

And now she couldn't work at all. Not for a while.

"Ned told me you established a victims' charity," Owen said.

"You're friendly with Ned?" Because of the strain between Ned and Cain she hadn't expected it.

He gestured with the spoon he still held. "We've both got kids in Little League. And he isn't so bad as long as Cain's not around."

Cain seemed to bring out the worst in Ned *and* Amy.

"More soup?" he asked, and she opened her mouth for another spoonful.

"Cain told me you're a doctor. That's quite an accomplishment," she said when she'd swallowed.

"Not really. I went to school for eight years to get where I am, but Cain probably knows as much intuitively."

He'd said it amiably, but Sheridan couldn't help wondering if he harbored some envy. "Does it bother you?" she asked. "That Cain's so good?"

"Of course not. He's my brother."

Cain was his *step*brother. They'd always stressed that in high school. It was almost as if the Wyatts, especially Owen's father, hadn't wanted to claim such a renegade. But Sheridan believed that his lack of acceptance in that family was what had *made* Cain a renegade. Although he'd played a few organized sports when he first moved to town, not long after his mother married John Wyatt, he'd quit them altogether. His grades began to suffer; he started acting out.

"What about *your* glamorous job?" Owen asked.

"What about it?"

"Tell me what working for your charity entails."

"I mostly act as a caseworker, which means I assess a client's needs, then fill in wherever possible. Sometimes that includes getting him or her a better lawyer or a different lab to analyze evidence. Sometimes it means getting a second opinion on a psychological profile or an autopsy, providing a safe house, a bodyguard, self-defense classes." She shrugged. "You name it."

"You like what you do."

It was a statement, not a question. "It's fulfilling.

The work's also frightening at times, and it can get pretty depressing when funds run low or we can't do as much as we'd like."

He adjusted the tray. "Must be difficult for you now, being on the receiving end of the equation."

"Being the victim instead of the helper? Definitely. But that only makes me more empathetic."

"Your work includes trying to put murderers and rapists and wife-abusers behind bars, right?"

She swallowed the next spoonful of warm chicken broth. "More or less."

"You're not worried about the danger involved in crossing people like that? I mean, couldn't one of them come after you?"

This was leading somewhere despite the benign expression on Owen's face. "Are you thinking that what happened to me might be connected to my work and not Jason's shooting?"

"I'm trying to figure out if it's a possibility."

She swallowed some more soup. "The timing and location argue against it. I'm from California."

"You could've been followed."

"I flew." And rented a car. She finally knew that much. She supposed her rental car was parked at her uncle's house, but she needed to ask Cain. He'd already said he planned to look for her purse and cell phone today.

"Doesn't matter. Anyone who knew your plans could've talked about them. It wouldn't be hard to figure out where you were going."

Sheridan studied him for a moment. "Then why

bother following me all the way here? Wouldn't it be easier and cheaper to take care of me in California?"

"Not all criminals are dumb and lazy. Ted Bundy, for instance." Owen blinked at her through his thick glasses. "He's an excellent example of a highly functional killer. If someone knew your background, knew you'd had trouble here before, this would be the smartest place to murder you. The police would naturally connect the attack to the incident at the lake. Especially if it's a small force like this one, with no experience in real detective work. And the change in jurisdiction would—"

"I wasn't having problems with anyone before I left," she broke in. She knew all about the difficulties of trying to get two police departments to work together, especially two departments located so far apart.

"But the scenario *is* possible, isn't it? Some man who abuses his wife isn't going to be happy about you getting involved and taking her side. You've probably done that at some point."

"Of course I have. More times than I want to count."

"See? Someone could be angry and desperate for revenge."

Was he *trying* to frighten her? She already felt as if the whole world had become unsafe….

"The degree of anger in what was done to you leads me to believe that whoever did it has something very personal against you," he said when she didn't respond.

Suddenly, Sheridan couldn't eat any more. The way he talked brought flashbacks of the beating. And it upset her that he seemed so insensitive to the fact that his words might cause her discomfort.

But he'd never really had social skills. Maybe the improvement she'd noticed when he first greeted her wasn't a true improvement, after all. Maybe he still didn't know what to say to a woman, to people in general. "You could be right," she said calmly. "There's always the possibility that what happened to Jason and me was completely random. I had no enemies when I lived here."

"No enemies that you *know of*," he corrected.

She let the spoonful of soup he held out dangle in midair. "What's that supposed to mean?"

"What if someone wanted you for himself and didn't like it when you went into that camper with Cain?"

Sheridan hadn't told *anyone* about the camper. Not a soul. Not until she was much older and far away from the whole situation. At sixteen, she'd been too paranoid about having it get back to her parents and too angry with herself for making such a colossally stupid mistake. She'd given Cain her heart at the same time she'd given him her body; he'd taken one and left the other without a second thought or a moment's hesitation.

But she'd always believed he'd at least done her the courtesy of maintaining his silence. "Who told you I went into the camper with Cain?"

"I was there."

Sheridan didn't know how to respond. "You were *where?*"

"Cain had insisted I get out of the house for a change and took me to the party. I wasn't enjoying myself, so I found a quiet spot where I could go unnoticed."

The thought of having a witness to the single most

intimate moment of her life made Sheridan sick. "*In* the camper?"

"Right outside it."

Sheridan wished she could trust him, but she felt sure he was lying. He'd brought it up for a reason, which could only be that he wanted to make her aware that it wasn't the secret she'd always thought. "What if I said we were just talking?" she asked.

"I wouldn't doubt you."

Yes, he would. He already knew the truth. She was even willing to bet he'd been *inside* that camper and had watched the whole thing—or listened to it. *God...* Her trip home was becoming more excruciating than she'd ever dreamed. "What does Cain say?"

"I haven't asked him. He wouldn't admit it, anyway. He doesn't need to boost his ego. He could have anyone. *You* were about the only girl I thought would rebuff him."

There was an underlying accusation in that statement. And she deserved it. She'd been no smarter than the others. But, even at this late date, she didn't want to embarrass her religious parents with rumors that might get back to them through old friends. *The Kohls thought their daughter was so good, but she slept with that Granger boy when she was only sixteen....*

Sheridan could easily imagine what Amy would do with that kind of news. "I knew better than to get involved with him," she hedged.

"With whom?" Cain strode into the room, clean-shaven and handsome.

"No one," she managed to say.

Cain had such presence. But she couldn't spare him

a smile. The old hurts and regrets and self-recriminations made her chest burn as if he'd pressed a branding iron into it, a branding iron with a giant *I* for *Idiot*.

Maybe he could feel the tension in the air, because he didn't push for a more satisfactory answer. "How're you feeling?"

"I...I'm getting shaky. I think I need to sleep." Taking the blankets with her, she turned onto her other side so she wouldn't have to look at him or his brother.

"How long has she been awake?" she heard Cain ask.

"Maybe thirty minutes."

"She didn't eat much." He wasn't pleased.

"Half a bowl of soup isn't bad. And I got some of your tea down her."

There was a pause. "I'll give her more later," Cain said. Then he called his dog and they went out.

8

"Later" seemed to arrive in the blink of an eye, but the sun was beginning to set so Sheridan knew it'd been hours.

"Time for dinner," Cain announced, gently shaking her shoulder.

The sickening realization of what Owen had told her was there, waiting to ruin the rest of her day. "I need a pain pill," she grumbled, fighting consciousness.

The rattle of dishes indicated that Cain had brought a tray and was setting it on the nightstand but she didn't bother to open her eyes. She wasn't hungry. Every time she thought of her conversation with Owen—every time she imagined him hiding out in that camper—she wanted to pull the blankets over her head.

"I'm taking you off Vicodin," Cain said.

This got her eyes open. *"What?"*

"It causes too much disorientation and can be addictive. I prefer to use herbs and other natural remedies."

He hadn't mentioned this in the hospital. "You're kidding, right?"

His expression said he wasn't kidding even before he spelled it out. "No."

"Why?"

"I told you, what I have is better for you. You'll heal faster. Trust me."

Healing fast sounded good. But trusting him? Trusting him in that camper had proved to be a disaster. "You're sure there'll be a real difference?"

"You'll see."

She eyed the mug on the tray he'd carried in. "More tea?"

"Yes. You'll have some with every meal." He waved at the dresser by the foot of the bed. "I brought your purse."

At last, a bright spot. Reassured that her driver's license and credit cards were now in the same general vicinity she was, Sheridan managed a grudging "thank you" despite her bad mood. She tried to sit up to see it for herself but fell back when black spots danced before her eyes.

"Take it easy," he warned and eased her into a sitting position by propping several pillows behind her. "Okay?"

She nodded, but the fact that he smelled so good— that even now she wouldn't mind burying her nose in his T-shirt—made her grumpier. "Where was it?"

"At your uncle's. Your stuff was spilled out on the kitchen floor."

"Was it actually spilled or was my purse ransacked?"

"Spilled, I think. Your money, credit cards—I'm pretty sure it's all there."

How had that happened? During a struggle? If only she could remember where she'd been, what she'd been doing, what she'd *seen*. "Did the police come up with prints or any other evidence?"

"No. Whoever grabbed you was wearing gloves.

There was some blood spatter near the sink. I'm guessing he got into the house while you were putting your groceries away. You saw movement or maybe his reflection in the window, turned and he hit you."

"So none of the blood was his."

"No."

Her abject despair must've shown on her face, because he seemed to want to cheer her up. "I brought your luggage, too. I thought you might like to get out of that hospital gown."

She felt exposed in the loose-fitting, tied-at-the-back gown, especially since she wasn't wearing anything underneath. But what she'd brought to sleep in was probably even less modest. She'd planned on being alone. "I usually wear a tank top and a pair of panties."

Their eyes locked and enough electricity to light up Manhattan seemed to charge through the room. But a moment later, Sheridan wondered if she'd been the only one to experience it.

"However you're most comfortable is fine by me," he said.

Was he pretending she didn't tempt him, regardless of what she wore? "Can you step out for a minute?" she asked. "I have to use the bathroom." He'd helped her before, but she was more lucid now and had added motivation to do it on her own.

He didn't go. He slid the tray aside so she wouldn't knock against it as she passed. Then he reached for the covers.

She quickly pulled down her flimsy hospital gown before his efficient movements exposed her bottom.

"Ready?" He started to slide a hand around her back, but she stiffened and did her best to move away. She wanted to stand on her own, but he ignored her resistance and swept her into his arms. Then he sat her on the toilet, making her feel about as powerful as a child.

Hating her own weakness and pain, Sheridan waited for the door to close, at which point she had some privacy. Still, she knew Cain was just on the other side, waiting for her to finish.

Why had she come home with him? What had she been thinking?

It was the drugs, she decided. They'd affected her brain. And the fear. She felt safer with Cain than someone like Ned, who was less intelligent, less aware, less capable and a whole lot less caring about the people around him.

When she was done, she used the walls and the sink to keep from falling and washed her hands. But once Cain heard the toilet flush and the faucet turn on, he opened the door and scowled when he saw her dragging herself around by the fixtures. "You could black out and hit your head. You know that, right?"

She pushed him away when he touched her. "I'm fine."

He didn't force her to accept his help, but he stayed close, watching her struggle with every step, inching along, clutching the walls and the furniture. She probably showed him an excellent view of her bare butt when she climbed into bed, but she didn't care. She'd made the trek on her own. That in itself was a victory—until the pain hit fresh and throbbing, punishing her for pushing herself too hard.

Wincing against a sudden wave of nausea, she closed her eyes.

"Are you okay?" he asked.

When she couldn't answer, he pressed a hand to her forehead, but she turned her face away.

"What's wrong?"

She smothered a groan and wiped her top lip, which was beaded with sweat. "Nothing." She shouldn't be sweating; it wasn't even hot in the room.

"You're not going to tell me?"

"What do you think? Everything's wrong," she snapped. "I need to move to a motel, where I can take care of myself."

She opened her eyes to see how he was taking this news and found him studying her with a frown. "You *can't* take care of yourself. Not yet."

He was right. It was stupid to argue. But acknowledging her inability nearly made her cry. She was so miserable and helpless. Someone had done this to her on purpose. Why? It made no sense. She hadn't been in town long enough to offend anyone.

"Will you please get me my Vicodin?" she asked. "A lot of it?" She needed to shut down. She was too aware of the pain, too aware of Cain, too aware of the past.

"Sheridan."

She wouldn't look at him. She could tell from the tone of his voice that he'd noticed the tears threatening to spill over. She'd come back to Whiterock to put the past right—at least as right as she could put it. She owed it to Jason to do everything in her power to bring his killer to justice. And now she couldn't do anything except depend on this man. The man who was the reason Jason had been at Rocky Point. She'd *used* Jason, trying to make him jealous. "What?" she muttered.

"I understand you feel like shit, okay? But it'll help if you eat. Then I can give you some tea to ease the pain. I also have an ointment. It doesn't smell great—it's actually for horses—but you'll see what it does for bruising."

Did he have something for heartache, too? She'd distanced herself from Whiterock for twelve years, and thought she was strong enough to finally come back here. And now this…

She rolled away from him. "Forget the food. Just give me whatever painkiller you've got."

Putting a hand on her back, he briefly brushed the bare skin in the gap between the ties of her gown. He was trying to soothe her, calm her as he would one of his injured animals. She had no illusion that his touch meant anything more. "You *have* to eat, okay? The tea might make you sick if I give it to you on an empty stomach."

"I'll eat tomorrow." Gritting her teeth so she wouldn't groan at the pain caused by her movements, she burrowed beneath the covers.

He pulled back. "Being uncooperative isn't going to help."

His voice had become stern, almost angry; and she welcomed that because it allowed her to be angry in return. "Leave me alone."

"No." As he drew back the covers, she felt cool air. "I'm in charge of your care now," he said, moving her firmly but gently into a sitting position and holding her chin so she had to look at him. "And you're going to eat a few bites."

"I don't even know what I'm doing here. Why are *you* taking care of me?"

"Because last time I checked, there wasn't a line forming!"

She brushed an impatient hand across her chin before her tears could drop onto her chest. "I don't have a single friend here."

"What have I done wrong?" he asked. "Because this sudden change in your behavior is confusing the hell out of me."

"*You're* confused."

"That's right."

She glared at him, and he glared back. Like most men, he was uncomfortable seeing her cry and wanted to do something to stop it. But his attempts to help hadn't worked and he was getting frustrated.

"Are you somehow blaming me for this?" he asked.

"The attack? No." She couldn't blame him. He'd saved her. And he'd been kind to her since. But she couldn't banish the images Owen had evoked. Through the years she'd replayed that act with Cain like a favorite, worn-out movie—and enjoyed it every time. Knowing Owen had been there ruined it, made her cringe in horror.

"Tell me what's changed."

She sensed that Cain's first instinct was to use his hands to calm her, but the way she'd responded to his touch made him rethink it.

Sheridan could understand why Cain's dogs obeyed

him. She felt the same compulsion. But it was that charisma, that magic *something* he possessed, that'd gotten her into trouble before.

Throwing back her shoulders, she swallowed hard. "Owen was watching us that night," she whispered.

Cain didn't immediately speak. He glanced away, rearranging the fork that sat on the plate, along with some steak he'd cut into bite-size pieces. "What're you talking about?"

"Oh, I'm sorry," she said with a bitter laugh. "I suppose with all the other girls, you must've forgotten. Just to refresh your memory, we made...we had sex once. In a camper. At a party. I was sixteen and you were—"

"I remember."

There was plenty of emotion in those two words, but Sheridan couldn't begin to guess what those emotions were. "Owen was there, too. He was watching us the whole time. Did you know that?"

"No." His complexion darkened. He was either angry or as embarrassed as she was. Except that Cain didn't get embarrassed. He was too indifferent for that.

"Yes," she insisted.

"How do you know?"

"He told me when he was here earlier." Her head hurt. Her whole body hurt. But she had to stop crying. She didn't want to cry in front of Cain. "He...he said he was outside the camper when we went in. It was the way he said it that led me to believe...he was there. Inside."

Cain folded his arms, but he wasn't relaxed. "Even if that's true, you don't have to worry. He hasn't told anyone. He *won't* tell anyone."

"That's it?" she said. "Don't worry about it? He was a witness to the most humiliating moment of my life!"

He rocked back as if she'd slapped him, the flash of pain that crossed his face surprising her into silence. Then he stood up and left the room, returning a few minutes later with her prescribed medication and a glass of water to wash it down.

"Here."

The harsh words she'd spoken had snuffed out the fire of her anger and resentment. But now she was cold and empty and ached with a sick sort of regret.

The pills were her ticket out. She needed them, needed the escape they'd give her. Taking them eagerly, she swallowed them both at once. Then, his jaw set, Cain took the empty glass and the tray and walked out.

Cain couldn't get hold of Owen. So he sat outside on the porch steps with his dogs, grateful for the cool night air. He'd spent the past eight days thinking about the man who'd hurt Sheridan, the rifle that'd been found in his cabin, his stepfather's deep-seated doubt and his mother. For some reason, being with Sheridan brought Julia back, made him miss her in a way that left him feeling as young and abandoned as he'd felt at seventeen. His mother had been the one right thing in his messed-up childhood, and he'd had to watch her waste away until she was gone.

He leaned back on his hands and gazed up at the starry sky.

Sensing his restless mood, Koda whined in commiseration, his tail thumping the wooden planks. Maximillian rested his muzzle in Cain's lap, and Quixote dozed at his feet. Cain preferred the simplicity of animals to the complexities of humans. He probably should've let someone else take care of Sheridan. Let Ned post a guard at her hospital room door. Something. But he didn't believe in a lot of the remedies used by conventional doctors. The chemical they prescribed for one malady only created another. Cain knew that with some work on his part and a little grit on Sheridan's, he could do a better job. Maybe he couldn't mask her symptoms quite so well, but he could heal her without causing other problems.

He wanted to do it, to give her a real chance at a full recovery. He supposed it was his way of trying to atone for corrupting her when they were younger, when he was so busy wreaking havoc with anything or anyone he could.

Nudging a rock out of the dirt, he tossed it across the clearing and listened to it land somewhere near the shed that housed his tools and lawn equipment. Owen had never mentioned the camper to Cain. Why would he tell Sheridan he was there? He had to know it would upset her, would upset any woman. It'd been her very first time, which made everything worse. And, apparently, it'd been humiliating. Cain had done his best, but...hell, he'd been a mixed-up seventeen-year-old back then. What did he know?

Grabbing the cordless phone he'd carried out with him, he tried Owen again. It was getting late, but he didn't think he'd be able to go to bed until he made his stepbrother answer for the stupid blunder. It was one thing that Owen hadn't made his presence known before any clothes came off, but it was even worse to embarrass Sheridan by telling her twelve years later.

This time the phone rang only once before Owen's wife picked up. "Hello?"

"Lucy?"

"Cain!"

He heard the smile in her voice. "How are you?"

"I'm okay," she said, "but I hear you have your hands full."

"Not really. I'm usually trying to heal something. A woman isn't so different." Well, maybe this woman was…

"From what Owen says, we're not talking about a sprained ankle. I can't believe anyone in Whiterock would hurt her like that."

"I wish I knew who it was."

"I do, too."

"Is Owen around?"

"He's in the bedroom. Just a minute."

A moment later, Cain heard her voice again. "Here he is."

"Take care," he said and the phone was transferred to his stepbrother.

"What the hell did you say to Sheridan?" Cain asked before Owen could say a word.

There was a long silence.

"Owen?"

"I don't know what you're talking about."

"You told her you were in the camper."

"I didn't tell her I was *in* the camper. I told her I saw her go in with you."

"She thinks you were inside, watching."

"I wasn't."

Cain hoped to God he could believe him. "So why bring it up?"

"Will you answer one question for me?" Owen asked.

"I'm pretty pissed off. That depends on what it is."

"How'd you do it?"

"Do what?"

"Get her to give it up to you? She hadn't even *kissed* a guy before you came along."

Cain had been her first everything. But Owen didn't sound as if he was speaking from conjecture or what he knew of her reputation. He seemed too sure for that. "What makes you think she'd never been kissed?"

Several seconds ticked by before Owen answered. Obviously, he'd heard the fresh suspicion in Cain's voice.

"I intercepted a note to one of her friends," he said at last.

"Which friend?"

"I don't remember. Maybe it was Lauren Shellinger. She and Lauren hung out a lot."

He was making it up. Cain could tell. "No, Owen. She told me that night. She told me that she'd never been kissed the way I kissed her, and you know that because you were there. Isn't that right?"

No response was as good as a confession.

Cain dropped his head in his free hand. "You were inside."

"I didn't dare say anything at the time, Cain. I would've blown it for you."

"How come we didn't see you?"

"I was in the bathroom."

"You've got to be kidding me." Cain had enough regrets about that incident without this. "You think I cared more about scoring than her privacy? Or the fact that you were far too young to be exposed to that kind of intimacy?"

"I didn't know what to do," he said. "I was glad you'd finally deigned to notice me, that you'd invited me to go with you. The last thing I wanted was to ruin your fun."

"So why mention it now? You haven't said a word for twelve years, Owen. Why did you have to let us know at all?"

When his stepbrother paused again, Cain suddenly thought of one very viable reason. "Wait a second... Dad thinks I killed Jason over Sheridan. He's telling you this, and you're remembering what you saw in that camper, and you're beginning to believe it."

"I *don't* believe it," he protested.

If that was true, he wouldn't have brought it up. Without Jason, what'd happened between Cain and Sheridan would have no more bearing on their lives today than Cain's experience with any other girl.

"Why'd you talk to Sheridan about it?" he pressed. "Why didn't you come to me?"

"I wanted to know how she felt about you, that's all. How involved you two were, if you had something going back then that no one knew about. Besides what I saw, I mean," he added awkwardly.

"That was a one-time encounter," Cain said. *The most humiliating moment of my life.* "I wasn't the least bit jealous that she was with Jason."

"You're sure."

"I'm sure."

"Early this morning, Maureen Johansen told Ned that you were at Rocky Point the night Jason was shot."

Cain stood so abruptly, his dogs scattered. "A lot of us spent our weekends at Rocky Point. That's part of what made Jason's murder so damn shocking."

"She thinks you saw Sheridan with Jason and it upset you. She said you were acting strange when you realized they were together. She said you even wanted to leave early."

It was true. For all his supposed indifference toward her, it'd bothered Cain to know she was with his stepbrother. But a goody-two-shoes cheerleader wasn't his type. Once he'd been with her, he knew she was as innocent as she appeared to be, and he wasn't interested anymore. Maybe *he* was self-destructing, but there was no need to take her with him. There were too many other girls to mess around with, willing, available girls who didn't have a reputation to protect.

Cain had hoped Sheridan would go on with her life as if the camper incident had never happened. He'd assumed that as long as she kept her mouth shut no one would know, because he certainly wasn't telling. But only weeks later, she and his stepbrother were shot and the mistake he'd made with Sheridan went beyond taking her virginity. Jason wouldn't have been there without her. Rocky Point was for rebels. It wasn't Jason's scene, or Sheridan's either, which was how Cain knew she'd been making a statement directed at him.

"And Maureen got all that from *what?* I didn't even speak to her that night."

"It's the ballistics tests on that rifle—and the attack on Sheridan. It has everyone stirred up. And Ned and Amy aren't helping."

"If Ned thinks I'm the one who hurt Sheridan, why'd he let me take her home?"

"He said it was her choice."

So the suspicion lingered. Despite the mysterious man who'd pushed and shoved his way out of the hospital. What, did Ned think Cain had paid someone to run through the hospital wearing a wig? "This is crazy," he muttered.

"Cain?" Sheridan's voice broke his concentration. It was reedy, thin, but filled with emergency. *"Cain?"*

Something was wrong. "I gotta go." Hitting the Off button without listening for Owen's response, he charged into the house, tossing the phone on the entry table as he ran.

"I'm here," he called and pushed the bedroom door open to find her lying on the floor. "What's wrong? What are you doing out of bed?"

"I have to…the toilet. I'm…sick."

Oh, boy. She was having a reaction to the meds.

Scooping her into his arms, he barely reached the bathroom before she started to vomit. "Go out," she said and weakly waved him away as she heaved.

But he couldn't leave her. She hardly had the strength to hold herself up. "I'm not going anywhere," he said and supported her weight until she'd finished vomiting. By then, she lay pale and limp in his arms.

"It's okay," he whispered, smoothing her hair off her sweat-damp face. "You're going to be okay."

A tear slid down her cheek, but she let her head fall onto his chest.

"Let's get you back in bed."

When he lifted her, she made a feeble attempt to resist. "No…not like this. I need…a bath."

But she wasn't strong enough to take one, and she wouldn't appreciate having him perform such a service.

After a moment of indecision, he set her on the bed while he collected the shampoo and soap, toothbrush and toothpaste. Then he carried her out of the house, across the clearing and down behind the clinic to the swimming hole created by a small, clear stream. It wasn't exactly a bath, but he knew the water would clean her and cool her at the same time.

Wading in, clothes and all, he let the water lap around them both.

9

The water soaked Sheridan's hospital gown, making it cling to her, but she didn't care. She needed the change of scenery, the chance to escape her bed.

With Cain's arms holding her at the knees and shoulders, she leaned back and let the current comb through her hair, loosening the dirt, cooling her hot scalp. Below her was nothing but water, above her an endless black sky shimmering with stars that looked like crushed diamonds. Cain was the only solid object in her world. Without him, she'd sink or drift away.

"Thank you," she said as he sat on a rock ledge and washed her hair.

He didn't answer, but when he was finished, he helped her brush her teeth.

The fact that it was Cain who'd stood with her through the worst days of her life made her feelings toward him even more confusing, more complex. Finally, her conscience overcame her desire to pretend she'd never mentioned their time together in the camper.

"Cain?"

He gazed down at her, his expression lost in shadow.

"I'm sorry," she said. "I…I didn't mean what I said to you earlier." But that was as far as she could go. She couldn't admit how much that night had meant to her. She was still embarrassed that, thanks to her naiveté, she'd fallen so hard. He'd laugh if he knew she'd pined for him until she was at least twenty-three.

"Forget it." His words sounded matter-of-fact, not grudging, but something had changed. He was formal, polite, kind and above all efficient—but the friendship that'd begun in the hospital room the night he'd stayed with her had been destroyed. He'd raised his defenses. He seemed…wary.

"I was upset about Owen," she tried to explain.

"I know. It doesn't matter. It was twelve years ago."

But it did matter. And it seemed like only yesterday.

Heal. That's all you should worry about for now. Heal so you can find the man who hurt you and put him away.

When Cain took Sheridan into the water, he hadn't thought about how he was going to get her dry. He hadn't remembered a towel. And the medication overtook her before he could bring her back to the house. She was limp in his arms, soaking wet, the ends of her hair dragging in the water.

"Sheridan?" Her head rolled onto his arm when he tried to make her look at him. "Can you hear me?"

No response.

Once he reached the back porch and stood there dripping, he admitted he had no choice but to change her. He couldn't put her to bed in a wet hospital gown.

And he couldn't leave her on the bathroom floor until she woke up.

Carrying her inside, he placed her on his leather couch. Then he changed into dry clothes, scavenged a clean pair of boxers and a T-shirt from his drawers for her and returned to get rid of that hospital gown.

He'd told himself he'd do this quickly and efficiently, like a doctor or a nurse. Dressing her was a practical matter—as long as he wasn't ogling her in the process. But the sight of her lying naked in front of him hit him like a right hook to the jaw. He hesitated even though he had the T-shirt ready in his hands—and let his gaze move quickly over her.

The phone rang almost at the same moment, jolting him back to his scruples. With a deep breath, he dressed her in the T-shirt and boxers, careful not to touch her anywhere he didn't absolutely have to.

By the time she was covered, whoever called had hung up, but Cain was grateful for the interruption. He didn't use sex as a weapon against himself and others anymore, but three years of abstinence was beginning to wear on him.

With a sigh, he got up and returned the call that'd come in. Beth Schlater wanted him to look at her dog in the morning.

But the change in focus didn't really help. Long after he'd hung up, he was plagued with the vision of Sheridan's nude body so close to his.

When Sheridan woke up, it was morning, but she wasn't sure of the day. She tried to do a mental calculation—had it been ten days since the beating?—but she'd been sleeping too much to be able to keep an accurate count.

She could hear Cain in the front yard, talking. The words "bacterial infection" came up and instructions to keep some dog on his medication.

Then everything that'd happened the previous day intruded, and Sheridan groaned. Learning about Owen in the camper. Getting sick and throwing up in front of Cain. Going to the pond and feeling weightless as she floated with only his hands to hold her up.

She tried to remember what'd happened after their swim and couldn't—but she was no longer in her hospital gown.

"Feeling better?"

It was Cain. He'd come in just as she was kicking off the covers to see what she was wearing. Outside, a car pulled away.

"These are *your* underwear," she said, stating the obvious.

He seemed reluctant to meet her eyes, which made her a little apprehensive. "I didn't feel comfortable going through your luggage so I grabbed something of mine," he explained as he stood on a chair to adjust the air-conditioning vent on the ceiling.

"It was too intrusive to go through my suitcase but you felt comfortable taking off my clothes?"

"You were unconscious. What else was I supposed to do?"

Sheridan didn't have a good answer. But she still

wanted some assurance that he hadn't taken advantage of her. "Maybe you could walk me through it."

He got down from the chair and opened the blinds. "Or maybe we could just forget about it."

"I can't forget about it. When I see these clothes, I want to know exactly how I got into them."

"I put you in some dry clothes. That's it." He sat in the chair near the nightstand and locked his hands behind his head. "Would you rather I'd put you to bed wet?"

"No...I...it just feels weird that I can't remember."

"You didn't miss anything."

"Except that one part."

"Which part?"

"The part where you took my clothes off."

"You're making a big deal out of nothing."

"Just tell me this much." She waited for him to meet her eyes. "Did you *touch* me?" She paused. "You know what I mean."

He frowned as if she'd offended him. "I'm pretty sure that would be a crime."

"So you didn't."

He blew out a sigh and extended his legs, crossing them at the ankles. "Of course not."

"But you *saw* me."

Ignoring the comment, he got up to straighten the bedding. "You hungry?"

"I'm starved, but first I want to hear your answer."

Propping his hands on his hips, he faced her squarely. "Okay. Yes, I saw you. Of course I saw you. I *had* to see you."

She wished she could read him better. "But you didn't *look* at me."

"I didn't look at you," he said. But a moment later, he rubbed a hand over his chin and, obviously chagrinned, reversed his answer. "Actually, I did look at you. But only for a second."

The honesty of that admission surprised Sheridan. And now that she knew, she wasn't sure how to feel about it. He'd done so much to help her. Did it really matter whether he'd indulged in a second of unnecessary gawking?

They were dealing with such subtle nuances here—did he see her or did he *see* her? And he was right; it wasn't as if she could've dressed herself. "Why?" she asked.

"Why what?"

"Why'd you look?"

"Are you kidding?" He shoved a hand through his hair. "Because I'm not dead from the waist down, that's why."

"Okay." She was ready to drop the subject. She'd asked. He'd told her. It was over.

But then she noticed that he was watching her with a contemplative expression. "Why don't you ask me what you really want to know?" he said.

The way his voice had lowered, grown huskier, made Sheridan more alert than she'd been since the attack. "What do I really want to know?"

A crooked smile lifted one side of his mouth. "If I liked what I saw."

"You're wrong. I don't want to know that," she said. "I have no illusions that I look good. I'm a mess of scrapes and bruises. That's partly why I'm so...uncomfortable with the idea. I feel...vulnerable."

His eyebrows went up. "It wasn't the scrapes and bruises that caught my attention."

Damn it, he was doing it to her again. She felt the same giddy excitement she'd experienced at sixteen, when she'd been wading in the shallow end of the public pool and his eyes had flicked over her as he sat on the lifeguard tower.

"You're saying you *did* like what you saw?"

His eyes glittered with enough predatory interest to make the tips of her breasts tingle. "Every inch of it."

"That doesn't mean anything," she said with a laugh. "You'd like a walrus if you thought you might get lucky." It was a defense mechanism, a way to depersonalize the attraction between them. And it worked even better than she'd hoped. The sexual energy in the room vanished as quickly as his smile.

"I'll get your breakfast," he said.

Cain had a chamomile salve he wanted to put on Sheridan's bruises but after their conversation this morning he preferred she be awake when he did it. He wasn't particularly proud of having looked at her while she had her clothes off last night, and he knew it would be smarter not to risk further temptation.

Problem was, she slept all afternoon and, after completing the reports that had to be turned in to the Wildlife Resources Agency, and watching a baseball game on TV, he was going stir-crazy. Normally, he didn't spend much time indoors. If he wasn't out at his clinic or somewhere else on the property, he was in the forest, patrolling the campsites, collecting fees, leaving vaccine-laced bait to prevent rabies, especially in foxes and raccoons. He also tracked various animals reported as unusually aggressive and made sure there weren't any picnic leftovers to draw the bears. But whoever had attacked Sheridan was still out there somewhere, so Cain didn't dare leave her alone. And he couldn't ask Owen to come back and sit with her. After what Owen had told her last time, he knew Sheridan wouldn't want to see him again.

Hell, *he* didn't want to see Owen after what he'd learned.

He was just trying to decide if Koda and Maximillian would be enough protection for Sheridan so he could go to the clinic for a while when he heard a car outside. Relieved that he'd get a break in the monotony, he went to the window, but when he saw it was Amy he had to admit he preferred the monotony.

Remembering the condoms in his truck, he grimaced as he watched her get out of her cruiser. She looked very official approaching the house with her thumbs hooked in her belt, but Cain found it rather frightening that Whiterock trusted her with a gun. He never knew which Amy he'd meet when she showed up—the one who wanted him back or the one who wanted to kill him because she couldn't have him back.

He swung the door open before she could knock. "Any news?"

"A little." Her lips pursed as her eyes swept over him, no doubt taking in his mussed hair, Tennessee Titans jersey, well-worn jeans and the fact that he hadn't shaved. "Sleeping late?"

"Working from home."

"How's Sheridan? She remember anything?"

She remembered the camper. "No. But she's improving. What have you found?"

"I'd like to tell you both at the same time. Can I see her?" She gave him a cynical smile. "Or do you have her chained to the bed?"

Cain lowered his voice in case Sheridan had heard the signs of a visitor and was starting to rouse. "I don't appreciate what you left in my truck," he said. Under other circumstances, he wouldn't have mentioned it. It was easier to ignore Amy than get involved in her psycho bullshit. But he was just bored enough to be open to an argument.

Her eyes, surrounded by the usual thick layer of eye shadow and mascara, narrowed slyly. "What'd I leave in your truck?"

"At Sheridan's uncle's place? While I was getting her things?"

"I have no idea what you're talking about. I was with my brother the day you went there."

"Quit pretending," he said. "I know it was you. There was a note, for God's sake."

"Did I *sign* the note?"

"You didn't have to. I don't know anyone else who'd present me with thirty-six condoms."

She laughed as if the jig was up. "Then I guess my next question is whether or not you've got any left."

"Give me a break. I haven't been with anyone in over three years."

She hesitated, but didn't have a chance to react before Sheridan called out from the other room.

"Cain?"

"She's awake. Let's hear what you've found," he said to Amy and led her into the bedroom.

Sheridan was more than a little surprised to see Amy Smith—Amy *Granger,* she corrected herself—walk into the bedroom wearing a self-satisfied smile. In the hospital, Amy had seemed terrified of Sheridan's spending time with Cain.

Something had changed. Sheridan hoped Amy had uncovered evidence that would eventually reveal who'd attacked her, but she didn't get the impression that was the case.

"Amy."

Amy nodded. "Sheridan. How're you feeling?"

"Better."

"What about your memory of the attack? Anything coming back to you?"

"Nothing that'll help. But I'm hoping you're here with some good news."

"That depends on how you look at it."

"Cain said you couldn't get any prints from the house."

"That's true."

Sheridan situated her pillows so she could sit higher. "What about trace evidence?"

"We don't have any of that, either. But we do have a witness."

"To what?" Cain asked.

Amy's pointed gaze cut in his direction. "Someone claims you had an argument with Jason just before he left to pick up Sheridan the night he was shot."

Cain's complexion darkened beneath his tanned skin. "Who?"

Triumph filled her voice. "Robert."

"My stepbrother was thirteen years old at the time."

"That's old enough to know what an argument is."

Cain stepped forward. "He wasn't even home that night! He was out with my stepfather."

Amy flicked a speck of lint from her uniform. "Are you saying your stepfather will back you up?"

A second's hesitation revealed Cain's lack of confidence in his stepfather's support. "Unless he's a liar."

"That's pretty funny, coming from you."

"What's funny about it?"

"You told me you didn't have sex with Sheridan in high school. You said you didn't sleep with her."

Cain's mouth formed a grim line, and Sheridan's heart began to pound. This wasn't something she wanted dragged out.

"Do you still hold to that?" Amy challenged.

He managed a stubborn nod.

"Then what do you make of this?" She pulled a piece of paper from her pocket and flattened it out on the dresser before handing it to him. He read it aloud.

"A few weeks after Jason died, I was lying on my bunk bed, with Owen in the top bunk above me, and we were talking about girls. He said he knew all about sex. I didn't believe him. He'd never had a girlfriend, and he was only fourteen. So I told him to quit acting like a dork. That's when he told me he'd watched Cain—"

Cain stopped, but Amy finished for him, as if she'd memorized every word. "—having sex with a girl at a party. And that girl was *Sheridan Kohl*." She smiled gleefully. "Robert signed it. It's a legitimate statement."

Sheridan's body grew so warm she thought she might spontaneously combust. Owen *had* told someone. He'd told Robert. And now Robert was telling everyone else.

"Amy, what're you doing?" Cain's voice was low, his words more of a warning than a question.

Her eyes narrowed with jealousy and hatred. "Why'd you lie?"

"Because I didn't want it to hurt her. Don't you understand that?"

"You don't care about hurting anyone."

"It was a one-time encounter. It had nothing to do with Jason's death."

"Don't kid yourself. It gives you the best motive we've found so far."

She reached out to grab the paper, but Cain held it away from her.

Her laugh sounded brittle. "Fine. Keep it. I don't need it. I can always get another one." She turned on Sheridan, mouth twisted in a sneer. "You don't deny it, do you?"

Sheridan wanted to, but doing so would be useless. She was sure her face had already betrayed her. "No."

10

Karen Stevens sat across from John at Ruby's Hideaway Steak & Seafood, which was the nicest restaurant in Whiterock. With the dark paneling and dim lighting, she could barely make out the expression on his face, but she thought he looked a bit pale.

"Is something wrong?" she asked.

He glanced up from cutting his meat. "No, why?"

"You seem…withdrawn these days. Restless." She knew it had to do with Cain and that rifle being found in his cabin, because that was when John had grown so reserved. The rifle incident had dredged up the pain of losing Jason. It also made the relationship between him and Cain even more difficult. She understood all that, but she didn't like the sense that he was shutting her out. At the very least she wanted John to be able to share what he was feeling.

"Robert's been drinking again," he said, shaking his head in resignation. "I think I have to get him into rehab."

John didn't need this on top of everything else, but Karen had to be careful what she said about Robert. She didn't agree with the way John handled his youngest son, any more than she agreed with how he handled his relationship with Cain—but for very different reasons. Robert needed to get out on his own and stop leaning on his father. Cain just needed love, but for some reason John couldn't give him that.

"Have you talked to him about it?" she asked.

"You know how he is. All he'll do is argue with me."

"He wouldn't listen even after he crashed into the shed?" She knew that hadn't been a minor accident. Robert's Camaro was still in the shop.

"He claims he won't drive under the influence again."

Karen was tempted to argue that John knew it wasn't true, but she wouldn't push him. Not tonight. He'd only clam up, and she wanted to talk. She missed the closeness they'd shared before that rifle showed up in Cain's cabin. Maybe she hadn't been interested in John when he'd first pursued her twelve years ago. But she was in love with him now.

"So what do you think?"

"I'm just frustrated. I can't tell you how many times I've visited his trailer to find him passed out in his chair. And he spent his last two paychecks on computer accessories *again*."

She chose her words carefully. "I thought you were going to make him start paying rent."

"He spent the money before I could even collect!"

"But the job he got over in Fernley is going okay?"

John shoveled a bite of potato into his mouth. "No. He got fired two weeks ago."

Karen saw John nearly every day. He was the custodian at the school where she taught. Besides that, he came over for dinner or spent the night at her place at least four times a week—during a normal week, anyway. He hadn't stayed with her since that rifle was found. "And you didn't think to mention it to me?"

"I didn't want to fight about it."

She'd told him Robert wouldn't be able to hang on to a job, especially one that required a commute. Robert couldn't even keep regular hours. He stayed up until dawn, then slept past noon. "What's he doing now?"

"I've told him he has to get a job by the first of next month or I'm kicking him out."

Karen would've been thrilled by this news, except she'd been through this cycle too many times. John would never follow through. He'd give Robert another chance and another and another....

"How are you and Cain getting along?" she asked.

A muscle flexed in his cheek as he held his fork in midair, and she clasped her fingers nervously in her lap. It was a risk just bringing up Cain's name. But she felt she owed him something. After what she'd done twelve years ago, she and Cain could never be friends, but she could use her influence to try and make things better between him and his stepfather. "I don't want to talk about Cain," he said as if he'd already made that clear enough.

"I'm just asking how you're getting along. That's not a big deal, is it?" She averted her gaze as she picked up her glass.

"I pretty much avoid him."

That didn't surprise her. "So you haven't asked him how he thinks the rifle ended up where it did?"

"Why would I? You figure he's going to admit to killing Jason?"

"I don't believe he killed Jason."

"And that's why I don't want to talk about it. You stick up for him every time I have something to say."

The accusation rankled. "I'm trying to help," she said. "You told me you haven't been sleeping."

"That's nothing new. I've had trouble sleeping for years. You know that."

She did know. That was the excuse he'd given her for staying away over the past several weeks. He said it helped him relax to be able to go out and work in his shed on his metal animals. Or he'd say he didn't want to keep her up with his tossing and turning. Bottom line, he was so preoccupied with blaming Cain that it was taking a toll on his health and creating stress in all his relationships. Including theirs. "I'm worried about you," she said frankly.

His expression lightened for the first time that evening as he reached across the table to take her hand. "Don't worry. I'm fine."

"Are you sure? I know you get depressed sometimes, over Jason. Is that what this is about?"

"I'm fine," he said again and gave her fingers a squeeze. "I love you. I've loved you from the first moment I laid eyes on you."

She smiled because she couldn't say the same. When she'd met him, he'd been cleaning her classroom at Whiterock High. She'd been twenty-seven; he was forty-two. She'd felt his interest right away but hadn't returned it. He was raising four boys, all of whom were closer to her age than he was—two of them became her students. And he was married to a woman who was dying of cancer.

She'd largely ignored his calls and letters. It wasn't just his situation at home that put her off. She'd been far more attracted to his charismatic stepson, who always sat in the back row of her class....

"Are we having dessert?" John asked.

Suddenly, Karen wanted to make love. It'd been too long. She needed reassurance—reassurance that John didn't know and would never find out the one thing that would, without doubt, destroy their relationship. "Let's have it at my place," she said.

It was late, but for the first time since the attack, Sheridan couldn't sleep. She kept hearing Robert's statement read aloud, kept hearing Amy proclaim that Cain had shot Jason out of jealousy. But that wasn't true.

She'd simply tell everyone what had happened and take full responsibility for it. She knew she'd have some explaining to do when her parents heard, and she felt terrible about the shame and embarrassment it would bring them. But if Cain was guilty of anything, it was abusing his sex appeal, not murdering his stepbrother.

She'd call Amy right now.

Leaning on the furniture and against the walls to stay upright, she got out of bed. Her balance was improving. It wasn't as difficult to walk as it had been just yesterday. Or maybe it was because of the drive she felt to control Amy's reaction to Robert's statement before this witch hunt could get any more out of hand. Either way, she made it to the living room and found Cain's phone easily enough. She didn't know Amy's number, but she was willing to reimburse him for a call to information.

Because she didn't have anything to write with, and her short-term memory wasn't what it used to be, she repeated the number over and over until she dialed it. Then the phone rang and she waited, eager to set the record straight.

But it wasn't Amy who answered. It was a man.

"'Lo?"

Sheridan paused. Had she dialed wrong? She didn't think so. "Is Amy there?"

"Who's this?"

"Sheridan Kohl."

"Sheridan." There was a soft laugh. "This is Tiger."

Of course. She remembered Cain's telling her that Amy and Tiger were seeing each other. Judging by the sleep in his voice and his confidence in answering Amy's phone, they were serious. "Hello, Tiger. How are you?"

"Better than when I knew you before, I can tell you that much."

Sheridan chose not to respond to the verbal jab. "I need to speak with Amy, if I could."

"I'm afraid she's pretty tired. She spent the whole evening laughing her ass off over the fact that your secret is out. The Virgin Queen was screwing Cain Granger. I found it amusing, too."

Sheridan swallowed hard. "That's what I want to talk to her about."

"Tell me something," he said.

She gripped the phone tighter at his intimate tone. "What?"

"Was it worth it?"

"I don't know what you're talking about. I need to speak with Amy."

"I'm talking about you and Cain." Obviously, he wasn't going to pass Amy the phone until he'd exacted a bit of revenge. "Was it worth breaking up with a guy who really loved you so you could screw someone who didn't give a shit about you?"

Sheridan drew a deep breath. *Don't react. There'll be more. A lot more.* Tiger was just at the front of the line. "You're right," she said. "Cain didn't give a shit about me. He got what he wanted and moved on. Does it help to hear me acknowledge it?"

He seemed surprised by her blunt response, and she took some small pleasure in knowing it didn't help at all.

"I would've treated you so differently."

Clearly objecting to Tiger's side of the conversation, Amy interrupted with a waspish remark. Tiger covered the phone, but Sheridan could still hear him. "I cared about her, okay? Certainly more than him. And she did me dirty," he added, saying this into the receiver.

Sheridan rolled her eyes. "You wanted the same thing he did, Tiger. You tried to put your hands up my shirt every chance you had."

"And you wouldn't let me so much as touch you! I couldn't even put my tongue in your mouth without you pulling away!"

"It's been twelve years. *More* than twelve years since we were together. What does it matter that I let him touch me?"

"It's just ironic. That's all," he said sulkily. "Goody-two-shoes won't part her lips for me, but Cain snaps his fingers and she spreads her legs?"

Sheridan rubbed her temples. "Are you finished making me feel like trash?"

He didn't answer, but Amy came on the phone. "Why are you calling here?"

"I'm trying to stop you from taking this too far. Yes, I slept with Cain. I even enjoyed myself. But he didn't care about me, and you know it. He took me to the camper, used me once and never looked back, okay? Are you happy? That was it. A boy doesn't kill another boy over a cheap lay."

She heard movement in the other room but ignored it. She had to convince Amy, had to stop this before Ned took the investigation down the wrong road. It wasn't fair to Cain. And she needed Amy and her brother to focus on the real killer, the person who'd put her in the hospital *twice*.

"There are other issues here, Sheridan," Amy said. "Issues you don't know anything about."

"Like the fact that you have an ax to grind?" she retorted.

"My personal life is none of your business."

"Then don't use what happened between me and Cain as a weapon against him."

"Stay out of it and let me do my job."

"You're not listening."

"Robert told me everything I need to hear."

Cain had come up behind her. Sheridan could sense his presence. He was standing a few feet away.

"Amy, this isn't right. You're the only one I know who's jealous enough to hurt somebody."

There was a long silence. Then Amy said, "I'm going to pretend you didn't say that."

"It's true. You're using a sixteen-year-old's—"

Cain took the phone from her, setting it on the cradle, and Sheridan glanced up in surprise. He was wearing a pair of jeans that weren't snapped all the way up—no shirt or shoes. Obviously, like her, he'd just gotten out of bed.

"Why'd you do that?" she asked.

"Because you were wasting your breath," he said. "It won't make any difference to her."

"But she's taking the investigation in the wrong direction! Meanwhile, there's someone who's *really* dangerous running around. I know. He used me as a punching bag."

Cain didn't respond right away.

"Are you listening to me?"

"How do you know it *wasn't* me who shot you and Jason?" he asked.

He was serious. She could feel his eyes boring through the dark, could feel his tension as he waited. But she didn't want to answer. "I just do."

"How?" he asked again.

"Because the boy who touched me for the first time was too careful not to hurt me," she finally said.

She thought he might insist on helping her back to bed. But he didn't. He walked out of the room without another word.

The next morning, Sheridan found a jar of ointment on the nightstand. "What's this?" she called.

The banging of pots and pans in the kitchen told her Cain was awake and making breakfast. "What's what?" he called back.

"This…stuff."

Koda and Maximillian nosed their way into her room and barked a hello. Quixote must've stayed with Cain, because Sheridan didn't see him.

"It's a salve I made." There was a brief silence as the water went on, then Cain added, "Take off your clothes and rub it everywhere. It'll help the aching and bruising."

She unscrewed the lid and sniffed. "Yuck! I'm not putting this on. It smells terrible."

He didn't respond. The phone had rung and he'd answered it. She could hear his voice drifting back to her and knew he wasn't happy with whoever it was.

Thinking it might be Amy, she set the jar aside and waited to see what was going on. Eventually, Cain came to the doorway.

"Bad news?" she asked.

Freshly showered, his jaw clean-shaven and his hair damp, Cain leaned against the lintel. "It's not good news. Ned's coming over. He wants to ask you a few questions."

She frowned. "About the night in the camper?"

"He says it's about the night Jason was shot, but we both know he'll approach it via the night in the camper. That's the only new information he's got. I almost told him no, but—"

"But if we cooperate, he might not make such a big deal of it."

"Exactly. At this point, our best move is to admit what happened and act as if it didn't matter, quit giving him and Amy something to go after."

And if their cooperation didn't appease Amy's

jealousy? Was Sheridan ready for Whiterock's response to her past sins? Her parents would just be getting back from their cruise....

Cain shoved away from the wall and came closer. "You might be well enough to fly home in a few days."

She opened the jar and, despite the smell, began applying the ointment to the ugly yellow bruises on her legs. "You're suggesting I leave town?"

"You could avoid the backlash that way," he said, watching her.

She arched her eyebrows at him. "Tired of baby-sitting me?"

"I just want to keep you safe." He picked up the jar. "Take off your shirt and lie down. I'll get your back."

Turning away so he wouldn't see her, she removed her top and did as she was told, mostly because she wanted to believe that if Cain touched her, it wouldn't mean more than when any other man did. "There are probably dozens of dangerous people in California who'd like to see me dead," she told him and flashed him a smile over her bare shoulder. "I seem to bring that out in a person."

His hands ran over her back, working the ointment into her stiff muscles. "So you're staying?"

"Until I'm done here, until I see this through."

"Then you're nuts."

"Maybe." She stifled a moan as his strong fingers focused on a knot in her neck. "But it doesn't make sense to save the fight for another day. Whatever trail my attacker left will only have grown cold."

"You know Amy will do anything she can to humiliate you."

It was all too easy to enjoy his touch. It'd been ages since she'd been with a man—and he wasn't just any man. "I deserve it. I was an idiot."

His hands stilled. "There's nothing wrong with innocence."

"Except the stupidity that so often goes with it. You've got to be laughing inside."

His voice grew deeper. "You think I like knowing I hurt you?"

"Not in a vengeful way, like Amy. I'm just saying you've got to be amused that a 4.0 student could be so gullible."

He began to rub her back again. "I'm amused that you think you're so much wiser these days."

"I am."

"Because now you know that all I care about is nailing another girl?"

She moved her hair to one side so he wouldn't get the nasty-smelling salve in it. "You don't seem to care so much about nailing girls anymore. I think you've changed. But, regardless, I don't regret the lesson you taught me. Just my own ridiculous reaction to it."

There was another slight hesitation in his movements. "What lesson did I teach you? That men are scum? That they're only after one thing? That sex doesn't mean what you thought it did when you were sixteen?"

She didn't want to get involved in a debate. She was still embarrassed over her puppy-love crush, the revelation of which made her look like a fraud, as well as a liar, to the whole town. "Fortunately, stupid and jaded are not the same thing. I merely learned what every woman should know."

"Which is…"

She let her eyes drift closed. "You have to be careful who you trust."

"Lucky me. I get the credit for that?"

His hands moved down both sides of her back, kneading her flesh. She thought about claiming she'd learned it elsewhere, too, but he was the one who'd forced her to take off those rose-colored glasses. "Like I said, it was a good lesson," she muttered into her arm.

"What you deserved for getting involved with the wrong boy."

She opened her eyes. Where was he going with this? "More or less," she said. "Anyway, now that our little mistake's out, they're going to be taking a hard look at you in relation to the shooting. You know that."

"They were already taking a hard look at me."

"There's no way Amy will let this go."

"I was keeping my mouth shut for your sake, not mine."

For some reason, she believed him. Maybe he hadn't fallen in love with her as she had with him, but he'd been honorable enough not to brag about what he'd done with her. "You're not worried?"

"I wouldn't go that far. I think you should get out of here before it gets any more uncomfortable."

"I refuse to let the person who chased me away twelve years ago make me run a second time. If I'm not equipped to take a stand now, after all my training, I never will be."

"What kind of stand?"

"I'm going to catch him."

"How?"

"I'll use myself as bait if I have to."

Cain set the salve on the nightstand and stepped back. "Don't even talk like that."

"Sometimes you have to fight fire with fire." Feeling oddly reckless, she rolled over and sat up—and began applying the ointment to the bruises on her chest as if he was no emotional threat to her at all, no different from a girlfriend.

"In case you haven't noticed, I'm still in the room," he said.

She hid a smile at his stunned expression. "So? You've already seen me. You said so yourself. And the past is behind us. I'm over my first-man-to-touch-me insanity."

"I get that," he said, taking the jar from her.

"What are you doing?" she asked, growing nervous.

"If I'm no temptation to you, I might as well help. This is purely clinical. It's like I'm a doctor and you're my patient. Isn't it?" His enigmatic green eyes were riveted on hers as his hands, covered with the slick ointment, slid over her breasts.

Arousal shot through Sheridan so hard and fast she could no longer breathe, and she was afraid he could tell. Especially when his palms scraped over her nipples.

"Sometimes fighting fire with fire means you get consumed in the flames," he murmured.

Stubbornly lifting her chin, she refused to flinch or cover up. She wanted to prove that she could take him or leave him, that *she'd* be the one to walk away this time.

But it wasn't long before she began to tremble. Taking the jar from him so he wouldn't notice, she forced a polite smile and moved out of reach. "I think that's enough, don't you?"

The doorbell rang but he stayed where he was. Lowering his eyes to what she'd revealed, he devoured the sight in a hot glance. And then he turned away—but turned back at the door. "Unless you plan on making love to me, don't ever taunt me like that again."

He wasn't joking.

Sheridan was so breathless, she wasn't sure she could keep her voice steady enough to speak. But she wasn't about to succumb to his temptation a second time. She'd already learned her lesson—the hard way. "Yeah, well, I'll call ya," she said.

11

Ned wrinkled his nose the moment he walked into her bedroom. "Smells terrible in here. What is that?"

Cain followed him but didn't seem to be in a particularly loquacious mood, so Sheridan spoke up. "Salve. For bruises."

"Where'd you get it?"

"Cain made it for his clinic, I think."

Cain didn't confirm her answer or offer an alternative. He obviously wasn't interested in making Ned feel comfortable.

"If the smell's too strong, you're welcome to come back another time," she said and prayed Ned would give her a brief reprieve. She was still jittery from the hormones that had flooded her system only seconds before he arrived.

"No. Let's get this over with." He looked around for a seat and pulled over the one Cain had used when he fed her. The padding flattened as he sank into it. Then he looked back at Cain, who stood resolutely at the door, like some kind of gatekeeper. "Could we have a few minutes alone?"

"No," he said, shoving his hands in his pockets.

Ned's frown said he wasn't pleased by this response, but Cain set his jaw, making it clear he wouldn't change his mind.

Grumbling under his breath, Ned faced Sheridan. "You probably know why I'm here."

"Of course."

"Good. Than maybe we can talk about what you didn't tell the police twelve years ago."

"I told them everything that mattered."

"You didn't tell them about your relationship with Cain in the weeks leading up to the shooting."

"We didn't have a 'relationship.'" How was a bad case of unrequited love a relationship?

"But you did have sex with him. Then you lied about it."

"I didn't lie."

He withdrew a small pad from his shirt pocket. "You didn't tell the police. Or it would be in the file."

"It's in the file now," Cain said. "I suggest you move on."

He shot Cain a dour glance. "From what I've heard, this happened at a party."

"That's true."

"Was Jason there?"

"No. Jason and Cain didn't really hang around with the same people."

"Were there any drugs at this party?"

"What does that have to do with anything?" Cain asked.

"I'm trying to establish whether either of you had a history of using drugs. That might tell me whether or not drugs were involved in the shooting."

"There weren't any drugs at the party. Cain had been drinking a little, I think."

"And you?"

"I didn't drink at that age."

Ned tapped his pen against his notepad. "Or so you say."

Sheridan clung tightly to her temper. "You know I didn't drink."

"I don't know anything. Until yesterday, I thought you never put out, either," he said with a bark of laughter.

Cain closed the gap between them so quickly Ned flinched and almost fell off his chair. "What?" he complained, dropping his pad on the floor.

"Either treat her with some respect or get the hell out of here."

The two glared at each other for several seconds, but it was Ned who backed down. "Fine," he grumbled. With a dramatic sigh, he focused on Sheridan again. "Did Cain ever mention to you that he and Jason were having problems?"

"No," she said. "As far as I know, they got along just fine."

"And you didn't feel you might be causing trouble between the two brothers by having sex with one and then the other?"

Anger sparked in Cain's eyes. "Damn it, Ned. Take it easy or I'll throw your ass out."

"I didn't have sex with Jason," Sheridan said.

"You were at a popular make-out spot. And, according to witnesses, the windows were thick with steam. No one could even see in."

"That doesn't mean we were having sex!"

"If you slept with Cain the first night you were together, what stopped you from doing the same with Jason?"

Sheridan pressed her palms to her eyes. "Jason was just a friend. We were only *talking*."

"About…"

"Life. School. Parents."

"That's it?"

She attempted a shrug. She didn't want to let him know how much this was costing her, but talking about Jason always made her feel sick inside. Why had she involved him in her childish attempt to get Cain's attention? How many times had she asked herself if Jason would still be alive today if she hadn't been so stupid and immature, if she'd been able to face the fact that Cain had merely used her?

"Did he know you just wanted to be friends?"

No. He had hopes of more. That was what made her cringe the most. "He—he wanted to kiss me," she admitted.

Ned scooted closer. "Could you speak a little louder?"

With effort, she raised her voice. "I said he wanted to kiss me, but I wouldn't let him."

"Why not?"

More skepticism. As she'd expected, Ned believed he'd uncovered a hypocrite. She hadn't been what she'd appeared to be, so she had to be the exact opposite. "Because I didn't really want to be there with him."

"Then why'd you go?"

She was desperate to see Cain and thought he might be at Rocky Point, and being with Jason gave her a legitimate excuse to be there, too. From the moment Jason had picked her up until the blast went off, Cain was all she could think about. "Cain didn't call me after the… after the incident in the camper. I guess I was…trying to see if it would bother him if I went out with someone else."

She could feel Cain's eyes on her but refused to look at him.

"So you tried to make him jealous with his own brother."

"Ned…" Cain warned.

Swallowing hard, hoping to relieve the terrible burning in her throat, Sheridan motioned to let Cain know she didn't need him to intercede. As ugly as it sounded, Ned had stated the truth, and she had to take responsibility for it. "That's *exactly* what I was doing, okay?" she said. "I was at Rocky Point with Jason that night because I was doing anything I could to get Cain to react."

Ned didn't bother to conceal his contempt for her behavior, but it didn't matter. His contempt was nothing compared to how she felt about her own actions.

"Did Jason have any idea he was a pawn?" he asked.

"That's it." In one swift motion, Cain lifted White-rock's police chief by the shirtfront and yanked him to his feet.

The chair hit the floor as Ned scrambled to get away. "What the hell are you doing?"

Quixote growled low in his throat, and Koda and Maximillian came to their feet, their ears back as they studied the situation for any sign of a threat to Cain.

Cain released Ned but shoved him toward the door. "Go."

"You can't attack a police officer!"

"I haven't attacked you. Yet."

Ned's gaze darted between Cain and his dogs. "You're in deep shit. You know that? I'm going to see that you finally get what you deserve."

"Just go," Cain said. "You're not here to investigate Jason's murder. You're here to make Sheridan feel like a tramp. And I'm done listening to it."

Amy sat in the booth next to her brother and across from Kent Lazarus, another police officer on their little force.

"He nearly hit me!" Ned said, telling them what'd happened at Cain's.

"What made him so mad?" Kent asked.

"He said I was humiliating Sheridan. But she might've caused Jason's death. She *should* be humiliated."

"No kidding." Amy couldn't believe Cain would stick up for Sheridan. Sure, she was pretty, but it wasn't as if they'd been friends back in high school. "She also pretended to be better than the rest of us while she was screwing my boyfriend behind my back."

"He wasn't your boyfriend," Ned grumbled.

Amy let the comment go because, technically, her brother was right. She hadn't managed any type of commitment from Cain until he married her. "But who would've thought she was messing around with Cain?"

"Her parents would've disowned her if they knew," he agreed. "They were so strict she had an eleven-o'clock curfew. She could only go out on one night each weekend. And they wouldn't allow her to date at all until she turned sixteen."

"Even then she could only double-date or go to official school dances," Amy chimed in. "You asked her out once, remember? She turned you down because it wasn't a school dance. And your reputation was much better than Cain's. They never would've allowed her to be with him."

"How'd Cain get in her pants?" Kent asked. He'd moved to town three years ago, well after Cain had started keeping a low profile, and didn't know him that well.

"Cain could've had *anyone* in high school," Amy said.

Kent snickered. "So was he sleeping with you at the same time?"

Amy wanted to reach across the table and smack him. "Shut up!"

"That's really what's pissing you off, isn't it?"

Ned interrupted before they could break into an all-out argument. "The question is, how are we going to make sure Cain gets what's coming to him? I'm not letting him get away with more of his bullshit."

Kent lowered his voice. "It shouldn't be too hard. The rifle was in Cain's cabin. Sheridan was attacked on Cain's land. Cain had the only motive we're aware of for killing Jason. Cain was at the hospital when that mysterious guy showed up. And we know Cain had emotional problems as a teenager. It's all Cain. He's the common denominator. I think we take what we've got to Judge Brown and try to get a search warrant."

Ned pursed his lips as he considered it. "If we could go through Cain's belongings, maybe we'd find the ski mask or a piece of bloody clothing or something."

Amy flicked the lid on the metal creamer. "Bloody clothing won't be enough. He carried Sheridan into his house the night she was hurt, so there's a legitimate reason for her blood to be there. Owen knows it, too. And he's loyal to Cain. He wouldn't talk to me about what he saw in that camper, and I got the impression he was pretty unhappy with Robert for telling us."

"So he'll testify that Cain was trying to save her, not kill her."

"Exactly."

"Who would've thought she could survive such an attack?" Ned muttered.

"It's a miracle she didn't die." Amy halfway wished she had. Then she wouldn't be at Cain's place right now and Amy wouldn't be spending every moment consumed with the fear that he might become emotionally attached to Sheridan Kohl.

"What if we found *Jason's* blood?" Kent asked.

"We're not going to. It's been too long." As much as Amy wanted to punish Cain for rejecting her, and as much as Cain's unapologetic and aloof nature inadvertently helped make him look bad, she knew he hadn't shot Jason. But her brother didn't, and neither did Kent, which made them perfect tools to badger Cain. He was going to need an ally soon; he was going to need *her.* She wanted that so badly she could taste his skin, his kiss—

"Then what?" Ned said.

"We keep talking to the neighbors, try to come up with someone who saw Cain in the neighborhood before Sheridan went missing," she responded.

Skepticism etched lines in her brother's forehead.

"But he has family there. His stepfather and stepbrother live a few doors down. Even if we find someone to place him on that street, he's got a good reason to be there."

"Robert's on our side."

Ned toyed with the sugar packets on the table. "Robert's an alcoholic, and alcoholics don't make the most credible witnesses."

Amy pushed the bowl of sugar packets back against the wall. She didn't want Ned to destroy every one of them. She had more coffee coming. "His statement got them to admit what they did."

"But John would be a more reliable witness," Ned said.

"He won't do it."

"He might. He wants to get whoever murdered Jason. And with the discovery of that rifle, he's beginning to wonder about Cain."

Amy shook her head. "He has Marshall to consider."

"What does Marshall have to do with anything? He's been over at Sunrise Vista ever since John's mother passed."

"Doesn't matter," Amy argued. "Marshall got a pile of money when he sold his hardware stores, and he won't leave it to John if John doesn't watch himself. Maybe John doesn't get along with Cain, but Marshall thinks Cain hung the moon."

"Maybe we could establish more testimony about Cain's presence at Rocky Point," Ned said. "Find someone who'll say he was enraged at seeing Jason and Sheridan together, that he made some threats."

The ice in Kent's glass clinked as he finished his water. "We already have Maureen Johansen."

"That's not enough," Amy said. "She won't go beyond saying she 'thought' Cain 'might' have been upset. If we're going to make a case out of circumstantial evidence, it needs to be overwhelming. We need more." More with which she could bring Cain to his knees.

Ned dropped the last mangled sugar packet she'd allowed him and rocked back. "We can find it."

12

"This is the girl?"

Marshall Wyatt studied Sheridan with his wise, old eyes, even though she suspected he couldn't actually see her very well. According to Cain, his step-grandfather had a cataract removed a few months ago, but still suffered from a bad case of glaucoma.

"This is the girl." Cain tossed the bag of pork rinds and the crossword puzzles he'd bought on the way over onto the old man's bed. "She's tough, eh?"

"She sure is." Marshall reached out a shaky hand. "I hear you've had a rough time of it since you returned to town, young lady."

Sitting in the wheelchair Cain had borrowed from the nursing home office, Sheridan pushed herself close enough to accept Wyatt's hand. "It was horrific," she said as he gave her fingers a brief squeeze. "If not for Cain, I wouldn't have made it."

"It's amazing what this boy will do for a pretty lady," Marshall said with a wink.

Earlier this afternoon, before Cain brought her to the nursing home, Sheridan had bathed in the pond again, only this time she'd worn Cain's boxers and T-shirt into the water and managed to dress herself afterward, donning a cotton summer dress with a pair of sandals. She couldn't raise her hands above her head for more than a few seconds, so Cain had helped blow dry her hair, but she'd washed her face and put on a little blush and lip-gloss. She didn't feel pretty—not with the lingering scabs and bruises—but she felt healthier than she had in a long while.

"He's turned out to be a very good friend," she said but avoided Cain's gaze. Ever since he'd put on that salve, she couldn't look at him without feeling a rush of desire. He'd affected her that way when she was sixteen; he affected her the same way at twenty-eight. She couldn't control the craving, so she was determined to hide it.

"You don't know who did this to you?" Marshall asked.

"No." When Cain had come into her room to suggest they take a short drive, Sheridan had jumped at the chance for a change of scenery. And she was glad she had. Although she'd never had any contact with Marshall Wyatt in the past, she already liked him.

"It's a tragedy," he said. "I can't understand it." Then he looked at Cain and waggled a finger. "And you. What're you doing sending that tea of yours over here? I'm not drinking that nasty stuff. I've survived eighty years without it, and I figure I'll take my chances from here on out."

"I can be just as stubborn as you," Cain told him.

For a moment, there was a standoff; then the old guy grinned. "I love this kid," he told Sheridan. "Doesn't matter that he's not really my own. If that John of mine had half a brain he'd realize what he's got here. What he's always had. But he's too big a fool, still livin' in the past, mournin' Jason. You can't get close to him for all that pain."

"We didn't come here so you could bore her with family business," Cain grumbled, but the glitter in his eye took the edge off his words and told Sheridan just how deeply he respected this man.

"So what *did* you come for?" Marshall said. "You'd better have more for me than those pork rinds and magazines. Where're my cigarettes?"

Now Sheridan understood the real reason they'd stopped at the convenience store on the drive over.

"You tell John I'm supplying you with these and he'll try to have me barred from visiting you." Cain dug the pack out of his pocket and tossed it onto his grandfather's bed with the other things. "You know that, don't you?"

"John?" Marshall nearly shouted. "That's what you call him now?"

"Come on. Don't start," Cain said. "Be happy that I smuggled in your contraband. I don't like going against your doctor's orders any more than he does."

"I don't care whether John likes it or not. You, neither. I'm an adult." Marshall jabbed a thumb against his own chest. "I've earned the right to decide whether or not I want to smoke."

Cain's smile slanted to one side. "Which is why I buy them for you. That and the fact I can't say no to you," he added under his breath. "How's that for tough love?"

"That's the kind of love I like," the old man replied,

laughing. "How come I'm the only one who sees it?" he asked Sheridan.

"Sees what?"

"That this boy has the softest heart of all." Recovering his pack of cigarettes, he placed them proudly in his front pocket. "Ah, that's what I needed," he said, giving them a satisfied pat.

"Fortunately, he likes having them more than he likes smoking them," Cain muttered to Sheridan, and she couldn't help grinning. This wasn't about smoking. It was about Marshall defying the people who said he couldn't, about asserting his will despite all the decisions that were being made for him.

"What'll the nurses say when they catch you with those?" Sheridan asked.

"Oh, they'll cluck and they'll cackle, but I won't let 'em give me too much trouble. They know who's boss around here." A noise drew their attention to the door. "Isn't that right?" he said to the nurse who appeared there.

"Isn't what right?" she repeated, coming into the room.

"That I'm the boss around here."

She opened her mouth to answer, then spotted the telltale bulge in his front pocket and scowled. "What's that you've got there?"

"You know what it is."

"Shame on you," she said to Cain. "How many times do I have to tell you? Cigarettes are against the rules here. Do you want him to die of lung cancer?"

"I want him to be happy for however long he lives," Cain said.

She didn't seem to have an argument for that, so she

sighed. "You're going to cost me my job someday." She was obviously exasperated, but she didn't really seem worried about losing her job, especially once she noticed Sheridan sitting quietly in the corner. "You didn't tell me you have a new girlfriend, Cain. Who's this?"

He didn't respond to the "girlfriend" part of her comment. "Sheridan Kohl, meet Candy Bruster," he said.

The short, middle-aged brunette offered Sheridan a sad smile. "I should've realized who you were when I saw the wheelchair. I heard about what happened. I'm so sorry."

"I was actually very lucky. If Cain hadn't been there, I probably wouldn't be alive right now."

"Makes you feel as if you're not safe in your own house anymore." Looking a bit haunted, she rubbed her arms. "I'm a single mother of three teenage girls. It's terrifying to think there's someone in our town capable of beating a woman to death."

"We're going to catch him," Sheridan said. "Don't worry."

"I hope you do." She pointed at the pack of cigarettes in Marshall's pocket. "I've got to finish my rounds. But if you don't want Bertha to take those away from you, you'd better put them in your drawer like you usually do. She's a lot stricter than I am." She grinned at Cain and Sheridan on her way out. "And he thinks I don't know where he hides them."

When she was gone, Cain nudged his grandfather. "How can you complain about this place? Looks to me like you've got everyone wrapped around your little finger."

Marshall's blue-veined hand found Cain's smooth,

strong forearm. "Only my favorite grandson," he said. "Can I give you money to take this beautiful lady to dinner?" He reached into his pocket to pull out some cash, but Cain stopped him.

"I don't need your money, Grandpa. I just need you to take care of yourself, okay?"

"You're a good boy," he said.

"Hey, be careful," Cain responded. "You'll ruin my reputation."

Marshall shook his head. "If folks don't know you by now they're more blind than I am."

Cain chuckled. "I've got to take Sheridan home. She shouldn't be out too long just yet."

"You two go ahead." Marshall waved them toward the door. "You know where I am."

Cain clasped his grandfather's hand and hugged him at the same time, then wheeled Sheridan from the room.

"What?" Cain asked when they were out in the sunshine again.

"What…what?" she replied.

"You're smiling."

"I'm glad you brought me. I like your grandfather— and it's wonderful to be out of bed."

"It's easy to tell you're from California."

"How?"

One finger lightly brushed her bare shoulder. "You've been indoors for ten days, but you still have a tan."

"I spent a week on the beach in San Diego before I came here."

He stared at her for several seconds—and didn't look away when she met his gaze.

"Cain?" She was growing self-conscious, but he didn't seem to mind the silence.

"You're even prettier now than you were then."

Sheridan was fighting a blush of pleasure when a car door slammed a few parking spaces away. Footsteps sounded on concrete, then a voice cut in. "Well, if it isn't my big brother."

The smile slid from Cain's lips as he turned and nodded in acknowledgement. "Robert."

"Spending time with dear old Granddad today, Cain?"

"We visited for a few minutes."

Robert tilted his head to be able to see around his stepbrother, who didn't bother to move. "Looks like you brought someone to meet him."

"This is Sheridan Kohl."

"I know." Robert bent his tall frame in a quick, mocking bow. "Her reputation precedes her."

He could've been referring to a lot of things—the shooting, the attack, even her work at The Last Stand. The organization had received a great deal of publicity over the past few years, mostly due to Jasmine, who freelanced as a forensic profiler and had been instrumental in solving several high-profile cases. But Sheridan could tell Robert wasn't referring to the attempts on her life or the work she'd done. In Whiterock, she was famous—or infamous, really—for her secret liaison with Cain twelve years ago.

"You sure know how to impress the ladies," she said in response to his sarcasm.

He clapped a hand to his chest. "Oh, no. Not like Cain."

Robert's sandy hair was greasy at the roots, and he

hadn't shaved. He was bigger than most men, had been a small giant even as a boy, but with his sagging chin, sunken eyes and jaundiced pallor, the stubble covering his jaw seemed sloppy and unattractive, not shabby chic.

"No," she agreed, chuckling softly. "Not like Cain."

His eyes narrowed at her frank honesty but Cain spoke before he could address her again. "Owen's letting you drive one of his vehicles?"

Robert glanced at the Toyota 4x4 he'd just parked. "I have to drive something, don't I? I can't find 'gainful employment' without transportation."

Cain hooked his thumbs in his pockets, but Sheridan sensed that he wasn't as relaxed as he wanted to appear. "Dad thinks you're out looking for a job?"

"I am out looking for a job."

Cain's eyebrows shot up. "So what are you doing here?"

"I can't visit Grandpa while I'm doing it?"

"Not if you're going to ask him for more money."

"I just need a short-term loan," he said. "I gotta get my car fixed."

"Can't you work it out some other way?" Displeasure sharpened Cain's voice. "Give the old guy a break?"

Robert shrugged his shoulders. "He's got nothing better to do with what he's got left."

Cain's right hand curved into a fist, but he didn't react to Robert's disrespectful and ungrateful statement. Shaking out his fingers, he changed the subject. "Why'd you tell Amy that Jason and I argued the night he was killed?"

The insolent grin that tugged at the corners of

Robert's mouth made Sheridan dislike him even more. "Because you did."

"How would you know? You weren't home that night."

"I was home right after school. And that's when you argued."

"It was a discussion, and it wasn't anything serious. We both wanted to use the truck. He told me he had a date, and I said I'd let him have it if he'd take me over to Scooter's before he left. That was it."

"I didn't say it came to blows or anything." Robert lifted his hands in mock innocence. "Amy asked me if you and Jason ever had any problems, and I told her the truth."

"The truth," Cain echoed in disgust. "And then you volunteered what Owen had told you."

"About the camper?" A lascivious grin spread over his face. "Amy asked if I knew whether or not you and Sheridan had a previous relationship, and I told her the truth about that, too."

"You're an asshole, you know that?"

His grin only widened at the knowledge that he'd hit his mark. "Gee, Cain. I didn't realize you expected me to lie for you."

Cain's chest lifted as if to take a deep, calming breath and Sheridan imagined him counting to ten. She was actually impressed with his patience, considering she wanted to punch Robert herself. "Whatever." He turned away, dismissing his stepbrother without a good-bye. But when Robert reached for the door to the nursing home, Cain whirled on him.

"What the hell are you doing?"

A flash of fear lit Robert's eyes, which looked out of

place on such a large man. But a second later, he managed to bury his initial reaction beneath a fresh dose of false bravado. "We already went over it. I need a loan. My car isn't drivable and I don't have the dough to fix it."

"I told you not to ask Grandpa."

Robert jutted out his chin. "I don't take orders from you."

"Then do it for him. The only time you come around is when you want something. He's got to be tired of it."

"Stay out of my business. He's not even your grandpa," Robert said and entered the building, where he'd be surrounded by people to protect him if Cain snapped and went in after him.

Cain stared at Sheridan but she knew he wasn't really seeing her. He was struggling with the desire to stop Robert from taking advantage of Marshall Wyatt. "There are days I hate him," he admitted when his eyes finally focused.

"I'm surprised there are any days you don't. Will your grandpa give him the money?"

"Probably," he said with a sigh. "He usually does."

Sheridan got out of the wheelchair so she could climb into Cain's truck. But he opened the passenger door and deposited her on the seat before she could take a single step.

After returning the wheelchair to the lobby, he got into the driver's side and started the engine. As he put the transmission in Reverse, she touched his arm. "Robert's intimidated by you. And envious. You realize that, don't you?"

"Robert's screwed up. That's what I realize," he said and didn't speak again the whole ride home.

Amy had to do something to get Cain to react. If he couldn't love her, she wanted him to hate her. Anything had to be better than the complete indifference with which he treated her now. He hadn't been with a woman for three years, yet he *still* wasn't tempted to touch her? What was that about? She wasn't even good enough for a casual screw?

Closing her eyes, she leaned her head back against the couch, remembering what it'd been like in the old days. The first time he'd touched her, they'd been out behind her parents' barn. He'd forgotten to take home the notes he needed to study for a test, a test he had to pass or he'd flunk the course, and he'd called to see if he could use hers. She'd had him come over, told her parents they were going outside to study and went into the barn, where she'd shown him what she was willing to give him. After that, she invited him over after parties, brought him home during school hours when her parents were working, even called and woke him up some nights so that she could sneak in through his window.

If only she hadn't lost his baby…

God obviously hated her. Or He wouldn't have taken the one thing that would've allowed her to keep some part of Cain, a part he could never take back. Having nothing was killing her. And it'd been killing her for years. When would the pain stop?

She couldn't go on like this.

"What's wrong?" Tiger wanted to know.

Amy slipped her bare toes under the blanket. Hot and humid as it was outside, she had her air-conditioning cranked high so she could cover up. It was too muggy to be close to Tiger and the heat his body generated without some air. "Nothing. Why?"

"You're fidgeting," he complained. "Sit still so I can watch the movie."

She gazed blankly at the screen. They were probably fifteen minutes into some terrorist DVD Tiger had chosen, but she didn't have a clue what it was about. People and cars were getting blown up. That was it. After the movie, Tiger would want to make love, and in order to get into it she'd pretend he was Cain. Then he'd go to sleep and snore until she was tempted to smother him to stop the noise. And, in the morning, she'd drag him out of her bed just in time for them to make it to work.

It was the same routine every day. But being with Tiger was better than being alone. When she was alone, she thought of Cain nonstop, drove up there even more often. Sometimes her presence made his dogs bark, but not always. They knew her. And, if it was really dark, she'd toss them each a dog biscuit so she could get close enough to see through the windows.

"Amy, stop it!" Tiger snapped.

She was fidgeting again. With a sigh, she got up and went to the kitchen. She knew she shouldn't eat. She was getting fat, which would make her even less appealing to Cain. But food seemed to be her only solace. And what did a few pounds matter if she didn't see any man other than Tiger? He was fat himself.

"You hungry?" she called.

"No, but you could bring me a beer."

Another beer? If he drank too many, she'd never be able to pretend he was Cain. Cain could be emotionally distant, but he was no bumbling, sloppy lover. "I'm out," she lied.

"Wanna run to the store?"

"Hell, no," she retorted, appalled that he'd even suggest it. But then she reconsidered. The prospect of seeing Cain had whetted her appetite for another visit to his house. She wanted to know what he was doing out there with Sheridan, wanted to see if he'd started using those condoms she'd left in his truck.

The thought of him in bed with Sheridan made Amy's stomach ache. Sheridan, always the golden girl, had managed to land on her feet—again. "Lucky bitch."

"What'd you say?" Tiger yelled.

"I said you're lucky. I've decided to go out and get you a six-pack. I have a few things to drop off at my brother's, too, so I might be a while. Hang out here and enjoy the movie, okay?"

"I'm not going anywhere," he said.

She wasn't worried. She'd have to undress in front of him just to get him off the couch.

13

"Don't do it."

Sheridan frowned at Cain, who sat across the table from her, then studied her cards again. They were playing poker, something she'd suggested they do. She wasn't strong enough yet to move around a lot, but she was tired of lying in bed and needed a diversion. Should she ignore him? She was about to raise her bet, but the caution in his voice made her hesitate.

Then it made her suspicious.

"What kind of poker player warns his opponent when he has a good hand?" she asked.

"One with a conscience, I guess," he said, shrugging.

She studied the pile of money in the center of the table. They'd each put in about $50—not a fortune but she couldn't afford to lose a lot of money. On her salary, she didn't *have* a lot to lose. "You? A conscience?" she teased. "I think you're bluffing. You've probably got a lousy hand, and you're hoping I'll fold so you won't have to."

A crooked smile curved his lips as his index finger tapped the table. "Do you want the truth?"

"Yes."

"I'm actually doing my best not to take advantage of you."

"You don't have to warn me. I can take care of myself. In case you haven't noticed, I'm a big girl now."

His eyes slid over her, making her heart pound. "I've noticed."

"But…"

He laughed. "But I've also noticed that you're a shitty poker player."

Stung, she muttered, "We've only been playing for fifteen minutes."

"I could tell in the first three."

"That's such bullshit!" She tossed a red chip into the center of the table. "I'll raise you ten."

"Suit yourself." With a sigh, he promptly threw in a blue chip.

"Wait. Don't you want to think about it? Obviously, I believe in my hand."

"I'm satisfied."

Damn. Now she was into the pot for another ten dollars, he'd just raised his bet by twenty, and she was facing the same decision she'd faced a moment earlier. Should she fold or raise again? "You think I should cut my losses."

He rubbed his jaw. "That's exactly what I think."

"But you could be bluffing."

"I could be, but I'm not."

She eyed him over her fan of cards. She was holding three eights, which was the best hand she'd had so far. She wanted to use it to win; if only to show him he didn't know everything. "I quit now, I lose sixty bucks."

"If you don't quit now, you'll lose more."

She bit her lip in indecision. "Oh, fine," she snapped and, with a sound of impatience, laid down her hand.

He glanced at the cards she'd revealed, smiled as if he'd expected as much, and fanned out his own hand. He had a full house.

"You weren't lying," she said as he raked the chips toward him.

"Nope."

"So why'd you warn me? You could've won a lot more."

"I don't want to financially cripple someone who reminds me so much of my mother."

She stopped kicking herself for not listening to him sooner. Cain rarely mentioned his past. "I remind you of your *mother?*"

"Yep."

Julia Wyatt had been beautiful. Sheridan would've been flattered if he'd said she looked like her, but she couldn't see how the two of them resembled each other at all. "In what way?"

"Everything you feel registers on your face. I don't think you could tell a convincing lie to save your life."

That was a problem. She was attempting to lie to him every day, wasn't she? By pretending he didn't affect her on a sexual level. By pretending she wasn't consumed with the thought of letting him touch her again. "It's a good thing when the people around you can tell how you feel. It means I'm not dark and moody, like you."

"Dark and moody?"

"Maybe not dark and moody, but…unreadable."

He cocked his eyebrow at her while dealing the next

hand. "Sorry, if you want to know how I feel, you're going to have to ask."

"Okay," she said. "I will. I have a few questions already."

"Like…"

"Like how did your mother and John Wyatt get together."

"What does that have to do with expressing my emotions?"

"I'm getting there."

"We were talking about poker."

"You have something else to say on the subject of poker?"

"I was about to express my emotions about it."

She folded her arms. "Fine. Go ahead."

His smile turned naughty. "I feel bad taking your money from you."

"That's…nice," she said, but she could tell there was more. "But?"

His smile showed more teeth. "But I wouldn't feel at all bad about taking your clothes."

"And this is you being honest about your emotions?"

Finished dealing, he put the rest of the cards in the center of the table. "I just wanted you to know that I'm capable of saying what I feel."

She couldn't help laughing. "Your depth amazes me."

"That wasn't the angle I was going after, but I'll take it. So what do you say?"

"If we changed to some other prize that made you feel less conflicted, I doubt you'd be warning me not to raise my bets."

"Hell, no," he said. "You can take care of yourself, remember?"

She remembered that she'd only won a single hand. "No, thanks."

"It'd make things interesting."

No, it'd make things dangerous. Sheridan wished it was her competitive spirit that was goading her on, but she knew the temptation came from farther south than her brain. "I'm not about to risk sitting here buck-naked with you sitting over there, wearing all your clothes and an 'I told you so' smile."

"There's that."

And there was also what would probably happen if she succumbed to the temptation. "What made your mother marry John Wyatt?" she asked.

Sobering, he sat back. "I was enjoying the other subject so much more."

"I'm curious."

"I think she loved him. At first. I also think she saw it as a way out."

"From…"

"From the life we were living. She was waitressing at a strip club in Nashville. It wasn't a good environment, but it was the only work she could get that paid enough to keep a roof over our heads and let her be with me at least some of the time."

"What about your father?"

"What father?"

"You've never heard from him?"

"Not a word."

"And your mother's family?"

"Her parents threw her out when she got pregnant with me, so she didn't have them to rely on, either."

Sheridan wondered if Julia was ever tempted to strip in order to make bigger tips, but she wasn't about to ask Cain that. "Have you met her family?"

"No. She was adopted as a baby, but the couple who took her in conceived right afterward, and she always felt overshadowed. If they could throw her out like that and never even try to track her down, I don't see any point in making contact."

"So John frequented a strip club?" Sheridan remembered that he'd attended church services as often as her parents did; the two images didn't seem to mesh.

"He tells everyone they met at a restaurant."

Sheridan tucked her hair behind her ears. "I'll bet your mother was excited that you were going to have a father."

"Some father," he said with a bark of derision.

"Did *she* feel she'd made a mistake?"

"I think she figured that out soon enough. The first year or two went smoothly, but John acted like a big baby most of the time and it became a serious problem. He demanded all her attention, which made him resent me. I'm sure she would've left him, but then she was diagnosed."

"So she hung on."

"She hung on because he wasn't abusive, as irritating as his self-pity and emotional rants could be. She didn't want to leave me alone, didn't want to die knowing I'd have no one, and she trusted that Marshall would do what he could for me, provided she stayed with John."

"What about John? If the marriage wasn't working,

why did he hang on? Why'd he take care of her all those months? Was it out of compassion?"

Cain picked up his cards and stared down at them, but Sheridan knew he wasn't really seeing them. "He was well aware that Marshall would cut him off if he walked out on her at that point. Marshall had already sold the hardware stores rather than letting John take over. He needed the money to provide for his retirement, but John didn't see it that way, so the relationship was strained. Besides, John liked coming across as a hero. Everywhere we went, someone clapped him on the back, applauding for his selflessness." He shook his head. "Letting us continue to live at the house was a small price to pay for the ego boost. It didn't cost him anything. Marshall helped out with the bills since my mother couldn't work, and John just went on about his business as if she wasn't even there."

"How sad for her."

Cain narrowed his eyes. "I hate him for treating her the way he did."

Sheridan wondered how Jason, living in that same house, remained so unaffected. She'd had a class with him. Occasionally, they'd met at the library to do homework together. Sometimes he'd called just to talk. He was popular and went out with a lot of girls, but she could sense that he was interested in her—maybe more interested in her than any of the others. She always had the impression that he was waiting for her to let him know she was ready to take their relationship in a new direction. But until she got involved with Cain, she was careful not to do that.

When Cain didn't call her after the camper incident, she'd cornered Jason and flirted with him just a little. And that was exactly the trigger she'd expected it to be. He'd asked her out, she'd agreed and everything had gone horribly wrong from that point on. But during all their conversations, Jason had never even hinted that there was any stress in the household. Cain's behavior was what told her that.

"Jason always acted as if everything was fine," she said.

"In his mind, maybe it was. His father worshipped him, would give him anything he wanted."

"Was John like that with Robert and Owen?"

"Not as much."

"So Jason was his favorite."

"By a long shot."

Sheridan had so many other questions she wanted to ask Cain. But the telephone interrupted them. Cain's chair squeaked as he shoved it back to grab the handset. "Hello?"

Sheridan toyed with the cards while she watched him. Her mind was still in the past, with Jason and what he must have been feeling, with Cain and Julia, with John and his selfishness. So it took her a moment to realize this call wasn't for Cain. It was her parents.

"…Cain Granger…That's right, Granger…She's doing better…I'll let her tell you about that…"

Swallowing a sigh, she accepted the phone. Her cell didn't work—Whiterock wasn't big enough to have its own accessory store so she still didn't have a new charger—but she'd used Cain's landline to leave her parents a message at home. They refused to get a cell phone, which meant she would've had to contact the cruise company if she wanted to reach them before they returned, and she'd decided not to do that.

"Hello?"

"Honey, are you okay?" She heard her mother's worried voice first, but it was only a second ahead of her father's. He'd picked up the extension.

"Your message said you were *attacked*. What happened?" he shouted. "Why didn't you call us?"

"There wasn't any reason to ruin your trip." After everything she'd been through, hearing from the two people who loved her most in the whole world nearly made her cry. She'd thought about contacting Jonathan, Skye and Jasmine plenty of times, but she'd been putting it off, probably because they'd think she was crazy for staying with Cain—and she didn't want to explain or defend herself. She preferred to pretend that it was the smartest thing to do. Not telling them allowed that. "I'm fine—well, better, anyway. When did you get home?"

"Just a few hours ago," her mother said. "There was an accident on the highway so we stopped to eat rather than fight the traffic. Had we known the news we had waiting for us—"

"How bad off are you?" her dad cut in. "Should we fly out there?"

"No. There's no need for that. Leanne's about to have her baby. You don't want to miss it, and I'm…all better."

Cain had stood up to mute the television playing in the background. "*All* better?" he echoed softly, setting the remote down as he slouched back into his chair.

She shot him a quelling look. "It wasn't as bad as it sounded," she said into the phone.

"But you mentioned a hospital," her father said. "If you had to go to the hospital, it was serious."

"That was just so they could check me out. You know how cautious doctors are about head injuries." The last thing she wanted was to make her parents miss the birth of their first grandchild—and land right in the middle of a scandal.

"So you're really okay? You're sure?" her mother said.

"I'm positive." Except for significant memory loss, the knowledge that someone in Whiterock was trying to kill her, Amy's attempts to destroy her reputation and the fact that she was staying with Cain Granger, who'd been the only boy capable of tempting her beyond her virtue twelve years ago… Except for all that, she was pretty much perfect.

"Then why don't you come here? I know Leanne would love it."

Not really. Leanne was stressed by the thought of having her in-laws visit from out of town. Sheridan didn't intend to add to the pressure her sister was already feeling. She'd spoken to Leanne before coming to Tennessee, and they'd agreed Sheridan should wait until the baby was a few weeks old. After Leanne had gotten into the routine of caring for an infant and her other company had departed, they'd be able to spend some private time together. "I plan to visit soon. But I have things I need to do here first."

"We can hire someone to get Uncle Perry's house on the market," her father said.

"I can do it, Dad. I'm already here, and I'm not leaving until I find out who's…harassing me."

"But it's not safe for you to be alone," her mother insisted. "And I don't think you should be staying with *Cain Granger.*"

She'd said Cain's name as if he were vermin. Lowering her head, Sheridan began to massage her temples. As much as she'd wanted to hear from her family, she was already beginning to regret letting them know she was having problems. "Stop it," she muttered but, as usual, her mother didn't listen.

"You're both unmarried, Sheridan. It doesn't look right. You need to come home before Pastor Wayne or someone else hears about it. That Granger boy has a terrible reputation—you know what folks will think."

"I'll talk to you about it later." She was hesitant to meet Cain's eyes for fear he'd immediately realize they were talking about him, but she chanced it—and found him sitting with one arm hooked casually over the back of his chair, watching her while waiting for their game to resume.

Clearing her throat, she pressed the handset closer to her ear.

"What does he get out of helping you?" her dad asked.

"Nothing. That's just it."

"He's in it for *something.*"

At that point, Cain got up and left the room. Sheridan wanted to believe he'd thought of some chore he had to do, but she was pretty sure he understood that she was in an uncomfortable spot.

"Would you guys quit?" she whispered once he was

gone. "Cain's been a good friend to me since I returned." Knowing how soon they were likely to find out about the past, she cringed. They'd be publicly humiliated in front of all their old friends, friends they'd hoped to impress by devout example. But that wouldn't be the worst of it. The worst of it would be the sense of betrayal they'd feel because she'd never confessed the truth.

She considered breaking the news to them now, before they could hear it from someone else, but decided against it. There was always the small chance that they wouldn't find out. She doubted she'd be that lucky but, just in case, she wasn't about to tattle on herself.

"You have to be careful not to get involved with the wrong man, Sheridan. You don't know how much unhappiness that would bring. You need to meet someone who's as religious as you are."

"You mean as religious as *you* are."

"Look at your sister. She's five years younger and she's starting her family. You want a family, too, don't you? If you married a man like Cain, you'd wind up divorced and miserable—if he even married you in the first place. And what if you had children? It's so important to marry a man who'll be a good father to your children."

"He's changed," she said, keeping her voice low. "He's not what you think he is."

"People don't change that much, Sheridan. He doesn't have the same background and beliefs you do."

It was no use. Nothing Sheridan could say would make the slightest difference. She could tell her parents that he'd saved her life, stayed with her during her darkest hour, defended her from everything, even ridicule. But he didn't go to church so it wouldn't matter.

They were probably right about one thing. Even if she got involved with Cain, their relationship wouldn't go anywhere. He wasn't the marrying kind. He belonged out here, alone in the forest with his dogs. "Gotta go," she said. "I'll call you later."

"So are you coming home?" her mother asked.

Had she been unclear in any way? "Not until I find out who hurt me."

"That could take days. Weeks."

"It might not happen at all," her father chimed in.

"So you think I should let him get away with it?"

Silence. Of course they didn't. Her folks were big on justice.

"If he'd been caught when he killed Jason, this wouldn't have happened," she added.

"You don't even know it's the same person, do you?"

"It has to be. It's too much of a coincidence that someone would come after me twice."

"Okay, but can't you stay with a woman?" her mother asked.

"What woman?"

"One of your old girlfriends."

"Lauren Shellinger moved shortly after we did. I checked when I first came to town. She's the only one I'd feel comfortable asking. You wouldn't allow me to keep in contact with any of my friends, remember?"

"The therapist said to make a clean break."

So much for that. Now she was back in Whiterock, and nothing had changed. Even her attraction to trouble.

"I'll bet Pastor Wayne would offer you a room," her mother said. "We still exchange Christmas cards every year."

Pastor Wayne was probably the one who'd wind up telling her mother that she'd lost her virginity to Cain at sixteen. "I'll keep that in mind, Mom. Wish Leanne luck with the baby."

"I will."

"What a scare you gave us," her father muttered.

"I'm sorry, Dad."

"I'm just glad you're okay, honey."

Her mother spoke again. "We'll call you when Leanne goes into labor."

"I'd appreciate that. Love you both," she said and disconnected. Then she sat in silence, wondering how she was going to find someone who'd already gotten away with murder and eluded detection for twelve years. Especially when she wasn't strong enough to get around on her own.

Had she overestimated what she'd learned about police work at The Last Stand?

Doubt was as big an enemy as fear. She had to do what she could—figure out *some* way to bring the culprit out in the open. She owed it to Jason, to Cain, to herself.

"Are you coming back?" she called.

Cain made no response. Careful not to fall, she moved into the living room, where she found him standing to one side of the window, peering through the blinds.

"What is it?" she asked.

"Someone's here."

"Why aren't the dogs barking?"

"That's what I want to know," he said. Then he went to his room and brought back a rifle.

Amy had dog biscuits in her pocket, but she didn't need them. As far as she could tell, Cain's hounds weren't in their pen. Which was good. Before Sheridan was attacked, Cain hadn't been particularly quick to come running every time the dogs barked. There were too many coons, skunks and possums in the area for that. But he was apt to be more vigilant now.

The constant jealousy Amy lived with jabbed her sharply as she thought about Cain looking after Sheridan so conscientiously. Mary Martinez had mentioned just this morning that Cain had told her he was taking a week off, so she'd have to take her cat to Peter Smoot.

Cain *never* took time off because his job wasn't like a regular job. It was his life. He did what he loved, what he'd do even if he wasn't getting paid for it. But for Sheridan, apparently, he'd stop the earth from spinning.

Grinding her teeth, Amy crept up to the back of the house, then around to the side to squint through the window into Cain's bedroom. His neighbors lived so far away he rarely bothered to lower his blinds. He'd come into his room, peel off his shirt and jeans, flop onto the bed in his boxers and turn on the TV. She loved catching him in those unguarded moments. Somehow it was enough just to *watch* him.

But he wasn't in his room tonight. The light spilling in from the hallway illuminated an empty bed.

Amy was creeping past the deck, hoping to catch a glimpse of Sheridan or Cain through the kitchen windows, when she heard the rattle of a chain-link fence—and froze.

Was it the dogs? She didn't think so. She didn't hear so much as an accompanying whimper. But she couldn't see them inside the house, either. What was going on?

Planning to check their pen, she came around the corner—and ran right into Cain. With a yelp of surprise, she jumped back. She would've darted away but he'd already seen her.

"What're you doing here?" he growled.

Calling up every ounce of nerve she possessed, she straightened her police uniform, which she'd donned for just such an eventuality. "Making sure the man who attacked Sheridan isn't paying you a return visit. What do you *think?* Jeez, you scared the shit out of me, Cain."

He hesitated, seemed to consider her response. "So you didn't shoot the dogs?"

"*Shoot* the dogs?" she echoed, shock in her voice.

"Someone put them to sleep, and I'm guessing it was with my own tranquilizer gun. There aren't a lot of those around."

"They're not dead—"

"No."

"Why would anyone want to put them to sleep?"

Cain was no longer looking at her. His eyes were scanning the darkness around them, checking the shadows, the trees. "To take them out of the equation. The real question is why whoever it was didn't just shoot them and be done with it."

"Maybe we're dealing with an animal lover."

"More likely we're dealing with someone who

knows a tranq gun is quieter. Whoever it was didn't want to alert me too soon."

There was a loud crack, then something whizzed past Cain and struck the side of his cabin with a *thwap*. Amy knew instantly that it was a bullet, but she didn't have time to check. Cain jerked her down and pulled her over against the shed, where they had some cover. "We have company. Do you have your gun?"

"Y-yes." Amy had her police-issue firearm. After what'd happened to Sheridan, she wasn't about to go skulking through the woods without it. But she'd never dreamed she'd actually have to use it. She'd been on the police force for six years and hadn't fired it once— except at paper targets hammered to a post in her brother's yard.

Rustling in the trees made Amy's heart skip a beat. There really *was* someone out there, trying to kill them.

"I'm going to flush him out," Cain murmured. "You go inside and stay with Sheridan. Don't let anyone get in. And keep low to the ground."

Amy nodded, but she had no intention of protecting Sheridan. Despite the adrenaline that made her legs as unreliable as if she'd consumed half a bottle of whiskey, she managed to stay on her feet as she headed around the front as Cain expected. Then, when he plunged into the foliage, she hurried around the dogs' pen instead. Moving close to the fence, she could see their inert bodies, which sent another chill down her spine.

Her car was parked about a mile away by road, near the Matherleys' cabin. She cut across state land, already planning what she'd say if Cain caught her. She'd tell him she'd left her keys in the car and was afraid the gunman might get away in it. Why should she huddle in the cabin with his real target? The sooner someone shot Sheridan, the better.

But Amy was terrified for Cain. It was entirely possible that he could die trying to defend the bitch who'd caused all this trouble. If only Sheridan had gone home....

Deciding to radio her brother from the car, she held up a hand to protect herself from the branches that scratched at her face as she ran. But when she reached the road, a dark figure darted out of the trees ahead of her.

Heart pounding, she raised her gun and placed her finger on the trigger. If it meant saving herself or Cain, she could kill without a doubt. But in that split second the moonlight hit the man's face and she recognized him.

"It's you," she said, holstering her gun in relief. "Damn, you scared me. What are you doing out here?"

He lifted the rifle he was carrying. "Probably the same thing you are. Cain called me about half an hour ago. Said he'd heard a strange noise. I came to help him check it out."

Breathing a huge sigh of relief, she studied the surrounding land. "Why didn't you call me?"

"I thought we could handle it."

"You haven't seen anything?"

He leaned his gun against her car. "No. And I've scoured this whole place. If somebody was here, they're gone now."

"I don't think so."

"Why not?"

She rested her hand on the butt of her gun as she

continued to eye the trees. "He nearly hit me a few minutes ago."

"You're kidding!"

"I wish I was. We have to keep searching." The sooner they apprehended whoever it was, the sooner Sheridan might be satisfied and go back to California.

"Then let's go."

He shoved off from the car and came toward her.

She opened her mouth to respond, but before she could say anything he grabbed her and yanked her back, pulling her pistol from its holster. Then he pressed the barrel to her temple.

"What're you doing?" She tried to resist, but it was useless. He was too strong. "Stop it! You—you're scaring me. This isn't funny."

"I'm sorry," he whispered. "I'm so sorry."

The anguish in his voice terrified her. But this had to be a joke. He wouldn't really shoot her—he wouldn't shoot anyone. "Let go!"

"I can't. Say your prayers, Amy."

Tears scalded her eyes. "But…I—I don't understand. W-why are you doing this?"

"Because you're in the wrong place at the wrong time," he said and pulled the trigger.

14

The crack of gunfire made Cain halt in his tracks. What was the reason for *that* shot? It wasn't aimed at him; it hadn't come from anywhere nearby. And it hadn't come from the direction of the house. Both of these facts brought him comfort—but not complete relief. Someone was still out there. Someone with a gun, and this time it hadn't sounded like a rifle.

Following the sound, he hurried through the woods, but when he reached the road he saw nothing unusual. Amy's car was there, but that was all.

With his rifle ready, he stepped cautiously beyond the cover of the trees, into the open. Silence. No movement or light or sound except for a sluggish wind that caused a dry leaf to skitter across the ground. He seemed to be the only person here. But he was positive that shot had come from this direction.

What was going on? Backing up so he could keep an eye out in case someone tried to surprise him, he felt the rear panel of the cruiser on the driver's side, then took two more steps and opened the door.

The keys hung in the ignition, but the cabin light revealed nothing other than an empty car. Everything looked just as it should—until he closed the door and crept to the front. Then he could make out the shape of a person lying on the ground about ten feet away, partially in the road, partially in the underbrush. And from the dark pant-legs of a police uniform, he knew exactly who it was.

Cain rushed back to the house. He wasn't leaving Sheridan alone, unable to defend herself or even run, the dogs out cold. He couldn't do anything for Amy; he'd already checked. She'd been shot in the head at close range and the bullet had probably killed her instantly.

Whoever had shot her had to be covered in blood, which meant he couldn't go unnoticed.

Or maybe he could. It was dark. All he had to do was slink off somewhere and wash up.

Cain wanted to search for the bastard before he could get away, but without his dogs he could tramp around the forest all night and find nothing. He couldn't risk the possibility that the culprit hadn't run away and was, right now, making another attempt on Sheridan's life.

"Cain! Cain, where are you?"

It was her. He could hear her calling him before he reached the clearing.

"Get in the house!" he shouted, but she was so unsteady on her feet he caught up with her before she managed to climb the porch steps. She was clomping around in his boots, which were way too big for her, and dragging his tranq gun.

"Why the hell are you out here?" he snapped. He was angry she'd made herself such an easy target. But he didn't wait for her answer. He grabbed her around the waist with one arm, carried her the last few yards to the house, and slammed the door behind them. Then he turned the dead bolt, brought her into his bedroom and sat her on the floor next to him, where he might be able to protect her. At least in the bedroom he had only one window to worry about and he could use the bed as a barrier.

"Did you call the police?" he asked.

"Y-yes." She was ghost-white and shaking. Was she in shock? It had to be *much* too soon to deal with something so traumatic.

"Where'd you find my tranq gun?"

"On the—the ground, at the edge of the clearing."

He took it and checked it over. His first thought was that he'd arm Sheridan, too, but it was out of darts. "Shit."

"What?"

"Nothing. Everything's going to be fine." He still had his rifle.

"You c-call this f-fine?" she said, laughing a little hysterically.

"Let me clarify. We have a weapon, and I'll use it if I have to."

The minutes passed with no noise from outside. Fairly certain that whoever it was had fled, he finally lowered his rifle and took one of her hands. It was ice-cold. "Are you okay?"

"The dogs…the dogs are dead." She sounded like she was hyperventilating. "I saw them—"

"No, they're just drugged. They'll be okay when it wears off."

That didn't bring her the relief he'd hoped. "But I was

afraid...I thought you were dead, too." She gulped for breath. "Or that you were lying on the ground some-where, b-bleeding, and I w-wouldn't f-find you in time."

She'd heard the gunshot and, when he didn't return, assumed he'd been shot. That was why she'd come after him, dragging a gun she wasn't strong or healthy enough to lift.

"I'm safe. I'm here." Gathering her to him, he held her tightly, telling her not to worry, that everything would be all right.

She started to calm down, but he didn't let go. He needed her for comfort as much as she needed him. No matter what he did, he couldn't block out the image of Amy's lifeless body dumped near his neighbor's long, winding drive, bathed in her own blood.

Cain had realized Ned wouldn't take the news well. But he hadn't expected the police chief to break down in tears. Because he and Ned had never liked each other, Cain didn't know what to say—what to do—when the other man's shoulders began to shake and he buried his face in his hands. Standing to one side, he waited for Ned to come to grips with his grief.

It was Sheridan who stepped forward to offer him solace. "I'm so sorry," she murmured over and over, rubbing his back. But when Ned looked up, he didn't acknowledge her.

"Why was Amy here?" he demanded, wiping his eyes.

"She said she was making sure whoever attacked Sheridan wasn't coming back," Cain told him, "but I don't know why she chose tonight. Maybe she's been patrolling regularly. Or maybe someone called her." He shrugged. "We didn't have the chance to say much. I went to see why everything was so quiet, found the dogs out cold and bumped into her while I was trying to figure out what was going on."

"You didn't ask her to come here?"

Cain chafed beneath such visible signs of Ned's grief. He hated tears, even from a woman. They made him feel so helpless. "No. As soon as I realized she wasn't the one who drugged my hounds, I knew someone else must be around. Then there was a shot and a bullet whizzed past my ear."

"So you sent Amy back to her car? That doesn't make sense."

She was a cop, she had a gun—and he'd been concerned about leaving Sheridan unprotected. "No. I didn't even know where she'd left it. I told her to go into the house and stay with Sheridan. I have no idea why she didn't."

"She never came to the door," Sheridan said, sounding as mystified as Cain felt. "I heard two gunshots, several minutes apart. That was it. No one knocked or called out."

When Ned didn't speak, Cain reluctantly met his red, swollen eyes. "What?"

"You never saw anyone else out there? Never spotted a vehicle?"

"Only Amy's cruiser. It's parked thirty yards or so from the turnoff to Levi Matherley's place, right by…right where it happened." His voice softened. Ned's job required him to go to the crime scene, where he'd meet the coroner and begin gathering evidence. He'd have to see his dead twin's body, document the scene with photographs, write notes about it....

"That's awful convenient, don't you think?" Ned's gaze lowered to Cain's shirt. Until that moment, Cain hadn't noticed that he had Amy's blood smeared across his chest. He'd rolled her over and pulled her into his arms to see if there was any hope. And then all hope had disappeared.

"What's convenient?" Cain heard the suspicion in Ned's voice but managed to hang on to his temper by telling himself that Ned wasn't thinking clearly. He was reacting to the pain and grief.

"People keep getting hurt up here. But you never see a damn thing."

"I live on 200,000 acres of forestland. How am I supposed to see everything?"

"It all happens within a mile of your house."

"That's not fair," Sheridan said. She tried to hold Cain back, but he stepped close to Ned, anyway.

"What're you saying?"

Fresh tears filled Ned's eyes but his voice remained truculent. "I think it's strange, that's all. That Amy was killed here, of all places. That there were no witnesses *again*. And that whoever did this had no compunction about killing a human being, yet merely tranquilized your precious dogs."

Cain clamped his jaw shut so he wouldn't say anything that could make the situation worse.

"What, no excuses?" Ned taunted.

With a sigh, he stepped back. "It wasn't necessary for

him to kill the dogs. He rendered them useless a far easier way."

"It would've been just as easy to shoot them." His eyes narrowed. "Unless whoever did this loved them too much."

"What if he was trying to set me up? Then he'd know better than to kill my dogs," Cain said. "Listen, you've blamed me for every bad day Amy's ever had, and I've let you do it. I wasn't a good husband, didn't love her the way she wanted me to, wasn't interested in trying to patch things up. I take responsibility for all of that. But I didn't kill her, Ned. If you continue to plow through this investigation with blinders on, you're going to miss something important. And none of us can afford that."

"Cain's right," Sheridan said. "You have to forget about holding a grudge. Try to be more objective."

"Just stay the hell out of my way," Ned snapped at them. "Whoever did this is going down, even if I have to kill him myself."

The slamming of the door echoed in the ensuing silence.

"It's not every day you hear a police chief threaten murder," Sheridan said as Ned's engine roared to life.

Cain couldn't conjure up a smile at her sarcasm, so he shook his head. "Poor dumb bastard. He's so busy trying to punish me he could be brushing elbows with his sister's killer and never know it."

Cain had often wished he'd never have to see Amy again, but he hadn't wanted anything like this. Her death was so sudden, so senseless, so…unbelievable. It was disgusting, too. He already knew he'd never forget the sight of her, missing one eye and half her head.

After checking his dogs for the fifth time to make sure they were all breathing and beginning to revive, he drifted around the house, searching for something to occupy his mind—the newspaper, paying bills, generating invoices for his sideline veterinary business. He couldn't focus long enough to finish a single task, however. He heard the police outside, digging that bullet out of the siding on his house, and wondered what was happening at the murder scene. And his thoughts kept returning to Sheridan. She'd gone to bed shortly after Ned's departure, but she wasn't asleep. Cain could hear her tossing and turning, knew she was as unsettled as he was. She'd left her door open as if she didn't want to be alone, and he felt the same way.

When he went to look in on her, she must've heard his footsteps because she rolled over to face him.

"You okay?" he asked, standing in the doorway.

"I think so. You?"

"I don't know." He'd never felt so at odds with reality.

"What you saw had to be gruesome."

"It was."

"But shouldn't you try to get some rest?"

"No point. I can't sleep." What he really wanted was to crawl into bed with her and pull her close, feel her breathing against him. But he knew what she'd think if he sought that kind of reassurance. "Want to watch a movie?" he asked.

She sat up. She'd put on a tank top—and what was she wearing below it? He couldn't help speculating.

"As long as it's not remotely violent," she said.

"A comedy?"

"What do you have?"

"I get satellite, so I'm not sure. But with over two hundred channels, we should be able to find *something*."

He wanted to support her as she made her way to the living room but didn't. She was capable of getting around on her own now. And, needy as he was feeling, it would be best to keep his hands to himself.

"So, what do we have?" She sat at one end of the couch and he sat at the other, reading the options listed on the programming guide.

"There aren't any comedies right now," she said. "At least no good ones."

"What about a drama? I've never seen *The English Patient*." He probably hadn't seen it because it looked like a chick flick. But he was in the mood for something sentimental, something that might fill the empty hole inside him. He'd found a woman murdered in cold blood not half a mile from his home. A woman he'd known most his life, someone he'd once created a child with. Before tonight, he'd felt safe living in the forest, safe and in control of his surroundings.

"I haven't seen it, either," she said.

"It started fifteen minutes ago, so we're coming in a bit late."

"But that's going to be the case with everything."

With a nod, he changed the channel and they began to watch the movie. It turned out to be so thoroughly entertaining that his tension finally began to ease—until Ralph Fiennes and Kristin Scott Thomas made love.

* * *

As Sheridan saw the lead characters take off their clothes and touch, it was as if she was experiencing the same desert heat, feeling the same passion and desperation they did. But she sat there rigidly, refusing to move, refusing to even turn her gaze in Cain's direction. Until Kristin Scott Thomas groaned in ecstasy. Then she couldn't stop herself from glancing at Cain. She wanted to catch a glimpse of his expression, see what he was feeling.

But he wasn't watching the film.

He was watching her.

"This might not be the best movie for us to see tonight," she said when their eyes met.

He didn't answer.

"Don't you agree?" she prompted.

"Why not?" he asked.

He knew, but he wanted her to spell it out for him, to see if she'd admit her own desire. "We're feeling a little…shaken and…disoriented after everything that happened tonight."

"Disoriented," he repeated.

"Yeah."

"I'll go with shaken, but I'm not disoriented. I know exactly what I want."

"Right. Well, I think I'll go to bed." She started to get up, but he reached out to stop her, and the moment his fingers closed around her wrist she felt reluctant to pull away.

His eyes ran over her tank top, then settled on the blanket she clutched around her waist. "Let go," he said.

She swallowed hard. "No."

"I want to see you."

"You already did when you dressed me after our dip in the pond, remember?"

"This time I want you to *show* me."

She told herself not to do it. She knew better than to take this any further. But she was transfixed by the desire in his eyes.

"Sheridan?" He sounded greedy, desperate.

Dropping the blanket, she stood in front of him wearing only her tank top and a pair of panties.

His sudden intake of air nearly melted the marrow in her bones. One finger flicked over the silk of her panties—and still she didn't step away.

"I can't stop thinking about you," he murmured.

It'd taken Sheridan years to recover from their last time together. But she wasn't sixteen anymore. She'd never been on the weaker end of a relationship since. She'd also never fallen in love again, which seemed unfair, but there was something to be said for emotional safety.

"Now's not a good time. I—I have too many bruises," she said, but it wasn't the bruises that worried her. Regardless of her self-talk, she was afraid of how a sexual encounter with Cain might affect her later.

"You think I'll hurt you?"

Not physically, which was what he meant. "No."

"So what're you afraid of?"

"Certainly not you," she lied. To prove it, she let her fingers delve into his hair and felt wildly powerful when he closed his eyes as if he'd actually been afraid she'd refuse him.

"I thought you were reformed," she breathed, watching the relief on his face.

"No, just waiting."

"For what?"

"For this." Holding her by the waist, he leaned forward and covered her right breast, fabric and all, with his mouth.

A tremor of pure pleasure made Sheridan too weak to stand. Cain must've felt her reaction because he supported her so she wouldn't have to stand on her own. Then he pressed her down onto the couch and raised her shirt.

"Wow."

She touched his cheek, and their eyes met. His were filled with a need she'd never seen there before. It was because of Amy. Finding his ex-wife murdered in the road had understandably shocked him, upset him, even though he hadn't been in love with her.

"Everything will be okay," she told him, and then he was greedily touching and tasting every inch of her bare skin.

"This is what I want," he murmured, and Sheridan groaned as his hand slid inside her panties.

She could comfort him this way, let him escape for half an hour and still distance herself emotionally, she told herself as he went to get a condom. But then he returned and their lovemaking escalated quickly, becoming so frenzied that her control slipped. When she felt the delicious pressure of him pushing inside her she realized she'd been waiting for this moment, too—ever since that night in the camper.

But she'd underestimated his power over her.

Because even as an adult, she couldn't be remote with him, couldn't reserve any small part of herself. She was falling in love so hard and fast she could feel the ground rushing up to meet her.

She froze at the thought, and he stopped moving.

"Am I being too rough?" he asked, his breathing ragged. "Am I hurting you?"

"No." He was doing the exact opposite, making her feel things she hadn't experienced since the last time he'd made love to her. She was twelve years older and *still* wanted to believe in what she felt, which was foolish. Trying to hold on to Cain's affection was like trying to capture sunbeams in a jar.

He pushed the hair from her forehead. "Tell me what's wrong."

"Nothing." She used her hands to urge him to continue, but when he tried to kiss her, she turned her face away. Then he froze, too, and fell silent for several seconds.

"Sheridan?" he said at length.

She could hear his confusion. Only moments before, she'd eagerly accepted his openmouthed kisses, matching his passion with her own. And now she was sick with a frightening sense of déjà vu. "What?"

He scraped his thumb along her bottom lip. In the flickering light from the television, she could see the furrow that'd formed between his brows. "What happened?" he asked.

"Nothing."

"Then why are you suddenly holding out on me?"

"I'm not holding out." She angled her hips to show him she hadn't brought him to this point only to shut him down. She knew that wouldn't be fair. But the attempt wasn't good enough to convince him.

"I don't want this to be a solo journey. I want to take you with me," he whispered.

She'd almost been there. She'd felt the tension building and bailed out at the last minute. Bringing her pleasure was too easy for him. She didn't want him to make her feel more than other men did. "It's not going to happen for me. Go ahead."

"It'll happen if you stop fighting it."

"No, I'm not even close." She lowered her eyelids so he wouldn't see it was a lie, but he knew anyway. He slowed down, as if they were starting all over, and although she wouldn't kiss him, he found plenty of other things to do with his mouth. "Do you like that?" he murmured as his tongue caressed the tip of one breast.

He knew she liked it. She couldn't help squirming beneath him, and she had goose bumps down to her toes.

"You're not playing fair," she accused him, and was rewarded with the sexiest smile she'd ever seen.

"No one said I had to play fair." His thrusts were slow and steady enough to make her crave the natural escalation they promised. "Quit denying yourself. Quit denying *me*," he said, and lowered his mouth to her neck.

She knew he'd leave a telltale mark and tried to stop him, but he'd succeeded in changing the focus of her defenses long enough to get what he really wanted. As she struggled to push his mouth away, he moved deeper and faster, and she could no longer resist the building pleasure. She cried out as her body convulsed—and he closed his eyes, as if it was all he could do to hold out for a few seconds more.

"That's it," he murmured. "There you go." But then he couldn't talk anymore because his body was doing the same.

15

*S*hit. She'd made the same mistake again. After twelve *years*. Given it all away without reserve, just like before. Now Cain was half lying on her, his naked body slick with sweat, his heart pounding as he recovered.

A little late to say no.

I'm an idiot. What was it about this man? Sheridan asked herself. With him, she couldn't think straight, make smart decisions or keep her clothes on.

"You'd better not have given me a hickey," she warned.

He chuckled, his breath warm on her shoulder. "You already have so many marks on you no one'll notice."

"Are you kidding? *Everyone* will notice."

"Mmm…" he muttered lazily. "Serves you right."

"How?"

"You made me do it."

"No, I didn't!"

"Yes, you did. You forced me—" he kissed the skin closest to his lips "—to take desperate measures."

Sheridan wished she could be angry. But she wasn't. She was caught in the blissful aftermath of lovemaking and wanted nothing more than to curl up with him and sleep.

He lifted his head to look at her. "Admit it—you're glad." He tried to peck her lips but she dodged him again.

His smile disappeared as his mood shifted from satisfied, even happy, to wary. "Why won't you kiss me?"

She didn't answer him directly; she wasn't sure herself. It just seemed the only way to hang on to a vestige of her resistance. "You're too cocky," she complained. "I'm going to bed."

He kept her pinned beneath him. "With me, though, right?"

"Alone." She needed time and space to reconstruct the barricades he'd just mowed down, to convince herself to be more careful in the future. It wasn't going to be easy. This had been the best sexual encounter of her life—probably because she'd never wanted anyone else so badly.

Some things never changed....

His expression grew unreadable. "Fine. Suit yourself." He moved so she could wriggle out from under him. But when he realized she was actually leaving, he came up from behind, lifted her over his shoulder and carried her into his own room.

"What're you doing?" she demanded.

"Taking you to bed."

His shoulder pressing into her stomach made it difficult to talk. "I can...see that. The question is...why?"

"Because I'm too exhausted to worry about you."

"What do you mean?"

He maneuvered carefully so she wouldn't hit any part of the doorframe. "You think I want to wake up to find you lying in the road, like Amy?"

"I guess that's one way…to get rid of…old lovers."

Horrified by her own careless remark, she knew instantly that she'd gone too far.

His step faltered. "On second thought—" he dumped her on the bed "—go put on some clothes."

Sheridan went into the living room and pulled on her T-shirt. Then she hovered in Cain's doorway. If she got in her own bed at this point, she doubted he'd stop her, but Amy's death had troubled him deeply. It troubled her, too, left her confused and sad and far too vulnerable.

The truth was, she didn't want to be alone any more than he did.

Finally lowering her pride enough to enter his room, she slipped into bed with him. She hoped he'd say something that would give her a chance to apologize, that maybe he'd throw out an arm to draw her closer. But he didn't. He hadn't bothered to put on any clothes, but he didn't touch her the rest of the night.

Sheridan opened her eyes to the large green numerals on Cain's alarm clock. It was after eight—not particularly early. But not as late as she'd wanted to sleep, either, considering what she remembered of last night. Was Amy really *dead?* Dead like Jason? Gone forever?

It didn't seem possible.

The phone rang. Cain stirred, then reached over her to pick up the handset. His bare chest came into contact with her arm, but she knew he wasn't naked anymore. He'd gotten up during the night at least three times to check on his dogs and had come back to bed in his boxers. "'Lo?… Right now?…We'll be there."

She felt the temporary weight of his body as he returned the phone to its cradle, but the contact between them didn't seem to affect him at all. Evidently, he was still angry with her.

"What was that about?" she asked when he got up.

"We have to go down to the station, make a formal statement." He went down the hall and into the bathroom.

"It was Ned?" she called after him

"No, Ian Peterson. I'm guessing Ned's still at the funeral home."

The funeral home. It was real, all right. Amy had been shot.

While Sheridan listened to the shower, she was relieved to hear the dogs outside. She'd been worried when Cain had gotten up so often.

Finally, she decided to bathe in the pond instead of waiting for a chance to use Cain's only bathroom. She needed to get out of the cabin, reassure herself that the whole world hadn't turned hostile. This would be the safest time. The cops were probably still at the crime scene less than a mile away. The killer would have to be an idiot to come anywhere close. And she already knew this killer wasn't stupid.

Taking Cain's rifle, just in case, she retrieved her toiletries from her suitcase and a towel from the linen closet and went to see the dogs before heading to the pond.

"Hi, boys." She hooked her fingers in the chain-link fence as she peered in at them. They seemed to be re-covered, all except Maximillian. He wasn't very energetic, although Koda and Quixote were definitely no worse for wear. Maximillian rested his nose on his paws as he watched her, his eyebrows tweaking quizzically; Koda and Quixote wagged their tails and begged her to let them out.

She took one of the leashes that hung on the fence nearby, then went into the pen and snapped it on Koda's collar. She had a good weapon, but figured it wouldn't hurt to bring an alarm, too. "Want to go for a short walk, boy?"

Koda barked in eager agreement, and she had to hold Quixote back as they passed through the gate. "I'll take you next time," she promised.

Koda wanted to run, but Sheridan wasn't up to that kind of exertion. She was feeling stronger, though. Last night had acted as a reawakening—a reawakening to the desires of a healthy body. And to the knowledge that she had to get well quickly before she wound up getting hurt again.

Sheridan examined the surrounding forest as she walked. It seemed that this killer could get away with anything. First Jason, then her attack, and now Cain's ex-wife….

She contemplated what her friends would say if they knew about this situation and nearly groaned aloud. She'd call them. Tomorrow. Tomorrow would be a better day to tell them. She knew they'd be frantic by then, especially Jon, but she couldn't deal with anymore right now.

Once she reached the pond, she tied Koda to a tree, set the rifle on a rock where she could grab it in a hurry, and dropped the towel she'd tucked around her waist. Surprisingly, thoughts of Amy—and even her own chagrin at getting more intimately involved with Cain— evaporated beneath a perfect sun, as round and as yellow as the yolk of an egg.

The creek trickling into the pond was the only sound she heard as she stripped down to a spaghetti-strap T-shirt and underwear. Then, with a warm wind caressing her skin, she waded into the water.

Koda sat on his haunches in the shade, watching her.

"You okay over there, Koda?"

He barked, and she smiled. "Good boy."

Knowing they had to be down at the station soon, she took a quick bath and was about to get out of the water when Koda lurched to his feet and began to strain at the leash. Fear-induced adrenaline shot through Sheridan as she started for the gun. But then she realized that wouldn't be necessary. It was Cain. He strode into the clearing, wearing a clean pair of jeans and a red T-shirt, his hair still wet.

"You couldn't have told me?" he said, obviously not pleased that she'd left the house without alerting him.

She nodded toward the gun. "I took precautions."

Cain didn't argue. He bent to pat his dog. She decided to get out while he was occupied, but he wasn't occupied long enough.

Glancing up, she met his enigmatic gaze and straightened, letting the water run off her, knowing it made her T-shirt nearly transparent. "You're staring," she breathed—and hoped he'd do a lot more than that. She pictured him striding toward her and taking her in his arms, as he had last night. But he didn't.

"You'll want to wear something to cover that love bite," he said. Then he untied Koda's leash from the tree while she dressed.

Last night had changed things between them—but by

how much? Cain was remote, guarded. And she knew he wouldn't touch her again, not unless she asked.

Sheridan didn't have anything with a high neck, so she had to resort to a colorful scarf to hide the hickey Cain had given her. She studied herself in the mirror, wondering if the purple and red scarf matched her pink spaghetti-strap T-shirt, tiered pink and red skirt and sandals. But in the end, she decided it didn't matter. That scarf was all she had to hide the evidence of their love-making. And this was going to be a difficult meeting as it was. She didn't want to walk into the police station only to have Ned and everyone else sneer at that mark and what it meant.

"I'm ready," she said, stepping into the living room.

At least she looked better than she had since she'd arrived in Whiterock. Her bruises were fading. But Cain barely glanced at her. He handed her a plate of scrambled eggs and toast and said simply, "Breakfast."

He had her eat in the truck as they drove and didn't break his silence until they pulled into Whiterock's small police station. Then he swore under his breath.

"What's wrong?" she asked.

He nodded toward an old brown station wagon. "My stepfather's here."

"Why?"

"I can only imagine," he said, and got out of the truck.

Sheridan followed him inside to find John Wyatt sitting there, looking far more distinguished than Sheridan remembered. Now gray at the temples, he had more lines bracketing his eyes and mouth than before, but he was still handsome in an even-featured, pleasant sort of way. And he had a nice physique for a man in his fifties.

"Cain, thanks for coming in."

Sheridan didn't recognize the police officer who greeted them, but she knew from his badge that he was the Ian Peterson who'd called.

"No problem." Cain's eyes cut to his stepfather, who stood, but they didn't embrace or even shake hands. They exchanged a slight nod of acknowledgement and Cain once again focused on Ian.

"What is it you need?"

"I'd like to ask you both a few questions, if you don't mind."

"And if we do?" Cain asked.

"We might think there's a reason."

"You'll think I'm involved regardless," Cain said, but he waved Sheridan ahead of him, and Officer Peterson showed her into Ned's office, where she took one of the visitor's chairs. The station wasn't big enough to have an interrogation room.

After closing the door, Peterson sat down at Ned's desk. "I understand you used to live here a decade or so ago."

She put her purse at her feet. "That's right."

He had a steno pad waiting, on which he recorded the date and her name. "You and Cain Granger had a sexual relationship at the time, is that also correct?"

Sheridan clasped her hands in her lap and straightened her spine. "Not entirely, no. We had a one-time encounter, an encounter that had nothing to do with anything before or after."

"And yet his stepbrother was shot within…" he opened a file that was also waiting on the desk, but Sheridan supplied the information before he could dig through its contents.

"Six weeks."

"And then you and your family relocated?"

"Two months later."

"Had you been planning to leave town before the shooting?"

"No. When the man who tried to kill me wasn't apprehended, my parents were concerned for my safety and decided to move."

"Did you keep in touch with Cain Granger once you left?"

"No."

"Not at all?"

"Not at all."

"Can you remember anything about the man with the rifle at Rocky Point?"

"Nothing that I haven't previously stated. Otherwise, I would've called and added it to the record. I want the man who shot me arrested as much as Mr. Wyatt or anyone else does."

"I'm sure you do." He put the file aside and focused on his steno pad. "How well did you know Amy Smith?"

"I remember her from high school, but we didn't hang out together."

"Had you seen her since your return to town?"

"Yes, twice."

"Was Cain present at either of those meetings?"

"He was at both."

"And yet you don't have a relationship with Cain Granger."

The hickey beneath her scarf seemed to burn. "He's been nice enough to take care of me while I recover. That's it."

"Out of the goodness of his heart."

"Basically, yeah," she said, glaring at him.

"Did you detect any animosity between Cain and his ex-wife in either of those meetings?" he asked, switching tactics.

"Not the kind you're obviously digging for."

He raised his hazel eyes from the lined paper in front of him. "Just answer the question, please."

"Amy was still in love with Cain. That created tension whenever they were together."

"You know this even though you've been gone for twelve years?"

She could sense Peterson's loyalty to his fallen comrade, and to his chief. "It was very apparent to me."

"In two short meetings?"

"You could tell in five seconds," she said with a pointed look.

"Would it be safe to say that Cain disliked his ex-wife?"

"I wouldn't call it *dislike*. I think he simply wanted her to forget the past, move on and leave him alone."

"And she wouldn't."

"No."

"So he killed her?" he asked softly.

Sheridan waited several heartbeats to give emphasis to her response. *"No."*

Peterson tilted his head. "How do you know?"

"Because he was with me the night it happened. We were playing poker when he realized the dogs were unusually silent. He went out to check on them, and then I heard the first shot."

"You don't remember Amy coming to the door? Or maybe giving Cain a call?"

"No. I heard voices outside, very briefly. But I had no idea it was Amy."

"Was that before or after the shot?"

"Before."

"What happened afterward?"

"Nothing for several minutes. Then there was another shot."

"When did Cain return to the cabin?"

Sheridan tightened her fingers, which were interlaced in her lap. "After the second shot."

"How long after?"

"Ten, fifteen minutes."

"What do you think he was doing during that time?"

Sheridan remembered seeing Cain enter the clearing, covered in blood; remembered the terror that'd gripped her until she'd realized he wasn't hurt. She'd already watched his stepbrother die. She didn't want to see another death—especially his. "He followed the sound of that shot—and discovered Amy lying in the road."

"He told you this?"

"I'm guessing."

"Exactly. You don't know what happened once he left the house."

"I know he couldn't have tranquilized his own dogs. He was inside with me when they fell silent."

"He could've done it earlier. Haven't you ever taken a sleeping pill? Some sedatives take time to work. Are you telling me he didn't go outside at all that evening?"

She couldn't make such a statement. Cain always went outside. He fed the dogs, let them in or out of their pen, watered or weeded his garden, performed small maintenance chores. "It wasn't him," she said.

Peterson meticulously rearranged the calendar, the pencil holder and the steno pad on the desk. "How are the dogs, by the way?"

"They're fine."

"All of them?"

"I think so. Quixote seemed a little lethargic this morning, but I'm pretty sure that was just because the sedative hadn't completely worn off."

He smiled, but Sheridan could tell it wasn't sincere. "Where do you suppose this person got a tranquilizer gun?"

"Cain checked. They used his."

"So now you're telling me Cain's dogs were shot with his own gun." That smile was back.

"Whoever did it broke into Cain's clinic and took the gun. You can see the damaged lock, if you want."

"We'll get to that in a minute. I'm still wondering about the dogs. They didn't go crazy with a stranger on the property? I thought they woke Cain up with their barking when you were attacked, which happened much farther away."

"Whoever did this knew how to handle them, I guess. Maybe he tossed some steaks inside their pen before he broke into the clinic. That would distract them until he could get the gun, don't you think?"

"I'm thinking it would be pretty easy for Cain to break his own lock."

"You seem pretty eager to believe Cain had something to do with Amy's death," she said.

"And you seem pretty defensive of him," he retorted.

"He's been a good friend to me."

"A friend." He nodded slowly. "I see. You're sure there isn't more to your relationship?"

"Like…"

"A closeness that would motivate you to lie for him?"

"I'm not lying!"

"But you've lied about your relationship with him in the past, correct?"

Sheridan unclasped her hands and curled her nails into her palms. "I didn't broadcast the fact that we slept together. There was no reason to do so."

He pursed his lips thoughtfully, but it was all for show. Officer Peterson seemed to think he was being clever. "Will you answer one more question for me, Ms. Kohl?"

"What is it?" She felt cornered and uneasy. She wanted Amy's killer found; she wanted the man who shot Jason and attacked her captured and punished. Instead, the cops were searching for evidence to charge *Cain*.

"How many people can you name who'd know which kind of sedative to use—and how much—in order to put a dog to sleep but not kill it?"

She glared at him.

"Ms. Kohl?"

"None," she admitted. "But all the supplies were

right there. And the amounts wouldn't be hard to figure out, especially if whoever shot Amy came prepared with a little information from the Internet and wasn't particularly worried whether or not the dogs died."

"You just said they survived. All three of them."

"Maybe we got lucky."

"Or whoever did it knew what he was doing."

"So now you're saying Cain killed his own stepbrother, nearly killed me twice *and* shot Amy?"

"You tell me," he said.

"*Why* would he do all of this?"

"He shot you and Jason out of jealousy."

She rolled her eyes but he lifted a hand as he continued.

"And he got away with it. What you told the police back then wasn't enough to cause him trouble, and you went away. It was over. Done. But then someone found that rifle, which he probably never expected, and you came back. It's logical to assume he'd be spooked."

"So why didn't he finish me off when he was beating me in the woods?" she challenged.

"He heard or saw something that led him to believe he'd been spotted, so he acted as your savior instead."

"Who could've seen him?"

"A hunter. A camper. A hiker." He paused. "Or maybe it was Amy."

Sheridan came to her feet. "*What?* Amy just happened to be randomly patrolling the forest near Cain's place at *midnight* and stumbled upon him beating me?"

"She went up there all the time. She was there last night, wasn't she?"

"Because she was making sure whoever hurt me wasn't lurking around. That's what she told Cain. Why else would she be there so late?"

He arched an eyebrow at her. "Knowing Cain, what do you think?"

They'd stop at nothing to disparage him. "He hasn't been sleeping with her."

"How can you be so sure?"

"Because of what Amy told me. Besides, she was a police officer. If she saw Cain doing something he shouldn't—"

"She was a cop, but she was a woman first. Maybe you don't know how much she loved him."

Sheridan did know. Unfortunately, she also knew that Amy wasn't the only one. "You're saying she was covering for him."

"That's exactly what I'm saying. Until last night. Maybe she threatened to come out with the truth and that's why he killed her."

16

When Peterson and Sheridan emerged from Ned's office, Sheridan didn't look happy. She sent him a warning glance, but Cain already knew things were going to get worse before they got better.

His stepfather was acting more remote, more formal, than ever. And he'd obviously come to the station for a reason.

"Cain, do you mind giving me a few minutes?" John motioned toward the now-empty office. "I'd like to talk to you alone."

Cain *did* mind. His emotions were so complex when it came to John Wyatt that even he didn't know how he felt most of the time. There'd been periods in the past when Cain had wanted to please him, to finally achieve the love and acceptance his stepbrothers took for granted. But everything changed once his mother got sick. Almost from the day of her diagnosis, John began to act as if she didn't exist. Maybe everyone else thought he was a saint, but Cain knew what he'd really been like.

With a curt nod, he headed into the office, then watched his stepfather slip past him and around the desk to take Ned's chair.

"Sit down," John said.

Cain didn't want to sit down. He was filled with too much nervous energy. First, that rifle had been found in his cabin. Then Sheridan had returned to town and nearly been killed. And Amy—God, Amy. Now that the shock was wearing off, what he felt about her death was a bleak sadness, a sense of waste.

"I'm fine the way I am." He folded his arms as he leaned against the wall, waiting to see what his stepfather would hit him with this time.

"Ned called me this morning," John said.

"Why would Ned call you?" Cain hated the sullen note that crept into his voice.

"He thought I should have a word with you before you spoke to anyone else."

"Spoke to anyone else about what?"

"About last night."

"I don't see how Amy's murder involves you."

"It does."

"Because…"

"Because I cared about her, too, damn it! She was like a daughter to me even before she married you."

Amy did anything she could to worm her way into his family's affections, to gain more ground in her attempt to possess him. Cain remembered her stopping by to clean John's house, bake him cookies, drop off some movies she thought he'd like. Cain had ignored it all, but John had reveled in her devotion and even suggested to Cain that he was foolish to "let her go."

Actually, she *used* to do all those things. It was hard to grasp that she was really gone.

"Beyond that, Ned believes, and I tend to agree with him," John was saying, "that there's got to be a connection between what's going on at your place these days and what happened twelve years ago."

What's going on at your place... Cain couldn't ignore the blame that tinged those words. "I agree, but I'm not that link," Cain said.

"Sometimes people make mistakes."

"Murder is more than a mistake."

John ignored his response. "It might feel as if there's no way out, but—"

"Just stop."

"If you'd listen to me and quit being difficult..."

"You think I killed Amy. How am I supposed to react?"

John's face flushed. This interview was gearing up to be the same power struggle they'd so often had in the past.

But then John closed his eyes and seemed to summon some patience. "I want you to know something."

Cain didn't bother asking what. It was coming whether he wanted to hear it or not.

"I want you to understand, *truly understand,* how hard it is to live each day without Jason. I miss him so much there are mornings when—" his eyes filled with tears "—mornings when I can hardly get out of bed."

"I miss him, too," Cain said, but he knew those words would sound insincere. John felt only his own pain; he'd never believe that Cain was capable of deeper emotion.

"It's not the same."

"Why not? Because I can't love as well as you do?"

"Quit putting words in my mouth!"

"I'm merely clarifying what you really said."

"All I mean is that it's difficult not knowing the identity of the man who killed my son, not having any closure, any sense of justice," he snapped. "I'm asking you to help me for once, damn it!"

How could he help? There was nothing Cain could do to assuage the pain John felt, nothing anyone could do. Cain wanted to know the identity of the man who'd killed Jason, too. Whoever it was had taken the only family member who'd loved him—besides Marshall, who'd been dealing with the onset of Alzheimer's at the time. "You think I did it," he said flatly.

John swallowed. "I'm beginning to wonder…."

"No, you've decided. That's why you're here. You believe Ned."

"Did you, Cain? *Did you kill my son?*"

The accusation brought a flood of the old anger and frustration. "No!" he said, but he knew John wouldn't believe him.

"That's it?"

"What more can I say?"

"I know things have never been smooth between us, Cain. I know you don't have a lot of respect for me. But I want you to understand that I did my best by you. When your mom got cancer, I was as devastated as you were—"

Cain raised a hand. "Stop! Don't tell me how broken up you were by my mother's last years. Not when I found that love letter you wrote to my high school English teacher barely two weeks after my mother's first chemo treatment. Not when I spotted you at the school, hoping to talk to your new love interest while my mother was wasting away."

His stepfather set his jaw. "I was reeling. I couldn't cope. Don't you understand that? I had children who still needed to be raised. I didn't know what I was going to do without her."

"So you were busy lining up her replacement?"

John shoved away from the desk and stood. "You little prick. You enjoy making me look bad, don't you?"

"Is that all you care about, John? How you look to other people?"

"I cared about your mother, too!"

Cared? He couldn't even say he loved her. Because he hadn't. Not in the end. Or, if he had, he'd loved himself more. But that came as no surprise. "Then, where were you?" Cain asked. "Where were you when she needed you?"

It was Cain who'd sat with her when the pain grew too great. Cain who'd tried to make her comfortable and dealt with the hospice care workers. Cain who'd refused to give up hope and hung on as long as possible. His stepbrothers and stepfather had acted as if nothing was wrong. They'd always had one excuse or another for being elsewhere. Even Jason and Marshall. Jason was too busy with school. And Marshall was still coping with Mildred's death; he was never the same afterward.

"Maybe I couldn't stand to watch it!"

Cain wished he could believe that. But it was an excuse. Eventually, his English teacher had admitted to him that John had been pursuing her for months. After learning that, Cain had spent an afternoon in her bed as a silent form of revenge. And she'd wanted him to come back. But by then the whole situation had turned Cain's stomach and he'd refused every request to "help with the yard work after school."

Karen Stevens had moved a few years after he graduated but she'd returned to Whiterock about six months ago. Now she was teaching at the high school again—and dating John. So John was finally getting what he wanted.

Distantly, Cain wondered what his stepfather would say if he found out Cain had slept with Karen. For one reckless moment, Cain was tempted to throw it in his face, to strike back. But he knew that in the end, he'd only feel worse, because he was ashamed of it and because it would hurt Karen. "If you expect my sympathy, you're not going to get it," he said.

"I don't want your sympathy," John spat. "I want the truth. It's time to come clean, Cain. It's the only way we can heal, the only way this community can get past what's happened." He reached out to grab Cain in a beseeching manner, and Cain forced himself to allow it, to do nothing more than stare down at the long fingers curling around his forearm. The only father he'd ever known believed he was a murderer. But then, John had never been much of a father....

"Think of Owen and Robert. Think of Grandpa."

"I didn't do it."

His stepfather's grip tightened. "Please!"

"I didn't do it!" He peeled John's hand away, then let the door slam against the inside wall as he stalked out.

* * *

Sheridan had heard Cain shout those last words. The whole office had.

"Yeah, right," Peterson muttered under his breath, but he didn't intercede. He didn't have the chance. Ned came in at that moment and drew his gun as soon as he saw Cain.

"You son of a bitch!" he screamed, aiming the pistol at Cain's chest.

Sheridan's mouth went dry as Cain stopped, heightened alertness brightening his eyes.

John Wyatt appeared in the doorway of Ned's office, looking pale and drawn.

"Chief, what're you doing?" Peterson's voice was low, cautious. "Put the gun down."

"He killed her." Ned's voice cracked with grief. "All she ever did was love him. All she ever wanted from him was a little bit of attention. And he killed her."

A muscle flexed in Cain's cheek, but he didn't deny Ned's charges. He didn't respond at all.

"He can't control who he loves any more than you can." When Sheridan stepped in front of Cain, he shoved her to the side, even tried to put her behind him. But she fought to stay where she was.

"You're not thinking right." Jerking out of Cain's grasp, she approached Ned. "You're exhausted and you've been up too long. Put the gun away before you get yourself in trouble."

"Sheridan, you're going to get hurt." Cain obviously wasn't pleased with her intervention, but she ignored him.

"Move." Ned waved the gun, indicating that he wanted her out of the way. "I won't let him get off this time. I won't see her buried and gone and watch him walk through town as free as a bird."

Sheridan expected Cain's stepfather to chime in. It was one thing to wonder if Cain was guilty, another to want him dead. But John didn't say anything. He stood there looking shocked, his gaze shifting from Ned to Cain and back again, as if he couldn't believe what he was seeing.

"He didn't do it." Sheridan knew what Cain had been like after he'd found his ex-wife last night, how upset and hurt he'd been despite his frustration with her relentless pursuit.

So how did she convince Amy's twin brother of that? With those dark circles under his eyes and what little hair he had left standing up on either side of his head, Ned looked like a crazy man. She didn't think she could make him understand.

"He did it!"

"We don't know that for sure, Ned. Not yet." Peterson inched closer. "Why don't you give me the gun so we can do this the right way? If Cain's guilty, we'll get him. You can bet your ass. I won't sleep until I do. I loved Amy, too. This whole town did."

John finally broke his silence. "Ned, stop it. Think about what you're doing. We've suffered enough losses."

Sheridan was all too aware of what he didn't add— that Cain would never hurt anyone. John's suspicion of Cain made it difficult to defend his stepson.

Sweat dropped into Ned's eyes, causing him to squint and blink rapidly. "He did it. I know he did." He reached into his pocket and tossed a letter onto the floor. "Here's proof."

Sheridan was tempted to pick it up, but Ned still had his gun pointed at Cain. She was afraid to allow him a clear shot. Instead, she watched as Officer Peterson retrieved the paper and read it aloud.

Cain,
Meet me tomorrow night at midnight, my place, or I'll tell them you did it.
Amy

Peterson slowly lowered the paper. "Where'd you find this?"

"It was in her purse. Along with a stack of pictures of *him*."

"Was she blackmailing you, Cain?" Peterson asked.

"No. She never gave me that note or any other like it. I don't know what the hell it's even referring to."

"She wanted him so badly." Ned's voice was a half wail. "Ever since I can remember. She was miserable. Miserable because of you!" His hand shook as if he itched to pull the trigger.

Sheridan cut him off when he tried to get around her. "But he didn't kill her," she said quietly. "This note doesn't mean anything."

"It means she had something on him—that's what gave him the motivation to kill her! Get out of my way!"

Sheridan didn't move. "Amy was desperate to see him and was using any means at her disposal. That's all. If you'd calm down for a minute, you'd see that, Ned. What about the pictures? She was obsessed with him, couldn't stop thinking about him."

Peterson set the note on the desk. "I'm afraid she's right, Ned. How do you know you're interpreting it correctly? It *could* be that Amy had something on him. But it could just as easily be that she was threatening to get him into trouble he didn't deserve. For heaven's sake, put the gun down."

"He blew her head off," Ned said, but he was no longer shouting. With tears filling his eyes, he finally lowered the gun.

Peterson rushed forward. "Come on over here and sit down, Chief."

Sheridan turned to Cain. It was time to leave. Ned needed a chance to deal with his sister's death, and Sheridan wanted to get Cain out of there. What if Ned changed his mind?

But when she tugged on Cain's arm, he didn't respond. He was staring at his stepfather, whose expression put a hard lump in her own chest. Maybe it was just for a second, but it was clear, even to her, that John had been hoping for another outcome.

Cain sat in front of the television, trying to get involved in the baseball game he'd turned on while Sheridan napped. She wasn't strong enough to make it through a whole day without a little sleep. But now that she was awake and sitting on the other end of the sofa, all he could think about was pulling her to him and burying his face in the indentation above her collarbone or running his lips over her soft, smooth skin. She could make him forget everything—his antipathy toward his stepfather, Amy's bloody remains, Ned's hand shaking with the desire to pull the trigger. *Everything.* When they were making love last night, the rest of the world could've been destroyed and he wouldn't have noticed. Or cared.

He craved more of that potent painkiller. But he wasn't going to touch her. She'd made it clear that she didn't want him to.

"Where were you?" she asked.

He allowed his eyes to move toward her, even though the sight of her in that sundress made him hard. "When?"

"The night Jason was killed."

He didn't want to talk about Jason, but at least that subject would obliterate his desire to make love. "I was at Rocky Point. For a while."

"I know that much. I saw you there. But then you left with someone before the..." He watched her draw a deep breath. "Before the shots went off."

He'd left, yes. But he'd gone alone. He'd seen her with Jason, assumed they were making out and couldn't stand the thought of it. So he'd told his friends he was going home. Since he'd come with someone who wasn't ready to leave, Amy had offered him a ride, but he'd refused. He knew what she'd want to do, knew he couldn't deliver—not when he was so upset about the idea of Jason kissing Sheridan. So he'd walked home. He hadn't known anything was wrong until he showed up at the house in time to receive a call from the police.

"I walked home by myself," he said. And he'd cut through the forest so he wouldn't be seen slouching miserably along the road—another reason he had no alibi.

"Where were Amy and your other friends?"

"They stayed at Rocky Point."

"What made you leave so early?"

He studied her. He didn't really want to reveal how he'd hated thinking of her in Jason's arms. It proved that everyone who claimed he was jealous was right. And it would let her know she'd been successful in making him feel what she'd been hoping he'd feel. But they were kids back then; he was too old to play games like that now. "You have to ask?"

She raised her hands in a defensive posture. "It had nothing to do with me."

He muted the television. "How do you know?"

"Because you couldn't have cared less about me. I understand that—now that I'm not so naive and stupid."

"What, you've slept around enough to become an expert?"

"No, but I have enough experience to know when to take something seriously and when to let it go."

She didn't know anything. Like his father and everyone else, she simply assumed the worst.

Shaking his head, Cain turned back to the television. "Don't tell me what I feel."

"I couldn't begin to guess what you feel. I'm just trying to figure out how to prove you weren't in the vicinity when that shot went off," she insisted.

"There's no way to prove it."

"Why not?"

"Because no one saw me from when I said I was leaving until I showed up at home after it was all over."

The phone rang. Using that as an excuse to remove himself from the conversation, he grabbed it. "Hello?"

"Cain? It's Tiger."

Not someone Cain wanted to speak to so soon after what'd happened. Tiger had to be as broken up as Ned. He'd cared about Amy, maybe even loved her. "Tiger," he responded, swallowing a heavy sigh.

"I just, I wanted to—" Tiger's voice cracked "—to ask you something."

Cain gripped the phone tighter. *Here we go again.* "What's that?"

"Did you call Amy last night? Did you ask her to come over?"

"No."

"That's what I thought." Tiger chuckled without mirth. "Would you believe she was supposed to be getting me some beer? I was sitting on her couch watching a movie while she sneaked over to your cabin."

Cain didn't respond. Nothing he could say would make the situation any better.

"Why is that?" Tiger asked. "Maybe *you* can tell me."

"It's possible someone tipped her off to trouble, I suppose."

"No." Tiger sounded resolute. "No one called here."

"It could've been after she left, maybe through dispatch."

"There's no record of it. Ned checked. She didn't receive any calls on her cell phone, either."

Cain propped up his forehead with one hand. "What're you driving at?"

"Why did she leave a perfectly comfortable evening with me to drive over to your cabin, where she was murdered."

"I can't answer that, Tiger. I have no idea."

Tiger gave another bitter laugh. "Don't pretend you don't know. *Please.*"

"I wasn't sleeping with her, if that's what you're getting at. I haven't touched Amy since before our divorce." Cain was facing a lot of doubt and accusation, but it somehow mattered that Tiger believe him on this.

"I know," he said.

Surprised that Tiger had accepted the truth so easily, Cain lifted his head, but Tiger continued before he could respond. "Unfortunately, I also know it wasn't because she didn't want to. She would've slept with you in a heartbeat if you'd given her the chance."

Cain didn't respond. He didn't have to.

"I thought I could eventually win her over, you know? I thought she'd realize you weren't going to change your mind, that I was the best thing she was ever gonna get. But she was such a stupid bitch." His words were harsh, but he was choking up when he said them.

"I'm sorry, Tiger. I wish the situation could've been different."

"That's the real kicker. I believe you on that, too." Tiger laughed again, then seemed to get hold of himself. "I have to tell you something."

Cain glanced at Sheridan, who was watching him intently. "What's that?"

"I saw a crumpled picture of Sheridan in the cab of Owen's truck yesterday afternoon."

Cain's heart skipped a beat. "Sheridan as a teenager?"

"Sheridan as an adult. As she is now. And someone had stabbed a pen or something through her face."

"Where were you?"

"At the baseball field. I went to watch my nephew's Little League game and ran into Owen in the parking lot. We were talking while his son got out of the truck. The picture nearly fell onto the blacktop, along with some fast food wrappers."

Cain could imagine the garbage in Owen's truck. It was so messy, his wife refused to ride in it. What Cain couldn't imagine was Owen in possession of a current photograph of Sheridan. *Why* would he have one? "Can you tell me anything about the picture? Where it was taken, maybe?"

"I think he printed it out on his computer because it was on regular paper. And I didn't get a very good look at it, but I could've sworn it was taken through the window of a house."

Which meant she didn't know she was being watched, let alone photographed. Cain couldn't believe it. Owen wouldn't stalk anyone. And he wouldn't skulk around the hospital wearing a wig or hurt Sheridan or anyone else.

But he'd feel at home in that particular setting. He'd worked at Mercy General once, for two years following his marriage. And Cain couldn't help remembering that he'd had trouble getting hold of Owen the night of Sheridan's attack. Had he spent all that time taking care of Robert, as he'd said? Or had he raced home to clean up?

The mere possibility infuriated Cain. "Was it my house in the picture? Or someone else's?"

"It wasn't your place. That's for sure. I think it was someplace in town. I didn't immediately recognize it."

Sickened by the thought that Owen might've had

something to do with the tragic events that had confused and hurt so many people, their family and Sheridan most of all, Cain fingered a hole frayed in his jeans. "You didn't ask him about it?"

"I said, 'Hey, that looks like Sheridan.' And he said, 'It's not.' Then he shoved it back in and shut the door."

"That's it?"

"That's it."

"Did you tell Amy?"

"Of course."

"What'd she say?"

Tiger's voice had choked up again. "She called to ask him. I checked her cell phone. His number was the last one she dialed. Based on the time, she must've been on her way to your cabin when that call was placed."

Shaking his head, Cain closed his eyes. Amy had called Owen about that picture. And now she was dead?

17

"Let's go," Cain said.

Sheridan blinked at him. "What? You're just going to hang up after that mysterious conversation and say, 'let's go'?"

"I can't leave you here alone. It's not safe."

"You could tell me *where* we're going."

He raked a hand through his hair. "My stepbrother's house."

"Owen? Why?"

Because Owen had had access to the cabin. He came and went from Cain's property all the time and could easily have put that rifle in the cellar. And after Cain's mother's funeral, when John was busy rekindling his love life, Owen had spent a great deal of time hunting and fishing with Bailey Watts, the man who'd first owned the rifle that had been used to kill Jason. But Cain didn't want to explain all that. He didn't want to entertain the thoughts that were going through his head. He only wanted to disprove them.

"I need to check on something."

She frowned. "What?"

Crossing to the bar that separated the kitchen from

the living room, he scooped his keys off the tile countertop. "Did you and Owen have much to do with each other in high school?"

She'd stood up when he told her they were leaving. Now she shoved her hands in the pockets of her dress and stepped in front of him as he moved toward the door. "Not much. Why?"

"He didn't ever follow you, or act as if he wanted to approach you, talk to you, be with you?"

"Not really. He wasn't interested in girls."

He was interested enough to watch them in the camper instead of making his presence known, wasn't he?

"He was too shy," she added with a dismissive shrug.

"No, not shy," Cain said. "Intimidated." His wife tells a funny story about how Owen haunted her classes for an entire year, hoping to date her, yet never asked her out. She finally invited him to the movies. She had to instigate the marriage proposal when the time came for that, too.

Sheridan took her hands out of her pockets and tucked her hair behind her ears. "Either way, he's not the violent type."

Cain tried to remember how his fourteen-year-old brother had acted after that camper incident. But he'd been so overwhelmed by his mother's death and trying to avoid any contact with his stepfather, he hadn't paid much attention to what Owen was or wasn't doing. His stepbrothers had had each other *and* their father. He hadn't been concerned about them. "I remember him studying, and reading for fun when he wasn't studying. That's all. That's why I made him go to that party. I thought it was time he got a life."

"He used to attend the football games," Sheridan said. "I don't think he missed one. He was always right there, sitting directly behind us—the cheerleaders, I mean."

"As if he'd come to see *you?*" Cain asked. That was the one thing missing from the puzzle. A motive. Why would Owen want to hurt Jason or Sheridan? And would the mild-mannered doctor he knew really be capable of something so horrific, especially at such a young age?

It was almost impossible to believe. But there had to be some explanation for that picture of Sheridan in his truck.

"I don't think so," she said. "Where else was he going to sit? The poor kid was two years younger than everyone else in his grade. He didn't have any friends to hang out with. And he knew me from the classes we had together. Being close to me probably made him feel more comfortable." She sounded confident in her answer, and yet a shadow passed over her face.

"What is it?" Cain had walked around her and was holding open the door.

"I guess there was *one* odd thing. But it didn't happen back then. It happened recently."

"What is it?"

"When he mentioned our—" she cleared her throat "—time in the camper."

"What'd he say?"

"He said, '*You* were about the only girl I thought would rebuff him,' as if I'd let him down by not doing so."

Cain dropped Sheridan off at The Roadhouse Café, which was well lit and public enough for him to feel confident that she'd be safe. She wasn't happy about being stowed there like baggage, but he had no intention of leaving her at the house alone, and he hesitated to take her with him to confront Owen. Owen would clam up if they had an audience, particularly a female audience. He'd never been at ease around females and, except for his wife, still socialized almost exclusively with men.

But Owen wasn't at home enjoying Sunday afternoon in his expensive air-conditioned home, as Cain had expected. According to his wife, he'd received a call from one of his patients and had gone to the office.

After playing with his three nephews for a few minutes, Cain thanked Lucy and drove to Owen's medical clinic, hoping to catch his stepbrother just after his patient had left. But whoever it was—a woman, despite the hoarse voice—was still there when he arrived. He could hear her and Owen talking behind the closed door that separated the reception area from the examination room.

You have strep, all right.

Lordy, it's the middle of the summer. Where'd I get that?

You could've picked it up anywhere. I'm going to prescribe an antibiotic that should make you feel better within twenty-four hours. If you don't notice a marked improvement, give me a call. And take some ibuprofen for the fever as soon as you get home.

Cain turned on the rest of the lights in the lobby and thumbed through a few magazines. Then he got up to see if Owen had bought any new fish for the giant aquarium that filled most of one wall, but he was watching the clock the entire time and brooding over Tiger's discovery. What would Owen's response be?

At last, the door opened and Dahlia Daugherty, a fiftyish woman Cain recognized as a checker at the Quick Shop, came out. Her watery eyes and flushed cheeks made her look as ill as she no doubt felt.

"Hi, Cain. When did you come in?" she asked when she saw him.

"A few minutes ago," he replied, but his attention was fixed on Owen, who stood behind her. His stepbrother didn't look surprised to see him—but he didn't look pleased, either.

"Lots of sleep and plenty of liquids," he reminded Mrs. Daugherty as she shuffled out.

"Hope you feel better," Cain called.

"Thanks."

The outer door shut behind her with a quiet *click,* leaving them in silence except for the whir of the ceiling fan.

Owen studied Cain through the gold wire-frame glasses he wore when he worked. "I take it you've heard from Tiger."

Cain nodded.

"What'd he tell you?" Owen hadn't bothered to raise the heavy blinds his assistants lowered before leaving every Friday afternoon, and even with the lights on, the place had a closed-up feeling.

"What do you think he told me?" Cain countered.

"About the photograph, of course."

It was always hard to tell what was going on in Owen's mind. He insulated himself from the world, hid behind those glasses and that lab coat. Formal, stilted and often easily out of his element—unless he was sitting at his desk behind a tower of books—he rarely revealed anything personal. But that was the worst Cain would ever have thought. That he was a bit antisocial, someone who took refuge in his professional status. Not that he was a killer. "He saw it in your truck."

"And you're here to find out why."

"I'm sure I won't be the only one who'll want to know."

"Have you told anyone about it?"

"Just Sheridan."

"I suppose now you think I'm the one who's been trying to frame you."

"I'm hoping you're about to convince me otherwise."

Owen tapped the pen he'd used to write Mrs. Daugherty's prescription on the counter and didn't speak.

"Well?" Cain prompted.

"I didn't take that picture."

Cain stepped closer. He'd been hoping for this, wanted to believe it. "Who did?"

His stepbrother blinked at him from behind those glasses. "It must've been Robert."

"Why?"

"I let him borrow my truck the other day."

Cain remembered. At the nursing home. He'd spent the past few days trying not to think about the amount of money Robert had probably wheedled out of Marshall. "And?"

"And he must've left it in there."

"I want to see it," Cain said.

"I don't have it."

"Unless you were covering for someone, yourself or Robert, you'd have it."

"I'm not covering for anyone. I've still got it. I hid it in my garage so no one else would see it until I figured out what it meant."

Cain blew out a long sigh and began to pace. "Does it tell you anything? When or where it was taken?"

"It's printed on regular eight-by-ten paper. There's no date. It was taken after Sheridan returned to town but before the beating. She has no visible injuries."

"What about location?"

"She's in her uncle's house. At the kitchen sink. Whoever snapped the shot did it from outside the window."

"Is it possible that Robert was stalking her? That he took that picture and left it in your truck? Intentionally or otherwise?"

"*Someone* was stalking her. I don't know if it was Robert. When I confronted him about it late last night, he claimed he's never seen that picture before in his life."

Cain didn't care much for Robert, but he had a hard time believing his youngest stepbrother would do anything as violent as what'd happened to Sheridan. And, provided there *was* a connection between the shooting and her attack, Robert couldn't have killed Jason. He'd always been large for his age. With a ski mask covering his face, he *might* have been able to pass for a small man at thirteen. But he'd worshipped Jason. There was no way he would've shot him. "When did you first notice that photograph in your truck?"

"When Tiger did, of course. Otherwise, I would've removed it a lot sooner."

"So why'd you act furtive, shove it back in and shut the door?"

Owen remained unflustered. "I didn't *act* furtive. I just didn't want him to see it. I was hoping he hadn't caught enough of a glimpse to know what he was looking at. I wanted to buy myself some time to examine it."

It was believable that Owen would treat the situation as he'd described. He was by nature private, methodical, judicious. But Cain had other questions. "Why didn't you come to me?"

Owen shoved his glasses on to the bridge of his nose. "Because I still don't know what it means."

Robert had been drunk the night Sheridan was attacked—so drunk he'd wrecked his car and banged up his face. Had he been so drunk he'd done other things, as well? Were some of his injuries due to Sheridan's attempts to fight him off?

But why would he attack her in the first place? And why would he beat her so badly? Whoever took her into that forest had either been out of his mind—or wanted to kill her. That much was obvious.

"Robert would never have hurt Jason," Owen said, echoing Cain's thoughts. "Which makes it unlikely that he was involved in the attack on Sheridan. But…"

Cain frowned as Owen's voice dwindled away. *But* they didn't have another explanation. That picture had come from somewhere. Cain wished he knew where. Was it Owen who was lying? Or Robert? Or was there some other answer?

"Was Dad around when you confronted Robert?"

"No, he was at Karen's. He spends a lot of his time there these days."

Cain recalled the awkward encounters he'd had with

his former English teacher since she'd moved back to Whiterock. The first had been at the grocery store. She'd whipped around a corner and nearly slammed into him with her cart. Blushing furiously, she'd mumbled an apology and hurried on. The next had been at the Roadhouse. He'd been having dinner alone, glanced up and caught her watching him from across the room.

But the last time had been the most uncomfortable. She'd accompanied his stepfather to a horse show in Kentucky, a show Cain had also attended. Since it was so far away, Cain hadn't expected anyone he knew to be there, but once John spotted him in the crowd, he and Karen made their way over and pretended to be excited about the chance meeting, even insisting they all have dinner together.

That was two months ago, during one of those rare periods when his stepfather was putting some effort into building a relationship with him. John did that occasionally. But such efforts were erratic, as if he wanted Cain to like him but simply couldn't hold out for the long haul.

Now that John thought he'd killed Jason, Cain doubted he'd ever bother trying again. Which, oddly enough, came as a relief. Cain couldn't forgive him for how he'd treated Julia. It was easier to avoid each other.

"So John doesn't know about the picture?" Cain asked.

"Of course not. No one does. I figured it was best to leave it alone until I could determine who the photographer was, and who might've left it in my truck."

"Do you lock your vehicles at night?"

He shook his head. "If someone was going to steal a car, I doubt it would be that one."

And he often parked it out by the curb, which meant practically anyone had access. But it seemed pretty far-fetched that someone would take that picture, poke a hole through Sheridan's face, then plant it in Owen's truck.

Could he believe Owen? It was impossible to tell. Owen was the most self-contained person Cain had ever met. He never gave anything away. Whether or not he'd wanted his father to marry Cain's mother. How he'd felt about skipping two grades. If he regretted graduating early. How much he missed Jason. Whether he'd resented Cain's presence in his life. Cain never knew how he truly felt about anything.

And yet he'd revealed *some* emotion to Sheridan. He'd let her know he was disappointed in her for sleeping with Cain. Was she the one woman he'd always silently admired? The one who, for whatever reason, could provoke him to violence?

"What'd you tell Lucy?" Cain asked.

"Nothing. She doesn't know anything about it."

Cain wondered if that was the case with a lot of things. Lucy admired her husband's intellect and praised his cool reserve. She'd been raised by a blustering drunk, a father who was occasionally abusive, and Owen appeared to be the complete opposite. But did she ever look deeper than his composed demeanor?

Cain certainly never had....

"Let's go," he said.

"Where're we going?" Owen asked.

"I'm following you home."

Owen's eyebrows lifted above the rims of his glasses. "What for?"

"I want that picture."

"What are you going to do with it?"

Cain snapped off the light. "I don't know."

"You won't show it to Dad, will you?" he asked without moving.

"You don't want me to?"

"He's really upset about Amy. Maybe you and Amy were divorced, but she treated him more like a father than—" He stopped before he finished the sentence, but he'd already said enough.

"Than me?" Evidently, Owen was more flustered than Cain had realized. Or it was a calculated blunder.

"They were close," he went on, his gaze steady. "She was his first daughter-in-law. And she came by all the time. Last week, she brought him a sack of peaches from her tree."

"So what does this photograph of Sheridan have to do with Amy?"

"I'm just saying that..." He seemed to grope for words. "Well, with her murder and...and the way Robert's been drinking lately...and Bailey's rifle being found in your old cabin, I don't think we should involve Dad in this. Robert told me Dad's been having chest pains again."

John had a history of high blood pressure. He also had some pretty severe sleep disorders. Cain could still remember him being up at night, walking the floor, taking a hot bath or making tea to help him relax. But Owen's explanation wasn't making sense. "If you and Robert have nothing to do with this, why are you so worried I might tell Dad?"

Owen didn't answer.

"Wait a second," Cain said. "You think it *was* Robert. You think it has to have been Robert. And you don't want Dad to draw the same conclusion."

"We don't know enough to make a big stink," Owen said. But Cain finally understood what was going on behind that purposely bland expression. Owen thought it was better for John to suspect Cain than to question his "real" son. Thinking Robert had done something so terrible, something that couldn't be fixed or covered up—as John had tried to fix or cover up his youngest son's other misdeeds and failures—might bring on the heart attack they'd feared for years.

"So I'm the sacrificial lamb," Cain said.

The angle of Owen's jaw revealed a hint of belligerence. "You don't care about him anyway!"

Owen was right. But he hadn't gone into the relationship assuming the worst. He'd been excited to have a father, had wanted John to accept him. But John had never given him anything to hang on to—no love, no emotional support, nothing. Owen had grown up in the same house, but he'd never understood Cain's thoughts, feelings or actions, and probably never would.

Cain told himself it shouldn't bother him to be blamed for the breach. It was just more of the same— another reminder that he was different from the rest of the family, separate.

"Fine," he said. "I won't say a word to *Dad* or anyone else about it. Not yet, anyway."

Owen couldn't quite hide his surprise. "You won't?"

"Not if you tell me why."

He shifted, obviously ill at ease. "Why what?"

"You're scared. There's more going on here than the photograph."

Now that the light was off, dark shadows fell across Owen's face, but Cain saw a hint of fear in his stiff posture. "There's nothing else."

"What aren't you telling me?"

"Nothing. Robert was too young!"

"For the shooting, not the beating. How does the shooting figure into this? That's what's really worrying you, isn't it? You've found some connection. And you're terrified it'll tear your family apart."

No answer.

"How does the shooting figure into this?" And then it occurred to him. "Where did Bailey's rifle come from?" he asked, lowering his voice.

"I don't know."

"Yes, you do."

Removing his glasses, Owen rubbed his eyes. It was a defensive movement, something designed to buy time, but Cain wouldn't allow him to stall.

"Tell me, damn it!" he shouted. "I want the truth!"

Letting go of a long sigh, Owen slipped his glasses back on his face. "I found it in Robert's trunk."

"What were you doing in Robert's trunk?"

"Looking for some jumper cables. Lucy's car wouldn't start and I couldn't remember where I put mine."

"But that was before the ballistics tests confirmed it was the weapon used in Jason's murder."

"There had to be some reason it was stolen. And when I found it in Robert's trunk I was afraid of what that reason might be."

18

The meeting between Cain and Owen seemed to be taking forever.

Trying to ignore the curious stares of the other patrons in the café, some of whom Sheridan recognized but didn't know well enough to greet, she watched the clock—twenty minutes ticked by, thirty minutes, forty. The waitress came around to see if she'd like more tea, but she covered her cup with one hand and shook her head. She didn't want anything except for Cain to come back and tell her what was going on.

Although it was getting late, and the stores closed early on Sundays, she decided to walk down Main Street and do some window-shopping to pass the time. But then Cain's stepfather walked in with Ms. Stevens, the high school English teacher she'd had for American Literature, creating an interesting diversion. She knew they'd dated briefly after Cain's mother died but thought they'd broken up. Apparently, they were back together because John was holding her hand.

They didn't see her at first. They were too busy talking. But when they began to look for a booth, they spotted her almost immediately.

Karen Stevens had been her favorite teacher. Sheridan smiled expectantly, but when their eyes met, Ms. Stevens glanced away. It even seemed as if she tried to distract Cain's stepdad by pointing to an open booth on the other side of the restaurant. But John Wyatt said something to her, then led her over.

"How're you feeling?" he asked Sheridan, his eyes somber, concerned.

She remembered him coming to see her while she was recovering from that gunshot wound twelve years ago, remembered how haggard he'd looked. With red-rimmed eyes, he'd asked her point-blank what'd happened. He'd needed to hear the sequence of events from her own lips in order to believe the unbelievable, needed to at least try and achieve the resolution he craved. And yet he'd been sensitive to her suffering, too. Rather fatalistic and subdued, he'd accepted what she said without blaming her for not being able to tell him more—or for coaxing Jason up to Rocky Point in the first place. She considered that a gift because it was hard not to blame herself for those things.

She would've liked John Wyatt, except that she felt so defensive of Cain. There'd always been a difference in the way John treated him as opposed to his own boys, and that bothered her. It'd bothered her even back in high school.

"I'm doing better," she said.

"Glad to hear it. I'm sorry for what you've been through. It's not fair."

"Unfortunately, people are victimized more often than any of us would like to believe."

"I'm sure that's true."

"Hey, John!"

Cain's father turned away to speak to a gentleman Sheridan didn't recognize. She heard the man ask if he'd be willing to say a few words at Amy's funeral in place of her own father, who'd died five years ago, and John readily agreed. At that point, Sheridan expected Ms. Stevens to focus on that other conversation and continue to ignore her. John had obviously forgotten about her. But her former English teacher seemed to rethink her earlier attitude.

"You still staying with Cain?" she asked.

"For the time being," Sheridan said.

Ms. Stevens looked over her shoulder, seemed reassured to see John engrossed in conversation, and lowered her voice. "He must be taking good care of you."

Sheridan sensed something strange behind that statement but she didn't know why. Ms. Stevens had always liked Cain. She'd taken a special interest in him when he was in high school, probably hoping to make up for what he'd been lacking at home.

"He is," Sheridan said. "He's a very kind person."

"I know." Ms. Stevens's smile grew sad. "Where is he?"

"He dropped me off a while ago. He had some business to attend to."

"I see."

After that, the silence stretched so long it grew awkward. Sheridan made an effort to come up with more small talk. "Are you still teaching?" she asked.

"I am. I'm actually chairman of the English department these days." She laughed. "Which isn't really saying a lot, since there's only me and Mr. Burns."

"I'm sure it keeps you busy."

"It's a good life. I know that now. I'm glad I decided to come back to Whiterock."

Sheridan hadn't realized she'd ever left. "Where'd you go?"

"To New York—for nearly ten years."

"What took you there?"

"I needed a break. This town is so small that everyone knows everyone else. I felt hemmed in, wanted to try the big city."

"You didn't enjoy it?"

"It had its positive side, but mostly it taught me to appreciate what I have here."

Sheridan had missed Whiterock, too. But she'd been so focused on running from the past and blaming herself for putting Jason in the wrong place at the wrong time that she rarely looked back. She'd been counseled not to even think about her hometown. Now she understood just how much she'd missed the life she'd known here.

The anger she felt toward the man who'd shot her and beaten her, if it was indeed the same person, nearly overwhelmed her. Those emotions sneaked up on her occasionally. One minute, she'd be fine, and the next she'd be overcome with rage. She tried to combat it by telling herself that she wasn't alone. Victims everywhere experienced the same helpless, futile anger. At least she was doing what she could to turn it into something constructive. She couldn't possibly have the kind of empathy she did for her clients if she hadn't gone through a similar ordeal.

"I can see why you like it here," Sheridan said.

Ms. Stevens toyed with the strap of her purse. "Will you be staying long? Or heading back to California? John tells me you're one of the founders of a high-profile victims' charity."

"The charity's been able to accomplish more than I ever dreamed. It's gratifying work. But I'll be here until I can figure out who attacked me."

"It's got to be tough not to have those answers, that sense of resolution," she said.

"It is."

"John feels the same way."

"He lost his son. He's a victim in this, too."

"And then there's Cain," she said, her voice falling.

Sheridan hesitated, trying to determine what that change of tone meant. "Excuse me?"

"Cain. It can't be easy to walk away from a man like that."

Obviously, she'd heard about the camper incident. "He's just a friend. There's nothing between us."

The bell jingled over the door and Sheridan looked over to see that Cain had finally returned. As his eyes met hers, her immediate reaction said she was a liar. She was still in love with him, maybe more than ever.

"Nothing?" Ms. Stevens said. "Judging by the relief on his face, I'd say he cares a great deal about you."

"What relief?" Sheridan frowned skeptically. If it was there, she didn't want to see it. It would only make resisting him that much harder. "He's…preoccupied. With whatever he's thinking about. That's all."

"But what he's thinking is, 'Thank God she's safe.'"

"Karen, are you ready to sit down?" Obviously eager

to move away before he had to confront Cain, John reached for her as the man he'd been speaking to left.

"I'm ready," she said, but she tossed Sheridan a barely audible parting comment. "You're a lucky woman."

Cain couldn't help noticing the snub. The moment his stepfather had spotted him, he'd turned his back without so much as a nod and headed to the other side of the restaurant, choosing a booth that was as far away as he could get. But in Cain's view, John had done him a favor. He didn't have anything to say to his stepfather, anyway. He felt infinitely more comfortable now that they were no longer pretending to be on semicordial terms.

"What'd you find out?" Sheridan asked.

Cain tried to ignore the fact that his stepfather was even in the restaurant. "It was Owen who hid the gun in my cabin."

"Owen?" Her eyes widened. She glanced toward John and Karen. They seemed engrossed in their own conversation—which appeared to be the beginning of an argument.

"Your stepbrother was trying to *frame* you?" Sheridan asked.

Cain motioned for her to keep her voice down. Most of the seniors who were the majority of the Roadhouse's clientele on Sundays had already finished the turkey and gravy special and were on their way home. But as much as he didn't want to acknowledge it, his stepfather was still around. "No. At least I don't think so. He claims he found the rifle in Robert's trunk and was trying to hide it somewhere no one would look."

"So he was protecting Robert."

"That part's believable enough," he added under his breath. "My stepfather and Owen have made a profession out of cleaning up little Robert's messes."

"But without ballistics testing, how would Owen know the rifle he found in Robert's trunk was the gun that killed Jason? I mean, to the naked eye, most rifles look alike, don't they?"

"Not if you've used a rifle before. Years ago, Owen went hunting with Bailey Watts. He recognized the gun as the one Bailey reported missing shortly after Jason's death."

"Still…Robert was so young when Jason and I were shot. He was, what, an eighth grader? Whoever wore that ski mask was the size of an adult."

"He's been the size of an adult since he was twelve. John used to call him Jethro after a character on 'The Beverly Hillbillies.'"

"But would he even know how to use a rifle?"

"My stepfather taught his boys how to shoot as soon as they could carry a gun. By the time John married my mother, Robert was seven and could shoot better than Owen."

Obviously troubled, Sheridan sat back against the booth. "But…why would he do that to his older brother? To me? He didn't even know me."

"Why would *anyone* do it?"

Kelly, the eighteen-year-old daughter of the widow who owned the Roadhouse, approached the table with a glass of water, which she slid onto the varnished tabletop. "What can I get for you, Cain?"

"Just a cup of coffee," he said.

She smiled and hurried away, and Cain returned his focus to Sheridan. "Not what you expected me to say, right?"

"No." Her cup clinked as she set it in her saucer. "So before we do anything else, we need to talk to Robert. Find out where he got that rifle."

"I just came from his trailer. He claims he found it in Grandpa Marshall's shed four years ago, when we were moving him into the nursing home." Propping his elbows on the table, he leaned forward. "He says Owen never told him he found the gun. It just went missing one day, leaving him to wonder what the hell happened to it."

"He didn't tell anyone he'd lost it?"

"No. It wasn't his to begin with. He figured, 'easy come, easy go.'" He took a drink of his water. "Interpreted, that means he thought he might've done something with it when he was drunk."

"But why didn't he speak up when it was discovered in your cabin?"

"He said he didn't realize it was the same gun."

"I don't believe him."

"I think it could be true, at least at first. Then, after the police proved it was the gun that shot you and Jason, he was too scared to come forward for fear the blame would shift to him."

"So he let everyone blame you instead."

"In case you haven't noticed, he doesn't give a shit about me."

"Why don't you and Robert get along?"

Cain shrugged. "He's a lazy slob. Even when he was

a kid we couldn't get him to help out with anything. All he wanted to do was play video games."

"So your relationship wasn't any better when you lived with him?"

"Actually, it wasn't so bad then. He was the youngest in the family. It was easy to make up excuses for him. We all pitched in, figuring he'd change as he grew up. But letting him lean on us for so long only made matters worse. He's still leaning on whoever will let him."

Sheridan seemed to weigh this new information. "So…about the gun…"

"What about it?"

"Why would your grandfather have it in his possession?"

"Who knows? Grandpa was a pack rat. Anyone could've stuck the rifle under one of the tarps that covered various boxes of junk he kept in his sheds. We don't even know for sure that Robert found it there, like he says he did."

"What about the picture in Owen's truck?" she asked.

Cain had explained his conversation with Tiger on their drive to town. "He's blaming that on Robert, too," he said, taking the picture he'd gotten from Owen out of his pocket and passing it to her. "That was Owen's truck Robert was driving when we saw him at the nursing home."

She unfolded it and stared down at herself, one hand over her mouth as she saw the holes in her face. "Does Robert have a digital camera?"

"He does. He fancies himself an amateur photographer and spends a lot of time tinkering with his photographs—when he's not playing Internet war games with his online buddies, that is."

"*War* games?"

"He's always been fascinated by military strategy and gaming."

They sat in silence for several seconds, that picture on the table between them. Cain wasn't sure he should've shown it to her—with those vicious-looking holes slashed in her face. But she had experience in criminal investigation. He thought it was important to disclose what he'd found.

"Robert lives right down the street from my uncle's place," she finally said.

Cain nodded. "He was probably one of the first people to realize you were back." He could easily have watched her, and taken that picture through the window. It wasn't as if he had a wife to wonder where he was. Or anyone else who kept track of him.

The waitress brought his coffee.

"Cream?" Sheridan offered him the bowl that contained plastic cups.

Cain shook his head. "I like it black."

She put it down and seemed to force herself to look back at the photograph. "Did he deny taking this picture?"

"Of course. He even handed me his digital camera, let me scroll through every shot. But that doesn't mean anything. He could've downloaded the file onto his computer and cleared the memory."

"He didn't offer you access to his computer, did he?"

"No. But I plan on checking when I get the chance."

She twirled her own water glass, making rings of

condensation on the table. "Your grandfather doesn't have many personal belongings in the retirement home. Just the basics. What'd you guys do with his stuff when you sold the house?"

"John took what he wanted for his own place, Owen chose a few keepsakes and Robert got most of the furniture because it was better than the junk he had in that old trailer. The rest they wanted to sell or give away. But it upset Grandpa to think that all his worldly possessions would be gone. So I packed them up and put them in the spare bedroom of the old cabin. Every once in a while I haul a box to the nursing home for him to go through. He really likes that."

"I can see why. It brings back fond memories and makes him feel secure, as if the things he cares about are still around, waiting for him."

Cain raised an eyebrow at the smile that spread across her face. "Why are you smiling?"

"You know how to take care of the people you love," she said quietly.

He scowled to hide his embarrassment at the compliment. "It's no big deal to store that stuff. I'm not even using the cabin."

"Doesn't matter. What matters is that you understand the small stuff that means so much."

For a moment, Cain forgot his stepfather was in the room. He even forgot what he'd recently learned from Owen and Robert and what it might mean. Forgot that he'd ever slept with Karen, that he felt partly responsible for Jason's death, that he still missed his mother. As deep as all of that ran, for this one second, it didn't touch him. Couldn't touch him. The look on Sheridan's face—as if she saw only the man he wanted to be and not the flawed human being he really was—protected him from all the mistakes, all the bitterness and grief, of the past.

A powerful desire to make love to her swept through him. But it had nothing to do with her physical beauty. There were plenty of beautiful women in the world. She had something else, something that promised him a more profound satisfaction.

His heart began to pound as their eyes met. He wanted her, and she knew it.

Her lips parted, but whatever she was about to say was lost when Karen stood up and shouted at John, "You can go straight to hell! Don't ever call me again!"

Surprised, Cain turned along with everyone else in the restaurant to watch her storm out.

When Sheridan emerged from the shower, she couldn't hear the television anymore. Cain had gone to bed. He'd turned off the lights. Except for the one in his bedroom. And he'd moved her suitcase in there with him. Which let her know where he expected her to spend the night. After what had happened to Amy, he wasn't taking any chances. He was keeping her *very* close. But she wasn't sure she could tolerate another night of sleeping chastely by his side. She already knew she'd lie awake, sensing his every move while dying to touch him.

But her alternative was to go to her own room. And she didn't really want to be alone, either.

After blow-drying her hair, she wrapped a towel

around herself and went into his room to get some clean clothes. Then she changed into her nightie in the bathroom and climbed into his bed.

Because he hadn't moved or spoken while she was preparing for bed, she thought he was asleep. But he wasn't. He changed his position as she straightened the covers. She thought—even hoped—he'd pull her to him. That glitter in his eye at the restaurant had revealed his hunger. But he didn't act on it. He faced the wall.

"Do you have enough blankets?" she asked.

"I'm fine."

"Okay."

In the silence she could hear the sounds of the forest. The forlorn hoot of an owl reminded her of the night she'd awakened to find a man in a ski cap digging her grave.

She moved a little closer to Cain. "Good night," she whispered.

He didn't respond. But when she moved closer still, and came up against his bare back, he rolled over and pulled her toward him so she could rest her head on his shoulder.

He was wearing his boxers; she could feel the fabric against her leg. She had nothing to worry about.

Shutting her eyes, she reveled in the smooth skin against her cheek. This was better. This was perfect. A girl couldn't ask for anything more. But memories of their lovemaking intruded.

Quit denying yourself...quit denying me, he'd said.

She lay there, barely breathing for probably fifteen minutes. She was waiting for the desire to dissipate, for Cain to go to sleep.

But it was no use. She knew what she wanted, and she knew she was going to take it.

Lifting her head, she pressed a kiss to his chest, then his neck and jaw. And finally she found his mouth.

Sheridan's hair fell around Cain's face, silky soft, as she leaned up on her elbows and touched her lips to his. It was a light kiss, sweet and unintrusive, but it surprised him that she'd initiated a kiss at all. He never expected her to make the first move; he thought she'd play it safe and go to sleep, and he'd been determined to let her. Instead, her hands moved over his chest, touching, seeking, testing him to see if he'd give her the response she needed.

His body responded, all right. But he held himself in check, touching her only as lightly as she touched him, giving her plenty of time to explore, to let the desire build. He'd made love to her twice; she seemed to want to be in charge this time.

She kissed him again, grazing his lips with the tip of her tongue as she did. With a helpless groan, he threaded his fingers in her hair and let her kiss him as she chose, which she did so gently he felt a sort of exquisite longing he'd never experienced before.

More, he thought. *Give me more.* But he resisted taking control.

"You taste good," she murmured. "And you feel good, too."

Closing his eyes, he clenched his jaw as he fought the urge to roll her beneath him. *Go slow.* He'd never been this desperate for a woman. He felt like he had to take what he could fast, right now—while Sheridan wasn't trying to reserve part of herself for someone else or for later or for never.

Afraid the opportunity to make love to her while she was this open to him might disappear, he slid his hands up her nightgown, massaging her back. He was so damn eager for the clothes to come off, but he wanted her to decide when that happened.

She didn't seem to be in half the hurry he was. Straddling him in her panties, she slowly ground her hips against him.

He put his hands on her waist to hold her still for a moment, just until he could stop shaking and his heart could slow a little. But then she bent forward and opened her mouth, kissing him deeply, the way he'd wanted her to the other night. Then he knew his heart wasn't going to slow.

"I can't wait," he whispered against her lips. "I want to be inside you."

She pulled back to look at him, and he thought he read confusion in her eyes.

"We'll do it slow later," he whispered. "I promise." And the next thing he knew, the clothes were gone.

19

"I wouldn't have pegged you as a premature ejaculator," Sheridan said.

Cain couldn't help laughing at the teasing note in her voice. "That was a pretty pathetic performance," he admitted.

She grinned down at him, her teeth glinting in the darkness as she played with his hair. "You're lucky I don't kiss and tell. That could ruin your reputation, Mr. Granger."

"Hey!" He scowled. "It's not over yet." He reversed their positions, rolling her onto her back, but she clutched at his hair, stopping him when he bent to kiss her breast.

"What if I want more of the real thing?" she challenged.

"You might have to be patient for a minute." He kissed her cheek, her neck. "But I can make sure you enjoy the wait."

He knew she was only giving him a hard time. He even liked the sassy flirting. But he was determined to turn the tables on her, to make her gasp and moan until she couldn't remember that she'd ever had a complaint. But then the dogs began to bark, and he heard a car in the drive.

Someone was outside. At this time in the morning? He checked the alarm clock. It was after three.

His heart started pounding again, but for an entirely different reason than it had a few minutes ago. After the attack on Sheridan in the forest, he had no idea what might be coming at him. He yanked on his boxers and grabbed the rifle he kept in his closet. "Get under the bed and stay there until I come for you," he whispered and headed for the door.

Cain stood sideways against the wall between his front door and living room window, peeking through the blinds. He didn't recognize the car, but he couldn't get a good look, either. The headlights nearly blinded him.

A second later, the lights went off but whoever was driving it didn't get out right away.

That made him very uneasy. What the hell was going on?

He heard some scurrying in the bedroom. "You're not under the bed?" he snapped at Sheridan.

"No. I'm calling the cops before you get hurt."

He wanted to order her back to safety, but he figured she was doing the right thing. "Then stay down."

Finally, he heard the car door open. Or he thought he did. It was hard to tell with the dogs yelping like mad. Cracking open the front door, he poked out the muzzle of his rifle. "Who are you and what do you want?" he called.

"Drop the gun," a voice returned. But it wasn't a man's voice. It was a woman's.

Completely baffled, he swung open the door a little wider. Yep, that was a woman. She was crouching behind the open door of her car, pointing a handgun at him.

He didn't lower the rifle one inch. "Who the hell are you? And what're you doing here?"

"I'm looking for Sheridan Kohl."

Sheridan slammed down the phone before she'd even finished dialing. "Skye?"

"Stay back," Cain warned. "She's got a gun."

"It's okay." She hurried toward him. "I know her." Shoving the muzzle of his rifle toward the ground, she flipped on the porch light. "It's me, Skye. I'm coming out!" she yelled and then she flung open the door.

"Sheridan?" the woman cried.

Cain wasn't about to let her go out there alone. He joined her, carrying his gun as she walked out with her hair mussed, wearing her nightie, which was on wrong side out, and her panties.

The woman slowly stood and lowered her weapon, but the expression on her face suggested she wasn't happy with what she saw. Her eyes moved between the two of them, obviously focusing on their lack of appropriate attire. "Let me guess. This is Cain Granger."

Sheridan nodded.

The woman Sheridan had called Skye muttered something under her breath as she put her gun in what looked like a police-issue shoulder harness. "I was afraid of that."

"So that's it? You're leaving?" Cain asked, leaning against the doorjamb while she packed her clothes.

Sheridan kept her eyes averted. She didn't want to see him standing there in nothing but a pair of jeans, didn't want to admire the way his hair fell across his forehead. She'd only want to touch him again if she did. "It's time."

"Time for what?"

Skye was sitting in the car, waiting for her outside. She had to hurry. "Owen told me I'm your 'bird with an injured wing.'"

"What's that supposed to mean?"

"I'm capable of flying again. And I need to get out on my own."

"But you don't have to go tonight. It's late. Why not have your friend come in? Then we can all get some sleep."

He'd washed some of her clothes—and folded them and put them in a dresser drawer. She scooped everything out and dropped it in her suitcase. He'd taken good care of her. He'd cooked and cleaned and nursed her and bathed her. And there'd been moments when he'd made her feel more alive than she'd ever felt before. But that was part of the problem. She was so vulnerable when it came to him. "Where would Skye stay?" she asked. "In the guest room?"

"That's what I was thinking."

She straightened and faced him. "And where would I sleep, Cain?"

"You could sleep with me if you wanted. It's not as if she's your mother. Or as if she doesn't already know we've been together."

Sheridan couldn't sleep with Cain while Skye was in the other room. She'd be too embarrassed. Sheridan knew she was grasping for something she couldn't catch, that she was asking for trouble. She'd been avoiding reality by not calling her friends. But now that Skye had arrived, the fantasy was over. She had to stop taking crazy, unnecessary risks. "I have to keep my mind on why I came here in the first place," she said. "I have to find out who's been trying to kill me, and then I have to go home."

He shoved his hands in his pockets. "Then sleep on the couch."

She shut her suitcase, left it on the bed and slipped past him to get her things from the bathroom. "We can't go on like this."

He followed her, watching as she gathered her toothbrush and makeup. She hadn't realized it until that moment, but her toiletries, her soap and deodorant and shampoo, were so mixed up with his it was almost as if they belonged there, as if she'd been settling in for good. "Like what?" he said.

"Condoms are only 85-98 percent effective." She knew that because she'd looked it up on the Internet yesterday. "If we continue sleeping together, which we would if I stayed here, we could wind up creating a baby, even if we continue to take precautions. And I already know how you'd feel about that."

"How do you know how I'd feel?" he asked with a scowl. "We've never even talked about it."

"What's to talk about? I'm twenty-eight. I'd keep the baby. That should be enough to scare you right there." Finished in the bathroom, she waited for him to move so she could return to his room for her suitcase.

"*Scare* me? If that happened, I'd support the baby," he said. "I made that decision before I ever touched you."

"Well, I don't want to become another woman to whom you feel obligated." It was better to leave him wanting more, better than ending the relationship on a note of bitterness. Or anger. And it had to end. She'd be returning to Sacramento. There was nowhere an affair with Cain could go, anyway.

She started to drag her suitcase from the bed, but he reached around her and picked it up. "You've got it all figured out, don't you?" he said.

"Not necessarily. It'll just…be better if Skye and I take off tonight. You and I both know this…*thing* between us wasn't serious. It was more of a—" she laughed uncomfortably "—a relapse, I guess. Now I'm well enough to move on, I need to do it. This had to happen eventually."

"Where will you go?"

"The motel, if we can rouse anyone to rent us a room."

The scowl that had descended a few minutes earlier remained.

"I'll be fine." She stood on her tiptoes to give him a quick kiss. That fleeting brush of their lips was her one concession to the sudden ache of longing. It was goodbye. "Thanks for everything," she said, offering him as bright a smile as she could manage.

He rubbed a hand over his face, sighed audibly and carried out her suitcase.

Cain sat on the porch, watching the taillights of Skye's rental car disappear. He couldn't believe Sheridan was actually leaving. One minute he'd had her naked body pressed up against his own. The next she'd dressed, packed all her belongings and climbed into the passenger seat of her friend's sedan.

Once the noise of the engine faded, he let his dogs out of their pen to keep him company. With Sheridan's attacker still on the loose, he feared for her safety. But the gun-wielding Skye Willis had insisted, in no uncertain terms, that she could protect them both. And she'd come all the way from Sacramento, so it wasn't as if Sheridan could just tell her to quit worrying and go home. Sheridan needed to spend some time with her friend, to explain.

Maybe she'd come back, he thought hopefully. But deep down, he knew that probably wasn't the case. *This had to happen eventually.*

"I don't think I like Sheridan's friend," he grumbled to Koda, whose tail thumped the floorboards of the porch. Recently, he hadn't given his dogs as much attention as they normally received. He couldn't imagine *they* were too broken up about seeing Sheridan go. But he felt strangely bereft. Even cheated.

So here he was, alone with time to think. About the man in the ski mask. About Jason and John and Owen and Robert. About Owen hiding that gun in his cabin. Cain believed Owen when he said he hadn't been trying to frame him. Owen wasn't malicious. But he hadn't come forward to protect Cain when the rifle was found, either. He'd chosen to continue covering for Robert, and that showed Cain where his true loyalties lay. Not only that, Robert had been more support to Amy than he'd ever been to Cain.

Even worse was that moment in the police station when Ned had drawn his gun. John had *wanted* him to fire. Cain had sensed his sudden eagerness, his reckless "just do it and end it all" attitude.

The memory of his mother's voice came into Cain's mind. "It's them, not you. If they knew you like I do, they'd love you every bit as much." For the sake of his relationship with Marshall, he'd made peace with his stepbrothers and father over the years. They spent Thanksgiving and Christmas together, and each year got a little easier. There were moments when Cain thought he might actually be able to forgive John. But then Bailey's rifle had surfaced and everything had snapped right back to where it'd been twelve years ago.

Quixote and Maximillian growled and got to their feet, their noses pointing toward the road. Koda lifted his head and flicked his ears. Cain thought maybe they smelled a skunk or some other small animal and told them to relax. With Sheridan gone, he didn't have to worry so much about every little sound or rustle of movement.

A few seconds later, however, he heard an engine and saw the lights of another vehicle coming down the lane.

When he recognized it as his neighbor's car, he got up and walked into the clearing.

Levi Matherley rolled down his window. His dark hair, laced with gray, stuck up on one side as if he'd recently been in bed. No doubt he had, since it was nearly three-thirty in the morning. Levi had a wife and two little girls to support. His feed store opened at six. Why would he be up and about at this time of night? "Hey," Levi called out.

"Hey, yourself. What're you doing here?" Cain asked.

"Vi heard something so I grabbed a flashlight and went out to check the yard." He sounded concerned and, after what had happened, Cain could understand why.

Squatting, Cain rested his elbows on the window ledge. "Don't worry. A friend of Sheridan Kohl's arrived a few minutes ago from California. She's not familiar with the area, probably made a wrong turn and ended up on your property before she found mine. That's all."

Levi's eyebrows went up. "Oh, really? Did she take time to stand in the woods and drink some tequila?" he asked and showed Cain a half-filled bottle he handled only by the very top.

Cain studied the label. "Where'd you find this?"

Levi pointed beyond the clearing. "In those trees behind your place. I've been tromping around back there with a flashlight. Didn't you hear the dogs?"

"I assumed they were barking at my guest."

"Lucky for me. I was afraid you'd think I was a threat and shoot me." He laughed uncomfortably. "That's why I decided to get in the car instead of approaching your place on foot."

"Good idea." He sighed as his gaze returned to the tequila. "We need to see if we can get some prints from this bottle."

Levi wedged the bottom of it carefully between the seat and the console, so the middle part, which would most likely hold prints, didn't touch anything. "I'll drop it off at the police station on my way to work in the morning."

"You don't have any idea who it was, do you?" Cain asked.

Levi didn't respond right away.

"Are you going to answer me?" Cain prompted.

"I think it's best to let the police handle it from here."

Cain touched his neighbor's shoulder. "What's wrong?"

A frown created deep grooves on either side of Levi's mouth. "Just a hunch."

"What kind of hunch?"

"I suspect it might've been Tiger Chandler."

Cain rocked back on his heels. "*Tiger?* What makes you say that?"

"I've seen his car up here a few times."

"What for?"

"What do you think?"

Cain was at a complete loss. He couldn't even remember the last time Tiger had been at his house. "I have no clue."

"He used to come up here fairly often. He'd park his car on the edge of my property and walk over to your place," Levi explained.

"He never came to the door," Cain said.

"I know. I confronted him about it once, as he was getting back in his car."

"What'd he say?"

"He claimed he was just out for some fresh air."

"What, the air's better at my place?"

Levi cleared his throat. "Come on, Cain. This is awkward enough. Stop pretending."

Cain felt his jaw drop. "Pretending? Levi, I don't know what the hell you're talking about."

"He knew about you and Amy, okay? He must have. That's why he kept coming out here, creeping around in the dark."

Cain couldn't have been more surprised. "Knew *what* about me and Amy?"

"I saw her, too," he said as if Cain's response had been deliberately misleading. "She came here quite often. That's the reason I didn't get up when I heard your dogs the night Sheridan was attacked. I figured it was Amy. Again."

"She used any excuse she could to see me." That was common knowledge. "But…are you talking about more than that?"

"I'm talking about when she came out here *at night.*"

"You mean…late at night?"

He lifted his hands from the steering wheel. "Yes, late. Once every other week, at least. I'm sure there were lots of times I didn't know about. But if you two had something going, it's none of my business. That's why I stayed out of it."

"We didn't have anything going!" Cain's patience was wearing thin.

Evidently, Levi could tell by his shock that he was being honest. "She didn't come up here to—" he lowered his voice, even though there was no one but the dogs to hear them "—you know, be with you?"

Cain scowled. "Not the way you think. I haven't slept with her since before we divorced ten years ago. And I've never invited her over at night. Hell, I didn't even invite her over during the day. If she came here, it was of her own accord. I'd already learned my lesson."

"What was she doing when she came here at night, then?"

That was what Cain wanted to know. "I have no idea," he said, but he thought it was high time he found out.

Sheridan sat on a double bed in the Fairweather Inn on Main Street, facing her best friend. She had the key to her uncle's place, but she wasn't ready to return there, wasn't sure she'd ever want to stay there again. The motel felt safer, more neutral.

"I can't believe you didn't call me," Skye said, still angry. "We've been so worried. Especially Jonathan. He's on an important case or he'd be here instead of me."

"I'm sorry. I...I didn't know what to tell you. Or him." She and Jon were no longer dating. They hadn't viewed each other in a romantic light for more than two years. But they were closer than ever, best friends. "I figured he'd try to talk me into leaving if I called him."

Skye glared at her without speaking.

"Besides, I don't have my cell phone," Sheridan continued. "The battery's dead and I have no clue where my charger went."

Skye's mouth twisted. "What about loverboy's phone?"

Sheridan shot her a dirty look at the loverboy reference. "I didn't want to use Cain's phone to make a long-distance call—"

"That's such an *excuse!*"

Why argue? It was a hundred percent true. She'd been hiding from everyone who might warn her against doing what she had, in fact, done. She'd never gotten over Cain. The impulse to stay with him had gotten the better of her common sense. That was all. And she didn't want to leave Whiterock for fear the mystery would drag on forever. She was determined to expose the man who'd tried to kill her, to keep fighting for the truth.

"Didn't you want a little emotional support? Or were you happy getting what you got instead?" Skye said snidely.

"Stop it." As chagrined as she felt for not being more

sensitive to her friends' concern, Sheridan was growing irritated with Skye's unrelenting digs. "You have no right to be such a smart-ass."

Skye almost flew off the bed. "I've got every right! You were nearly beaten to death *two weeks* ago. You don't think that's something I should know? What if Cain hadn't taken such good care of you? What if you'd *died?* You're one of my best friends, damn it!"

"But it's my life! I can screw it up if I want to!"

Skye flounced back on the pillows and used the remote to turn on the television. "Well, I hope it was worth it."

At this point, Sheridan was pretty sure it had been. An interlude like the one she'd shared with Cain was difficult to regret. She'd never enjoyed making love to anyone the way she'd enjoyed it with him. That had to count for *something*. There were people who went their whole lives without experiencing that sense of giddy excitement, that bone-melting desire. So what if it couldn't last? At least she'd *felt* it. At least she knew it was possible, that it was *real*.

But she'd caused Skye a lot of worry, trouble and expense. She owed her an apology for that. And she'd probably upset Jonathan even more. "Skye, I was completely out of it for probably…I don't know, eight or nine days. You can't hold the first week against me."

Skye sulked as she watched some movie on TV. "You could've had Cain notify your family and friends."

"The police tried to contact my parents, but they were on their cruise."

"What about me and Jon?"

"I was getting around to it," she mumbled.

She tossed the remote onto the bed. "When? Next month? After we'd filed a missing person report and mourned you as *dead?*"

Sheridan got up and rummaged through her suitcase for a nightshirt. "Will you please calm down?"

Taking a deep breath, Skye frowned but didn't say any more until the next commercial break. Then she attempted a calmer approach. "That's how I learned you were hurt," she said. "I finally got through to your parents."

"They told you where I was?"

"They said you were staying at Cain Granger's until they could make other arrangements for you. But that was enough to tell me you were in trouble. It isn't as if we don't know about him, Sher. He's almost all you talked about in that victims' support group where we met. I know what he means to you and how guilty you feel…."

"So you came to rescue me from him."

"I came to see what the hell's going on and to bring you home. It was me or Jon, and he couldn't leave, not really. Jasmine wanted to join me, too, but she's in Virginia."

Sheridan changed into a T-shirt of Cain's she'd accidentally grabbed while packing. "If you talked to my parents, you knew I was okay."

"Did I?" Skye challenged. "Let me tell you something. Jasmine called me this morning—" she glanced at the clock "—I mean, yesterday morning."

A tremor of foreboding went through Sheridan. Jasmine had undeniable psychic abilities, which she used to help police solve various crimes, many of them high-profile. Sheridan didn't really understand how Jasmine did what she did, but she'd seen her friend's visions come to pass often enough that she no longer questioned them. "What'd she say?" Sheridan had to ask, even though she dreaded the answer.

"She said you're in trouble, Sher." Skye's voice was beseeching now. "She said she keeps seeing visions of you with blood running down your face. Lots of it."

Sheridan rubbed the goose bumps away from her arms. She could imagine how Jon had reacted to that. "There *was* lots of blood. She's probably talking about the beating."

Skye shook her head. "No, there's more. She keeps seeing you dead in the forest."

That brought the goose bumps back and made Sheridan nauseous. But it explained why Skye was so upset. And why she'd hopped on a plane, rented a car in Nashville, driven half the night and shown up at Cain's cabin regardless of the hour.

"I should've called," Sheridan conceded. She didn't add that she'd been afraid to hear what Jasmine might have to say, that it was part of the reason she hadn't contacted them. And she felt safe with Cain. Maybe even *safer.* Skye prided herself on her defense skills. She could probably handle a pistol better than Cain, since Cain rarely had occasion to use one and Skye taught shooting classes at the range every week. It was just that Skye represented all the cases Sheridan dealt with in Sacramento where the good guy hadn't won and never would.

"You *should've* called," Skye repeated.

Sheridan crawled into bed, and they watched TV for several more minutes. Then Skye glanced over again. "You okay?" she asked, finally calm.

"I could be better."

"What do you think we should do?"

Sheridan pleated and unpleated the edge of the coverlet, trying to figure things out. "You want me to go back to Sacramento, right? Isn't that where you're going with this?"

"That's exactly where I'm going."

"I can't do that," she said.

Skye muted the television. "Why not?"

"Because it's not just about me anymore."

"Of course it is. It's about keeping you safe! It's about making sure Jasmine's vision never becomes reality!"

"No, it's about keeping *everyone* safe. Someone killed Amy Smith. We can't simply forget about that and walk away."

Skye nibbled her bottom lip. "Who's Amy Smith?"

"An old acquaintance. There's a connection between what happened to me and what happened to her. I *know* it."

"Why can't the local police handle it?"

"Are you kidding? They're completely inexperienced in homicide."

"They can ask for outside help."

"They don't even realize they need it. Anyway, is that what you'd tell me if I was a stranger who came to you for help?" she asked. "Leave it to the police?"

Skye watched the silent television screen. "You know I wouldn't."

"Because we help victims. That's what we do. So why wouldn't that go for me, too?"

Skye's voice fell to a whisper. "Because you're closer to me than my two sisters. I couldn't bear to lose you."

"But I need closure as much as anyone. Whoever shot me and killed Jason has been free to go on with his life for *twelve years* while I've been dealing with the repercussions of what he did. And that's not the worst of it. Because he wasn't caught back then, someone else is dead. *Dead,* Skye! We have to stop him. If we don't do it, I doubt anyone else will."

Skye pinched the bridge of her nose. "Just tell me one thing."

"What's that?"

"Are you taking this risk *only* because you want to find the man who killed Jason and Amy?" she asked, dropping her hand.

"Why else would I be staying?"

"I can think of one very gorgeous reason. The same reason who was standing in his boxers not too long ago, showing me a little too much of his rifle *and* his incredibly muscular body."

"Cain."

"Have you fallen in love with him again, Sher?"

"Again?" Sheridan laughed softly, hugging his shirt even closer to her body. "I never *stopped* loving him, Skye. I don't think I ever will."

A spark of compassion changed her friend's expression. "So it's about closure there, too."

Sheridan blew out a sigh. "Maybe."

"Don't let him tempt you into making a mistake. Don't stay here and fight this battle because you think you might have a chance with him. Not at the risk of your life."

Sheridan raised her chin. "I know what to expect— and not expect—from Cain. I find the bastard who nearly killed me twice, who murdered Jason and Amy, and then I go home."

"Promise?"

"I promise." Then she could say goodbye to Whiterock without any regrets. Then she could leave because she'd chosen to leave and not because fear had chased her away.

"Fine. Just call Jon and let him know you're safe. He's left me three messages since my plane took off."

"At *this* hour?"

"He doesn't care what time it is. He wants to hear from you."

Bolstering herself for more anger, Sheridan called Jonathan—but he was too relieved to yell at her. "God, you had me scared," he said.

"I'm sorry. I was out of it for quite a while, but I'm better now."

"Do you need me to fly out there and kick some ass?"

She chuckled. "Skye says you're on an important case."

"Nothing's more important than my friends."

"Stay there and do your job," she said with a smile, missing him. "I'm going to be okay."

"Let me know if that changes."

Hearing the fatigue in his voice, she decided to let him go. He worked too hard, and slept barely five or six hours a night as it was. "Get some rest. I'll call you again tomorrow."

"Right. Talk later," he mumbled.

She hung up and slid back under the covers. But eventually her thoughts reverted to Cain, and she couldn't help feeling cold and lonely without two hundred pounds of warm male beside her.

20

Cain knocked on Tiger's door at seven in the morning. His eyes sockets felt like they were filled with sand because he hadn't bothered to go back to bed last night, but he wasn't the least bit groggy. For reasons he refused to explore, he was angry that Sheridan's friend had shown up and dragged her off. And he was determined to find out what the hell Levi had been talking about.

From the look on Tiger's face when he answered the door, he wasn't pleased to be rousted from his bed so early.

"Why are you pounding on my door at the freakin' break of dawn?" he snapped, wincing against the sunlight as if he had a headache—or more likely a hangover.

"I assumed you'd be up and getting ready for work." Tiger owned a transmission shop in town and repaired tractors, too.

"I'm taking the whole week off." He scratched his stomach. "So what do you want?"

"Were you at my place last night?" Cain asked.

Tiger didn't answer. Behind him, his two-bedroom house was completely dark, and it reeked of alcohol and sweat.

"Tiger? It was you, wasn't it? Drinking tequila and watching my house?"

With a sigh, he pressed his palms into his bloodshot eyes. "Yeah, it was me. So what?"

"So what?" Cain echoed. "So I want to know why. My neighbor claims you've been coming up there quite often. He says Amy visited even more."

Tiger's lips twisted into a bitter sneer. "You can't seriously need *me* to explain that."

"You told me on the phone that you know I didn't touch her."

"I do know that. I also know she was in love with you." His expression was so sullen, he looked like a thwarted child. "She would've taken you over me any day of the week and twice on Sundays."

Cain had always assumed Tiger was oblivious to Amy's true feelings. He'd certainly acted that way. At times, Cain had pretended to be oblivious himself, mainly to salvage Tiger's pride. Which was why he chafed at such a bald admission—and hesitated to examine it further. He hadn't asked for or wanted Amy's undying love. He found it more annoying than flattering. But something was going on that made it impossible for him or Tiger to ignore or deny the truth any longer. "That doesn't tell me what she was doing up at my place so often."

"She was peeking in your windows, Cain," he said, spelling it out as if he was addressing a five-year-old. "Watching you. Hoping you'd undress or touch yourself." He lowered his voice. "Pretending you were touching her, no doubt." He snorted. "Isn't that fucking amazing? That a woman could be so clueless when you didn't even care enough to notice?"

No, it was sad. What had he done to trigger her obsession? Sure, he'd stupidly gotten involved with her early on, but he'd been honest from the start. And as soon as he realized he couldn't love her the way she wanted him to, he'd backed off. She'd been the one who kept coming on to him, pulling at his clothes, begging to make love. The fact that he'd indulged her had been an even bigger mistake. That was how she'd ended up pregnant.

Cain felt guilty about all the mistakes he'd made in his life, but he knew with Amy he didn't have anything to feel especially bad about, not in the last ten years. "So you followed her to see what was going on?"

"I was afraid you might break down someday. That you'd get lonely enough out there to decide that maybe she was better than nothing. So I bought a pair of binoculars and watched her watch you." He laughed without humor. "We were both pathetic, eh? She was up there probing her worst pain and I was doing the same."

"What was there to see?" Cain asked. "I don't do anything very interesting. I eat and work, like everyone else."

"She would've been happy just to watch you sleep. Her favorite spot was right outside your bedroom window."

Cain grimaced at the image that conjured up in his mind. Too bad he hadn't built the dogs' cage on the other side of the house. "Why didn't you tell me so I could put a stop to it?"

Despondency seemed to replace Tiger's anger. "I wanted to win her over. I wanted her to think of *me,* desire me, without you having to chase her off. And I felt like that was happening. She quit going to your place so often. I actually believed she'd finally stopped. The last couple of times I checked, she wasn't there. And then this past week…it proves she was still waiting for you. I was never good enough." A muscle flexed in his cheek as he challenged Cain's gaze. "The only two women I've ever loved both wanted you."

Cain rubbed his neck. "You're talking about Sheridan."

"You took her virginity as if it was nothing. And I would've given anything to be in your place."

Once again Cain had to face what he'd done as a screwed-up kid. "It wasn't nothing," he said.

"How was it different?" Tiger asked. "She was just one of many."

She'd been different. Very different. But Cain wasn't about to discuss that with Tiger. "It was a long time ago—"

"So? Why couldn't you have stuck with those other girls? Did you have to have her, too?"

"Tell me one thing," Cain said.

Tiger leaned back to grab an open beer from a side table. Who knew how long it'd been sitting there. He didn't seem to care. "What's that? If I had it to do over again, would I have moved the hell away from here, from you *and* Amy? You bet. Now look at me. She's dead, and I'm the only one of us who even gives a damn. That's fucking sad."

"I didn't want anything like this to happen to her, Tiger."

"But you're glad she's gone, aren't you?"

Cain wasn't going to get anywhere with him, not

when he was like this. "Just tell me why you were at the house last night."

Tiger scraped a hand over the whiskers on his chin. "Damned if I know."

"As far as I'm concerned, you're the only one who *would* know."

"I guess it was my way of saying goodbye to Amy— and admitting at the same time that I was stupid to try winning her away from you." He downed the rest of the beer. "Shit, that's warm," he muttered in disgust.

Cain didn't want to deal with the jealousy issue. Amy was gone. It no longer mattered whom she'd loved the most. They had other things to worry about right now. "Do you know who might've killed her, Tiger?"

He stared off into the distance.

"Tiger?"

With a blink, he focused. "Whoever it was knew her well."

"What makes you say that?"

"He wrote something in the dirt not far from her body."

"I didn't see anything."

"Ned stumbled on it. But not until dinnertime yesterday. He went back to the scene after everything was cleaned up, to take another look around, and spotted it about twenty feet from where you found her body."

Cain hadn't seen anything like that. But then, it'd been dark and he'd been so horrified by her murder he'd only been looking for danger. The minute he realized Amy was dead, he'd panicked and run back to the house to make sure Sheridan was safe. "What'd he write?"

"I love you, Amy."

Cain shoved his hands in his pockets. "That's some love."

"Love is cruel," Tiger said and shut the door.

It wasn't the sight of her uncle's house that did it. It was the smell—a mixture of old furniture, new polish and the scent of roses wafting in from the open door behind her.

Sheridan stood inside the front entrance and braced against the wall in the entryway while the memories came tumbling back. As Cain had supposed, she'd just returned from the supermarket when she'd been attacked. She remembered that clearly now. She also remembered that she'd carried her groceries into the kitchen and was putting them away when she'd seen a shadow move along the side of the house.

Curious and a little unsettled, she'd walked to the living room window and gazed out at the side yard. In the deepening dusk, she could see the trash can and the empty newspaper recycle bin, but not much else.

Trying to shrug off a sense of unease, she'd told herself her misgivings were merely the effect of an overactive imagination. Her line of work tended to make one over-cautious. And it wasn't easy coming back to the town where she'd been shot and nearly killed. All kinds of nostalgic, poignant emotions had surfaced as soon as she'd driven past that Welcome to Whiterock sign, especially when she began to notice the changes to her hometown.

With a new gas station at one end of Main Street, the motel recently refurbished, and the only bar in town boasting a new neon sign, there was plenty of evidence that everyone had carried on very handily without her.

"What's wrong?" Skye cut into her thoughts. Her friend had gone in ahead of her, but once Skye realized Sheridan had stopped, she returned. "You okay?"

Sheridan nodded, but she was afraid of the other memories—the ones that were quickly coming into focus. They brought back the sudden terror and helplessness she'd felt.

"I locked the door," she said.

Skye angled her head quizzically. "You what?"

"I wasn't stupid. At least I locked the door."

"You're talking about the night you were attacked?"

Sheridan drew a deep breath and nodded again. "I thought I saw something, couldn't really confirm it, but I came back and locked the door, anyway."

Skye drew her into the living room, where Sheridan sank onto the stiff old couch. She refused to even look at the kitchen. She knew now what had happened there, remembered turning from the counter to be confronted by a man wearing a ski mask. Seeing a figure so similar to what she'd faced when she and Jason were shot had stolen the strength from her limbs. Because she knew he'd come back to kill her.

"How'd he get in?" Skye asked, gently touching her shoulder.

"He had a key," she whispered.

"How?"

"Cain said there was one under the mat. I never thought to check. My family knows better than to leave a spare in such an obvious place. The tenant must've left it behind when he moved out."

"Did you hear this person come in?" Skye was trying to pull the details from her. But it wasn't easy to sort through so much mental debris.

Sheridan wrapped her arms around herself. "No. But he must've come through the door. There was no breaking glass, no forced entry. As a matter of fact, I heard nothing until the floor creaked right behind me. And then it was too late." She closed her eyes, wishing she didn't have to relive those minutes. But she knew it was important to examine every detail.

"What'd he do, Sher?"

"He shoved me. I tried to fight him off, but he put his hands around my neck and squeezed until…until everything went black."

"Then he could take you from the house."

"He tied me up and gagged me first." She licked her dry lips, tried to regulate her breathing. "The next thing I knew, he was carrying me through the woods. I had some kind of cloth stuffed in my mouth. My hands were tied, but not my feet."

Skye's voice was low, intense. "Was he still wearing the mask?"

"I think so." Sheridan concentrated, wishing she could remember more clearly. "Yes," she said confidently. "I wish that, once I freed my hands, I'd grabbed for it, but at that point all I could focus on was escape. I knew my life depended on what I did in the next few minutes, maybe seconds."

"What *did* you do?" Skye asked, taking her hands.

Sheridan watched her friend gently squeeze her fingers. "I shoved at his chest. I wasn't the only thing he was trying to carry. He also had a—a shovel or something. Yes, that makes sense. He had a shovel later. That must've been it."

Skye waited with an anxious expression but she didn't interrupt.

"Anyway, when I woke up, I started working at the ropes. I couldn't believe it when I felt them loosen. He probably tied me very quickly and didn't expect me to be in any position to get free. So when I began to kick and fight, it took him by surprise, sent him off balance. He stumbled and fell, and I went sprawling to the ground." The words were coming faster as memories intensified. "That gave me a chance to get up and run. I took off, but it was so hard to move my legs. They felt as if they weighed a hundred pounds each. And branches kept gouging my face and cheeks and arms."

"He must've come after you."

She swallowed hard. "He did. A minute later he grabbed hold of my clothes." She fell silent, trying to come to terms with what he'd done next. She'd never been through anything more harrowing in her life. Even the shooting at Rocky Point hadn't been as traumatic— not at the time. Because it had happened so fast. She hadn't felt the bullet for several seconds.

This attack was different. She'd known from her first glimpse of that mask that she was in trouble. And she'd never felt more fear than those few minutes when the man who'd choked her was chasing her through the forest.

Until he caught her.

"Is that when he started hitting you?" Skye asked.

Sheridan pulled her hands away so she could cover her eyes.

"Sher?" Skye moved closer, and rubbed her back soothingly.

"Yes," she breathed. "He—he picked something up. Like a bat, but it was probably a—a heavy stick or piece of wood. He hit me with it. Again and again and again. Until I couldn't see because of all the blood in my eyes. My ears rang and I couldn't think straight. I didn't know where I was, *who* I was."

"What made him stop? Did you pass out again?"

"No. I knew I had to quit fighting, make him believe he'd won. So I went limp."

"Did it work?"

"He kicked me to see if I'd move, but I didn't. I had nothing left. I just lay there. I felt as if I was floating outside my own body, watching this brutality."

"Did he say anything? Did you hear his voice?"

"He said, 'Stupid bitch. Now you're going to pay.' As if *I'd* done something to *him.*"

"What was his voice like?"

"A hoarse whisper. That was all. It was barely audible."

Skye cursed in frustration and disappointment, but she wasn't willing to give up. "And then what'd he do?"

The rest was a blur. Sheridan supposed she'd faded in and out of consciousness during the next few minutes. "I don't know."

"What do you *think* he did?"

"I assume he went back for the shovel, then dragged me deeper into the woods. Because the next time I came around, he was digging my grave."

"God." Tears filled her friend's eyes. "He was going to bury you? It's a miracle you're alive."

Sheridan thought of Cain. *I can't wait. I want to be inside you…* He was inside her, all right, in her heart, in her blood. And she doubted she'd ever get him out. "I wouldn't be, if he hadn't been interrupted."

"Interrupted?"

"We were on Cain's property. When his dogs started barking, he got out of bed to see what was going on. Then the man with the shovel ran away. At least, I think he did. I don't remember anything other than staring up at the stars—until my hospital room came into view."

Skye plucked at the worn edge of the sofa. "Cain got you to a hospital?"

"Yes."

Blinking away tears, Skye shook her head. "You almost died."

Sheridan didn't respond. Skye was only reacting to her own fear and anger—but pointing out how close she'd been to death wasn't making her feel any better.

Skye seemed to understand that they had to focus on some more constructive goal. She cleared her throat. "Do you recall anything unusual about the man who attacked you, Sher? A…a mannerism? A smell? A sound? His clothing? The way he moved? His size? Anything?"

"He had an average build. He was quiet and cautious but very, very determined. And he wore gloves—I remember the feel of them around my neck." It wasn't much, and Sheridan knew it.

"That's it? What about his vehicle?"

"I don't remember a vehicle. I mean, he had to get me from here to Cain's property somehow. It's a fifteen-minute drive. But I didn't come around until he was carrying me into the woods."

"There has to be something else," Skye pressed. "Something distinctive."

Sheridan wracked her brain for the tiniest detail. She remembered her attacker's grunts as he struck her, his palpable rage, his unyielding response when she began to plead.

And then a memory that'd been lost in the deep well of her unconsciousness floated to the surface.

"The bastard had to have it all."

"What?" Skye said, leaning closer.

"That's what he whispered when I went limp. He was standing over me, holding whatever he'd been using for a club, breathing heavily, and he muttered, 'The bastard had to have it all.'"

"Who was he talking about?"

"I don't know. Maybe Cain. We were on his property."

Skye waited, obviously hoping for more. But there was no more. Tossing her purse on the coffee table, she finally got up and crossed the room to look out the window. "Have the police been here yet?"

Cain had said they'd been there but hadn't found anything of importance. "Yes."

Skye glanced around. "Who cleaned up?"

"The police?"

"Are you dreaming?" She turned back to the window.

Skye was right. Sheridan had never known the police to clean up a crime scene. That was typically hired out. Or a family member had to do it, even with the most gruesome of murders. But this was a small town, and small towns had their own way of doing things. It was possible that someone on the police force had been kind enough to clean up the mess, but somehow she knew it was Cain. He seemed to take care of everything.

Hands on her hips, Skye pivoted to face her. "So what do you think? Are you really going to be able to tolerate sleeping here?"

Sheridan was well aware of the money it would cost them to stay at the motel, but she wasn't eager to be back in this place. "How long are you planning to stay?"

"A week. Maybe two."

"What about David and the kids?"

"They'll be fine. It's not as if I go out of town very often."

"I don't think you've ever left them before."

"But I can trust David to look after himself and the kids. I want to help you. I want to solve this so you can go home with me."

As touched as Sheridan was by her support, she couldn't let Skye put her life on hold for more than a few days. "No, Skye, you have to go back sooner than that. We can't both be gone from The Last Stand at the same time. Ava's new. She's probably in a panic. And you said yourself that Jonathan's on a big case. What help can he be to her?"

Skye arched an eyebrow at her. "They'll manage, okay?"

Obviously, Skye was refusing to be practical. She was letting her heart rule her head—but she'd have to reverse that eventually. "This isn't convenient for you."

"And it's convenient for *you?*"

Sheridan stood and began to wander around the kitchen. The fridge held a few of the groceries she'd bought. She didn't know what'd happened to the rest. There was no garbage or dishes in the sink. "You could get hurt if you're mixed up in this, Skye. I can't worry about you in addition to everything else."

"I can take care of myself."

"But cases like this drag on. You know that. What are the chances we'll solve it quickly, even if you get involved?"

"Better than if I don't." She clapped her hands. "But let's not worry about that right now. Let's see what we can dig up and go from there."

Sheridan leaned on the back of a kitchen chair. "You're crazy," she said, but what she really meant was, "I'm glad you're my friend."

"You'd do it for me," Skye responded.

"But I don't have a family at home."

"Doesn't matter. You're not getting rid of me anytime soon, so you might as well quit trying. Just tell me whether we should stay at the motel or move back here."

That was the decision Sheridan didn't want to make. Whoever had tried to kill her had known where to find her and had invaded her space so easily—*this* space. She didn't feel safe here. But she hadn't been expecting trouble at the time, so she hadn't been prepared to defend herself. And murders happened in motels, too. It was more about watching her back than staying in one place instead of another. If whoever had attacked her really wanted to, he'd find her no matter where she went.

"We might as well save a few bucks," she said with a shrug.

"I agree." Skye started for the door. "Come on, let's get our suitcases."

Wondering if she'd be able to live with her choice, Sheridan lingered in the kitchen—until she heard someone at the front door.

"Well, *hel-lo* there. Who're *you?*"

It was a familiar voice, but Sheridan couldn't immediately place it. Turning the corner, she saw Cain's youngest brother standing on the stoop, lowering his sunglasses in order to give Skye an appreciative once over.

Dressed in a Harley T-shirt with the sleeves ripped out and a pair of jeans, he was wearing flip-flops that revealed disgusting feet with overgrown toenails. A dragon tattoo covered the upper part of one arm; *R.I.P. Jason* in blue and red ink covered the other.

Sheridan watched Skye return the exaggerated perusal. "I'm Skye Willis," she replied. "A friend of Sheridan's from Sacramento. Are you the man who attacked her?"

Robert shoved his sunglasses back up to the bridge of his nose. "Um…no," he said in obvious surprise.

"Good." Skye nodded decisively. "Then I won't have to shoot you."

He laughed as if he didn't know whether she was joking. Sheridan wasn't completely sure herself. "She's spunky," he told Sheridan as he spotted her. "I like that."

"She's also married," Sheridan said. "Skye, this is Cain's youngest brother."

"*Step*brother," Robert clarified.

"*Step*brother," she repeated, but she had to hide an ironic smile at his concern about the distinction. She could understand Cain's being reluctant to claim Robert, not the opposite—but then, if Robert could really see himself, he'd probably clip his toenails.

"What can we do for you?" she asked.

"I was on my way home, saw some activity over here and thought I'd stop by and welcome you. It can't be easy coming back to this house after what happened." Apparently, it was Sheridan's turn to be checked out because the sunglasses slid down again. "Hey, you're looking better. The bruises are fading."

It was a struggle to keep her indifference toward his opinion out of her voice. "Thanks."

"I also wanted to let you know that I'll keep an eye on the place from now on," he added with a wink that did absolutely nothing to allay Sheridan's fears.

"Robert lives in a trailer behind his father's home across the street and four houses down," Sheridan explained to Skye.

"It's the one with the metal dinosaur out front," Robert said. "My dad makes those."

"Did you see or hear anything unusual the night Sheridan was attacked?" Skye asked, obviously uninterested in John's hobby.

"Not a thing. Cain stopped by earlier that evening, but that was about it."

Sheridan couldn't help resenting the way Robert kept trying to connect Cain to everything that had happened. He'd told Amy about the argument between Cain and Jason the night Jason was murdered. He'd blabbed what Owen had told him about the camper. And now this.

She folded her arms. "Does he come by very often?"

She hoped to get a positive answer, so she could accuse Robert of highlighting details that were irrelevant. If Cain visited the house from time to time, it wasn't remarkable that he would've been there the night she was attacked. But given his relationship with his stepfamily, he probably didn't go to their place often.

"Not really," Robert said.

"So this was unusual?"

"Sort of. We certainly weren't expecting him."

"What'd he want?"

"He came to talk to my dad about Grandpa."

That sounded like Cain. Sheridan was tempted to smile at his love for Marshall. But then Robert continued.

"He didn't stay long enough to say much, though. Karen Stevens showed up a few minutes later and as soon as he saw her—" Robert clapped his hands for emphasis "—he took off."

Skye's gaze shifted between them. Obviously, she was drawing her own conclusions about Robert. But Sheridan was too preoccupied to guess what they might be. "Are you suggesting he left *because* of Karen?" she asked Robert.

"That's exactly what I think. Happens every time. For some reason, he hates even being in the same room with her."

"But Karen used to be Cain's favorite teacher. Why would her presence bother him?"

A devilish smile twisted Robert's lips. "Maybe he liked her a little *too* much. Maybe he wasn't just cleaning her erasers after school."

Sheridan's stomach tightened. When she and Cain were in high school, Karen Stevens had dated John Wyatt soon after Cain's mother died. Their relationship had started clear back then. Surely Cain and Ms. Stevens hadn't crossed *that* line….

But now Robert had mentioned it… Sheridan recalled that Ms. Stevens had shown unmistakable favoritism toward Cain. That kind of history would make sense of her manner and her words in the restaurant. *It's not easy to walk away from a man like that….*

"Are you intimating that they had an inappropriate relationship?" Skye asked. She could obviously tell how hesitant Sheridan was to voice her thoughts, how badly she didn't really want to know.

"I'm not *intimating* anything." Robert's eyebrows knitted in mock innocence. "Imagine how upset my father would be if he heard such a thing."

Robert hadn't appeared at her door through any desire to be neighborly; he'd come to make trouble for Cain. Sheridan had expected as much, but she hadn't expected *this*. Ms. Stevens? What did Robert expect her to do with this information?

And then it dawned on her. He knew about the camper. He was hoping her wounded pride and outrage would provoke her into exposing this—further damaging Cain's reputation. Maybe Robert claimed he didn't want his father to know, but he did. He just didn't want to be the one to tell him.

"Why are you trying to leak this?" she asked.

"I'm not," he said.

"You want your father and Karen to break up, is that it? And if you can make Cain look bad at the same time, even better."

"Stop it. You're being paranoid!"

"What's wrong? Don't you and Karen get along?"

"It's no secret that I think she's a bitch, but my dad has his own life to live. I don't care who he's with."

Unless he married her, of course. Sheridan was sure Karen wouldn't be thrilled to have John's twenty-five-year-old son living in her backyard. If the relationship became that serious, Robert would have to move, maybe even support himself for a change.

"Well, thanks for the distasteful mental picture," Sheridan said, "but I don't believe it. Even if I did, I wouldn't tell anyone. I'm sure you understand what'll happen to your father's relationship with Karen if a rumor like this were to get started."

"Which is why I haven't mentioned it."

She rolled her eyes. "You just told me," she pointed out.

Attempting to look sincere, he shoved his hands in his pockets and jingled his change. "You know, there are times when I wonder if hiding something like this from my dad is really doing him any favors. Sex with a student is pretty scandalous. Cain was underage. And Karen was in a position of authority. I've seen teachers go to prison for less."

Skye put her hand on Sheridan's arm to act as a warning: *Hold your temper.* "Is that what you'd like to see?"

"Whether I want to see it or not, the truth usually comes out. One way or another, people get what they deserve, don't you think? I mean, take what happened to you, for instance."

"You think I got what I *deserved* when I was attacked?"

His lips pressed tight against his teeth. "According to what Amy told me before she was killed, you lured Jason to Rocky Point just to make Cain jealous. Is that true?"

Sheridan couldn't answer. She kept seeing the barrel of that rifle in the open truck door, hearing the blast....

"You cost him his *life*," Robert went on. "Because of Cain."

Sheridan felt as if he'd just slapped her. She was guilty as charged, but she'd never had Cain's stepfamily throw it in her face.

"I think you should leave," Skye said quietly, but he made no move to go.

"Women and my stepbrother," he said with a disgusted shake of his head. "I wish you could see how silly you look, lusting after him, jumping into his bed every time he snaps his fingers."

Sheridan jutted out her chin. "Do I sense a bit of jealousy on your part? Is it eating you up inside that your older brother is everything a woman wants, everything *you'll* never be?"

"I'm everything I need to be," he retorted. "You're the one who's always pretended to be something you're not, the very picture of innocence during the day, panting for Cain at night. It's no wonder someone hates you badly enough to—"

"*Was that someone you?*" she shouted.

He lowered his voice. "If I'd attacked you, you wouldn't be around to tell."

"Go home." Skye shoved him in the chest. "Now. Do you hear me? Before I shoot you, after all."

Chuckling that he'd managed to elicit such a strong response, Robert dropped his hand and walked toward Owen's truck, which he'd parked haphazardly at the curb, the engine still running.

He turned back after taking only a few steps. "Oh, I should leave this with you while I'm here," he said and reached into his back pocket to toss a folded flyer on the ground by their feet.

Sheridan was so furious she didn't bother retrieving it until he'd gone. Then she opened it and smoothed it out: It was Amy's funeral announcement.

21

There was another note under her doormat, the second in the past five days.

Returning home from school, her arms laden with papers, grade books and progress reports, Karen Stevens could see the white corner sticking out and felt her steps automatically slow. She didn't want to pick it up. She knew what it would say. But she had to get rid of it before John arrived. He was stopping by at 4:30. He wanted to make up after their argument in the restaurant, but that wouldn't happen if he learned what she'd done with Cain. It didn't matter that the incident had occurred twelve years ago. John had so many issues with his stepson, he'd never forgive her. It was Cain they'd argued about at the restaurant the other night. She'd encouraged him to acknowledge his stepson, saying it was ridiculous for them to live in the same town without speaking to each other. He'd flatly refused, saying he wanted no contact with "that murdering son of a bitch." Which had motivated her to try convincing him that Cain couldn't possibly have killed Jason. Which made him angry that she was taking Cain's "side." Which caused her to say that Cain was twice the man Robert was—words she'd been biting back for months. Which led him to insist he couldn't be with anyone who didn't understand his responsibilities as a father. Which provoked her into telling him to go to hell. Then she walked out.

It was basically the same argument they'd had before. And yet it was different. Somehow the stakes had been raised. And that was what scared her.

After checking to make sure none of her neighbors were watching, she shifted her load so she could bend down. Then she grabbed the note, hurried inside and locked the door behind her. Someone was bent on terrorizing her. Why? And how had whoever it was found out? She was almost positive Cain hadn't told anyone. Maybe he didn't care what John thought—although she suspected that, on some level, he did—but he definitely cared about Marshall's opinion. He wouldn't want his grandfather to know what they'd done. Neither would he want to give those he associated with every day, and the police, another reason to think the worst of him.

Closing her eyes, she pressed a hand to her pounding heart and tried to stop shaking. When she'd returned to Whiterock she'd believed the past would remain in the past, that it could be forgotten. Cain had never tried to contact her. There wasn't even a hint that anyone knew about her terrible mistake. Until recently, she'd thought she was safe.

Tempted to call Cain, she glanced at the phone. But she didn't move toward it. She'd tried to make herself get in touch with him before and always chickened out. She owed him an apology for what she'd done. He'd been a seventeen-year-old boy, desperate for love and attention and she'd—

Too embarrassed to think about it, she cringed, imagining her behavior exposed to the entire town. She'd been nominated for Teacher of the Year last term, for crying out loud. If the truth came out, she'd look like the biggest hypocrite on earth.

She could already see the headlines: Teacher of the Year Hides Dark Secret. She'd be publicly humiliated, fired from the school district, possibly imprisoned, maybe even forced to register as a sex offender. And if Cain hadn't been too hurt before, he'd be hurt now. It would jeopardize his relationship with Marshall, a man he loved more than any other, by giving Marshall reason to finally side with John.

After setting her books and papers on the counter, Karen sank into her most comfortable chair. Lizzie and Pepe Le Pew, her cats, welcomed her home, brushing up against her legs, but Karen was too numb, too dazed to pet them. What was she going to do? She had a terrible feeling the notes wouldn't stop, that eventually the sender, whoever it was, would reveal her shame.

She had to put an end to this—but how? Whoever was leaving these messages gave no clue to his or her identity. Karen had no way of determining the author, so she couldn't even contact him or her to plead her case.

Slowly, she unfolded the paper to see what had been written this time. True to form, the note was produced on a computer and was unsigned. The first two had been very brief: *I know how Cain became teacher's pet...* and *Do you miss Cain, Ms. Stevens?*

Do you dream about him coming over after school to cut your grass?

This one was a little longer but even more painful to read: *Do you still fantasize about Cain? Or is he too old these days? Maybe what you really want are the boys in your class. You'd better be careful or I'll expose you. Just watch me.*

That someone would think she'd victimize her students made her physically ill. She wasn't like that and didn't understand how she'd ever made such a terrible mistake. But at least it had only happened once. She wanted to believe it wouldn't have happened at all had she really been interested in John. Fifteen years her senior, he'd seemed too old for her, too staid. He'd been through two marriages and had a family of nearly grown children, while she'd never even been engaged. When she became so hopelessly infatuated with Cain, she'd been reliving her own high school years, but she knew he'd never returned her interest.

That was the most pathetic part. Maybe she could attempt to justify her actions if they'd fallen in love, if Cain had pursued the relationship. But, after that one time in her bed, he was the one who'd told her no. Repeatedly. And that had only made her want him more.

The difficulty of trying to reconcile how she could be both a caring teacher who loved her vocation and a predator who'd lured one of her students into a sexual relationship was the reason she'd left Whiterock. She'd only returned after John had found her on MySpace and started e-mailing her again. He hadn't gotten together with anyone else in the years she'd been gone, said he missed her and wanted to try again, and she'd begun to realize how much she missed *him*.

Now she was back, hoping to get it right. Instead, the mistake she'd tried to forget was back, too.

She folded the note into a small triangle. She needed to get up the nerve to ask her neighbors if they'd seen someone approach her house today. In the past, she'd been too frightened to question them, in case they kept an eye out in future and picked up what was left behind. But maybe that was a risk she'd have to take.

The doorbell rang, and Karen's heart jumped into her throat. It was 4:00 p.m. John was early.

Getting to her feet, she rushed to her bedroom and hid the note in her underwear drawer. She'd burn it later, like the others. For now, she had to calm down and appear as normal as possible. And that wasn't easy, because she'd fallen in love with John. She couldn't bear the thought of losing him.

How ironic...

"Karen?" John was knocking again.

Taking a deep breath, she squared her shoulders and opened the door. "Hi."

He offered her a sheepish smile. "Did you get my message?"

He'd called to tell her he was sorry about Sunday. He was always short-tempered when Cain was around, but he'd been especially irritable at the diner. For different reasons, the stress of having Cain so close had made them both touchy.

"I did. I'm sorry, too." Neither of them had meant the things they'd said, but she knew they'd probably argue about the same subject again. Robert wasn't a problem that was going to disappear. Apparently, neither was Cain.

"You have to understand that it's hard to hear you criticize my children," he said.

And *he* had to understand that Cain wasn't the bad guy he wanted him to be. John was trying to justify the fact that he'd never been able to love Cain. But after abusing her position as Cain's teacher, Karen felt obligated to make it up to him, and that included trying to show John the extent to which prejudice tainted his feelings about his stepson.

She didn't mention that right now, however. After finding a third note on her doorstep, she didn't want to risk another argument. She needed to feel John's arms around her. "I know. I'm sorry," she said and slipped into his embrace.

"Hey, what's wrong?" he said when she clung to him longer than usual.

She dashed a hand across her cheeks to wipe away the tears that'd begun to stream down her face. "Nothing."

His eyebrows drew together. "Bad day at school?"

"No. Not that. I just…I don't like it when we fight."

He stepped inside and closed the door behind him. "I don't like it either, babe. As a matter of fact, I think it's time we stopped letting other people cause problems between us."

Did that mean he was finally going to do something about Robert? She doubted it. More likely he'd suggest a truce: If she didn't say anything bad about Robert, he wouldn't say anything about Cain. He'd once asked her why they couldn't simply pretend the two men didn't exist, and she'd tried to explain that they didn't live in a vacuum. By virtue of Cain and Robert's connection to John, they were also connected to her. But she was too rattled to be so pragmatic at this particular moment. *She* wanted to be the dreamer for a change.

"That would be good," she agreed.

"And I think it'll be easier if…"

When he paused, she drew back to look at him. His body language and tone of voice suggested he was gearing up to say something profound.

"If we get married," he finished.

Her jaw dropped as he pulled a velvet box from his pocket. "You're *proposing?*"

He flipped open the lid to reveal a shiny solitaire set in white gold. "Will you marry me, Karen?"

Stunned, she reached for the box. "You're serious…."

"I've never been more serious. I'm in love with you. I've been in love with you for twelve years. It's time I made you my wife."

Even with that note hidden in her underwear drawer, she wanted to say yes. Maybe she felt such eagerness *because* of the note. Marriage would bind them together, make it more difficult for John to leave her. But she'd risk having her husband come home to one of those notes on the doorstep. She couldn't let that happen.

"What do you say?" he prompted, his eyes dancing with excitement as she stared at the ring.

Her chest had grown so tight she could hardly breathe. Two weeks ago, she would've been thrilled. But that was before the past had snuck up on her.

"Aren't we moving a little too fast?" she asked, stalling so she'd have time to think it through.

He chuckled and cupped the velvet box in her hand, smiling as he gazed down at it. "Are you kidding? We dated for four months twelve years ago. We corresponded for a long time while you were gone and we've been together for six months since you came back. How long should it take to know we're in love?"

"But—" She was reeling, caught between hope and fear. "We haven't even *talked* about marriage before."

"We're talking about it now. It has to start somewhere. Are you going to try it on?"

She took the ring from its padded box and slipped it on her finger.

"How does it fit?"

"Perfect." The weight of it felt so satisfying, so right.

"Do you like it?"

"I love it." It was the very ring she'd admired in a jewelry store window when they'd gone to Kentucky. How thoughtful of him to go back for it. "So...where will we live?"

"In my house, of course. You're only renting."

But he had his twenty-five-year-old son living in the backyard. Karen didn't think she could tolerate having Robert so close. Still, they'd just agreed not to talk about Robert. Or Cain. And she didn't want to ruin this moment. "When would we do it?" she asked.

"I've always thought Christmas would be nice for a wedding."

Christmas. That gave her a fairly long engagement. Surely within six months she'd have figured out *some-*

thing. Maybe whoever was leaving her the notes would get distracted and move on with his or her life, or make a conscious decision to let it go. Bringing up that… incident served no good purpose and stood to hurt other people besides her. "Okay, Christmas," she breathed.

He tilted up her chin. "That's a yes?"

"That's a yes," she said with more conviction. But she knew a lot had to happen before then. If she couldn't find out who was tormenting her, she'd have to tell John what she'd done. Otherwise, this person might tell him for her, and that would be much, much worse. *I'll expose you. Just watch me.*

Imagining her confession made Karen's heart pound with fear. John could surprise her and be forgiving. At times he was so kind, so generous. In this situation, however, it was far more likely that the truth would always stand between them, even if they tried to go on. And if John was ever vindictive enough to take what she confided in him to the police, her life would be ruined.

Could she trust him that much?

She believed she could—if her indiscretion had involved anyone but Cain.

Cain had spent most of the past two days in the woods with his dogs, searching for evidence. And he'd discovered a footprint that matched the ones by the creek the night Sheridan had been attacked. Ned had come out to make a plaster cast of what looked to be a size ten tennis shoe, worn down along the outside heel.

He stayed so busy in the daylight hours that he had

little time to miss Sheridan. The nights were long, however, and the house felt empty without her.

But that was just because he was worried about her, he told himself. Robert had confirmed that she was once again staying in the house where she'd been attacked.

He turned up the TV and flipped to a new station. *She'll be fine.* Her friend Skye had a gun and obviously knew how to use it. But it would be far too easy for Sheridan's stalker to shoot her through a window before anyone saw it coming. There was so much activity in the crowded neighborhood; how would anyone know when someone didn't belong? Would Skye really be able to protect her?

Cain had asked Ned to have someone patrol the area, and Ned had acted as if he'd already planned on it. He wanted to find Amy's killer, and he believed Amy's killer was also the man who'd hurt Sheridan, so Cain knew he'd follow through. But having someone cruise down the street was no guarantee of her safety.

Tossing the remote aside, he got up from the couch and paced for several minutes. The more he thought about how vulnerable Sheridan was, the more worried he became that it'd been a mistake to let her leave with Skye.

Of course, he hadn't had any choice in the matter. It wasn't as if he could restrain her.

When the phone rang, he grabbed it, hoping to hear her voice. She hadn't called since she left, which bothered him as much as everything else.

"Hello?"

"It's your fault she's dead."

Tiger. His words were slurred. He was drinking again.

"I didn't ask Amy to come up here, Tiger."

"You didn't have to," he said and hung up.

With a curse, Cain put down the receiver. Emotions were running high in Whiterock. Ned and Tiger were both pointing a finger at him for Amy's death, but she'd come out to his place on her own, many times according to his neighbor. And the night of the shooting, she hadn't gone to the house, the way he'd told her to, but in the opposite direction. Not only that, he'd begged her, for years, to forget him. How much more could a man do to get out of a romantic entanglement?

Nothing. He'd never given her false hope or made promises he didn't keep. Even in high school, when they'd been sexually involved, she'd known his heart wasn't in it.

He didn't feel responsible, he felt sad—sad that she'd loved him so much with absolutely no encouragement, sad that he couldn't return her feelings, even though he'd sometimes thought he should try. Sad that someone could end her life as if it was nothing, and afraid the same thing would happen to Sheridan if he didn't do something to stop it.

He considered calling her, but her cell phone was still out of operation. And he didn't have Skye's number.

Reclaiming his keys from the top of the refrigerator, he decided to drive to town. He doubted Sheridan's friend would be very happy to see him. Skye seemed particularly distrustful of him. But he didn't care. He'd never be able to relax if he didn't achieve some type of assurance that Sheridan was safe.

He'd just reached the front door when the phone rang

again. Expecting more drunken accusations from Tiger, he wasn't in any hurry to answer. But after two more rings, he walked over to check caller ID.

It wasn't Tiger. The screen read K. Stevens.

Why would his former English teacher be calling him? He wasn't any more eager to speak with her than he was with Tiger or Ned. Even less, in fact. But she hadn't called him since she'd been back. He figured this must be important—in a bad way.

Sitting on the arm of the closest chair, he answered the phone. "Hello?"

"Cain?"

"Yes?"

"It's Karen."

"I know."

"I—I'm sorry to bother you. Especially so late."

He didn't know how to respond. He didn't harbor any hard feelings toward her, but as far as he was concerned, they couldn't even be friends. There was too much history between them.

"No problem," he said, but he was waiting for whatever she'd called to impart.

"Your stepfather asked me to marry him today."

Last he'd heard, they'd had a blow-up in the Roadhouse. Karen had told John not to contact her again, and Cain had been hoping that was the end of their relationship.

But of course it wasn't. This was the bad news he'd been expecting for a long time.

Remaining silent, Cain tried to imagine what their marriage would mean to her, to him, to his stepfather

and stepbrothers. At the very least, it would complicate
relationships that were already complicated enough.
What if Marshall dragged him to Thanksgiving dinner
come November? He pictured himself sitting across
from Karen, seeing the guilt in her eyes, a constant
reminder of the terrible secret they were keeping from
John. And that was the better of two unattractive possibilities. It was more likely that Karen would eventually break down and tell John. That was what most
wives would do, wasn't it? And then John would finally
have irrefutable proof that Cain was the bastard he'd
always accused him of being. He'd use it to poison
Owen against him. And he'd go to Marshall.

Cain couldn't help wincing at the thought. "Did you
answer him?" he asked, dreading her response.

"Yes." There was a pause. "I agreed."

Cain closed his eyes. Just what he needed right now.
Why the hell didn't he simply walk away from the
Wyatts? Why did he let them matter?

Because he *couldn't* walk away. Not as long as
Marshall was alive. And he owed Owen some sort of
loyalty, too. He and Owen had never had any significant
trouble between them.

"When's the wedding?" he asked, sick at heart.

"December."

He kneaded his temples. "Are you in love with him?"
He silently pleaded with her to hedge or say anything
that might indicate she wasn't genuinely committed.
Maybe she was lonely and needed the companionship.
Maybe she thought he was the best she'd be able to get.
Anything short of what it would take to make a mar-

riage like this work… Then he could oppose it, feel vindicated in disparaging the idea. But her sincerity disarmed him.

"Yes. I have been for a while, although it was a gradual thing for me, much more gradual than it was for him."

Damn it! "So why are you calling me?"

He could tell that his brusque response made it difficult for her to go on.

"For several reasons," she said at length. "First—" her voice dropped to an agonized whisper "—I owe you an apology."

"Don't." He could sense her shame—because he shared it. He didn't want to hear that she was sorry; he just wanted to forget. He'd been trying to distance himself from his past for a long time. Why allow it to catch up with him now?

"Please, let me talk about this. It's been bottled up inside me for twelve years."

Did he have to?

When he said nothing, she haltingly continued. "What happened was my fault, Cain, not yours. I—I was your teacher, for God's sake. I should've been protecting you, guiding you, not lusting after you."

He opened his mouth to interrupt but forced himself not to speak. *Let her finish, let her get it off her chest.* Maybe it would help *one* of them.

"It's just that…well, you've got to be aware that you're a very charismatic person. And you seemed so old for your age, so streetwise. Despite the age difference between us…and all the things that should've stopped me, I had this…this silly crush on you." She laughed in a self-deprecating way. "I guess I can understand how Amy felt. You were all I could think about and I—"

Unable to listen to anymore, he finally interrupted. "Karen."

She didn't answer immediately. She'd broken down in tears. The sound of her weeping was even worse than the apology.

"I knew what I was doing," he said. Maybe he was the one who owed *her* an apology. He'd never felt any attraction to her. He'd done what he had so he could take what his stepfather wanted instead of his mother. He'd used Karen to strike out at John. He couldn't place all the blame on her doorstep.

"Then we both made a mistake," she muttered.

"Apparently."

She sniffed. "People make mistakes sometimes, don't they?"

Was he ever familiar with *that* concept! He'd made more than his share. And considering the fact that everyone in town seemed ready to suspect him of murder, he was still paying for the past. "So…are you going to tell John?" That had to be where this conversation was going. He could tell that their actions weighed heavily on Karen's conscience and guessed she wanted to unburden herself. So her answer surprised him.

"No. I'd never do that to you."

Her conviction caused him to sit up straighter, but she continued before he could respond.

"But I'm afraid someone else will."

"Who?"

"That's what I'm calling to ask you."

She thought *he* might break his silence? If he was going to do that, he would've done it at the police station when, once again, he'd been tempted to use his transgression with Karen to hurt John. "I won't say anything. He'd never be able to touch you again without thinking of me." Without knowing she'd wanted him first. That was the real revenge. But it was a revenge he'd never used and never would.

"Then who have you told?" she asked.

"I haven't told anyone."

"No one? Not a single soul?"

"No," he said, wondering why she seemed so unwilling to believe him.

"That can't be true."

Cain had assumed she'd merely been trying to reassure herself that it was safe to proceed with the engagement, that he wouldn't sabotage her. He hadn't expected this. "Excuse me?"

"There's someone else, someone who knows."

"What makes you think so?"

Another long silence ensued. Then he heard her sigh. "Can you meet me at the corner of Rollingwood and Old Schoolhouse Road?"

"What for?"

"I have something to show you."

22

Cain waited at the appointed place for nearly an hour, but Karen didn't show up. Frustrated, he finally got in his truck and drove to her house to see what was going on. And then he knew. John's car was parked out front. His stepfather had probably surprised Karen; with John there she couldn't even call. Cain didn't have a cell phone, anyway.

Wondering what Karen needed to show him, and why she was so adamant that, after twelve years, someone knew about their afternoon together, he headed over to Sheridan's. It was too late to knock at the door, but at least he could make sure no one was lurking about.

He parked across the street, in plain sight in case Sheridan or Skye came to the window. He wasn't trying to frighten them or get himself shot. He only wanted to check on their safety. But as soon as he left his truck, a voice issued out of the darkness.

"Well, if it isn't the man of the hour."

Tiger was in the side yard, leaning against the fence. So this was where he'd decided to get drunk. "Last I knew you didn't live in this area."

"Neither do you."

"I'm here to make sure everything's okay."

"Did Sheridan ask you to do that?"

"No."

"Are you two seeing each other?"

Cain couldn't decide what to make of his and Sheridan's relationship. He definitely wanted her back in his house, back in his bed. But he couldn't say how much of that was due to what had occurred in the past and the fact that they'd already been intimate, and how much to the unusual circumstances that had put her in his care.

Was it even worth deciding? About the time he figured it out, she'd be leaving town.

"We're friends."

"That doesn't seem to matter to the women you know. They want you, anyway."

"I'm sorry about Amy, Tiger."

Tiger stared at him, then his face crumpled. "Damn. Why can't you give me a target?"

"I'm too busy providing a target for everyone else at the moment."

Tiger's smile revealed the chipped tooth he'd had for so long Cain couldn't remember what he'd hit, or what had hit him. "Yeah, you've been catching more than your fair share of hell lately, haven't you?" He gulped down some of his beer. "I guess it's easier to pile on than to accept the truth."

The acknowledgement was enough for Cain. He knew what Tiger was going through. "You speaking at the funeral?" he asked.

"I'm saying a few words, yeah. Her mother wants me to give a 'life portrait.'" He eyed his bottle in the light coming from the porch, obviously measuring the amount he had left, annoyed that it wasn't more. "Will you be there?"

Cain was well aware that Ned, Amy's parents and probably even Tiger, would rather he stayed away. But considering what Amy had wanted from him, and the little he'd been able to offer, he felt he owed it to her to pay his final respects. "Yeah, I'll be there."

"That should make it fun," Tiger said dryly. "You're a glutton for punishment, you know that?"

"I have as much right to say goodbye to Amy as anyone."

"I guess you do."

The door opened, and Skye stuck her head out. "You two going to stand in the yard all night? Or are you coming in?"

Cain smiled at the invitation and raised questioning eyebrows at Tiger.

"I'll go in," Tiger said, pushing away from the fence. "Why not? I've made my peace with you. Now maybe I can finally bury the hatchet with the other girl you stole from me."

Cain decided to let him do that, even though he was dying for a glimpse of Sheridan himself. "I think I'll go say hello to Robert."

Tiger toasted Cain with his bottle. "You're not threatened by leaving me with your girl?"

Cain didn't bother to contest the "your girl" part. Tiger was just provoking him, trying to get a reaction. "No. Keep her safe while you're there, though," he said. Then he waved at Skye and walked away.

* * *

Robert wasn't home. Neither was John. Cain was just cutting across the lawn to the street when he succumbed to the inner voice that told him he was squandering a fabulous opportunity. Robert claimed he hadn't taken that digital picture of Sheridan, yet he had a digital camera, a computer and a color printer, and because he lived down the street from her, he also had access. He claimed he hadn't known the rifle he took from Marshall's shed was the one that had killed Jason. Yet he'd never mentioned finding it *or* losing it.

Cain didn't believe his youngest stepbrother was capable of life-threatening violence, especially against Jason, but something about Robert wasn't right.

On the other hand, he'd never seemed completely right. His behavior could easily be the result of alcoholism or the mood swings he'd exhibited for years. It didn't necessarily mean any more. But Cain knew he'd feel better if he checked Robert's recent picture downloads. Just in case.

Problem was, he had no idea when his stepbrother might return. Robert could be out for a late night of drinking or merely running a quick errand.

He hesitated on the front lawn, eyeing the metal dinosaur his stepfather had made not long ago, trying to decide. Then he turned back and walked around the house to the trailer.

"So...are you planning to attend Amy's funeral?" Tiger asked.

Sheridan sat with Skye on the sofa, facing Tiger, who'd chosen the recliner.

"I am. I didn't know her that well, but I feel terrible about what happened." She also wanted to see who else showed up and how each mourner behaved. The fact that the person who'd shot Amy had taken the time to write "I love you" in the dirt, suggested it was someone she'd known well. Someone who'd probably be missed if he didn't come to her funeral.

"Who do you think killed her?" he asked.

"Not Cain."

He finished the beer he'd carried in and set it aside. "He was running around the forest alone."

"Not really. Someone else was out there."

"According to him. We have no other witnesses."

"Someone else *had* to be there. They drugged the dogs. Those hounds went silent before Cain ever left the cabin."

"Are you sure?"

"Of course I'm sure," she said, but she wasn't. She hadn't noticed when the dogs went silent; Cain had.

"He was never out of your sight?" Tiger pressed. "Couldn't have drugged them himself while you were in bed or watching television?"

Sheridan remembered how engrossed she'd been in the conversation with her parents, how concerned that Cain might overhear. After he'd walked out of the room, there'd been no noise to indicate his whereabouts for several minutes. Still, she *knew* it wasn't him. "He's not the one who beat me up. So why would I believe he'd create such an elaborate scheme to kill Amy?"

"Because it wasn't elaborate. It was very simple— and you gave him an alibi."

"Stop it!"

"Ned can't place anyone else in the area."

"Cain saved my life, Tiger."

"Or pretended to."

Sheridan couldn't keep the exasperation from her voice. "If he wanted to kill me, he could've done it while I was recuperating. I was out of it for days."

Tiger shook his head. "That'd be too obvious."

"You don't like Cain, do you," Skye said, entering the conversation for the first time since the initial introductions.

"Sure, I like him—for the most part," Tiger responded. "Other times I'm stinkin' jealous of him. But what else would you expect? The woman I planned to marry couldn't get over him enough to commit to me. And he's the reason Sheridan broke up with me in high school, even though she didn't tell anyone at the time. Isn't that right?" He turned to her with an expectant expression.

He knew it was, but apparently he wanted to hear it from her own mouth. Sheridan didn't see the point, but maybe it had to do with some sort of closure. If that was what it was going to take him to forget about their high school involvement and move on, she was more than willing. "Yes."

"And you're still holding that against them both?" Skye cut in.

Tiger chuckled at the censure in her voice. "The male ego is a sensitive thing."

"Apparently *your* ego is," Sheridan said. "You refused to talk to me for months afterward, wouldn't even say goodbye."

"I was determined to punish you, make you sorry

you'd pushed me aside." Growing philosophical, he pursed his lips. "That plan was doomed from the start, of course. You have to care in order to be sorry."

"I was too concerned with other problems by then," Sheridan pointed out. "Maybe you don't remember this amidst all your own pain, but someone had just tried to kill me—and succeeded in killing Jason."

He didn't react to the sarcasm in her voice. "I remember."

"It wasn't you, was it?" Skye inserted.

Sheridan hid a smile. Skye had asked the same question of Robert; she'd probably ask everyone she met.

"Nope. Can't help you there. I really liked Jason."

"And me?" Sheridan drew his attention to the obvious slight.

He grinned. "Not so much at the time."

"So you have a sensitive ego and you hold a *very* long grudge," Skye said.

His voice turned sulky. "No one likes to get dumped on."

"Getting dumped and getting dumped *on* are two different things." Skye looked directly at him. "She liked someone else, so she broke up with you. She had the right. Get over it."

He tilted his head. "I can tell you're the sentimental type."

"In my line of work, I've seen some *real* suffering."

Sheridan noticed that Skye didn't include herself in that category, even though she'd gone through a harrowing ordeal when a man with a knife suddenly appeared in her room in the middle of the night and tried to rape her. "I don't have patience for so much self-pity."

"Ouch," he said, laughing. "Your friend is brutal."

Crossing her arms, Sheridan leaned back with a smile. "You should see her when she's angry."

"So, are you ever going to forgive her for breaking your boyish heart?" Skye asked.

"I don't know." His eyes seemed to focus on the spot below Skye's left eye where her intruder had cut her five years ago. "Some scars are hard to get rid of."

Skye smiled back. "Those are the ones you learn to live with."

The only light in Robert's trailer came from his computer monitor. It grew bright and then dim, and turned from red to blue, creating shifting patterns on the front window. Robert had such an abundance of computer equipment and spent so much time online that he no longer relegated his equipment to the spare bedroom. What he fondly called his "command center" sprawled across the entire living room. Why walk those extra few steps? Why cram a scanner, a regular printer, a color printer, two old monitors, two working CPUs and three that were torn apart, two modems, a power surge protector, shelves of software manuals, electric cords and chargers into an out-of-the-way corner? Robert didn't need a sofa or a coffee table because he didn't entertain, and he didn't have a TV. He used his computer screen to see pirated movies, chat online, hack into various systems and play interactive video games. The digital world was *his* world.

Cain watched the moving image on the window as

he tried the front door. It was locked, but he knew Robert kept a spare key hidden under a rock beneath the wooden steps leading to the entrance. He'd had to use it before, to get Robert a change of clothes when the police picked him up on a DUI six months ago. Robert hadn't been able to get hold of John or Owen and had resorted to calling Cain.

It took only a moment to retrieve it. Then Cain let himself in and frowned at the mess. Apparently, his stepbrother had given up cooking and cleaning. Fast food wrappers and takeout boxes from Sicilian Pizza and Susie's Sandwiches filled garbage cans that over- flowed onto the floor, and beer cans cluttered every surface. But that wasn't the worst of it. The worst was the flies that crawled over the half-eaten food drying on the counter and the ketchup-smeared bath towel tossed over a broken lamp. Robert didn't need to worry about keeping his towels clean; he generally showered at John's so he wouldn't have to do any of his own laundry.

"*Nice,* bro," Cain muttered. For a second, he asked himself why he'd even decided to poke around this cesspit. He knew Robert was weird, lazy and dysfunc- tional, but if Robert had the dark tendencies of a murderer, he was pretty sure there would've been some sign of it before that rifle turned up.

Cain figured he was probably wasting his time—but it didn't hurt to do a little searching while he was here. Clearing garbage out of the way so he could see what lay beneath, he eventually located a cord that seemed like the type used to download pictures. But it wasn't attached to anything.

Studying several photographs of strangers that Robert had enhanced in odd ways and taped to his wall, Cain sat in front of the primary computer and jiggled the mouse to dispel the psychedelic screensaver. The geometric shapes flying toward him dissolved, and Pink Floyd's *Off the Wall* suddenly came on. *Hello... hello...hello...Is there anybody in there?*

Cain jumped at the noise. He would've chuckled at his own reaction, except the computer was asking him for a username and password, and he didn't have either.

He was dead in the water before he even got started.

"What would you think is clever?" he muttered aloud. He attempted a few combinations he thought Robert might use, but he knew he wasn't likely to crack the password. He didn't spend enough time with his stepbrother these days.

With a sigh, he gave up and twisted around in the seat to survey the room. Wondering if he might stumble across a discarded picture of Sheridan, he checked the garbage but came up with nothing. He was about to leave—he didn't need to get into an argument with Robert over invading his privacy—when he decided to take a quick peek at Robert's shoes, just to verify that none of them fit the wear pattern on those footprints on the muddy road and at the creek.

He went to his stepbrother's bedroom and examined the tread on all the shoes he could locate amid the clothes heaped on the floor, but they didn't match the prints that'd been found near Amy's body.

Relieved, he started back down the hall. Robert's bathroom was filthier than the rest of the house. The smell alone made Cain eager to leave. But he paused when he saw that the door to the spare bedroom was closed.

Just to be thorough, he pushed it open—then froze. There was a computer inside. Only this one had four monitors above it, attached to the wall.

And they were showing live feed.

"What's wrong?" John asked, leaning up on his elbow in bed. "You seem…distant."

Karen knew that wasn't good. They'd just made love. But she hadn't expected John to show up tonight, and she'd been watching the clock over his shoulder the whole time. She was ninety minutes late for her meeting with Cain. Surely he'd left by now. "I'm tired, that's all."

He pulled her into his arms for another kiss. "Happy *and* tired, I hope."

She'd be much happier if she didn't have to worry about whoever was sending those notes. *I'll expose you. Just watch me.* Was it Robert? And if so, how far would he go to make sure she didn't threaten his way of life? Would the news of their engagement make him reveal what he knew to John? "Of course. We're going to have a storybook ending."

"It's about time. It's taken me twelve years to convince you that I'm the man for you."

She grinned. "The most powerful bonds are the ones that grow slowly."

"If you say so." He kissed her neck, her collarbone, her lips. "When should we make the announcement?"

"Don't you think it would be best to take your boys aside and tell them first?"

He gazed down at her. "That's a good idea. Do you want to tell them together?"

"I think Owen would be receptive to that. He and I get along well. But Robert?"

Scowling, he let go of her and sat up. He thoughtlessly dragged most of the bedding with him, but Karen didn't complain. It was warm in the room, despite the swamp cooler in the hallway. "Robert will be fine with it," he said.

"Robert doesn't like me."

"Don't start with that. Why ruin the evening?"

Because she had a note in her purse that could ruin more than their evening. She had to handle this marriage announcement right. "I'm just saying I think you should visit with him alone, tell him we're in love and would like to get married. Try to get his blessing."

He pulled on his boxers. "I suppose you expect me to ask Cain for his blessing, too."

"It'd be nice if you spoke to him, made him feel like part of the family," she said as she watched him dress.

"No way. As far as I'm concerned, he can find out when everyone else does."

There was that prejudice again. "Do you *really* think he shot Jason, John?"

"I think he's capable of it, and that's enough for me." Taking his keys from the nightstand, he dropped a kiss on her forehead. "Get some sleep. I'll talk to the boys tomorrow."

Karen listened to him lock up as he let himself out, then she went to the phone and tried Cain's house. He wasn't home.

23

"What the hell?" Cain whispered, gazing at several different views of John's house.

Pink Floyd was singing *I've become...comfortably numb*...but in the next second, the music snapped off. Cain stiffened, wondering if Robert had come home, but he didn't hear any movement. "Robert?"

Nothing.

Returning his attention to what he'd found, Cain sat at the desk and studied each monitor. Apparently, Robert had installed a security system. But why? And why hadn't Cain ever noticed the cameras before?

Probably because he didn't come by very often and wasn't in the habit of looking for such things. Still, Robert must've hidden them well or he would've noticed *something*. The fact they were there at all was astonishing enough—but it was the *reason* for the security system that really stumped Cain.

As far as he knew, John had never been robbed. If Robert was worried about a break-in, why hadn't he put up a camera that focused on his own front door? Robert's computer equipment meant more to him than anything. He spent every dime he made on either hardware or software. And yet none of the monitors showed the approach to the trailer—or covered the trailer at all.

"This is weird."

As Cain watched, a Toyota Prius came down the street shown via a camera filming John's front lawn. Although it was impossible to discern many details about the driver, there were enough streetlights to reveal the color of the car. It was a car Cain recognized. The town librarian, Marian Welton, lived on the corner and drove a charcoal Prius. If Cain could freeze the screen and magnify the picture, he was fairly sure he'd be able to identify her, maybe even read the license plate number.

Was Robert recording all of this or just using these monitors to keep an eye on the place while he was home? So many cameras would require an equal number of recording devices. If the tapes existed, and they were date-stamped, it was possible that his stepbrother had recorded footage of the man who'd kidnapped Sheridan from her uncle's house—or at least his vehicle.

Pulse racing, Cain opened the cabinets beneath the desk that contained the CPU. Nothing there. But a second later, he found what he was looking for in the closet—a tape for each camera and a red light that indicated the system was recording.

"I'll be damned." Why hadn't Robert said anything? What was the purpose of all this?

Regardless, he had to get his stepbrother to let him view the tapes from the night Sheridan was attacked.

But Robert didn't have a cell phone. He wasn't away from home enough to need one.

Back in the kitchen, Cain called Owen. "Where's Robert?"

"What?"

Owen's groggy voice told Cain he'd gone to bed. "I need to talk to Robert."

This time Owen sounded more alert. "What's he done now?"

"I'm not sure."

"Why do you want to talk to him?"

"Did you know about the security system?"

"The *what?*"

"The security system. Robert's watching Dad's house 24/7."

"Oh, that." Owen yawned loudly. "It's nothing, just Robert's new toy. I don't have to tell you what a techie he is."

"Why would he put up a system to monitor Dad's house and not his own?"

"It's nothing, really."

"Then tell me."

"I don't know if you've heard Dad ranting about it lately, but he saw some story on the news that convinced him banks are no longer safe. He withdrew his entire savings and invested it in silver coins, which he's keeping at the house."

"Oh, brother," Cain grumbled. "If he was going to do that, why wouldn't he put it in a safety deposit box?"

"I guess he wants it accessible. He talks like he's preparing for the end of the world."

"How long has Robert had this system in place?"

"Three or four weeks."

"Any chance his cameras might've been recording the night Sheridan was kidnapped?"

"I don't see why not," he said. "But, like you mentioned, those cameras are aimed at Dad's house. How's that going to help?"

"One camera catches a section of the street. It might tell us more than we think."

"I doubt it, but—" he yawned again "—you can definitely ask Robert."

"Do you know where he is?"

Before Owen could answer, headlights bore down on the trailer as a car pulled up.

"Never mind. He just got home."

"Wait…"

Cain hesitated. "What is it?"

"Where are you calling from?"

"Robert's."

"What are you doing there?"

"Snooping," he admitted.

"Shit, don't let him know that."

"I don't think there's any way to avoid it, since I'm standing in his kitchen and he's parking out front."

"Say I told you about the system and you wanted to see it," Owen said quickly.

Robert would refuse to help him if he admitted the true motivation behind his visit, so Cain agreed. "Good idea. Thanks for the cover." He was about to disconnect, but Owen stopped him again.

"Whatever you do, don't fight with him. I really don't

want to drag myself out of bed right now. And I'd hate to see what you could do to poor, stupid Robert."

Cain peered out the window to see his youngest step-brother climbing out of the truck he occasionally borrowed from Owen. "I won't touch him."

"If he's drunk he might get in your face—"

"I said I won't touch him," Cain repeated and hung up just as Robert threw open the front door and let it bang against the wall.

"What the hell are you doing in my house?"

He didn't sound drunk, but the vein popping out on his forehead put Cain on notice that he was more than a little upset. "Take it easy." Cain lifted a placating hand. "Owen told me about the security system, and I came by to talk to you about it."

"Where do you get off letting yourself in?"

"You weren't home, and I wanted to see it."

His stepbrother tilted his head. He seemed to believe this response, but then his eyes narrowed in distrust. "I didn't see your car parked in the drive."

"Because I walked down from Sheridan's." At least that part was true.

Robert dropped his keys on the counter and ditched the anger and suspicion—but not the belligerence Cain encountered even on good days. "That system's none of your business."

"From what I saw, there's a camera angled across the front yard."

Robert went to the fridge and took out a beer. "So?"

"So I'm thinking you might've inadvertently recorded the guy who kidnapped Sheridan."

There was a crack and a hiss as Robert popped the top of his beer can. "You think you're the only one smart enough to consider that, do ya?"

"Quit being an asshole and tell me if it's possible."

"Yeah, it's possible. I burned the footage from that night on a DVD." He raised his beer in a mocking gesture before taking a long drink and wiping his mouth. "But I've already gone over it a dozen times. There's nothing that shows who dragged her from the house."

"Can I see it?"

His glower returned. "I just told you, there's nothing on it."

Cain drilled him with a look. "I want to see it, anyway."

Robert thrust out his chin as if he was tempted to refuse. Then he seemed to think better of it. Shrugging, he actually smiled. "Suit yourself." He crossed to his desk, opened a drawer and rummaged around, closed it, searched another drawer, closed that one too, and eventually located it in his computer. "Here you go, *bro*."

"Good thing you're so organized," Cain said.

Robert made a rude gesture. "That's what your opinion's worth to me."

Cain tapped the DVD with one hand as he jerked his head toward the overflowing trash. "You're going to catch a disease living like this."

Robert propped his feet on a chair. "So what? My *real* brother's a doctor."

Cain chuckled and turned to go but paused at the door. "What does Dad think of the security system?"

"He doesn't know about it."

"You're kidding, right?"

"No, I'm not kidding. He's not worried about anyone breaking in. He'd consider it a waste of money, and I don't want to hear him bitch at me for spending this much."

"Sounds like he'd prefer your help came in the form of a rent payment."

"Yeah, well, I guess we can't all be as self-sufficient as you. Anyway, I'm pulling my weight by watching out for him. He's got a lot of valuables in that house."

Cain wondered if Robert knew that John had proposed to Karen but didn't dare mention it. If John hadn't made the announcement yet, he'd place himself in the awkward position of having to explain how he'd been the first to hear. "How do you like Karen?" he asked instead.

Robert rocked back in his chair. "More than you do."

"What's that supposed to mean?"

"I've noticed how you avoid her."

Leery of the smugness in Robert's voice, Cain continued to act as indifferent as possible. "I don't avoid her. Dad and I haven't been getting along that great the past month, so I rarely see her."

"Don't bullshit me."

"I don't know what you're talking about."

"There's some sort of history between you two."

Shit—Robert knew, or at least he suspected. Maybe this was what Karen had wanted to convey. "She used to be my English teacher. What kind of history are you suggesting?"

"Amy said something strange to me once."

Amy. Cain had never been able to escape her lovesick eyes and grasping hands. She'd given every detail of his life her undivided attention. If anyone had guessed what happened that afternoon with Ms. Stevens, it was her. Simply because she'd always watched him so closely, known him so well, guarded him so jealousy. In the end, she'd even found out about Sheridan. That incident with his English teacher and the encounter in the camper were the only two secrets he'd ever bothered to keep. And now, there was a chance they were both out. "What'd she say?"

"She said she intercepted a note that invited you to come over and 'help out' after school. It wasn't signed, but she recognized the writing."

Amy hadn't intercepted it; she'd probably taken it from his locker. She used to stand over his shoulder to learn his combination. He knew because she'd left him plenty of her own invitations, cookies, pictures of herself. "So? I once earned ten bucks mowing Ms. Stevens's lawn," he said. It was after the lawn-mowing that she'd served him a cold drink and let him know what she wanted by the way she brushed up against him and touched his hair or his arm.

"That's it?" Robert said.

"That's it."

An evil grin curved his lips. "Would she say the same?"

Forcing a laugh, Cain rested his hand on the doorknob. "You'll stoop to any level to break them up, won't you?"

The sudden uncertainty in Robert's face provided a modicum of relief. Cain wished he could say, "The past is the past. Leave it alone and let everyone move on." But Robert would take that for the confession it was, and he wouldn't be content with using it to hurt Cain. He'd go after Karen, which would cause John suffering, too. And for what? The past really was the past. That afternoon had been a one-time foolish mistake made in the stupidity of youth, a knee-jerk reaction to the overwhelming anger he'd lived with in those days. Karen felt terrible about her part in it, too.

"Way to turn it on me," Robert said, belligerent again.

Cain lowered his voice to increase the impact of his meaning. "Bottom line, whether it's true or not, we'd all be smarter to stay away from that one, don't you think?"

Robert shot out of his chair. "Are you threatening to take me down with you?"

"I'm saying that in your eagerness to hurt others, you might wind up hurting yourself. If you love your father, mind your own business and quit digging for dirt." He held up the DVD. "Thanks for the recording," he said and walked out.

24

"I've got something you'll want to see."

Sheridan stood at the door, telling herself that she shouldn't be nearly as excited or relieved to see Cain as she was. But ever since Tiger had left, she'd been keeping an eye on his truck, which was still parked across from the house. "What is it?"

He held up a DVD. "A recording of the street the night you were abducted."

"Where'd you get it?" She stepped aside to let him in.

"From Robert."

Sheridan knew Skye would want to be part of this, but her friend had gone to bed, and Sheridan wasn't about to get her up. It was her fault that Skye didn't like Cain. She'd done too good a job convincing her friends that the mysterious Cain Granger from her troubled past was a playboy, a mistake. But accepting responsibility for Skye's feelings didn't change the fact that, at the moment, Sheridan preferred not to deal with her disapproving glances. She'd told Skye that Cain had changed, but after tumbling out of his house in her underwear, she had no credibility. Skye insisted that Sheridan was seeing what she wanted to see.

And maybe she was right.

Sheridan could smell Cain's aftershave as he passed and was tempted to reach out and touch his arm. She'd missed him. But she told herself that was her sixteen-year-old self talking and kept a two-foot buffer between them as she closed the door and followed him into the living room. "Robert's been filming the street?" she asked when he turned to face her.

"He put up some security cameras a few weeks ago. One of them catches a large section of the street." He gave her a penetrating look, as if he was trying to sense what she was feeling, but she averted her gaze and waved him toward the kitchen, where Skye's computer was set up.

He means nothing to me. I will never be such a sucker again. Even if he'd changed as much as Sheridan believed, her life was in Sacramento. And she had to admit the thought of him with Ms. Stevens upset her, even if that was twelve years ago.

She tried to focus strictly on the subject at hand and not the undercurrent of attraction that seemed to flow so powerfully between them. "What does he need a security system for?"

"He says it's to make sure my father doesn't get robbed." He passed her the DVD.

She checked both sides of it. It came with no case—and there were no markings. "Have there been recent burglaries in this neighborhood?"

"Not that I've heard of. Robert's always loved electronics. It's probably more about playing with a new toy."

She opened Skye's CD-ROM and slid in the DVD. "But why didn't he say something before now?"

"He claims he watched the recording, that there's nothing interesting on it. And I don't know any different, so don't get your hopes up."

She could feel his closeness as she sat down and he bent over her shoulder, looking at the screen. "He's watched it?" she repeated to hide the shiver that went through her when his warm breath stirred the tendrils of hair that'd fallen out of her ponytail.

"Quite a few times, apparently. But that doesn't mean we shouldn't look at it, too. There might be something here that'll trigger a memory for you, or be more significant to you than anyone else."

They fell silent as the image of the street materialized on the computer screen. There was no audio, of course. But a time and date stamp in the bottom left corner showed it to be the evening of the day she'd been dragged into the woods. "The camera's angled away from my house," she said.

"It's supposed to be covering my dad's drive. But whoever kidnapped you had to have had transportation. I'm hoping it caught his vehicle."

"He didn't park in front of the house. I would've seen him as I was putting away my groceries."

"But once he tied you up, he had to have some way of transporting you to the woods."

"Who's to say he didn't drive out of the neighborhood in the other direction, though?"

"No one. We have a 50/50 chance, that's all."

They stopped talking as headlights appeared on the screen. Sheridan held her breath when she saw a car roll into view but released it, once she realized it was only Robert. He pulled into his own drive, then went out of range.

The seconds and minutes crept by as they continued to stare at an empty street. A neighbor walked by with his dog on a leash. Karen came to John's house, went inside for a brief visit, and left. Ten minutes turned into fifteen, which turned into twenty.

"I think it's past the time I was attacked," she said, disappointed.

"When did you get back from the store?"

"Around eight-thirty."

The tape showed eight forty-five, and the street was still empty.

"Let's give it another couple of minutes," Cain said.

"He must've gone out—"

Another pair of headlights lit up the screen. They belonged to a truck. But not just any truck. Once she'd gotten a good look at it, Sheridan shifted in her chair to see Cain's face. "That's Tiger, isn't it?"

There were lines of concentration on Cain's forehead. "Back it up."

She reversed the DVD and played that part again. Sure enough, a vehicle resembling Tiger's traveled down the street—very slowly.

"Can you freeze it?" Cain asked.

It took several tries to get the playback where they wanted it, but soon they were staring at a fuzzy image of what appeared, based on size alone, to be a man behind the wheel of a black 4x4 with a lift kit. "Does anyone else in town drive a black 4x4?" she asked.

"There might be one or two, but—" he pointed to the lower portion of the screen "—see that dent?"

She could, now that he'd brought it to her attention. "Yeah…"

"The white paint on it is from an accident at the Roadhouse. I was there when it happened. That's Tiger's truck, all right."

A hard knot formed in the pit of Sheridan's stomach. "What would he be doing in this neighborhood that particular night?"

"I don't know. It isn't as if he has friends here."

Cain would certainly be aware of it if he did. He'd grown up on this street, still visited on occasion.

She pushed the play button. "Let's see if there's anything else."

There was more—more of Tiger. He drove by three times in the next five minutes, going slower with each pass.

Uneasy, Sheridan rubbed her arms. She'd just entertained Tiger in her living room for thirty minutes and thought they'd made peace. As they'd talked, she'd recognized signs of *some* lingering resentment. But, for the most part, she'd gotten the impression that Amy's death had made him realize how unimportant such petty grudges were.

Or had that been fun and games for him? Was he enjoying the fact that he could attack her one night and sit in her living room like a guest two weeks later?

"You don't think…" She couldn't even finish the sentence. Although it was years ago, she'd been his girlfriend. Surely, he wasn't the one who'd tried to kill her, who'd taken Jason's life.

Cain's whiskers rasped as he rubbed his chin. "Bitterness is a powerful emotion."

Tiger had been bitter—but bitter enough to shoot her and Jason for being together at Rocky Point? "Do you know where Tiger was the night Jason and I were shot?"

"I doubt anyone's thought to ask him. Why would they?"

"I think it's time we posed the question, don't you?"

"Damn right." Cain frowned at the screen. Sheridan had left the DVD running after the third sighting of Tiger's truck, but nothing else showed up. Robert pulled out of the drive about nine-thirty and didn't return before the taped segment came to an end. That was all.

"You told me Robert watched this, right?" Sheridan said.

Cain made a sound of acknowledgement.

"Didn't he find it odd that Tiger would drive by *three* times?"

"I'm sure he can't imagine Tiger attacking you or killing Jason. He and Jason were good friends."

"Maybe that's what enraged him."

"You two broke up months before the shooting."

"That doesn't mean he was over it." Yes, some feelings faded over time. Her brief infatuation with Tiger had disappeared in a matter of three months. She'd only hung on longer than that because they were comfortable together and she didn't want to risk losing his friendship. But sometimes things just were what they were, regardless of the passing days, weeks, months. When she'd first returned to Whiterock, the thought of encountering Cain had evoked a response despite twelve years of having no contact.

Remembering how angry Tiger had been when she broke up with him, how sullen and withdrawn he'd acted afterward, she said, "Maybe he's twisted. Maybe no one knows how twisted."

Cain reached around her to start the playback over again. "Twisted enough to kill the woman he loves?"

As Sheridan watched Tiger's truck pass her uncle's house yet again, she knew Cain was thinking of that note in the dirt. "Maybe he got tired of the fact that Amy wouldn't let go of you and decided this trip to your cabin would be her last."

"I suppose it's possible."

"That he'd do it on your land is even a little poetic, especially the part where he sets you up to take the blame. Maybe he feels you deserve it because you were the obstacle standing between them."

"I don't know how I could've tried harder to get out of the way," Cain said.

Sheridan knew he didn't fully understand Amy's fixation. How could he? As far as she knew, he'd never fallen so hopelessly in love.

But she could relate, to a point. She had too much pride to allow herself to be an unwanted nuisance, but she'd loved Cain almost as long as Amy.

The humid, stagnant air in the four-foot crawl space beneath Sheridan's uncle's house made John sweat. But he wasn't about to open the heavy plank door to the side yard, which was how he'd gotten in. The neighbor next door might see it if he left it hanging that way. Besides, uncomfortable as he was, he was too preoccupied with trying to hear what Cain and Sheridan were saying to step away from the hole he'd drilled in the living room floor.

"That seems like a pretty elaborate system just to protect a few thousand dollars," Sheridan was saying.

"Maybe he has more than a few thousand," Cain responded.

"Why wouldn't he stash it somewhere safer?"

"Owen said he doesn't trust banks anymore. But I don't know when that happened. He's never indicated a thing like that to me."

That surprised Cain? They never even talked anymore. John wished he could cut Julia's son out of his life permanently.

"You're telling me he doesn't know that Robert's installed security cameras around the house?" Sheridan again.

"According to Robert, he doesn't. And, if he did, I think I would've heard *something* about it, if only a complaint that Robert was spending money he should have put toward utility bills or groceries."

"But how could John miss the cameras?"

"Robert hid them well. I scanned the eaves on my way out. It was dark and he was watching from his trailer so I didn't stop, but even knowing they were there, I couldn't find them."

That Robert could be so sneaky made John a little uncomfortable. If he hadn't come across the wrapping materials for that equipment stuffed in the recycle bin outside, he might not have known what Robert was up to.

But it didn't take him long to figure out that recording everything around the house had its benefits.

"Are you going to confront Tiger?" Sheridan asked.

"Definitely," Cain said.

"When?"

"After the funeral tomorrow."

A few minutes ago, John had overheard them say that Tiger had driven down the street a number of times the night Sheridan was attacked. Was it because he'd seen something through the window of Sheridan's house? And, if Robert knew Tiger was around, why hadn't he said so? He could've claimed to have seen Tiger's vehicle without giving away the fact that he had a security system in place.

Cain and Sheridan's voices grew louder.

Holding his breath, John pressed closer to the peephole he'd created, hoping to catch a glimpse of them. They were walking back into the living room, but he couldn't see them yet. The hole didn't give him that much range.

"I don't want to leave you here alone," Cain said.

"I'm not alone. Skye's in the other room."

"Whoever's doing this could kill you both. You realize that."

He and Sheridan had finally come into view. Cain was leaning against the wall with his hands in his pockets, obviously in no hurry to leave, although he looked absolutely beat.

God, he was a tough son of a bitch. No one knew that better than John. He'd never forget the time Cain had challenged him over the funeral arrangements for his mother. John had been trying to save a few bucks. Most kids wouldn't have been paying attention, but

Cain wasn't like most kids. He always paid attention, and he wasn't afraid to insist. He'd basically shamed John into providing what he called a "decent" coffin and a "respectable" marker by saying he'd raise the money for those things himself, if he had to. John couldn't lose the commiseration and support of the whole community. So he'd agreed. But he resented the way Cain had forced his hand, just as he resented most things about Cain.

"It's late," Sheridan was saying above him. "You've got to get some sleep. You're nearly dead on your feet."

Not as dead as John wished. Even when Cain was young, he'd made John's life miserable, but not for any reason John could clearly name. That was what he found most frustrating. Cain's effect on him was so... subtle. He made John feel inferior without even trying. The day Julia and her boy moved in, John had brought home some flowers and a box of chocolates he'd actually bought for another woman, who'd refused them because she'd heard he was getting married. There was no way Cain or Julia could've known the history of those gifts, and yet the moment John gave them to Julia, Cain's eyes had connected with his as if he could read the truth—

John jerked himself out of his thoughts. Sheridan and Cain weren't making small talk anymore. The tone of their voices had changed, grown softer in volume.

"At the restaurant, Karen told him never to contact her again."

"I guess they made up."

"When are they getting married?"

"Sometime in December."

John's heartbeat thudded in his ears. How did Cain know about the wedding? John had just left Karen's. She made it sound as if she hadn't told a soul, and John knew *he* hadn't mentioned it to anyone.

"How do you feel about that?" Sheridan was searching for something deeper than "fine." John could hear it in her voice.

"I'm not sure."

Why would he care? What business was it of his? John ground his teeth, irritated that Cain actually thought there'd be implications for *him*.

Sheridan moved; then John couldn't see her anymore. He could, however, see his stepson's troubled face.

"Is there a reason you wouldn't be happy for them?" she asked. What was she seeking? John wondered. She seemed oddly nervous, as though she dreaded the answer. But why—

Then they were interrupted. "Isn't it getting a little late to be visiting an old friend?"

A third voice came from the direction of the hall and whatever Cain was about to say wouldn't be said tonight.

"Yeah, it's late," he replied. "I'd better go." He turned to Sheridan. "Sure you're both okay here?"

The other woman's strident answer overran Sheridan's. "We're *fine*."

John could see them again. He watched Sheridan put out her hand as Cain opened the door, but let it drop before she touched him. "Good night."

"Night," he muttered and the sound of the door closing echoed in John's brain, along with the question that made him sick with suspicion: Now that he'd finally convinced Karen to marry him—how come Cain was the first to know?

He'd almost told Sheridan. Cain had wanted to open up and share what had really happened the afternoon Ms. Stevens had invited him over to mow her lawn. He'd always been too ashamed to even think about what they'd done. As soon as an image from that encounter crossed his mind, he'd flinch and shut it out, refuse to remember. But he wanted to tell Sheridan before she found out some other way, wanted that chance to explain.

Which made no sense at all. What could he say? It wasn't as if he could deny it.

He hesitated on the front lawn. Whether he told her or not, he wanted to protect her, wanted to *be* with her. It'd been almost impossible to keep his hands to himself while they were standing in the living room. The memory of her soft skin against his was too addictive; he imagined slipping his hand up her shirt to caress her while he kissed her.

But he'd always known she was meant for someone better, someone more like Jason. He'd understood that even back in high school. And yet he'd taken her virginity. He'd known how selfish he was being, even at the time. His determination to ignore her afterward only made matters worse. He could hardly expect her to trust him now.

Recalling the "you're not worthy of her" accusation in Skye's eyes, he forced his legs to carry him to his truck. Sheridan's friend was right; she was better off without him.

With a final glance at the house, Cain got behind the wheel. He saw his father's station wagon at home, parked in its usual place out front so that Robert could get in and out. The lights were off.

Karen was probably asleep, too. She'd either be going to Amy's funeral in the morning or she'd be at school. But Cain needed to hear what she had to say.

25

"Are you mad at me?"

Sheridan stared at the television, struggling to answer Skye in a way that would satisfy her so she'd go back to bed. Sheridan needed time alone. Ever since Cain had left, she'd felt so unsettled. "No."

No? That was the best she could do?

Skye arched an eyebrow at her. "Maybe you could say that again and be a little more convincing."

"I wanted to go home with him, Skye. It's that simple." Sheridan had to fight the urge to drive out to Cain's cabin—and not only because she wanted to sleep with him. She felt as if he'd been reaching out to her tonight, as if he needed her.

But that was crazy. Cain never needed anyone.

Except the night Amy was murdered. Sheridan would never forget the way his hand had shaken as it covered her breast. He'd needed her then—to block out the bad and help him remember the good, to celebrate the pure essence of life. But she wanted something more lasting, didn't she?

"So why didn't you?" Skye asked.

"Because I'm getting too involved with him. It's putting me right back where I was twelve years ago."

"That's not why."

Sheridan watched her friend dubiously. "It's not?"

"No. You would've taken that risk. You didn't go because I'm here, and you feel obliged to stay with me."

Headlights swept along the street. Half hoping it was Cain, although she knew that was highly unlikely, Sheridan stood up to see the car.

"Who is it?" Skye asked.

She recognized the station wagon. "Looks like John's going somewhere."

"This late?"

"I'm sure he goes to Karen's at all hours." Sheridan sat back down and continued to watch television, but Skye interrupted again.

"What I'm trying to say is that I'm not helping you, Sher."

Sheridan suddenly felt guilty. Skye had come halfway across the country, motivated by love and concern, and she couldn't even act grateful. "What do you mean? Of course you're helping me."

"No." Skye twisted her long hair into a knot. "I've come to the conclusion that this is something you have to wade through yourself. As much as I'd like to do it for you, I'm just making things more difficult."

"Don't say that."

"It's the truth. You need to go back to Cain's, see where it leads."

"It'll lead to the bedroom," she muttered.

"You told me he's changed."

"And you told me I'm seeing what I want to see."

"Maybe I was wrong. Regardless, my being here isn't going to save you from him. And he's ready and willing to save you from everything else. I should go."

It wasn't practical to keep Skye away from her family. Sheridan had been aware of that ever since Skye showed up. "I won't go back to Cain's cabin," she said. "Now that I've moved in here, I'll stay and get the house ready to sell, like I promised my parents."

"If you're going to do that, you should take this." Skye went into the kitchen and returned with a Kel-Tec P-3AT semiautomatic handgun.

"I don't want a gun, Skye," Sheridan said, refusing to take it.

"I know you don't like them. But I also know you're a decent shot, and it might save your life."

"What if I'm overpowered before I even get a shot off? Then that gun could be used to kill me instead of save me."

"What's your other option?" Skye asked.

With a sigh, Sheridan took the semiautomatic and placed it under a couch cushion. "Fine."

Skye frowned in disapproval. "You're going to put it *there?*"

"It'll be more accessible. Otherwise, I could be caught without it, wondering where I left my purse. And even if my purse is handy, I'd have to dig around, among all the other junk I've got in there."

"I guess you've got a point."

"So you're leaving right away?" If Skye was relinquishing her gun, she wasn't planning to stay much longer.

"Tomorrow, as soon as I can get a flight." She

laughed, slightly embarrassed. "It's not all you. I miss my husband and my kids."

"I know." Sheridan met her friend in the middle of the floor and gave her a fierce hug. "I'm sorry I'm so torn. I understand how frustrating it must be for you."

"You don't have anything to be sorry about. I've been through this myself, remember? Just catch the son of a bitch who tried to kill you." Skye pointed to the couch where Sheridan had hidden the gun. "And promise me you'll use that if you need to."

"I'll use it," she said.

When Karen found Cain on her doorstep, she became more conscious than ever of their age difference, and the toll those extra years had taken on her body and her face. Maybe it was because they were alone for the first time in twelve years and she'd probably never be completely immune to him. Her reaction had nothing to do with John. She loved her fiancé. He evoked an entirely different set of emotions—peace, a calm contentment and appreciation for his companionship and support. John was the kind of man a woman married; Cain the kind of man she dreamed about.

That was the insight a little maturity had brought her. If only she'd known twelve years ago what she knew now. Back then, she'd cared only about obtaining the object of her desire. She hadn't realized that being with someone less perfect, who accepted her and her flaws, would provide more satisfaction in the long run.

With a quick glance outside to make sure the lights were off in her neighbors' homes, she pulled her robe more tightly closed and gestured him inside. "I'm sorry I couldn't meet you earlier. John stopped by unexpectedly." He'd brought a bottle of champagne to celebrate their engagement. It'd been a sweet, romantic gesture, and they'd made love for the second time in one day, which rarely happened. Maybe because he was older than she was by a decade and a half, John seemed content with sex a couple of times a week. He liked to cuddle or watch TV with her almost as much as anything more physical, which suited her fine. But he hadn't been himself lately. Finding that rifle in Cain's cabin had created a sense of urgency in him, an anxiety that had left him off balance.

Cain stepped inside, his eyes passing over her living room before taking in her appearance. As satisfied as she was with John, Karen wished she was more beautiful, more desirable—even irresistible. She didn't want to be with Cain anymore, but she would've been flattered to see some appreciation in that handsome face, maybe a hint of regret for so easily passing up everything she'd offered him.

Instead, she noticed some very obvious signs that he didn't want to be where he was—the slight rumpling of his eyebrows, the stern set to his jaw, the worry in his green eyes. "What'd you want to show me?"

Tucking her disheveled hair behind her ear with one hand, she raised the other in the classic stop signal. "Wait here. I'll be right back." She hurried to her bedroom, found the note in her purse and brought it to the living room.

His eyes fixed on her engagement ring for a moment when she handed it to him. But then he opened the note.

A second later, his gaze lifted to meet hers. "Where'd you get this?"

"It was on my doorstep when I returned from school today."

"You don't have any idea who put it there?"

"None. But it's not the first one I've received."

His glower darkened considerably. "Where are the others?"

"I burned them. I—I had to get rid of them. I hoped…I don't know what I hoped. That whoever it was would simply stop and it would be over, I guess."

"It's Robert," he said.

She tightened her belt again. "Robert?"

"Amy said something about it to him once. He just mentioned it to me tonight."

"How did Amy know?"

"I don't think she *knew.* I think she suspected."

Of course. She was so hyper-focused on Cain she could almost *smell* the interest of a rival. "And voiced those suspicions to Robert."

He nodded.

Her knees went weak at this news. Robert was the last person she wanted connected with these notes. He competed with her for John's love and attention and resources. He'd use what he knew to destroy her if he could. "He's trying to get rid of me. That's why he's sending the notes. It's a way to scare me off without involving John. But he'll involve him if he has to. I have no doubt of that."

As Cain studied her, she wished he'd give her arm a comforting squeeze or her shoulder a pat—something to indicate he'd forgiven her and that they could at least be friends. She felt like such a fool for making the mistakes she had, for putting herself in this unenviable position.

But Cain didn't touch her. He maintained a very careful distance. "He's not sure," he said. "And going to John could make it look like he's out to get you any way he can."

She couldn't help wringing her hands. "So what do we do?"

"Deny it. If you love John, it's your only choice."

"And these notes? Should I go to Robert, tell him it's not true?"

"No. If it's not him, and he finds out there's someone else who suspects the same thing, it'll give him even more power."

"What if whoever it is won't stop? John could stumble on one of the notes, and then…" She didn't need to explain what would happen "then." They both knew.

"You'd have to do everything you could to convince him it's a lie."

Karen wished there was another way. She wanted to be honest, to confess her big sin and be forgiven, especially by John. Hiding the truth made her feel like such a hypocrite. But John would be hurt right along with them, and he didn't deserve that.

"I'm so sorry I caused this," she murmured.

"My best advice is to forget it." Cain started for the door, but she stopped him with a question.

"Are you in love with her, Cain?"

Karen knew she had no right to ask. But she had to wonder if someone had finally captured the uncapturable. And she wanted Cain to be happy. She thought it might be easier to forgive herself if she knew he'd settled down.

"Who?"

She smiled and shook her head. "You know who."

"I'm not sure I know what love is," he said. But it was merely an evasion. He knew what love was. He'd just never been consumed with it himself.

Karen had a feeling Sheridan was about to change all that.

He opened the door, but she stopped him again. "I'd like to be a friend to you, Cain. If we can ever get to the point where...where we can forget. I don't want to come between you and your family. I'd like to...to facilitate a better relationship between you and John, if I can."

She expected him to continue walking out and shut the door without a response. Or say something cynical like, "You've done enough already." But Cain proved himself more generous than that. Turning, he gave her a half grin. "Marry John and be happy," he said. Then he took her hands and pulled her toward him just long enough to peck her on the cheek. And she stood at the window crying with relief as she watched him leave.

Sick to his stomach, John hid in the bushes as Cain drove away. Karen's porch light winked off, but he didn't move. He remained crouched in the shadows of her yard, listening to his heart thud in his chest. He hadn't been able to see anything, but he'd heard Karen's soft "goodbye" before the door closed. It had been filled with emotion—*positive* emotion.

What the hell was going on? John couldn't think of a single good reason for Cain to visit Karen's house in the middle of the night.

Anger, now a living, breathing monster inside him, drove him to the door. The two of them had to be up to something. What was it? Were they sleeping together?

That thought made John want to throw up. If Karen was playing him for a fool, laughing behind his back while he handed her his heart on a silver platter, he'd make her pay. She'd be sorry.

He didn't bother to knock the way he usually did. He had a key. Letting himself in, he moved as quietly as possible to her bedroom door, where he could see the outline of her body in the bed. She was asleep. Already.

"Karen?"

She rolled over as if he'd startled her. "John?"

"Surprised?" he said.

She didn't reply, and that made him angrier still.

He stepped to the side of her bed. "Aren't you excited to see me? I'm the man you love, remember? Your new fiancé?"

"I wasn't expecting you. What…what're you doing here?"

He could feel her fear. "A better question might be what was *Cain* doing here?"

Silence. "He, uh, stopped by."

"Does he do that often, Karen? In the middle of the night?"

"No." She sat up and shook her head. She seemed frantic to make him believe her, but she wasn't explaining. Why wasn't she explaining?

"Are you going to tell me why? Or would you rather leave that up to my imagination?" *Say something, damn it. Say something I can believe, before I beat it out of you.*

"It's not what you think. He…he wanted to wish us well. That's all."

The breathless quality of her voice caused a muscle spasm in John's cheek. "He drove over here to wish us well," he repeated. What a lousy liar she was. What had he seen in her, anyway? If she cared about him, she wouldn't be lying to him. She wouldn't be entertaining the one person he hated more than any other at three o'clock in the morning. Where was her loyalty?

"I—I called him earlier," she said.

John sat on the bed next to her. "Because…"

"To tell him about our engagement, of course." She laughed, but it came off as unbelievable as all the rest.

"Somehow, I find it odd that you'd want him to be the first to know. We decided I should talk to Robert and Owen before telling anyone, remember?"

She was weeping now, but John felt no sympathy. She didn't deserve his love, didn't deserve the life he'd envisioned for them. "Shh…" he admonished. "Calm down. I'm just asking you to tell me what's going on."

"Please, John." She sniffed and gulped for air. "Try to understand. I—I feel sorry for Cain, that's all."

He laughed. "Then you're one in a million, Karen, because he doesn't inspire pity in too many people."

"Listen to me." Her fingers curled around his forearm. "He loved his mother so much, and…and he lost her."

He stared down at the ring he'd given her. "I'm not

asking you to recite his history, Karen. I only want a reason." He looked into her eyes and enunciated very carefully. "Just one reason explaining why he was here tonight."

She released his arm and wiped her tears, his diamond sparkling as she moved. "The only thing he ever wanted from you was a little love and approval."

"He came over here to tell you *that?*"

"No, I—I called him to...to tell him about the wedding. I didn't want him to think he'd have any less of a chance to...to have a relationship with you... because you were marrying me."

"I don't see the connection." There wasn't one, of course. She was speaking gibberish. What obligation did she feel toward Cain? Who gave a flying fuck what he thought about their marriage?

"Cain was my student, John."

"The truth, Karen," he chided. "We still haven't reached the truth."

"John, please. I don't want to tell you!" she blurted. "Just trust me. Can you? Can you trust me, John?"

"No," he said simply. Not when it was about Cain. He couldn't trust anyone.

Shaking from her sobs, she put her arms around his neck, but he couldn't respond. "Tell me."

"You won't understand. You... It'll ruin what we have. Please, I'm begging you. Let it go! Let's move away from Whiterock. Then you won't have to see Cain. Neither of us will ever have to see him again."

John had ice in his veins. Cold, sludgelike blood that was freezing up his heart, which seemed to be beating very, very slowly…. "You slept with him," he said. "You slept with my stepson."

She froze, as if shocked by his statement.

"That's it, isn't it? You probably stood in line behind all the other women he's been with to have your turn." He got up because he couldn't sit any more. "Was it tonight? How long has this been going on?"

"Nothing's going on!" she cried.

Grabbing the thin fabric of her nightgown, he hauled her up onto her knees. "Don't lie to me! Whatever you do, don't you dare lie! I know you slept with him. I can see the guilt on your face!"

"But n-not tonight. N-not now."

"When?" He dug his fingers into the flesh of her arms, demanding a response.

"A long time ago! It happened *once,* John. We—we haven't been together in twelve years. It was a mistake. That's all. I didn't realize what I was doing. I was confused and Cain came in every day and sat at the back of my class—"

John grasped at fleeting hope. "Are you telling me it wasn't your fault? That he forced you?"

As she stared up at him, the shine of her tears reflected the moonlight streaming in through the window. *Please say yes.* That was all he needed. Then he could blame Cain and Cain alone. Then he could take Karen and her testimony to the police and finally destroy the one person who'd been destroying him, inch by inch, for years.

But she wasn't answering. "Did he rape you?" he shouted, shaking her hard.

Rattled by his rough treatment, she could barely talk. "N-no. It—it was my fault. I...I wanted him. I was confused—"

"You wanted him." John let her go, and she fell back on the bed.

"It was a long time ago, John. It has no bearing on our current relationship. None at all. I've been over Cain for years."

"You wanted him," he said again. "He was sleeping with you while I was going crazy trying to get you just to go out with me."

"It only happened *once*. That was before I knew you like I know you now. That was before I fell in love with you."

He gaped at her. "But...don't you understand? I'll never be able to believe it's really me you want. You're settling. You're settling for me because you know he'd never want you for more than a quick piece of ass. Especially when he could have someone really beautiful. Someone like Sheridan."

She gulped at his words. He'd shocked her with the truth. Well, it was his turn, wasn't it?

"John, I-let's calm down before we say things we'll regret," she said, attempting to gain control of the situation. "I know you're hurt and you want to be cruel. But listen to me. It was a mistake, nothing more."

"Because you refused him afterward?" he asked softly.

He could sense how badly she wanted to say yes. He could also sense the decency in her warring with a desire to blame it all on Cain. "No," she admitted.

"If it was up to you it would've continued."

She didn't respond.

"Answer me!"

"Probably." She'd spoken so low he had to strain to hear her.

"That's rich, isn't it?" John laughed without mirth. "You're the only woman I've ever really wanted, and now I find out you're Cain's sloppy seconds. What am I supposed to do about that? I certainly can't marry you."

She clutched at his shirt. "Forgive me, John. Please. I—I've wanted to tell you the truth for a long time. I've thought about it again and again."

"That's why you called Cain over here in the middle of the night? Because you wanted to tell me?"

"I didn't call him over here."

"He came on his own?"

"No, I—I called him earlier. I needed to talk, to discuss what we should do. And we decided it would be best not to tell. We knew it would only cause you pain and doubt for nothing."

"*We.*"

"Not we, necessarily. *Me.* I didn't know what to do, okay? What happened between Cain and me that one time was just a stupid mistake. Can't you see that? It's over. I love *you.*"

"You don't love me!" He slapped her before he even knew he was going to do it. Her head whipped back with the force of the blow; then her jaw dropped and she stared at him, fingering the mark he'd left on her cheek.

"I hope you feel better," she whispered.

He didn't. Not in the least. He kept seeing her taking off her clothes for Cain, welcoming him into her body, wrapping her legs around his hips and moaning, just as she did for him....

He had to get out of here. If he stayed, there was no telling what he might do.

The telephone woke Cain almost as soon as he fell asleep, but he immediately scrambled to get it. The shrill sound jangled his nerves, made him think immediately of Sheridan. He shouldn't have left her. Had something happened?

"Hello?"

When he heard nothing, his heart jumped into his throat.

"Sheridan? Are you okay?"

There was some noise—like muffled crying—then a whispered, "It's Karen."

Cain glanced at his alarm clock. He'd only been home half an hour, just long enough to fall asleep. "What's wrong?"

"He knows."

John. The secret was out. Taking a deep breath, Cain dropped his head into his hand and massaged his temples. "How?"

"He saw you here tonight. N-nothing I said made any difference."

Other than that small quaver in her voice, she sounded oddly subdued. "What happened?"

She sniffed. "Nothing more than I deserved. Anyway, it's over between us."

"You've had other fights. Maybe he'll come around." Cain didn't really believe it. He'd known what this would mean, to both of them. But he wanted to offer her some hope. She was obviously crushed.

"No. He has too many hang-ups about you. He'll never be able to overcome them," she said and disconnected.

26

Sheridan sat next to Skye in the last pew of the church she and her family had attended when they lived in Whiterock. The funeral service hadn't even begun but already the building was packed to overflowing. The sensational way Amy died had sparked more interest than Sheridan had expected.

She glanced at the people crowded along the back wall.

"Looking for Cain?" Skye asked, interrupting her search.

That was exactly what Sheridan had been doing, but she didn't want to admit it. "Just wishing I could stand up, too. It'd be easier to see everyone."

"Why don't you?"

"You have to ask?" Sheridan gestured at her shoes. "I'd never make it." She hadn't planned on attending anything formal in Whiterock, so she and Skye had had to purchase the clothes they were wearing. Skye had chosen a simple black skirt, white cuffed shirt and black vest; Sheridan had bought a black sheath dress, as well as a strand of fake pearls and strappy shoes. The shoes were far too high to be comfortable for long, but she'd done the best she could with what she'd had to choose from. She was pretty sure Petra, the woman who owned the small boutique in town, had been a prostitute in an earlier life. To her, simple and elegant meant drab. It was all Sheridan could do to get out of the shop without fishnet stockings. "You need…something," Petra had said, frowning at her ensemble.

"So…do you see anything unusual?" Skye asked now.

"Not particularly."

"Tell me who everyone is. The only person I'm sure I know the identity of is the poor woman lying in the casket."

Sheridan tried not to point as she indicated Ned in the front row. "That's Amy's brother. His wife and kids are on his left. His mother is on his right."

"Who's the guy on the platform who keeps looking over at the casket?"

"The one in the tweed jacket and blue tie? That's Cain's stepfather, John Wyatt. You know Tiger, and Pastor Wayne greeted us on the way in."

"I remember. He's the one who said he has an extra bedroom for you if you need it."

Sheridan rolled her eyes. "You gotta love my parents."

Skye laughed. "Aren't you glad I showed up at Cain's house instead of them?"

Sheridan nudged her. "Do you have to keep bringing it up?"

"That's what friends do. I'll be teasing you about it for the rest of your life."

"Good to know."

"Cain's stepfather is quite distinguished-looking, isn't he?"

"I guess. I like the silver at his temples."

"How old is he?"

"Fifty-four or so. The woman he's marrying is quite a bit younger."

"Your former English teacher?"

"That's right."

"Where is she?"

Sheridan couldn't find Karen Stevens. "I don't know. But she's attractive, too."

They lapsed into silence as they waited for the service to start. The door opened and closed several times, but Cain didn't come in. Sheridan picked Owen and his wife out of the crowd. Marshall was with him, and Robert sat in the same pew, looking sloppy despite his tie, which wasn't long enough to reach over his bulging stomach. The police officer who'd questioned her that day in the station was just across the aisle from her, and she recognized several other people, most of whom she hadn't seen in more than a decade. Many of them smiled or waved, but the atmosphere was as subdued as a funeral should be.

"This is just tragic," the older lady on her right murmured to the man sitting next to her. "What's the world coming to?"

"It's really getting hot in here," Skye grumbled over whatever the man said in response. "Are they ever going to start? At this rate, I'll miss my plane."

Sheridan's eyes skimmed over the flower arrangements as a lady at the piano played another hymn. "You don't fly out for three hours."

"Exactly."

Fifteen minutes later, the scent of carnations had become so oppressive Sheridan could think only of Jason's funeral. She'd smelled the same scent there. Five minutes after that, most people were using their programs as fans, but at least the service was getting underway. His features arranged in an appropriately pained expression, Pastor Wayne adjusted the microphone at the podium as he waited for the crowd to quiet down.

The moment he'd finished praying, the door opened again, and Sheridan knew before she even looked that it was Cain. She heard the rumble of voices, could tell plenty of folks had been speculating on whether or not he'd have the nerve to show up.

Sheridan glared at the people who turned to stare at him, but he seemed impervious to their attention. No doubt he'd expected it. She'd heard Ned spouting off about Cain when she and Skye walked in, saying Cain had better watch out because Ned was going to see him in prison someday.

That kind of tough talk made Ned feel as if he was doing something about his sister's death, but it merely proved to Sheridan that he had no viable leads. Otherwise, he would've had something more constructive to say.

She wondered what Ned would think when Cain told him that Tiger had driven past her place three times the night she was attacked. Tiger was probably the only one who knew where to find Amy the night she was shot— because he'd followed her there before. And he had reason to be angry about Sheridan's being with Jason twelve years ago. In Sheridan's opinion, he was as likely a suspect as anyone.

Cain moved to the far corner of the building instead

of trying to find a seat, but if he'd hoped to blend in, he hadn't succeeded. He was several inches taller than most of the other men and far more attractive. He wore black dress pants and shoes, along with a black tie and a crisp white shirt, rolled up at the sleeves. And unlike the rest of them he hadn't been cloistered in the church long enough to start sweating. Sheridan couldn't help thinking how pleased Amy would be that he'd dressed up just for her.

Maybe he wasn't the type to marry and settle down, but he was a good man, Sheridan thought. Regardless of their history, she hoped they could be friends—

She caught Skye watching her with a quizzical expression. "What is it?"

"Nothing," she whispered. "I think he's handsome, too."

Considering how passionate Skye felt about her husband, that was quite an admission.

Sheridan didn't respond because Pastor Wayne was talking about how terrible it was to lay Amy to rest at such a young age. A few people around her were already sniffling, and Ned had broken down again. His wife put her arm around his shoulders to console him. Then it was Cain's stepfather's turn to talk.

"I lost my son twelve years ago. And now I've lost a daughter," he began. "Amy was sweet and unselfish and made Whiterock a better place for having lived here. The most difficult part of this for me, for all of us, is the one question no one can answer at this point. Why?"

When he choked up, Sheridan felt a lump in her own throat. Everyone was taking it so hard.

"He seems like a nice guy," Skye murmured. "Why don't he and Cain get along?"

That was something Sheridan had asked herself many times. "I'd say he blames Cain for Jason's death," she whispered back, "but whatever the problem, it started long before that."

Sheridan noticed Tiger staring at her. His face was puffy, but he wasn't crying, like almost everyone else. He sat there stoically, looking uncomfortable in a new suit that was a bit too tight, waiting his turn.

When Cain's stepfather finished, Tiger got up and said, "I loved Amy and I'm going to miss her. Probably more than anyone. But the only person she ever truly loved was Cain Granger."

This bald admission was hardly the "life portrait" anyone had expected to hear. Or maybe it was *too* true to life. Most of the congregation began to murmur and twist in their seats to see Cain's reaction.

Cain remained where he was, eyes glittering with determination as he withstood their scrutiny.

Then Tiger went on. "Maybe he got sick of her and shot her. I don't know anything about that. But I know she had no business being where she was that night. And I can tell you that he didn't kill Jason."

The movement and noise grew so loud, Tiger held up a hand so he could be heard. "She told me on a number of occasions that he didn't do it, that he'd never do such a thing. And I believe she knew him better than anyone, especially back then."

Ned was on his feet. "This isn't a testimonial for Cain! This is my sister's funeral, for God's sake."

"That's why I said what I did," Tiger told him. "I know she'd want her true thoughts on the matter to come out at last."

With that, he sat down and Skye leaned close. "I don't care whether he drove by the house fifty times that night. It's not Tiger," she said.

Sheridan finally let go of the breath she'd been holding. "I know."

Ignoring all the speculation in the church around him, Cain's eyes sought his stepfather's. Surely after what Tiger had just said, he'd *have* to believe Cain was innocent. But it didn't matter. John had something else to blame him for.

He knows.... Karen's words from last night came back to Cain. At least he was actually guilty of what John held against him now.

Turning his back on the whole congregation, Cain stalked out, hanging his tie on a tree branch as he wound his way down the path to the parking lot. He didn't need John Wyatt, or Owen or Robert or Marshall. He didn't need anyone. Even Sheridan.

Especially Sheridan, he decided. She threatened him on a level no one else could.

Karen stared at herself in the mirror. She hated missing Amy's funeral. But she couldn't go looking like this. John had hit her hard enough to bruise her cheek, and her eyes were red and swollen. Everyone she saw would want to know what was wrong. And the mere question would make her cry. That was why she couldn't go to school, either. She'd taken a personal day just to sit at home.

Using the last of her tissues, she blew her nose for the umpteenth time and turned away from her blotchy reflection. What was going to happen next? She was afraid to find out. She wanted to believe that John would come to his senses and forgive her, but deep down she knew he wouldn't. Her confession had severed the bond they'd formed. She'd seen a side of him she hadn't known existed and no longer felt sure he was the man she'd thought he was. Even if they managed to patch things up, it couldn't last. Cain made him too crazy. John would watch every nuance between them, read far more into their relationship than was there. And he'd use her past sins against her every time he got angry. What he knew would eat at him until the contempt she'd witnessed last night rose to the surface again.

She couldn't expect them to pick up where they'd left off. But she had to at least try to talk him out of ruining her reputation. After so many years, she doubted any D.A. would prosecute her. But if John told anyone, she wouldn't be able to hold her head up in Whiterock. The school board wouldn't allow her to continue teaching. And once the word was out, she suspected she'd never get a job in any other school system, either.

The clock said it was almost two; John should be back from the funeral. Grabbing her purse, she wiped her face one last time and headed out.

As impatient as Sheridan had been with Skye's reaction to Cain, it wasn't easy to let her friend leave.

"You're going to be okay in Whiterock without me, right?" Skye said as Sheridan helped unload her bags.

"Of course," Sheridan said. But she wasn't so sure. She'd driven separately so Skye could return her rental car to the airport, which meant she still had her own car for transportation. They'd found a cell phone store along the way so she had a new charger. She also had the gun Skye had insisted she keep, still tucked under the cushion of her couch. Even better, she was stronger and wiser.

And yet she had plenty of misgivings. Was she foolish for staying? Did she really believe she could solve a crime with no real leads?

"Sheridan?" Skye angled her head to look into her face. Sheridan blinked. "What?"

"Are you having second thoughts? Because if you are, I'll gladly return to Whiterock and help you pack."

"I am having second thoughts," she admitted. "But…I don't think I can walk away from what's happened. As soon as I get home, I'll only want to come back. Maybe it'd be different if I had some confidence in Ned and his force, but…"

"But Tweedledee is dead and now you've just got Tweedledum."

"Skye!"

She raised a hand. "I know, I'm sorry. It was disrespectful. I'm just saying Whiterock doesn't have much of a police force."

"It used to be that they didn't have much crime, either. I want to see my hometown safe again. I want to put whoever attacked me, and killed Jason and Amy, behind bars."

Skye hefted her purse higher on her shoulder. "I can't promise you won't see Jonathan. As soon as he's finished with the case he's working on, I'm sure he'll come out here."

"He's a damn good investigator. I could use his help if he's interested."

"We're all interested. Just busy."

"I can do it."

"I know you can. And I guess now's the time. I've watched you kick yourself for too many years over what happened to Jason not to realize how important this is to you. But, jeez, Sher—"

"I know. Be careful."

"Be more than careful."

"I got rid of that weird flasher guy who was stalking me last year, didn't I?"

Skye's eyebrows shot up. "The guy broke into your house, and you hit him with a can of chili because you wouldn't use your gun. Are you sure you want to use *that* incident to bolster my confidence?"

"That can of chili really hurt! You should've seen the bruise. Besides, he was more odd than dangerous. He wasn't trying to kill me."

"Just don't forget that this guy's playing for keeps."

The eyes that'd stared at her so intently as she struggled to free those strong hands from her throat flashed in Sheridan's mind and sent a shiver down her spine. "I won't."

"So use your gun this time."

"Okay. You've got to hurry," Sheridan reminded her. "You're going to miss your plane."

"Right." Skye hugged her goodbye and started off, then turned back. "What am I doing? I should be staying here. You can't shoot anybody."

An old man who was passing by stopped to look at them.

"She's talking about pictures," Sheridan explained. "I'm a photographer."

Shaking his head, he gave them both a wide berth.

"You have children at home, Skye," she went on. "They need you."

"But I'll never forgive myself if anything happens to you."

"We take these kinds of risks every day. It's our job. It's nothing new. Like you said, Jonathan will come when he can."

An announcement telling travelers to keep their luggage with them at all times came over the PA system. Skye waited through it, still undecided, until Sheridan gave her a little shove. "Go! I'll be home in a couple of weeks, probably before Jon can even finish with his case." She knew that was optimistic, but it was all she could say to reassure Skye.

"I really hope I don't regret this." With a final hug, Skye wheeled her luggage into the terminal. And then she disappeared into the crowd.

"Tell me I'm not crazy," Sheridan muttered as she got back into the car.

Cain hadn't spent much time working since Sheridan's attack, but he wasn't worried about losing his job. He had more vacation days accrued than he'd ever need. And as long as he checked the campgrounds and turned in his reports, he'd be fine. There was no one looking over his shoulder; he'd been part of the agency too long for that. His boss knew he could be trusted to care for this land as if it was his own.

It felt good to be back in the forest. This was where he belonged, where he felt the most clarity and freedom. He wasn't sure how he'd let himself get so caught up in the no-win issues involving his stepfather and Amy and Ned. He'd learned at a young age to avoid such emotional entanglements. But that damn rifle had drawn him in. Amy could've stood by him; she'd known all along that he wasn't the one who'd shot Jason. Instead, she'd let him wriggle on the hook, which didn't really surprise him. It was her own brand of punishment. But he thought it was generous of Tiger to come forward with her real opinion, and to pick a public forum to do it. No one could question Amy's opinion on this because half the town had heard what Tiger said.

Including Sheridan.

Briefly Cain allowed himself to imagine her in that black dress she'd worn with her hair up. She'd looked far too refined for a hick town like Whiterock. He pictured her in a more intimate setting, closing her eyes and parting her lips as he buried himself inside her and, even now, felt himself go hard. She'd always been a distraction, the only girl who was out of reach, the only girl he shouldn't touch.

And yet he had touched her. And that made him crave her all over again.

Koda barked at a squirrel and Quixote and Maximillian gave chase. Cain didn't bother calling them back. They weren't going to catch it. It skittered up a tree, clung to a branch and chattered at them as if mocking their attempt while Cain stopped to look inside his pack. Before he left the cabin, he'd taken his heavy-duty flashlight off its charger—but had he actually put it in with his supplies?

He hoped so. It wasn't dark yet, but he was planning to check the backpacker campsite several miles into the forest, which meant he'd probably spend the night out here. He did that occasionally, especially in summer. There was a lake not far away, and he figured he'd sleep there. With Skye in town, it wasn't as though he needed to worry about Sheridan. There was nothing he could do for her from his cabin, anyway.

Sure enough, the flashlight was right next to the plastic tarp he'd rolled up to put under his sleeping bag.

Perfect. Reclaiming the rifle he'd set on the ground, he whistled for his hounds, stepped over a fallen log and hiked farther up the mountain.

27

John wasn't home. Karen had no idea where he might be. The truck Robert had been using since the accident was parked in the drive, so she knew the funeral was over.

She grimaced as she thought of Robert sitting in his trailer. Was he the one leaving those notes on her doorstep? She considered confronting him. If he hadn't been harassing her, she and John would still be engaged. Her life wouldn't have changed so drastically in a matter of twenty-four hours. But she couldn't go after him. She still had too much to lose. That was why she'd come, why she was growing more frantic by the second.

Would it be too late by the time she talked to John? How many people had he already told? He loved complaining about Cain, loved to paint Cain as the evil stepson, with himself as the long-suffering parent. Would he exploit her secret to serve his ego, even though it would ruin her in the process? She never would've expected such behavior, but she wasn't sure she really knew him anymore.

As she waited in her car at the curb, she bit the cuticles on her left hand. It was an old habit, one she'd managed to break—until now. But she was so nervous she couldn't stop herself. She had to reach him, needed some type of assurance that she wasn't going to become a pariah in Whiterock.

Don Lyons, John's next-door neighbor, drove down the street and waved at her before turning in to his drive. When he got out of the car, she could tell from his formal attire that he'd probably been at the funeral.

She averted her gaze, hoping he'd go into his house and leave her alone. But he didn't. He walked over and rapped on the window.

Cursing silently to herself, Karen rolled it down and looked up at him. "Hi, Don."

"Hi, there." He was smiling but did a double take when he saw her cheek. "Oh, wow, what happened?"

"I walked into a door, can you believe it?" She knew it was a lame excuse, one battered women used all the time, but she also knew he'd never suspect the reality.

"Jeez, that must've hurt."

"It did."

His thin strands of gray hair, which he combed over a mostly bald dome, glistened in the sunlight. "We missed you at the funeral today."

"I haven't been feeling well. My, um, accident's given me a pretty bad headache."

"No surprise there. I'm sorry about that." He bent closer, seemed to take particular note of her red, watery eyes. "Are you okay?"

"I'm fine." If she could just convince John to keep what he knew to himself. "How was the service?" she asked, changing the subject.

He shoved his hands into the pockets of suit pants that

had to be as old as his divorce, which had happened around the time Cain's mother had died, and rocked up onto the balls of his feet. "I think we gave her a good send-off. Amy would've been proud to have such a showing."

"Have you seen John?"

"Not since he spoke at the service. Boy, did he do a great job."

"I'm glad to hear it."

He straightened his tie. "She was like a daughter to him."

"He's mentioned that."

Another neighbor came down the street in a Prius and waved, and Karen decided to get out of her Mustang. She couldn't sit in front of John's house, chatting with his neighbors. She'd skipped the funeral because she didn't want to be seen.

"I think I'd better wait inside. I'm feeling a little light-headed." She was pretty sure Don had been in the middle of telling her about something Tiger had said when she piped up with that random comment. But she was too preoccupied to feign interest. She longed to go where it was quiet and dark and she could be alone with her worries.

"Can I get you an aspirin?" he asked. "A glass of water?"

"No, thanks. I'll talk to you later," she muttered and left him standing on the lawn, staring after her.

Letting herself into John's house with the key he'd given her months ago, she breathed a sigh of relief once the door was closed. But only a moment later her throat grew tight and she began to cry again. This place was so familiar to her. Although they'd spent more time at her house, she'd expected to move in with John someday....

She stood at the piano and studied the array of pictures he had displayed there. Mostly, they were of the kids when they were young. Jason in his football uniform. Jason in his soccer uniform. Jason in the old car he'd bought with the proceeds of his after-school job. Jason grinning as a six-year-old boy, missing his two front teeth. There was one small photo of Owen when he'd graduated from med school, one of Robert at a science fair, and one of her and John at a restaurant. But there wasn't a single photo of Cain or his mother— which was a bit ironic, considering the piano had belonged to Julia.

"I bet you hated having to leave your son," she murmured and set the ring John had given her right beside Jason's picture.

From there, she rambled through the house, looking for ways to distract herself from the gut-wrenching worry— until she saw Robert through the side windows. She suspected he was coming around the house to the front door, so she ducked into the garage. She didn't want to face him, didn't want to have to explain the large bruise on her cheek or admit that her relationship with John was over. Robert would be all too happy to think he'd achieved his goal; she couldn't deal with that in addition to everything else.

"Karen?" He called her name from somewhere close to the garage door. Then he moved farther away. "Karen?"

Her car was out front. Had he spotted it as he came onto the porch? It didn't matter. If he didn't find her, he'd have to assume she'd merely parked it there and left with John or someone else, wouldn't he?

It sounded plausible to her. But he seemed so darn determined to continue looking for her.

"Karen? I know you're here." He was just on the other side of the door again. "Where are you?"

She slipped into John's little workroom as the door handle began to turn. Then the light went on. "Karen?"

She held her breath. She definitely didn't want him to catch her now. He'd know she'd been hiding from him.

Closing her eyes, she said a quick prayer that he'd go away, and a few seconds later he went back inside.

Breathing a sigh of relief, she sat on John's workbench and stared at the mess. John wasn't the type to do any major cleaning. He kept the main rooms of his house devoid of clutter by tossing everything he didn't want around into the garage, which was so full of junk he couldn't fit a car inside. He also used the back bedroom as a storeroom. It was a miracle he could find *anything* when he needed it, she thought as she eyed the vast assortment of boxes and tools, extension cords, holiday decorations that probably hadn't been used since Julia died, car-cleaning supplies and—

Her eyes returned to a shovel propped against the wall in the corner. Most of the gardening tools were piled next to the side door, where John tossed them when he finished the yard each week. But finding a shovel here wouldn't have been odd in and of itself. What drew her attention was the handle. It appeared to be covered by a dark substance that looked an awful lot like...*blood?*

Curious, and more than a little surprised, Karen maneuvered through all the junk littering the floor in order to get a closer look. But she stopped before she reached it. There, sticking out behind some shelves not far from the shovel, was a black ski mask.

Without Skye's reassuring presence, Sheridan knew it was going to be too difficult to go back to her uncle's house. Just thinking of being alone there reminded her of the way the floor had creaked right before she'd turned to see a man wearing a ski mask standing in her kitchen. Obviously, she'd been unrealistic when she'd told Skye she wouldn't move. Gun or no gun, she'd already changed her mind.

But where was she going to go? To Cain's? Or to a motel?

She knew which place she preferred, but she wasn't at all sure Cain would be pleased to see her. He'd left the funeral early, and she and everyone else had seen his tie hanging on a tree as they came out of the church. She didn't know what that signified, but she had a feeling it wasn't good.

Her cell phone rang. She dug it out of her purse, then glanced at the LED screen, frowning when she saw it was her parents. They'd definitely have an opinion on where she should stay....

Using the hands-free device she'd bought when she purchased her new charger, she punched the Talk button. "Hello?"

"There you are," her mother said. "Where've you been?"

"What do you mean?" It wasn't as if she hadn't kept

in touch. She'd called her family twice in the past three days, just to let them know she was safe.

"We've been trying to reach you all day. Your sister just had her baby."

"That's wonderful! How's the new mom?"

"Great. She was only in labor for eight hours. And you should see little Evangeline. She's so beautiful."

"How much does she weigh?"

"Nine pounds—can you believe it?"

"That's a big baby."

"They should've induced a week ago. I tried to tell her doctor, but he refused to listen to me."

Sheridan wanted to get her mother off that particular tangent. "But the baby's healthy?"

"Perfect. She's got a head of dark hair, just like you did when you were born."

Sheridan felt a twinge of envy. At twenty-four, her sister was married and already had a baby. And here she was at twenty-eight, fighting rapists and murderers— hardly conducive to family life.

"I'm thrilled for Leanne. How did Kyle handle the whole coaching experience?"

"He turned green and nearly passed out when they asked him to cut the umbilical cord. So I got to do it," her mother said proudly.

"Good for you!"

"How are things in Whiterock?"

Since her day had been spent attending a funeral and putting her best friend on a plane, Sheridan thought things could be better. But she didn't want to ruin her mother's excitement. "Fine," she said quickly.

"Do you have any leads on the man who attacked you?"

"A few," she hedged.

"You're not staying with that Cain Granger, are you?"

That Cain Granger? The way her mother referred to Cain irritated her, but she preferred to avoid an argument. And because she hadn't decided what she was going to do, Sheridan told her mother what she wanted to hear. "No."

"That's good. Because an old friend called just before I left for the hospital this morning and had the nerve to imply you're sexually involved with Cain—and that you were when you were younger, too. Can you believe it? I told her she must have you mixed up with someone else."

Sheridan caught her breath, wondering how to respond. Fortunately, she didn't have to. Her parents were still basking in the afterglow of their first grandchild's birth. Someone said something in the background, which distracted her mother. Then her father came on the phone.

"How's my girl?" he asked.

"Hanging in there. You?"

"We've had a bit of excitement today."

"That's what I hear. How are the in-laws behaving?"

He lowered his voice. "Leanne is ready to strangle Kyle's mother. But his dad's okay."

"What's wrong with his mother?"

"She's a bit…overpowering."

"In what way?"

"She's rearranged the furniture twice. All the comfortable chairs are in the living room now, where you can't see the TV. And she reorganized the cupboards. Leanne can't find a damn thing."

"Sounds like fun."

"Marriage is a give-and-take," he said with a sigh and Sheridan smiled because she knew he was thinking of his own mother-in-law.

"Give Leanne my love."

"You're coming here soon, aren't you?"

"As soon as I can."

"I'll tell her," he said.

Sheridan was still smiling when she hung up, but she sobered as soon as she spotted the turnoff to Cain's place. What was she going to do?

She told herself to drive right by and get a room at the motel. But she slowed and put on her blinker anyway.

Karen couldn't have said how long she stood there, staring at the ski mask. She was trying to convince herself it was merely a coincidence that she'd found this…this thing in John's workroom. But she couldn't. Her mind was throwing up questions—questions she was almost afraid to answer. Where was he the night of Sheridan's attack? Were they together?

Now that she took the time to think about it, she remembered him telling her he had to work late. She'd stopped by to bring him a coffee and discovered his station wagon parked out front. But he wasn't around. When she'd mentioned her visit the following morning, he'd told her he'd gone for a walk. Then he'd launched into all the other stuff that'd happened later, with Robert crashing into the garden shed and Owen coming over to check out Robert's injuries.

She picked up the mask, noticed some dots of reddish

black, now dried and crusty, around the cutouts for the eyes, nose and mouth and immediately dropped it. Blood spatter?

Her stomach churned as she looked at the shovel. What did these things mean? Sheridan had been beaten by a man who'd started to dig her grave, a man wearing a ski mask. But that man *couldn't* have been John.

Could it? What reason would John have for hurting anyone, especially Sheridan? Logic suggested she'd been attacked to keep her from sharing anything she might've remembered about Jason's murder. That was what the police believed. There'd been a story about it in the paper. But John was convinced he knew who'd killed Jason, and he definitely wanted Cain to be caught. Sometimes it was all he talked about.

Did he want it badly enough to frame him? That had to be it. John would never have hurt Jason himself. He'd worshipped that boy. So the two incidents were connected but not as directly as everyone thought.

Still…angry as John was with Cain, much as he might want revenge, he wasn't a violent man.

Or was he? She touched her cheek, and the memory of John's rage caused goose bumps to rise on her arms. He'd wanted to hit her again. She'd seen it in his eyes—

A car pulled into the drive. Karen could hear the engine, then the slamming of the door. Was it him? Who else could it be? Robert was already home.

Heart pounding, she wondered what to do. She couldn't confront him with what she'd found. She might not live to tell about it if she did. She had to get off the property without being seen. She'd always known John was obsessed when it came to his stepson, but until this moment she hadn't understood the depth and breadth of that obsession.

Forcing herself to retrieve the mask, she stuffed it into her large purse. Ned would want to see it and, even though she hated what this would do to John, she had to turn it over to the proper authority. She couldn't allow a man who'd done what he'd done to remain free.

As her fingers came into contact with the rough-feeling droplets on the knitted fabric, she shuddered. That had to be Sheridan's blood.

Obviously, John would stop at nothing to see Cain punished.

John had spotted Karen's car the moment he turned down the street, but he wasn't happy that she was at his house. What did she think she was doing? He'd told her it was over, and he meant it. He'd never forgive her for making such a fool of him. As if their encounter hadn't been bad enough, when he'd gotten home last night, he'd found a typewritten note on his doorstep: *Cain was Ms. Stevens's pet for a reason.*

Those words indicated that someone else knew. And if that was true, it was only a matter of time before everyone did. She'd allowed Cain to humiliate him, and his shame would soon be public.

Just the thought of being embarrassed like this was driving John crazy.

The house was unlocked, but Karen didn't answer when he called her name—Robert did.

"Where is she?" he asked as soon as his youngest son

appeared at the entrance to the hall. For some reason, Robert had been in the back bedrooms.

"I don't know," Robert said. "I can't find her."

"Are you sure she's here?"

"That's her car out front, isn't it?"

"Maybe she's talking to one of the neighbors."

"No, I saw her come in."

Via the security cameras. Of course. "Maybe she went back out and you missed it on those little monitors of yours," he said wryly.

If Robert was surprised he knew about the surveillance, he didn't show it. "If anyone ever tries to break in, you'll be glad I have those monitors."

"I'm already glad. Someone left a note on my doorstep last night. I want you to tell me who it is."

"I-I'm not sure the cameras picked that up."

Doubt caused John to take a closer look at his son. "Sure they did. They pick up everything, right?"

Robert flushed but didn't respond.

"You know, don't you? Who was it?"

Again, no answer.

"Robert, you're going to show me those tapes, so I'll see for myself soon enough."

"Fine, it was me," he admitted, hanging his head. "I-I don't have proof, but Amy once told me she thought Cain and Karen were involved, and…I thought you should know."

He couldn't have made him aware sooner? Before he'd bought an engagement ring? "Your note was a little late. She'd just told me herself when I found it," he said.

"She did? And—"

"And we broke up, so you can be happy about that."

"I wasn't trying to break you up."

"Right," he said, letting the sarcasm that boiled up inside him drip onto the word.

"Dad—"

"Just tell me where it is." What kind of game was Karen playing?

"I don't know, but she's here somewhere. I saw her arrive, but she didn't leave."

Motioning for Robert to hand him the phone, John dialed her cell and was rewarded by a barely audible jingle.

Coming from the garage.

28

Karen's cell was in her purse, along with that ski mask and a million other objects. She had no chance of finding it and silencing it before the sound gave her away. So she acted on instinct. Ducking out of the workshop, she tossed her purse toward the side door, which stood open to the backyard. The resulting clatter told her everything had spilled out as it fell, but she didn't have time to worry about what she might lose. She'd already stepped into the workshop and hidden behind the door.

Someone came into the garage—she didn't know if it was John or Robert. Her cell phone still chimed, despite hitting the concrete floor. She could hear rustling as someone navigated the mess and picked it up.

Pressing a hand to her chest as if she could slow the galloping of her heart, Karen squeezed her eyes closed. *Please think I dropped it as I ran. Please go out after me.*

"What's going on between you and Karen?"

Robert was asking the question. His voice came from the entrance to the house, so she knew it was John who finally silenced her cell. "We broke up."

"Why?"

He didn't answer right away. Karen could hear him

moving around and guessed that he'd walked over to the side door to search for her. "Damn."

"What's wrong?"

"She's gone."

"Are you going to tell me what happened?"

His voice grew angry, strident. "She's been screwing Cain. That's what happened."

Anger made Karen's eyes and mouth fly open at the same time. That wasn't true! She *hadn't* cheated on him.

"When did that start?" Robert asked.

"Twelve years ago, when Cain was in her class."

Karen nearly whimpered. Robert hated her. If he wasn't the one who'd already known, he knew now. This was all she needed to seal her fate. Her future in Whiterock was ruined.

"Somehow that doesn't surprise me," Robert grumbled.

"Why?"

"Something Amy said."

John cursed. "And you didn't tell me?"

"Cain denies it."

"Of course he denies it. He's lying. They both were. God, I hate them. I'll hate them till the day I die."

A tear slipped down Karen's cheek. John had asked her to marry him only yesterday. How could one mistake, one mistake twelve years ago, destroy everything he'd ever felt for her?

"So…if you're not together, why'd she come here?" Robert asked.

"That's what I want to know." Someone, probably John, pushed the garage door opener and the gears began to grind. "Her car hasn't been moved."

"Maybe she left on foot."

"Must have."

"What's this?" Robert had come into the garage.

Karen held her breath, knowing instinctively what Robert had found, but John wasn't paying attention. "She'll be back."

"Look here," Robert said. "Where'd this ski mask come from?"

That got a reaction. There was some more movement; John, when he spoke, sounded as if he was just on the other side of the Sheetrock wall. "Where'd you get that?" he asked Robert.

"It was hanging out of her purse."

No response.

"That's weird, isn't it?" Robert probed. "That she'd be carrying a ski mask in the middle of summer?"

"Maybe she was trying to get rid of it for Cain."

There was a moment of shocked silence before Robert reacted. "Whoa! You really think so?"

"You know the kind of effect he has on women," John said. "They'd do anything for him."

Sheridan found Cain's house dark and locked. The dogs were gone, and so was his truck.

She sat out on his porch for almost an hour, wondering whether or not to head into town, but decided to see if she could get inside instead. She knew he wouldn't mind. He was the guardian of this forest, taking care of anything sick, injured or frightened.

She missed him and his care.

Hanging his tie, which she'd retrieved from the tree

at the church, on the front doorknob, she walked around the place. Several windows were open to catch the breeze. But she didn't want to ruin any screens by trying to get in through a window, and the back door was as tightly locked as the front. She thought she might find a spare key at the clinic, but it was locked, too. The windows there weren't even open.

Disappointed that she'd made the trip for nothing, she got back in her car. But just as she drove out of the clearing, she remembered Cain's old cabin. He'd said he used it on occasion. Maybe he'd be there. And even if he wasn't, she figured it was about time she examined the scene where that rifle had been found.

Karen stayed where she was for at least fifteen minutes after John and Robert had left. They'd lowered the automatic garage door and flipped off the light, so she was crouched in darkness, but that shovel was only three feet away. Positive that it'd been used to dig Sheridan's grave, she was too terrified to emerge. John had the ski mask—he knew she'd found it. And Robert believed it had come out of her purse. With all the prejudice and suspicion surrounding Cain, and the string of women who'd fallen so hard for him, how was she ever going to convince Ned that she'd discovered the mask in John's garage? John would claim she'd been planting it for her lover, as he'd suggested to Robert—that she was striking out because he'd broken up with her.

And Robert would be right there to back him up. No doubt they'd say the same thing about the shovel. Even if it originally belonged to John, there was nothing to prove that he was the only one who'd ever touched it. Cain *could* have used it. He'd grown up in this house and definitely had access to it.

Think! She had to devise a plan before John remembered that shovel, came back to remove it and found her cowering in his work shed.

But she was too nervous and scared to form much of a plan. She trusted the evidence—still quaked with fear, having experienced John's violent rage last night—but she loved the man she'd thought he was. There were moments she felt sure she was crazy, assuming such terrible things.

That doubt could get her killed. She had to leave and get ahold of Cain or Sheridan, someone who'd believe her.

Grabbing that shovel, she moved cautiously, trying to keep quiet as she made her way through the mess. She was tempted to pause long enough to search for her phone and her wallet, but because there were no windows in the garage, it was far too dark to see such small items. She was better off leaving them behind, for now.

The backyard appeared to be empty. She waited at the open side door, listening for sound or movement, but heard nothing. Stepping out into the late-afternoon sun, almost blinding after the darkness, she squinted against the glare and put her head down. She couldn't go to her car. She no longer had the keys. They were lying on the garage floor somewhere, or John had taken them. She suspected the latter. It was going to be tricky, but she had to get down the street to Sheridan's house before John or Robert could spot her.

It was only a few doors away. She could do it, she

told herself, and opened the gate. But no sooner had she passed through than a hand darted out to grab her elbow. And she knew that touch so well she didn't even have to look up to realize it was John.

The old cabin was locked up, too, but there was only a piece of plastic covering a window that'd been broken at some earlier time. Sheridan easily pried the tape away, then rolled a log close to the building so she could climb in without cutting herself. She fell on her butt but was pretty proud of herself for sustaining no injuries.

Dusting off her hands, she got up and looked around. She'd landed in the living room on a wood floor not far from a potbellied stove. The kitchen was part of the same room. A quick peek in the back revealed two bedrooms and a bathroom. Both bedrooms were being used for storage.

As she'd expected, this cabin was smaller and more primitive than Cain's new house, but it had a futon couch that folded into a bed, a bucket of wood by the stove, and some matches and a jug for water on the counter. Not a bad place to camp out, she decided, and started looking for access to the cellar, where Cain had told her the rifle was found. She'd searched for outdoor access already and found nothing.

A small door off the kitchen led into a sort of lean-to designed to keep the extra wood dry. She poked her head into it, figured there were probably more rats and spiders in that pile than she wanted to deal with, and almost went back inside—until she spotted the outline of a small door with a latch. Kicking aside the few logs that'd tumbled off the main pile, she unlatched it and opened the door so that it rested against the house.

Wooden stairs descended into darkness. She could feel the cool, damp air wafting up toward her. It was a refreshing change from the heat and humidity of the day, especially what she'd endured in that church during the funeral, and the earthy smell was equally inviting. Only the dark put her off. This cabin didn't have running water or electricity, like Cain's new place. She needed a flashlight.

Returning to the kitchen, she went through cupboards and drawers until she came up with one. The beam was dim, which meant the battery was low, but a weak beam was better than no beam at all. She took it with her as she went back into the lean-to and descended into the dank, dark space beneath the cabin.

Karen tried to jerk away, but John was too strong. "You must think I'm an idiot," he said.

She didn't know where Robert was. She didn't see him. She just reacted. Raising the shovel she was carrying, she swung it at him like a bat.

The metal end made a sickening sound as it struck him in the head. Obviously, she'd surprised him. His eyes widened, then rolled back and he crumpled to the ground.

Karen had no idea how badly he was hurt. But she couldn't risk having him wake up and grab her, so she turned to flee—and ran right into Owen as he was coming across the grass.

"Stop! What're you doing?" he cried.

Tears rolled unheeded down Karen's cheeks. She

knew she looked like a maniac. She'd dropped the shovel when she hit John and was desperate to escape. "He—he tried to kill me!" she shouted. "He tried to kill Sheridan Kohl, too! I—I found his mask and the—the shovel, and he…he hit me last night!"

She was spilling it all out, but maybe she wasn't making any sense. Owen didn't seem as shocked as she'd expected. He frowned as his gaze dropped to his fallen father, then he beckoned her toward his truck.

"Come on," he said. "I'll take you to the police."

Handmade racks lined the cellar walls, racks that held wine, preserves, canned tomatoes and pickles. Sheridan was pretty sure Cain hadn't canned the food himself. He'd probably bought it from Ron Piper, who owned a farm on the outskirts of town. Ron grew more food than his family could eat, so his wife and kids sold produce all summer via a little stand on the highway. What they didn't sell, Sandy and her girls preserved. Some of her recipes were becoming legendary, so she'd taken to selling the canned goods, too.

Sheridan picked up one of the jars and held it in front of her flashlight. Sure enough, it bore the Piper Farms label. Cain had obviously raided these shelves—there wasn't a lot left. Or, more likely, the boys who'd found the rifle had broken some of the jars just for the hell of it. The smell down here suggested spoiled food.

Angling the beam of her flashlight into the corners, Sheridan tried to figure out where the gun had been. Perhaps Owen had simply leaned it up against the shelves. But that didn't make sense. Wouldn't he try to hide it?

And then she saw a patch of dirt where there'd been some digging. Maybe the rifle had been buried. It seemed possible, considering the recently disturbed earth. But why would two teenagers start randomly digging in a cellar?

The floor above her creaked. Wondering if she'd imagined that noise, Sheridan held her breath and listened. Because of what had happened to her already, she knew she was jumpy. But discounting her reaction didn't stop the chills that ran through her. Did she have company?

No. She had an overactive imagination.

But then she heard another creak and another.

Yes. Someone was walking across the kitchen.

Karen didn't know she was in trouble until Owen steered his truck right instead of left as he drove out of his father's neighborhood.

"Where are you going?" she asked.

He locked the doors. "We've got a problem."

She knew they had a problem. His father was homicidal. They needed to go directly to the police station. Instead, they were heading into the mountains. Why? There was nothing out this way except wilderness.

And then other details began to occur to her. Owen had left his father lying on the ground without even attempting to get help, without even stopping to see if John was still breathing. He'd heard what she had to say and hadn't questioned it, even though it must have sounded crazy. And he'd picked up the shovel she'd dropped and put it in the back of his truck.

Turning, she saw it vibrating in the bed of the truck

as they drove. Maybe that should've alarmed her from the beginning, but she'd been so shaken by what she'd just discovered, she'd thought Owen had the same idea she did—that the evidence needed to be shown to the authorities.

"Take me back to town!"

He didn't look at her. "I'm afraid I can't do that."

She glanced at the shovel again. She was sure it had been used to dig Sheridan's grave. Was it now intended to dig *her* grave? "Why not?" she asked.

"Because you've been snooping around, haven't you, Karen? You've been sticking your nose where it doesn't belong."

"That was *your* mask."

No answer.

"You put those things in your father's workroom so they wouldn't be on your own property."

"It's not like I was setting him up," he said, as if he was more offended by that accusation than the accusation of attempted murder. "I just didn't think anyone would look there. I mean, who'd ever suspect him of hurting anyone?"

She had. She'd seen how John had reacted to the news about her and Cain and assumed the worst.

"Who'd think twice about any of the junk in that mess?" he went on. "I don't know how he functions in such a chaotic environment. He and Robert." He shook his head.

"And Cain?"

"Cain's not like the rest of us. He's not related."

"Is that why you didn't mind setting *him* up?"

"He deserved it. He *asked* for it."

She wondered how quickly she could unlock the door and get it open. Would she have any chance if she jumped? They were gaining speed, going at least forty miles an hour. But he'd have to slow down once they hit the winding part of the road. That was probably her one opportunity. There'd be rocks, branches, pinecones, trees and stumps all along the shoulder. But if she got lucky, if she hit a soft patch, she might survive the fall.

"Don't even think about it," he said mildly.

She released her seat belt. "Why not? It might be my only chance."

"I'd find you and kill you anyway."

"What about Jason?" She wanted to distract him, keep him talking while she searched for another opportunity. "Did you kill him, too?"

He didn't answer.

"Did you shoot Jason?" she repeated.

"Cain shot Jason."

She inched closer to the door. "That's not true, and you know it. Cain didn't shoot anybody."

His gaze slanted her way. "Of course I wouldn't expect you to believe me. You're one of his many conquests, after all. My dad told me at the funeral. He was very upset, you know. He said you fell for Cain just like Amy did. And Sheridan. I thought she was different, too good for him. But no…she proved herself to be no better than the rest."

"Is that why you did it? You were angry that Cain had been with Sheridan?"

"No, I was disappointed in her. I thought someone would finally put him in his place. But Sheridan had nothing to do with it."

"Who did?"

No answer.

"You're not going to tell me?"

"You wouldn't understand even if I did. You have no idea what it's like always living in someone else's shadow."

"Cain casts a big shadow."

"Cain?" He laughed. "Cain's shadow wasn't half as big as Jason's."

"You were jealous of Jason?"

His knuckles whitened on the steering wheel. "You would be, too, if you saw how my father worshipped him. Robert couldn't do anything right. I could see why he might pale in comparison. But Jason wasn't nearly as smart as me. I skipped *two* grades, for crying out loud. I graduated from med school at twenty-two. You'd think my dad would be proud of that."

"He *is* proud of you, proud of what you've accomplished. Why would you ruin it? Why would you take the one thing he—" She caught herself, but Owen finished for her.

"The one thing he really loved?" He chuckled bitterly. "You understand more than I thought."

"No. I can't comprehend how one brother can kill another, regardless of what his father thinks. There's something wrong with you, Owen. You have to get help."

He looked wounded. "There's no need to be unkind," he said. "This isn't personal."

"Living is personal to me."

He smiled. "That's a good comeback. I've never been quick with that sort of thing. Maybe that's why Dad liked Jason better. Jason had a quick comeback for everything."

"Maybe he liked him better because he wasn't a psychopath."

"You're making me angry," he said, but she couldn't have told from his voice. He spoke in the same monotone he always used.

Karen could feel the metal of the door latch against her upper arm. "If it was Jason you wanted, why'd you shoot Sheridan?"

"I couldn't make it too obvious. I'm not that stupid."

"But you went after her again when she returned!"

"That was Ned's fault. He told me she knew something she wasn't saying. He told me she was going to crack the case. And I'm still worried that might be true. You never know what little detail might give the truth away. If she remembers something, I could be in trouble."

"So you decided to make sure she never did."

"I have a family now," he said. "I have a successful practice, too. I can't go to jail."

"And what about Amy?"

Regret flashed across his face. "Amy got in the way. I didn't want to kill Amy."

"They'll catch you this time, Owen. Robert was home when we left. He might've seen us together."

"I'm sure he did. He's got the whole exterior of my dad's place on camera surveillance. Did you know that?"

This surprised Karen. She'd never seen any cameras during her many visits. But it explained how Robert had known with such certainty that she'd gone into the house and not over to a neighbor's. "What're the cameras for?"

"He's protecting the place from burglary. Dad has most of his money in silver, sitting right there in the house, in case you weren't aware of it." He adjusted his rearview mirror. "They're both a little weird, if you ask me. But I'm not one to point fingers."

Karen stared longingly at the passing landscape. "Weird?" she echoed weakly.

"That was a joke," he said. "Funny, huh?"

Karen didn't find it funny at all. She found it terrifying. "If you hurt me, you'll go to jail, which is exactly what you're trying to avoid."

He smiled confidently at her. "You got into my truck on your own. It wasn't as if I dragged you in. And the cameras will prove it."

"They'll also prove that you were the last one to see me before I disappeared."

"So they'll come around to ask why. And I'll simply tell them that you and my father were fighting—the tape will show that, too—and I got you out of there before you could swing that shovel again."

"It won't be that easy. They'll want to know why you weren't more concerned about your father."

"It won't be that hard, either. I'll say I could tell he wasn't seriously injured. They'll believe me because I'm a doctor. And Robert was there to look after him."

They probably would believe him. As far as Ned and the police were concerned, he'd have no motive. She and Owen had always gotten along just fine; it was Robert who'd never liked her.

"Even if they suspected me, they'd have to prove it," he added.

And he was too smart to leave any evidence behind. He'd gotten away with two murders already.

They came up on another truck that was going much slower, and Owen put his foot on the brake.

"Aren't you going to pass them?" Karen wanted him to do something that might attract the driver's attention. If the driver looked over at her, maybe she could signal to him.

"I'm not in a hurry," he said. "People get sloppy when they hurry. I'm the kind of person who likes to take his time."

Her fingers twitched, wanting to reach for the door handle. But the truck was still going too fast. She needed Owen to either speed up, so she could get the attention of the driver in front of them, or slow down so she could jump. "Where are we going?"

"Not far. Any little side road will do."

Panic surged through Karen. He intended to kill her. And he didn't have a twinge of conscience about it. She could imagine him talking about her as distantly as he did Amy. "It was unfortunate, but she found the shovel and the ski mask so I had to take care of her…."

Grabbing the steering wheel, she jerked it to the right. He cried out and tried to fight her off, to straighten the tires.

Karen heard the squeal of brakes, smelled burning rubber as they spun. Then she saw the steep drop-off falling away to the river below, just before he got the truck under control.

They were both breathing hard as they came to a stop in the middle of the road. Fortunately, there was no one behind them. Gratitude for that filled Karen with hope, gave her the presence of mind to go for the door handle.

But Owen grabbed her and punched the gas pedal. They lurched forward, gaining speed as they wrestled.

Somehow, he managed to fend her off, drive and pull a gun from under his seat almost all at the same time.

Karen's heart jumped into her throat. She saw her mother standing over her, kissing her goodbye before sending her off to kindergarten, the principal of her high school as she was awarded her diploma, her boyfriend in college laughing as he tackled her under a tree, Cain sitting in her class, doodling, John smiling as he proposed. The images rushed toward her in the split second she realized she was about to die.

Then the gun went off.

29

Cain had spotted Sheridan's car out front. He knew she had to be here somewhere. But he couldn't see her anywhere inside and, other than the plastic that was missing from the window, nothing seemed disturbed. He wished he hadn't let the dogs go home ahead of him. They'd smelled familiar ground and been so eager to run he'd given them the whistle that sent them off before they'd reached the old cabin. When he didn't arrive behind them, they'd eventually backtrack, but they weren't here now and he could've used their incredible sense of smell.

He poked his head into the woodshed attached to the kitchen and saw that the cellar door was open, but it was completely dark inside.

A sick feeling settled in the pit of his stomach as he went to retrieve his flashlight from the backpack he'd left on the counter. Was Sheridan in that hole? Someone had been here; he knew he'd closed the door when he'd cleaned up after the kids who'd broken in and vandalized the place—and discovered that rifle.

If she was down there, what would he find? Sheridan

on the ground, bloody and bruised and nearly dead, like she'd been in the woods?

Or would she *be* dead this time?

Why had she come here? And where the hell was Skye and that trusty gun of hers?

Snapping on the flashlight, he went back to the cellar door and angled the beam down into the hole. He couldn't see anyone. But neither did he find a body.

"Sheridan?"

"Cain?" A wan light went on as he descended the stairs, and he sighed in relief. She was wedged into the corner between two shelves. How she'd managed to get into such a tight space, he had no idea, but it wasn't easy for her to get out.

"What're you doing here?" she asked.

He'd planned to stay out in the woods, to escape all the turmoil that recent events had caused inside him. But it didn't bring him the peace it used to. He'd changed since Sheridan came to town. All he could think about was her. "This was on my way home. I was heading back."

"You scared me!"

"I could say the same! Do you know what I imagined when I couldn't find you upstairs and I saw the cellar door open?" His voice was a little too gruff, but he'd been so busy fearing the worst that his heart was still pounding.

"It must not've looked good."

"No." Someone else could've run into her here—the man who'd nearly buried her the night Cain's dogs went crazy. That was what upset him so much. "You shouldn't be running around out here alone. It's not safe."

"I just wanted to see where those kids found the rifle.

It's odd that they uncovered something so well hidden, without doing any damage or rummaging around the place or anything."

"They did plenty of damage. I cleaned it up."

"Oh."

"Where's Skye?" he asked.

"She went home."

"I thought she was going to stay. At least for a while."

"She wanted to. But she has a young family and a lot going on at The Last Stand. And our partner, Ava, is new. There's no way she could handle our cases as well as her own, especially the ones where she was coming in late on the action."

"You should've gone with her," he said.

She stared up at him, her eyes defiant. "Is that what you want? You want me gone?"

"I want you safe."

Her flashlight dimmed and went out. Cain had his pointed at the ground. "And if I'm gone, then you're safe, too, is that it?"

He'd be safe from the worry, safe from the fear. And maybe he wouldn't think about her every time he closed his eyes. "I'm safe, regardless. You're just another woman to me." He scowled and looked away, hoping to appear as indifferent as his words, so she couldn't read that statement for the lie it was.

"You haven't changed? Making love is still all fun and games to you? You won't invest any emotion, won't form an attachment?"

It was safer to let her believe he was that shallow. Then she'd go away and never contact him again. And he wouldn't be tempted to risk more of his heart than he'd ever risked before. "Quit blaming me," he said. "You've known all along that I'm not the kind of man you need."

She frowned at him. "Did you sleep with Karen Stevens?"

He didn't answer.

"Cain?"

"What do you think?"

"You did."

He wanted to tell her how much he regretted it, what a mistake it had been, but he refused to hide behind excuses. "That's right."

"Recently?" she pressed.

"God, give me some credit." He turned to go up the stairs, but she grabbed his arm.

"If I don't mean anything to you, what's wrong with here and now, Cain? Why not take what you want one more time? What do you have to lose?"

Everything. He lost a little more of himself with every touch, was already consumed by the thought of her. "I'm not in the mood."

She lifted his hand to the soft flesh of her breast, and he felt his body instantly react. It was all he could do not to back her up against the wall.

"You're going to get hurt, and then you're going to blame me," he said.

Her voice held a mocking note. "What makes you so sure you won't be the one to get hurt this time?"

He knew better than to rise to the challenge, but his libido demanded a different answer. "Don't say I didn't warn you," he said and snapped off his light.

* * *

Owen was breathing hard as he stared at the blood spatter on his passenger window. Karen's death wasn't supposed to go like this. He'd hoped to take her out into the forest, where he could shoot her without worrying about being seen or heard. Instead, he'd made a mess in his truck.

Checking to make sure the vehicle ahead of them hadn't seen them spin out and stopped to help, he got back on the road. He definitely didn't want to be straddling the highway when the next driver came up behind him. Not with a dead woman slumped in his passenger seat.

He glanced at Karen. Boy, had she surprised him. He'd never expected her to be so strong. She was almost as strong as Sheridan. But he'd been lucky in one regard: he was pretty sure the incident had gone unobserved.

Problem was, the bullet had traveled through her chest and lodged in his seat. How was he going to explain that?

He told himself he'd think of something. First things first. Stay organized. And that meant he had to dispose of the body before he got distracted by other concerns.

Giving the truck enough gas to come up to a reasonable speed, he laid the gun in his lap as he tried to decide where to dump the body. He had a shovel. He could go someplace and dig a shallow grave. But that would take a lot of time. The night he'd tried to bury Sheridan was too fresh in his mind. Digging was harder than he'd realized for a man who wasn't used to physical labor. And he had so much to do. He had to clean his truck, hide that bullet hole in the seat and invent some kind of excuse for Karen's disappearance—all before his wife began to wonder where he was.

He needed a place where he could get rid of the body fast without worrying about being observed. A place where it wouldn't be found until he could cover his tracks.

He smiled as the obvious occurred to him. Now that Sheridan was staying in town, Cain's focus was on her. Which meant Owen could dump Karen in the cellar of Cain's old cabin and leave her there until Lucy fell asleep tonight. He had a key; Cain had given it to him years ago.

Yes, that would work. Later, he could get "called to the office." As the town's only doctor, he was on duty 24/7. His wife had quit trying to keep track of him at night.

The darkness embraced Sheridan seconds before Cain's arms went around her and his mouth crushed hers. He kissed her with soft, pliable lips, meeting her tongue with his as his hands slipped up the back of her shirt. "You think you're tough, huh?" He sounded breathless as he kissed her neck, cupped her breasts.

She caught his bottom lip between her teeth. "I'm as tough as you are."

He laughed. "I don't doubt it. Should we go up to the futon?"

"No." She liked it right here, where it was so dark neither of them could see. There was something erotic about such absolute blackness, about darkness so thick it felt tangible. She could throw her head back and cast all reservations aside because she didn't have to worry about giving too much away.

"This is no place for a nice girl."

"I think I've already proved I'm not so nice."

"You don't mind getting messy?"

"I like messy." Her hands were under his shirt, too. She closed her eyes as she swept her fingers over his flat stomach, traced his pectoral muscles and explored the ropey muscles of his neck and shoulders.

He pulled his shirt off, and she didn't bother using her fingers anymore. She used her mouth.

"You make me so hot," he whispered.

She moved lower, which became the trigger that threw everything into fast-forward. They couldn't get naked fast enough, couldn't touch enough, couldn't get close enough. He paused only when their clothes were off, and he was lifting her onto him. She sensed a strange hesitation, a desire to say something. But she didn't want to let him think, didn't want to let herself think, either. Wrapping her legs around him, she pulled him inside her.

"That's what I want," he said.

"I want it, too," she whispered. But then it hit her: Birth control.

"Cain?" she gasped.

His face was buried in her shoulder while he supported her weight. "What?"

"What about a condom?"

He stopped, but the way he squeezed her bottom told her it hadn't been easy for him. "Don't you have anything in your purse?"

"No."

"Do we really need it?"

She thought he was joking. "Unless we're willing to risk a baby, we do."

She'd said it flippantly, but he remained serious. "Would you trust me that much?"

Sheridan stiffened in surprise. "What did you say?"

"You heard me."

"We've been over this. We're talking about a lifelong commitment, Cain. I'd want to keep the baby."

"I understand that." His chest rose and fell as he recovered his breath. "I won't leave you high and dry. You know that, don't you?"

She clung to his shoulders. "But you already got stuck with this problem once. You don't want to do it again."

"This isn't the same."

"How's it different?"

He touched her forehead with his own. "I was lying when I said you don't matter to me." He hesitated, as if his next words were difficult, but that made them sound all the more sincere. "I'm in love with you."

Sheridan didn't know how to react. It was the last thing she'd expected to hear. "Cain…"

"I tried to warn you."

"You told me I was going to be hurt."

"You probably will be hurt. I make a terrible husband."

"It's been eleven years since you were married. And you were so young. How can you say that?"

"Because it's true."

"At least you're good in bed," she teased. "We'll always have that."

He took her words for the cue they were, only this time he moved much more slowly, drawing it out. "So what do you say? Wanna make a baby with me?"

It was probably the most reckless thing she'd ever

done. They lived across the country from each other, and she had no idea how they'd work out the logistics. Would he move to California? Would she move to Tennessee? How would her family react? Was this something he'd said in the heat of the moment? Would he want to marry her ten minutes from now?

She didn't know the answers to any of those questions. But she knew she wanted Cain's baby. He was the only man she'd ever loved. And, after twelve years, she'd only fallen harder.

"Yes," she said and then he finished so tenderly she knew he wasn't going to change his mind.

John wasn't sure exactly what hit him. All he knew was that Karen had been there one moment and was gone the next. "Where'd she go?" he muttered and realized from the frustration on Robert's face that it wasn't the first time he'd asked.

"You must have a freakin' concussion," he said. "I told you! Owen took her somewhere."

They were standing in Robert's trailer, but John couldn't remember walking there, and he couldn't clear his head enough to think straight. Pain radiated from behind his eyes; he had to squint just to see the screen Robert was trying to show him.

"He's right there." Robert pointed to a grainy figure crossing the front lawn. "That's Owen."

"I see him. But where's his truck?"

"It's not in the picture. I'm guessing he parked it across the street."

"You weren't there?"

"I was watching for Karen to come through the house, like you told me to."

"So..." John struggled to recall if he'd asked this before. "Did you see her hit me?"

"No! When I came out, you were lying on the ground and there was no one else here."

He gingerly touched the swollen lump on the side of his head. "What'd she hit me with?"

"A shovel, I think." He touched one finger to the screen. "Owen picked up something right here." He froze the playback. "That looks like a shovel to me."

John couldn't argue with that. It looked like a shovel to him, too. But why would Karen be carrying a shovel? "Where are they now?"

Robert's eyebrows drew together. "I don't know. Owen's not picking up his cell phone. He's not at home. And he's not at the office."

Robert was getting at something. That much was becoming clear. "So?"

"I'm worried."

"Why?"

"That mask we found in her purse?"

John finally conjured up the knitted ski mask in his mind. "Yeah?"

"It had blood on it."

"She wouldn't hurt anybody." He remembered the news she'd imparted last night. "Not physically, anyway."

"I'm not sure the mask belonged to her, Dad."

"It probably didn't. She's covering for Cain." Cain was the bad guy here—had been since he was a kid. But he wouldn't get away with the things he'd done. John was determined to attain justice. He'd sit in the crawl-space beneath Sheridan's house all summer if he had to, but he'd eventually see or hear something that would put Cain away.

"What if it wasn't Cain, Dad? What if…what if it was Owen?"

John gaped at his son. "What reason would Owen have for shooting Jason, for God's sake?"

Robert stared at his feet for several seconds, then raised his head. "If you want a reason, go take a look at the piano."

"The *piano?* What are you talking about?"

"You worshipped Jason. Owen could never compete, Dad. Not at anything. Neither could I."

Owen's cell phone rang. He didn't want to answer it. He had too much to do, needed to stay focused. But he was almost out of range, and he knew it would be smarter not to go missing for that long. "Hello?"

"Owen?"

It was his father. "Hi, Dad."

"Where are you?"

"Driving around, looking for Karen."

There was a slight pause. "Why are you looking for her?"

"It was the craziest thing," he said. "I was walking up to the house to visit you, and she came running out of the backyard, screaming. She had a big bruise on her face and she was obviously hysterical, so I had her get in my truck."

"You didn't see me there? Lying on the ground?" he cut in.

"I saw you, but I knew she couldn't have hurt you too badly and that Robert would take care of you. I knew you wouldn't want the neighbors to hear what she was yelling. I planned to take her to the office and give her a sedative, calm her down and see if anything was really wrong with her, but when we were driving to town, she jumped out of my truck. By the time I got turned around, she'd disappeared into the trees, and I've been looking for her ever since. I'm wondering if she was attacked by the same man who beat Sheridan."

There was a long silence. Then John said, "Have you called Ned?"

"No. To be honest, I'd rather find her first."

"Why?" His father pounced on the statement, but Owen wasn't worried. When he was finished, there'd be no evidence linking him to this crime, either.

"Because she was claiming *you* hit her, Dad. I didn't want her telling that to Ned."

"Owen, quit looking for her and come home. Do you hear me? Come back right now."

Owen frowned and glanced at the clock. He needed more time. "What did you say?"

"I said come home!"

"My phone's cut…out…. I'll…later." Owen punched the End button. Then he smiled at the bloody mess that was Karen. "He'll buy it," he told her. "He hates Cain so much he's blind to everyone else. I can get away with this, no problem. I walked right into the hospital where Sheridan was—and walked out again while everyone was searching for the man with the wig. I swear I'm invisible sometimes. I'm whatever I have to be. I'll fix this." He winked even though she was no longer alive to see it. "You just watch me."

30

Cain lifted his head from the futon where he was lying naked with Sheridan, and kissed her forehead. After making love in the cellar, they'd gone upstairs, where they could be more comfortable, and fallen asleep. The sun was going down, so it had to be at least eight-thirty. "Hey, we gonna sleep here for the rest of the day?"

"Mmm…" She snuggled closer. "Maybe."

"But I missed dinner. And sex makes me hungry," he said.

Although her lips curved into a smile, she didn't open her eyes. "Then you must be starving."

"I am. And I'm not interested in the granola I put in my pack. What about you?"

"Sex makes me tired."

He carefully eased himself out from beneath her. "Fine. You stay here and sleep while I run home and make us something to eat. By the time you wake up, I'll have a picnic ready."

"Sounds good," she mumbled.

He went back to the cellar and brought up their clothes. Then he dressed and covered her with the blanket that had been folded at their feet. "Where're your keys? It'll be faster if I drive."

"I left them in the car. I wasn't planning to stay long."

"See you soon." He started for the door, then turned back to look at her. He was going to marry her. Even a few days ago—certainly a few weeks ago—the idea of marriage would have panicked him. But he'd made the decision in a moment of clarity during which he realized he'd never felt this way about another woman.

It didn't matter how quickly he'd made the decision. Or whether or not she was pregnant. He wasn't frightened at all. The only thing that scared him was the thought of *not* being with her.

"He's gone," John told Robert as he hung up the phone.

"Is he coming back?"

John didn't think so. "He's looking for Karen."

"Where is she?"

"I don't know." It didn't make sense that she'd jump out of Owen's truck and run into the trees. But nothing made sense anymore. Not since last night. "It's Cain. It *has* to be Cain," he muttered.

Robert frowned at his bank of monitors. "I'm not so sure. I'm the one who first found that rifle, Dad."

John's muscles bunched with tension. "What are you talking about?"

"I didn't know it was the gun that killed Jason. All I saw was a rifle in Grandpa's storage. And I didn't see any point in letting it sit there and rust. I thought I'd use it for some target shooting now and then. So I took it and put it in my trunk."

"How'd it wind up in Cain's old cabin?"

"I was as surprised as anybody. It just disappeared one day. That's another reason I put up the security system—to prove when I was home and when I wasn't. I was scared to death someone would use that gun and I'd be blamed because my fingerprints were all over it. I never dreamed Owen had taken it."

"You think he's the one who hid it in Cain's cabin?"

"That's right. And he wiped it clean. When those kids came across it, there were no prints—except for theirs."

"How does that prove Owen put that gun in the cabin?"

"Cain came to me a little while ago to ask where I'd gotten it in the first place. He said Owen told him he'd found it in my trunk, recognized it as the one that'd belonged to Bailey Watts and hidden it in the cabin. But the police hadn't tested the rifle yet, Dad. Only the person who'd used it would know to get rid of it right away—would know for sure that it was the gun that killed Jason."

John didn't want to hear this. He was tempted to walk out. But he couldn't. He'd craved the truth for too long. "No! That rifle went missing before Jason was shot with the same type of weapon. This town isn't so big that rifles go missing every day. Owen guessed, that's all."

"Then why didn't he say anything to me when he found it?"

"He was probably afraid *you* were to blame," he said, grasping for an explanation. "So he got rid of it." Owen wasn't the type to hurt anybody. He didn't have Cain's temper, Cain's confidence or Cain's strength.

"But after that I found a picture of Sheridan stuffed under the seat of Owen's truck."

"That doesn't mean anything, either."

"It was taken not long ago, through the window of her uncle's house. He was watching her, and she didn't know it."

"So? She's a beautiful woman, someone he knew in high school. Sometimes a marriage can begin to feel… confining. Everyone fantasizes now and then."

"But someone had stabbed a pen through her face— then crumpled the photograph. You wouldn't do that unless you hated the person. But Owen's always said he liked Sheridan."

John felt as if he were falling, spiraling down into a bottomless pit. "Maybe he's not the one who defaced the picture."

"Then who did? Lucy never drives his truck."

"Doesn't mean anything," he said numbly.

"I've been telling myself that, too." Robert let go of an audible sigh. "But there's something else."

This was it. John could sense it coming. "What?" he said, his voice cracking as he forced the word out.

"The footprint they got from that tennis shoe?"

"Owen's not the only size ten in Whiterock."

"But today at the funeral, I asked Lucy what she had planned for the rest of the afternoon. She said Owen had to work but she was going shopping in Nashville."

"Go on," John said, bracing for the worst.

"I asked her what she was looking for." He took a deep breath. "And she said 'Owen lost his tennis shoes. He asked me to pick up a new pair.'"

John could feel the sweat running down his back. "How does a grown man *lose* his tennis shoes?"

"Exactly."

Cain's dogs were milling around the yard as the sun set, waiting for him. "Too tired to come back for me, eh?"

Quixote barked and trotted over, and Cain scratched his ears, which brought the others. He spent a few minutes giving them the attention they demanded, then stood. "I suppose you're all hungry."

Their tails wagged at the mention of food.

Cain fed them and put them in their pen. He was pretty sure he and Sheridan would be staying at the old cabin, and he'd rather not worry about the dogs taking off after a raccoon.

"Rest up," he told them, then found his tie on the doorknob and chuckled as he went in.

His phone rang while he cooked, but he ignored it. There was no one he wanted to talk to. And he was enjoying the anticipation of presenting his meal to Sheridan.

As he finished and began loading everything into grocery bags, however, the phone was ringing again. And this time it wouldn't stop.

"What the hell?" he muttered and finally walked over to answer.

"Hello?"

"Cain?"

It was his stepfather. Cain's hand tightened on the receiver. After the past few weeks, what could John possibly want with him? "Yes?"

"Where have you been? I've been trying to reach you for over an hour."

"You're lucky I picked up now. Why are you calling?"

"It's Karen."

"I don't want to talk about her. Whatever she told you is whatever she told you."

"Listen to me." The strangled sound of John's voice made Cain's heart beat a little faster.

"What is it?"

"She's gone."

"Well, she's not over here," he said. He was on the verge of hanging up, but John's sense of panic was genuine enough to make him hesitate.

"I…I'm afraid something might've happened to her."

Cain sank onto the couch. "What makes you say that?"

"She got into the truck with Owen more than an hour ago."

"So?" Cain could barely hide his irritation. He had Sheridan waiting for him. He wanted to be with her instead of dealing with these same old suspicions.

"I think Owen's the one who shot Jason."

Cain sat without moving. Surely he'd heard wrong.

"Are you listening?" John asked.

"I'm listening," Cain said. "But you must be losing your mind. First it was me, and now it's Owen? Owen wouldn't hurt anybody." Cain had briefly wondered, when he'd first learned how that rifle found its way into his cabin, but he'd never actually *believed* it.

"I hope you're right. Oh, God… But I'm at Karen's and…she's not here. No one knows where she went. She was last seen getting into Owen's truck."

This wasn't an apology for misjudging him. So what was it, exactly? "Why are you telling me?"

"I saw something on television once. About killers."

Killers... The word sounded so strange coming out of John's mouth, especially in relation to Owen. "I'm waiting."

"They often return to familiar ground."

"Which means..."

"Owen put that rifle in your old cabin. He took Sheridan to your land."

"If he has Karen, you think he might be bringing her *here?*"

"Somewhere close by. It's possible. I don't know where else to look. Robert and I have been all over town. Can you check the forest? It—it might be our only chance of saving her life."

He was serious. As hard as it was to process what he'd just heard, his father's heartbreak came through clearly, convincing him. *What would it be like to wonder if your son was about to kill the woman you loved?* "Has anyone seen Owen's truck?"

"It was spotted leaving my neighborhood. Lyle Porter said he had a woman with him, couldn't tell if it was Karen. But I know it was. Lyle told me he turned toward the mountains."

The mountains... "I'll call you later," Cain said and hung up. He wanted to help Karen, didn't want to see anyone else hurt. But if Owen was anywhere near his place, he didn't want Sheridan sleeping at the old cabin alone.

* * *

Sheridan heard the car pull up, was surprised Cain had returned after only thirty minutes. "It feels like you just left," she murmured. But she was glad to have him back. It was dark now. She didn't like being here alone after dark. And she was getting hungry.

When he didn't come in right away, she got up to see if he needed help carrying in their dinner and saw that it wasn't Cain at all. It was Owen. The cabin light in his truck gave her a glimpse of him just as he was climbing out.

Ducking so he wouldn't see her naked, she scrambled to dress and smooth down her hair. She thought she'd be lucky to repair her appearance before he knocked at the door. But she didn't hear from him even after she'd finished.

What was taking so long?

Another peek through the window told her he was getting something from his truck, so she went out to give him a hand. "Hey, stranger, what're you doing here?"

She expected him to say that Cain had suggested they meet here. Or that he'd been looking for her because Ned had discovered something new about the investigation. She expected anything—except what she saw.

Obviously, she'd caught him unawares. He turned and stared at her, then quickly tried to shove whatever he'd been wrestling with back inside his truck. But he lost his hold, and it fell against him, knocking him back into the door, which opened wider. Then a body tumbled out onto the ground. Although it was unnaturally limp and covered in blood, Sheridan was close enough to recognize it in the pale glow of the same interior light that had let her identify Owen.

"Ms. Stevens," she breathed in absolute astonishment.

Owen didn't respond. He stepped over Karen as if she were nothing and reached inside his truck. But Sheridan didn't wait to see what he was after. He'd killed Karen. He was probably the one who'd nearly killed *her*.

That thought galvanized her into action, and she took off for the forest. She knew better than to go back into the cabin. He'd only corner her there, and she didn't have a weapon. Skye's gun was at her uncle's place, under the couch cushions. She might've regretted leaving it there, but putting it in her purse wouldn't have helped. Her purse was in the rental car, which Cain had taken.

Unfortunately, she didn't have any shoes, either. The soles of her feet screamed in pain with every pinecone, sticker and sharp rock she landed on, which hampered her ability to move very fast.

She could hear Owen charging through the trees behind her. He was quicker than she'd expected. And she knew from experience that he was stronger than he looked.

Her lungs pumping like pistons, she ignored the pain in her feet and dodged right, then left, threading her way through the trees toward Cain's new cabin. He was her only hope. She couldn't outrun Owen indefinitely, not without protection for her feet. And maybe not even then. She wasn't back to full strength.

"Stop! Let me explain," he called after her.

Explain why he had a bloody corpse in his truck? Hell, no! She kept running.

Like her, he was already winded. "I didn't…hurt you when I…fed you that…soup…did I?"

Because she'd recovered sufficiently that it would've been a little obvious had she died in his care. He wasn't stupid enough to give himself away. He'd been biding his time, waiting for a safer opportunity.

"Sheridan?"

Her name weighed on her like lead.

"Do I...have to...resort to...other tactics?"

Cain's cabin was too far away. She wasn't going to make it.

"Are you...listening? I'll kill...Cain!" he threatened.

She believed he was capable of it. But at the moment it wasn't Cain's life that hung in the balance.

"It'd be...easy. All I'd have to do is...knock...pull out a gun...and shoot."

Sheridan blanched at the image his threat created. But how did she know Owen wouldn't do it regardless? He'd proven he had no conscience.

Tears came to her eyes, blurring what she could see of the ground, but she forced herself to keep running. Afraid that leading him to Cain would only get Cain killed, she was heading away from both cabins now, plunging so deep into the forest that the canopy of pine trees towering overhead completely blocked out the moonlight. She could no longer see the obstacles in her path. Branches caught at her clothes and scratched her face, reminding her of the sheer terror she'd faced in this same forest weeks before—terror and pain she'd experienced because of the man chasing her now.

Soon her legs felt so heavy she could barely lift them. She wasn't going to make it out of here alive. She had to do something else, think of some way to stop him.

Ducking, she grabbed a handful of whatever her hands came up with—dirt and rocks and leaves—and threw it to the left. Then she cut immediately to the right and hunkered down behind the wide base of a tree.

Owen was still coming. She could hear his footsteps drawing closer and squeezed her eyes shut as she tried to smother the sound of her own labored breathing.

Please, God. Help me...

He slowed, then stopped. She imagined him listening for her, trying to determine what direction to take. But he didn't fall for her ruse. He started batting through the trees nearby, feeling his way....

Sheridan was tempted to move. He was too close. Fear insisted he'd find her if she stayed, brought to mind what he'd done to her last time. The club...the digging...the rain...

But as much as she wanted to scramble away, darkness was her only protection. Darkness and silence. She couldn't move, couldn't make a sound.

"Sheridan..." He tried to regain his breath. "Don't be stupid. This doesn't have to be so hard."

She clamped her teeth down on her bottom lip. He was *so* close. Barely two feet away. Could he see her somehow? It felt like it, even though she couldn't see him.

"If you don't come out right now, I'll have to kill Cain. And I don't want to do that. Contrary to how the rest of my family feels, I've always been fond of him."

She hunkered lower, praying that something would frighten him away. The movement of an animal, the flashlight of a neighbor. She kept seeing Karen Stevens's sightless eyes staring up at her.

"Sheridan? Do you *want* me to shoot him? You're forcing my hand, I hope you know that."

Thump, thump, thump… Each heartbeat vibrated through her whole body.

"Fine. Have it your way," he said and stalked off.

Sheridan waited until she could no longer hear him, then rested her head against the tree as her tears fell. The hoot of an owl sounded somewhere overhead, an eerie call in the darkness, but at least Owen was gone. She was safe as long as she stayed where she was. But it was too easy to imagine what Owen might do to Cain. Cain wouldn't be expecting it. He'd open the door to his stepbrother and then…

She whimpered at the image of a bullet hitting him the way a bullet had struck Jason. She'd watched Jason *die.* She couldn't let Cain die, too, regardless of the risk to herself.

Relinquishing her hiding place, she began limping back as carefully and quietly as possible. If only she could find one of Cain's neighbors so she could call his house and warn him. But what few neighbors he had up in these mountains were so spread out. She didn't even know which direction to travel. She was so turned around, so confused….

Help. She had to find help.

But she didn't get the chance. She'd gone about twenty feet when Owen jumped out of the darkness. He'd been waiting for her all along.

31

John was right—Owen had come to the mountains.

Cain could see the light inside Owen's truck glowing through the trees as he raced to the old cabin. In the backseat of Sheridan's rental, his dogs barked and stepped over one another in an attempt to reach the open window, which Cain had lowered to allow for the muzzle of his rifle. They could sense Cain's nervous energy, his absolute focus and intensity, and were responding to it, shivering and shaking in their eagerness to get out and do their job.

Had Owen already found Sheridan?

Cain knew the answer to that question as soon as he turned into the clearing. Of course he'd found her. The front door of the cabin was wide open.

"Shit!" He threw the car into Park, grabbed his gun and jumped out. He opened the back door so the dogs could scramble out, too, but instead of heading for the cabin or the forest, they immediately surrounded a limp human form that appeared to have fallen from Owen's truck and barked as if to say they'd found what he wanted.

The metallic taste of fear rose in Cain's mouth, but as he drew close, he could tell it wasn't Sheridan. It was Karen. Dead.

"No," he murmured, but mourning would have to wait. If he hurried, he might be able to get to Sheridan in time. And right now that was all he cared about.

He had his dogs smell Sheridan's car to pick up her scent, then ordered them to find her. They began to track, going to the cabin first. Cain knew her scent was strong there, but she wasn't anywhere to be found.

Killers often return to familiar ground. John's words seemed to reverberate in Cain's head as he called her name. If only he hadn't left her; if only he'd stayed here....

But he didn't have time to berate himself. He had to find her, had to reach her before it was too late.

Charging through the house, he ducked into the woodshed and shone his flashlight down the stairs. But he couldn't see anything except one of Sheridan's shoes. He must've dropped it when he carried up their clothes.

Just to be sure, he sent Koda down, but the dog came right back up.

"Nothing?"

Koda whined and led him to the front door. So Cain whistled to stop Quixote and Maximillian from searching the cabin. If Sheridan was there, they would've found her already. Which meant she had to be in the forest.

With a whistle, he sent the dogs into the trees and ran behind them.

Only a few seconds later the report of a gun echoed against the night sky.

Sheridan was hit, but she'd knocked Owen off balance and the bullet had merely grazed her arm. She felt the sting as she shoved him. She wanted to run, but she couldn't see well enough to avoid the trees. Her only chance was to stand and fight. Knowing she couldn't stop him with her bare hands, she sank to her knees and groped for a weapon.

Owen fired again, but it was a random, desperate shot. She couldn't tell where the bullet had gone. She could sense him aiming lower, however, and knew the next one would hit her if she didn't somehow get out of the way.

Covering her head, she somersaulted to the right as the gun went off. The sound, so close, made her ears ring. But her hands finally landed on a broken branch and she came up swinging.

He stumbled and fell when she hit him. She heard him cry out as he sprawled on the ground. But she didn't back off. As long as his breathing or movement gave her a target, she swung her club and managed to hit him one more time.

He must've dropped his gun in the scuffle because the next thing she knew he was wrestling with her. But she could hear dogs in the distance. Cain was coming. She was going to live, she told herself. She was going to make it—if she could hold out long enough.

Owen noticed the beam of light before he heard the dogs. That was strange. Sheridan must've hurt his hearing when she hit him with the club he'd finally wrested away from her. Or he was hyper-focusing again. Now that she was lying limp on the ground, however, he couldn't miss the dogs.

They circled and yelped and had no trouble seeing in the dark. Owen thought it might help that they knew him, thought he'd be able to talk to them, calm them down. But it didn't help as much as he hoped. He'd never been good with animals, and they were more riled than he'd ever seen them—probably because of Cain's panic when he'd found the cabin empty. And the blood, the blood they could smell on Karen and on his clothes.

Dogs were so damn smart, especially Cain's dogs.

Owen shouted for them to get back and began swinging the club Sheridan had used on him, but the aggression worked against him. The lead hound—was it Quixote?—lunged and latched on to his ankle. But he didn't bite very deep. Even though the dog's senses told him to fight he was confused; he'd been familiar with Owen for years—and he didn't yet know what Cain wanted him to do.

Kicking free, Owen scrambled to find his gun. He was going to need it to go up against Cain.

Cain was close now, the beam of his flashlight brighter, more blinding. Once again Owen couldn't hear the dogs, even though he knew they were still barking. He'd found his gun and all his attention was focused on moving it slowly behind his back.

"You're too late," he said as soon as Cain reached him. Actually, he was guessing it was Cain because of the dogs, but he couldn't see the looming figure well enough to identify him.

The beam of Cain's flashlight swept over the ground, and stopped at Sheridan. Then, for the first time in Owen's life, he heard a sound of true agony from his step-brother—and grimaced. Cain was usually better at hiding his feelings. Owen had always admired that about him. This grief was distasteful, made him seem so…weak.

"Sorry," he said. "But she was a problem."

The muzzle of a rifle appeared in the light. But Owen wasn't worried. He *wanted* Cain to shoot. He'd known it might come down to this, because there wasn't any way he'd let them take him alive. He wasn't going to prison; he wouldn't last a day there.

"Go ahead," he said. "Shoot. I strangled her with my bare hands. I killed Karen, too, in case you didn't see the mess back at the cabin. You wouldn't believe what she did. I had to shoot her while I was driving. Crazy, huh? We spun around and nearly crashed down the mountain. But I got everything under control."

He knew the pride in his voice would provoke Cain, and he wasn't disappointed.

"Pretty proud of yourself, aren't you, Owen?"

"Most people would've gone off the cliff. Or let her get away."

"You're not as clever as you think," Cain said. "Dad knows."

This bothered Owen. He told himself it shouldn't. His father had never really loved him, not like he'd loved Jason. But it'd been a lot of work establishing his reputation. And now it was gone. Just like that. "I'm sure you're happy he knows it wasn't you," he said. "It makes you look oh-so-good by comparison, doesn't it? But he's never going to love you. Jason was the only one of us who mattered to him. And that didn't change after he was gone."

"You need help, Owen," Cain said.

"I think it's a little late for that, don't you?" Lifting the gun, he managed to squeeze off a round. Cain was close enough that it should've killed him—and would have, if not for Koda. The dog had leaped toward Owen the moment he sensed the threat, and the bullet struck him instead. He fell to the ground with a whine. And, almost simultaneously, Cain's rifle went off.

There was a deep hole, and she was at the bottom of it. Sheridan could hear Cain calling her name, but she couldn't seem to rise to the surface, to break free of the darkness.

"I love you. Come back to me," he said. And she fought harder. She could make it. She was a survivor.

With supreme effort, she opened her eyes to see him standing over her. She was in the hospital again; she recognized the wallpaper.

"Oh, no," she murmured. "What happened to me this time?"

Cain looked pale beneath his tan, but he smiled. "You were out doing your superhero shit again. You've really got to stop that."

She tried to laugh, but her head hurt too much. "Am I as badly beat up as the last time?"

"No. The doctor says you should be able to go home with me tomorrow."

Surprised, because she felt as banged up as ever, she managed to lift her hands to her face. "What are these bandages hiding?"

"All superficial wounds that have just been cleaned. A bullet passed through the flesh of your arm—that was the worst of it. And the cuts and bruises on your feet."

"My throat hurts."

"But it's not seriously injured. The doctor thinks you passed out before Owen did much damage. He certainly didn't do what he thought he did."

She remembered the dark forest, the barking dogs, the bouncing light coming toward them. She'd been trying to hold out until Cain arrived, but Owen had overpowered her at the last minute.

"Where is Owen?"

"He's in a different hospital, in a room with an armed guard."

"So I hurt him that bad?" She grinned weakly.

"You definitely left a few marks. But that's not why he's in the hospital. They're taking out the bullet I put in him when he shot Koda."

"What?" Alarmed, she struggled to sit up.

"Shh, it's okay." Cain rubbed her arm in a reassuring manner. "I've got him patched up. He's going to be fine. But if John hadn't arrived when he did, I doubt either Koda or Owen would've made it."

"That must've been quite a scene."

"It was, but it showed me something."

"What?"

"As much as I love Koda, you were all I cared about at that moment."

Their eyes met and Sheridan felt a tightening in her chest. She'd had strong feelings for Cain for so long she almost couldn't believe he loved her back. "How's John dealing with the truth?" she asked.

"He's struggling. He's lost two sons and Karen." Cain closed his eyes for a moment. "Her funeral's in two days."

"Why'd Owen do it?" she whispered.

"He wasn't just 'different' as we've always assumed. He has no conscience. Jason was the golden boy. He had the position Owen wanted in the family—so Owen killed him. I provided a convenient scapegoat. All the suspicion swirling around me kept the focus off him, so he lived with minimal fear of discovery. Until you returned. Then Ned started shooting off his mouth about how you were finally going to solve the case, and it spooked him. He didn't know what you might've remembered, whether something around here would trigger a memory, or what you were capable of doing now that you have experience working with the police."

"That's why he tried to kill me. I get that part. It's sick, but understandable, you know? It's the reason he killed Amy and Karen that mystifies me."

"They got in the way. According to Robert, Karen had found the shovel Owen used to dig your grave."

"How does he know it was the same shovel?"

"Someone had attempted to wipe it clean, but if you looked closely enough you could see blood."

"*My* blood?"

He nodded, and she swallowed to ease the soreness in her throat. She was probably pushing herself too hard, but she had to have answers before she could rest. "Why wouldn't Owen have put it somewhere safer?"

"He thought he was being smart by hiding it in plain sight. He didn't expect anyone to notice it. And if it *was* found, he figured people would think I put it there."

"So why didn't he try and blame you? Why'd he kill Karen?"

"She came out of the garage screaming that John had attacked her and you, and murdered Amy. With her pointing a finger in another direction, I'm guessing Owen panicked."

Sheridan closed her eyes for a few seconds, but her mind was still whirring with questions. "What about Owen's wife and kids?"

"I think he must love them, as much as he's capable of loving. But they're the ones I really feel sorry for. Lucy was completely clueless. I don't think she believes he did what he did, even with all the evidence."

She opened her eyes again. "She needs grief counseling."

Cain gave her a quirky smile. "Maybe you could start up an outpost of The Last Stand in Tennessee and take care of that."

His words reminded her that she had a difficult decision to make. She loved him, but giving up her job wasn't going to be easy. "We need to talk about that."

He slipped his fingers through hers. "Don't worry, I'm just kidding. After everything you've been through, I wouldn't expect you to live here."

What did that mean? Was he saying they should part? She was afraid to ask. Her work was important to her, but she didn't want to give *him* up, either. "I can't see you living anywhere other than where you live now," she admitted. "You belong in the forest."

"There are forests in California." He reached over to the counter and showed her a magazine he'd picked up somewhere. *California Dreamin'*. "We could live in the Sierras."

Sheridan was excited that he seemed open to the possibility, but there were things she needed to know. "It's different there, Cain. If you wanted to be a vet, you'd have to go through all the schooling and licensing."

"I could do it. But I'm actually considering becoming a dog breeder and trainer."

Sheridan liked the idea. "In the Sierras, huh?"

He turned to a beautiful picture of Emerald Bay. "Right here."

She couldn't help laughing. Obviously, he didn't know how far Lake Tahoe was from Sacramento. "That'd be a three-hour commute for me each day. Would you consider someplace in the foothills?" she countered.

He studied the picture wistfully. "Would it be anything like this?"

She took the magazine and thumbed through it. "It'd look a lot like *this*." She tapped a page showing Apple Hill in Placerville.

"I could live with that," he said, his eyebrows raised in interest.

Sheridan relinquished the magazine as her exhaustion edged closer. "I want plenty of babies, too," she told him.

"How many is plenty?"

"Four, five, six."

He laughed. "Good thing kids and dogs go together." He showed her a picture of a cabin with a great view and lots of glass. "Maybe I'll build us a home like this one to house our brood."

She smiled as she imagined them in such a place, nestled in the foothills with their babies and their dogs. Now that she thought of it, now that she knew Cain was willing to move, she could see him fitting in there just fine. There was only one problem....

"What about Marshall?" she asked. Cain wouldn't want to leave him.

"We'll bring him with us, if he agrees. He needs a change."

"John won't like that."

"John's going to be moving, anyway. He said he can't stay here, not after what's happened."

"Won't he take Marshall wherever he goes?"

"Maybe. We'll leave that up to Marshall."

"Won't you miss John and Robert, at least a little?"

"I doubt it," he said. "It's just never been there. I was forcing it because of Marshall, but..."

"I understand," she said.

He set the magazine aside. "By the way, someone named Jonathan's been trying to reach you."

Sheridan had planned to check in with Jon the moment her cell phone became functional, but she'd received that call from her folks and hadn't had a chance.

"Is this the guy in the picture you've got in your wallet?" Cain asked.

Sheridan sensed a tinge of jealousy in those words. "He's the private investigator who works for us when we need him. He used to charge us by the hour, but he's gotten so involved that he mostly donates his time these days."

A muscle flexed in Cain's cheek. "Involved with the charity or...with you?"

"We used to date a couple of years ago. We're still close, but now he's more like my brother."

"Nothing I should worry about, then."

She laughed. "Definitely not. What did he want?"

"The same thing your other friend, Jasmine, wanted. They were trying to warn you to stay away from any cabins."

Sheridan waved at the hospital room. "Did you tell them they're a little late?"

"I told them you're safe. And that you'll call them in the morning."

"That's good."

"Jasmine's an interesting individual," he added.

Sheridan tucked his hand under her chin as she curled up. "Why do you say that?"

"I've never known anyone with psychic ability."

"You might be a skeptic. But, trust me, you can take what she says to the bank."

He bent over to kiss her forehead. "I'm glad to hear it."

Sheridan detected amusement in his voice. "Why's that?"

"Because she said we're going to live happily ever after."

* * * * *

New York Times **bestselling author**

BRENDA NOVAK

**continues her Last Stand series
with three suspenseful new novels.**

**"Brenda Novak expertly blends realistically
gritty danger, excellent characterization
and a generous dash of romance."
—*Chicago Tribune***

**Available now
wherever books are sold!**

REQUEST YOUR FREE BOOKS!

2 FREE NOVELS
FROM THE SUSPENSE COLLECTION
PLUS 2 FREE GIFTS!

YES! Please send me 2 FREE novels from the Suspense Collection and my 2 FREE gifts (gifts are worth about $10). After receiving them, if I don't wish to receive any more books, I can return the shipping statement marked "cancel." If I don't cancel, I will receive 3 brand-new novels every month and be billed just $5.74 per book in the U.S. or $6.24 per book in Canada. That's a saving of at least 28% off the cover price. It's quite a bargain! Shipping and handling is just 50¢ per book in the U.S. and 75¢ per book in Canada.* I understand that accepting the 2 free books and gifts places me under no obligation to buy anything. I can always return a shipment and cancel at any time. Even if I never buy another book, the two free books and gifts are mine to keep forever.

192 MDN E4MN   392 MDN E4MY

Name	(PLEASE PRINT)
Address	Apt. #
City	State/Prov.	Zip/Postal Code

Signature (if under 18, a parent or guardian must sign)

Mail to The Reader Service:
IN U.S.A.: P.O. Box 1867, Buffalo, NY 14240-1867
IN CANADA: P.O. Box 609, Fort Erie, Ontario L2A 5X3

Not valid for current subscribers to the Suspense Collection
or the Romance/Suspense Collection.

**Want to try two free books from another line?
Call 1-800-873-8635 or visit www.morefreebooks.com.**

* Terms and prices subject to change without notice. Prices do not include applicable taxes. N.Y. residents add applicable sales tax. Canadian residents will be charged applicable provincial taxes and GST. Offer not valid in Quebec. This offer is limited to one order per household. All orders subject to approval. Credit or debit balances in a customer's account(s) may be offset by any other outstanding balance owed by or to the customer. Please allow 4 to 6 weeks for delivery. Offer available while quantities last.

Your Privacy: Harlequin Books is committed to protecting your privacy. Our Privacy Policy is available online at www.eHarlequin.com or upon request from the Reader Service. From time to time we make our lists of customers available to reputable third parties who may have a product or service of interest to you. If you would prefer we not share your name and address, please check here. ☐

Help us get it right—We strive for accurate, respectful and relevant communications. To clarify or modify your communication preferences, visit us at www.ReaderService.com/consumerchoice.

MSUS10

J.T. ELLISON

Homicide detective Taylor Jackson thinks she's seen it all in Nashville—but she's never seen anything as perverse as The Conductor. He captures and contains his victim in a glass coffin, slowly starving her to death. Only then does he give in to his attraction.

Once finished, he creatively disposes of the body by reenacting scenes from famous paintings. And similar macabre works are being displayed in Europe. Taylor teams up with her fiancé, FBI profiler Dr. John Baldwin, and New Scotland Yard detective James "Memphis" Highsmythe, a haunted man who only has eyes for Taylor, to put an end to The Conductor's art collection.

the cold room

Available wherever books are sold.